say i do

LUCY KEVIN

say i do

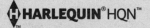

ISBN-13: 978-0-373-77901-7

SAY I DO

Copyright © 2014 by Harlequin Books S.A.

The publisher acknowledges the copyright holder of the individual works as follows:

THE WEDDING GIFT
Copyright © 2012 by Oak Press, LLC.

THE WEDDING DANCE
Copyright © 2012 by Oak Press, LLC.

THE WEDDING SONG
Copyright © 2012 by Oak Press, LLC.

Recycling programs for this product may not exist in your area.

Printed in U.S.A.

CONTENTS

Dear Reader,

If you have got this book in your hand right now, I'm guessing that you love romance and weddings and happy-ever-afters as much as I do. That is why I wrote this series of books that are all focused around brides and grooms and their own special love stories.

Julie, Phoebe and Tyce each work at Rose Chalet, a fictional wedding venue in my hometown of San Francisco. Like most of us, my characters wonder if they will ever meet that one special person—the person who makes their heart skip a beat, the person who makes their life complete. We all love reading about how people met their significant other, and we know that sometimes the road to true romance can be a little rocky. *Say I Do* reaffirms the fact that, if you are patient, your perfect someone could be right around the corner.

It was so much fun writing these stories and creating happy endings for everyone at the Rose Chalet. I would love to hear from you! Please contact me at www.lucykevin.com.

Happy ever after,

Lucy Kevin

THE WEDDING GIFT

CHAPTER ONE

Delgado's Restaurant: 2 stars out of 5
By Reviewer Andrew Kyle,
Host of *Edgy Eats*

San Francisco's restaurant scene is amazing, and we diners are spoiled for choice. It is always exciting to try a new place and it was with this thought in mind that I made a reservation at Delgado's.

When I dine out I have certain expectations. On this occasion I expected the first course—a seafood bisque—to be well prepared. I wanted the chicken to be perfectly roasted, and the home-made ice cream to be sweet and cold. On top of all that the service had to be professional and friendly. Delgado's, the new kid on the block here in San Francisco, met all those expectations.

Unfortunately, simply meeting expectations isn't enough anymore. Chains and fast-food joints do that. To survive and do well, restaurants must offer more than bland food. A special night out should provide a culinary experience that demonstrates the owner is passionate about food and the restaurant business.

That passion for food didn't come across at Delgado's. Judging by the many empty seats in the dining room, it appears as if other customers have likely felt the same way.

Perhaps in future, the owner will couple her obvious skills with a more imaginative menu, but for now, Delgado's is one to avoid.

Unmemorable.

"COME ON, JULIE, you're going to be late if you aren't careful. You know I—"

"—was never late," Julie finished. "Yes, Aunt Evie, I know. I'm meeting new clients at The Rose Chalet today and I really want to make a good impression. Do I look okay?"

Julie's aunt was in her sixties now, with gray hair and a slight stoop caused by too many years of bending over hot stoves. But she still looked good for her age, and she still had that same no-nonsense attitude she'd had when Julie was a child.

Even though Julie was twenty-eight now, Evie still didn't hesitate to wipe off a spot of smudged makeup from her cheek.

"You look lovely, sweetheart."

"Are you sure?"

Julie checked her appearance in the mirror hanging by the door one more time, knowing everything had to be perfect for today. She usually tied her dark hair back when she was cooking, but she'd left it down this morning, knowing she made a better impression on strangers when it was falling down around her shoulders. She'd decided on a simple combination of a navy blue sweater and dark pants for the day, because they were practical enough to cook in while still looking professional.

Aunt Evie nodded. "Of course I'm sure. Though you

could do with putting on a few pounds. Whoever heard of a thin cook?"

"This from the woman who wouldn't dream of missing her exercise class twice a week?" Julie laughed. She glanced at her reflection again and ran one hand over her hair. "Maybe if I—"

"I'm not going to stand here complimenting you when you should already be on your way to work," Aunt Evie said. "You have had breakfast, haven't you?"

"I'll get something later," Julie promised.

"Probably from one of those food trucks you seem to love so much." Her aunt harrumphed.

Julie gave her aunt a kiss on the cheek, then ran out to the car she was borrowing. Her beloved Mustang had gone the way of her old apartment, sucked away by debts when the restaurant went under.

Julie wove through traffic, hoping she wouldn't be stopped while she completely ignored the speed limit in an effort to be on time. As Aunt Evie had pointed out, *she* had never been late in all the time she'd worked at The Rose Chalet, and Julie now had her aunt's old job...sort of.

Actually she was just filling in. Rose Martin, the owner of the wedding venue, had been clear about that. She only wanted someone to help out with one wedding. Then she would start looking for someone permanent to head up the catering department at The Rose Chalet.

Julie couldn't afford to screw this up. Not if she wanted a chance to turn temporary work into a permanent job.

As she parked her car in front of The Rose Chalet a few minutes later Julie thought, again, what a beautiful place it was. The building had a refined, old-fashioned elegance, surrounded by small but elegant grounds that were expertly maintained. It was exactly what a bride and groom would want in a wedding venue: a little slice of paradise carved out of the middle of a big city.

At present, however, the reception area was a bit chaotic. Rose was there, looking as pristine and lovely as ever, her red hair carefully arranged, her delicately patterned dress suiting her perfectly. She was standing at the bottom of a stepladder while RJ, the handyman/gardener, worked to replace some damaged wooden scrollwork up near the ceiling. Given that he was both muscular and good-looking, Julie could think of a few women who wouldn't mind holding ladders for him, but apparently Rose didn't agree.

"Could you hurry up, RJ?"

RJ flashed a smile back down at Rose. "I would hurry, but I know you couldn't live with yourself if I fell off this thing and broke my neck. Just hold it steady for a few more seconds, boss."

Julie wasn't sure if Rose was going to start yelling or laughing at that point. No question about it: RJ was very charming. But Julie knew that as an employee she'd never dare to speak to Rose like that.

"I have some very important prospective clients coming today and I want to make sure everything is perfect for them—" Rose broke off to look over at Julie. "Oh, good, you're finally here. How is Evie doing?"

"Much better," Julie said with a smile. "I'll let her know you asked."

With that, Rose pulled out her phone with her free hand and scrolled through her calendar. "The couple and some of their family will be coming by this afternoon. Before they arrive, I'd like you to produce the tasting samples for the food options, along with an overall menu. I'm going to coordinate all the other things they are here to review, as well as finalize the budget. I've got about a dozen other things to do before I head out for my lunch date with Donovan."

"I'll be ready," Julie promised. "Why don't I hold the ladder and you can take care of your preparations?"

Rose looked at RJ for a moment before nodding. "Thanks."

Julie took her place by the stepladder while Rose bustled off. She always seemed to be in a hurry.

"Good to see you again," she said to RJ once Rose was gone. "So, who's Donovan?"

"Donovan McIntyre is Rose's fiancé. He's a plastic surgeon. Look, I only had Rose holding this ladder to get her to take a break. She's been working since the crack of dawn, and I bet you've probably got more important things to do than stand around and watch me work."

He was right; for one thing, she had a whole menu to prepare. Not that she could cook most of it until early afternoon, of course. That was one of the things about cooking: she could do all the preparation she wanted, but she'd still end up trying to control about five things at once as she rushed to get it all ready at the same time.

Despite the challenges, Julie enjoyed the pressure. No, she *loved* the pressure—the rush of working with ingredients she could transform into something special while under serious time constraints. It always amazed her that with heat and spices, and unique presentations and food combinations, she could turn something ordinary into something spectacular.

Today, all she wanted was to make sure everything went smoothly so she would have a chance of impressing Rose. Impressive enough to turn a one-shot-deal into a permanent gig at The Rose Chalet.

"Yes, I probably should get going," Julie said. "I would hate to disappoint Rose."

RJ smiled down at her from atop his ladder. "Don't worry about Rose. Her bark's worse than her bite. She just wants everybody's special day to be—"

"Special?" Julie broke in with her own grin.

"I was going to go with *perfect*. Good luck with the menu."

Julie hoped, as she made her way over to the Chalet's kitchen, that she wasn't going to need luck.

The kitchen was a big space, well up to the task of producing food for several hundred wedding guests. It was quite a bit bigger than the kitchen at Julie's old restaurant, but it was quiet now in the early morning hours in a way that Delgado's had never been. She'd loved the constant activity of her restaurant's kitchen— a half dozen people working together to feed hungry customers.

Julie shook her head. She'd promised herself she wouldn't think about the past. She couldn't allow herself to falter because of everything that had happened. This was not the time for regrets.

Working at The Rose Chalet could be a fresh start— a pathway to getting out of Evie's guest room and back on her own feet.

Purposefully, she turned her focus back to the job at hand. The menu itself was pretty straightforward. After all, when a bride and groom had friends and relatives coming to San Francisco from every part of the country, they would want to serve food and drink that everyone would enjoy. Julie had decided on seafood and a salad as options for the first course. The entrée would be either duck in plum sauce or pesto pasta. And dessert would be a selection of individual mousses that would nicely complement the wedding cake.

By lunch, Julie had most of the preparations completed. She'd prepped samples of two different types of chocolate mousse and they were now cooling in the walk-in fridge. The duck was slow-cooking in the oven, and there wasn't anything that could go wrong with it. The vegetables and other ingredients for the main course were ready. The pasta would be cooked right before she was nearly ready to plate everything, and the combination of fish and scallops for the appetizer was ready to go. Now all she had to do was wait for those manic last twenty minutes when the final cooking and plating would be completed. With all that done, now would be the best time to go get her own lunch.

Julie loved the food trucks that lined the city's streets. Over the past few years they'd popped up, one after the other, serving all kinds of food, from greasy to gourmet, American to international fare. She'd known exactly where all the best trucks were parked within a twenty-minute walk of Delgado's, but she didn't know the area around The Rose Chalet quite as well. She was hungry and she hoped she would find a good food truck nearby.

Julie headed out just in time to see Rose leaving for her own lunch date. She was accompanied by a blond-haired guy with looks to die for, driving a sports car that practically screamed "successful surgeon."

No wonder Rose had been so eager to make the date despite her busy day. Lord knew Julie had been without a date of her own for a long time. Given the opportunity, she would have done the same thing.

Fortunately she didn't have time to mull over her pathetic love life. Right now her every thought was focused on impressing the socks off Rose's clients in a couple of hours.

Five minutes later Julie found a truck selling the best falafel she'd tasted in a long while. She enjoyed it while sitting on a bench in a nearby park that looked out over San Francisco Bay. Still, she didn't linger long over lunch and when she returned to The Rose Chalet after thirty minutes, Julie was surprised to see that Rose was also returning from her lunch date with the doctor.

If this was how fast Rose always moved, Julie mused, no wonder RJ had to scheme to get her to stand still for a few minutes.

Sleeves rolled up, RJ was constructing frames for a couple of the flower beds and he nodded hello to both of them. "How was lunch?"

"Great, thanks," Julie said.

Instead of answering him, Rose turned to Julie. "Our guests will be here soon. Julie, is the food ready?"

"It's all prepped," Julie said. "I just have to finish it off once the bride and groom arrive."

Rose nodded, clearly making check marks on a long mental list. "I'll phone you on your cell the moment they arrive, and we can go from there. Oh, and could you make sure that everything is fine in the dining room? I checked the layout, but—"

But a small tornado might have hit in the meantime so you want me to check it again? Julie shook off her snarky thought. Rose was right—everything should be perfect for a bride and groom on their wedding day and her job was to help achieve that.

After verifying that everything in the dining room was indeed perfect, Julie headed for the kitchen. She was almost at the swinging door when she realized, with no small amount of horror, that she'd forgotten about the duck. Thank God, she hadn't lingered over her lunch!

In the nick of time she pulled the bird from the oven, sustaining only mild burns to her fingers. Right then her cell phone rang. It must be Rose. Julie picked up, barely remembering to mumble a hello as she sliced into the bird and confirmed with a loud sigh of relief that it was fine.

All of which was why it took her a few beats longer than it should have to register what Rose was saying to her. "They're here already?"

"*He* is," Rose corrected.

"The bride sent the groom over alone?" Julie couldn't keep the surprise out of her voice. What bride wouldn't be there for the planning of her own wedding?

"The groom's brother, actually," Rose said. "We'll go through to the dining room in about fifteen minutes."

The groom's brother?

Julie pushed the question aside as she hurriedly got to work putting the final touches to the appetizers. When she was finished, she balanced the plates expertly in one hand and took the short walk out to the dining area.

Rose and the groom's brother were just coming in, and Julie had a quick glimpse of a well-dressed, dark-haired man who appeared to be in his early thirties. She bent over her plates for a few moments to make sure there were no errant splashes of dressing or seasoning along the rims.

Rose made the introductions. "This is Julie. She'll be handling the catering for your brother's wedding. Julie, I'd like you to meet Andrew."

Julie looked up, her best smile in place as she met the newcomer's dark eyes. She was instantly aware of his strong, handsome features with just a trace of stubble, his dimples, and how his well-tailored suit showcased his athletic frame. Normally, Julie's smile would have widened at least a little in feminine appreciation.

Instead it faltered on her lips, and it was only by the faintest thread of control that she managed to hold it in place at all.

Julie recognized those features. It was hard not to, really, when she had spent so much time staring at them. This was the face that beamed out at her, and thousands of others, from the Cuisine Channel. They were the features of a man that virtually any chef in the city would have dreaded having in their dining room.

And…they just so happened to be the picture-perfect features that had accompanied the restaurant review that had ruined her life.

"You're Andrew *Kyle*."

"It's a pleasure to meet you, Julie."

Andrew Kyle was the very last person Julie wanted to see but, she had to get ahold of herself. She clasped his outstretched hand. She couldn't just ignore the brother of a potential customer, especially with Rose watching.

That was no excuse, however, for noticing how strong his hands were, his palm and fingers slightly scarred from the old burns and cuts that anyone who cooked for a living acquired along the way.

"Have you been working here long?" he asked.

How could Julie answer that? *"Ever since a two-star review wrecked my life"* lacked a certain something. The same went for her next thought, which was to go the silent-movie route and simply dump a plate of salad over his head.

In the end she had to settle for mumbling a tame, "No, not very long."

"Julie has graciously agreed to help us out with this

one wedding now that her aunt has retired," Rose supplied, obviously determined to make up for Julie's lack of social skills.

Julie managed to nod. "Sorry," she said. "If you'll excuse me, I need to get back to the kitchen to check on the other courses. Enjoy the first course."

Unfortunately the odds of Andrew Kyle enjoying anything she cooked were so remote that they probably had Ozark mountain men living in them.

Back in the kitchen, she leaned against the door and took a deep breath. The worst part, she was shocked to realize, wasn't so much that she'd been surprised by Andrew's sudden appearance at her new job.

It was that he hadn't even recognized her.

Pulling herself together, Julie knew there was still a lot of work to do to finish prepping both the main courses and the desserts. She also knew the *worst* part would be yet to come if she served poorly prepared food to one of the biggest celebrity chefs on the west coast.

Not only would Andrew know he'd been right about her substandard cooking, but Rose would undoubtedly fire her.

CHAPTER TWO

IT WASN'T EASY trying to finish off the main courses and desserts, knowing all the while that Andrew Kyle was probably out there telling Rose exactly how awful Julie's food was. And Rose would listen, of course, because what else would she be able to do in the face of a triple whammy: celebrity chef, the groom's brother and great dimples?

Enough about the dimples, Julie ordered herself. *Just remember what he did.*

It was pretty hard to forget. One review from the city's most prominent TV chef, and her business had come crashing down around her ears. The faint trickle of new customers Julie had hoped would widen into a stream dried up completely. Her entire dream had gone south in a matter of weeks, all thanks to the man who was currently sampling Julie's seafood platter.

Well, she couldn't let him ruin this dream, too. Which meant Julie couldn't do anything horrible to his food, even if a small part of her wanted the revenge.

The truth was, the best revenge would be to show him just how wrong he had been. All she had to do was present him with the best plates of food in her life, and then force him to eat his words.

Easy.

Though if it was that easy, why was her hand shaking while she finished the duck? She needed to focus, take her time and—

"Is everything okay?"

Julie jumped at the sound of Andrew's voice, almost slicing a finger open in the process.

What was he doing in her kitchen? Had he finally realized who she was? Had he come to gloat?

Or, maybe, to apologize for what he'd done?

Knowing anything she really wanted to say to him would get her instantly fired by Rose, Julie responded with a clipped, "I'm not sure you should be in here."

"No, it's fine—"

"Julie," she reminded him in an even more clipped voice this time, hardly able to believe that he'd already forgotten her name. "Julie Delgado."

Was there a flicker of recognition in his eyes?

Then again, why would there be? He was a famous chef. She was a nobody who couldn't keep her own restaurant kitchen open and was now cooking for scraps at a wedding venue.

"I asked Rose's permission to see the kitchen where the food for the wedding might be prepared."

"*Might* be?"

"My brother and his fiancée deserve the best. I promised I'd cast my chef's eye over the food. Which is why I'd appreciate it if you would bring the desserts out with the main courses and then stay with us as we go through everything." He flashed that brilliant smile of his. "After all, I'm sure the two of us will have a lot to talk about."

For a moment Julie wondered if he was referring to the damning restaurant review, but those darn dimples of his were turning her brain to mush so that all she could manage to say was, "Will we?"

"Sure," Andrew replied with another smile.

Oh, my God, after all he'd done, was he actually flirting with her?

Julie just barely resisted the urge to hit him with the nearest thing on hand, but only because it happened to be a saucepan full of steadily reducing plum sauce. Of all the arrogant...

Again, Julie took a deep breath and reminded herself that since she obviously wasn't important enough for the big star to even remember her name, why *wouldn't* he pull out the charm to cover his tracks? The same charm that had everybody else fooled.

"I'd be happy to bring out everything at once," Julie said, if only because it seemed like the quickest way to get him out of her kitchen. "Just give me a minute or two."

Actually, it was more like ten, but at least for those blissful minutes, Julie didn't have to worry about anything more serious than whether her food was perfect or how she was going to deliver it all intact. As fun as it might be to dream of "accidentally" tripping and covering Andrew Kyle with food, Julie knew perfectly well that she wasn't going to do it.

In the end she was surprised when Andrew got up to help her with the plates and even made a second trip to the kitchen to bring out the desserts.

Once they were all seated, Andrew examined the plates with a critical eye. Beside him, Rose's expression was indecipherable. Of course, she was clearly as concerned as Julie that this tasting go well. If she'd ever read one of Andrew's restaurant reviews, Rose would know how harsh his judgments could be.

Taking a spare seat at the table, Julie looked at the

plates that held the first course and wondered what Andrew was thinking.

It was impossible to tell with any certainty. He hadn't eaten much of each dish, but he'd clearly tasted *some* of everything, so maybe that was a good sign. Julie fidgeted, then clasped her hands under the table to keep them still.

"I've tried the seafood and salad, but let's move on to everything else and then I'll give you my thoughts."

Watching Andrew Kyle eat was an experience. He didn't talk between bites, as though that would in some way spoil his concentration. Instead he assembled the food carefully on his fork, closed his eyes and let his nose take in the scent for a moment. Then he finally pushed it into that sensuous mouth.

Julie found herself briefly entranced by the way he involved as many of his senses as possible. He really did treat food as something truly important.

Of course, that didn't make up for the way he kept Julie and Rose waiting while he tasted everything. In fact, the only time he spoke at all was about halfway through, when he glanced up and raised an eyebrow.

"Aren't you going to join in, Julie?"

"Worried I might have done something to the food?" she replied.

Andrew laughed at that but Rose was obviously less than pleased by the barely veiled testiness in Julie's question.

"Come on, join me. I always feel weird tasting things alone. Rose?"

Rose held up her hands. "I just had lunch."

Andrew returned his gaze to Julie. "Looks like it's just you and me, then."

It was clearly a challenge. Besides, Julie knew she

was never going to get away with the same excuse as Rose.

She picked up a fork and enthusiastically sampled the dishes she had produced. She'd always eaten with gusto—Aunt Evie sometimes laughingly asked if she thought her food was going to be snatched away.

Julie worked to concentrate on the taste of everything, looking for anything that the celebrity chef might try to pick up on. Were the scallops perfectly seared? Was the texture right? Was there any little mistake at all that was going to cause a problem?

She almost sighed with relief as she tasted the results of her efforts. As far as she could tell, everything had come out without any problems at all.

Poke holes in that, Andrew Kyle.

Apparently, Rose was as eager to know the outcome as Julie was. "What do you think?" she asked Andrew.

Julie couldn't help noticing the way Rose's tone became so much more formal around an important client.

"Is everything to your satisfaction?"

Andrew put his fork down carefully. "It's all well cooked," he said. "The scallops are nicely done and the fish goes well with them. The salad is crisp and fresh. The plum sauce with the duck is just right, and I like the richness of the gâteaux."

"Well, that's great," Rose said. "I'm sure that Julie can produce everything to exactly the same standards on the actual wedding day."

"I'm sure of that, too," Andrew said.

But, somehow, the compliment didn't make Julie feel as warm and fuzzy inside as it should have. Maybe it was the tone in which he had said it.

Rose seemed determined to ignore his less-than-thrilled tone. Or maybe she just hoped that if she pressed on, everything would be fine. "Why don't you sign off on the menu, then, Mr. Kyle, and we'll—"

"I'm sorry, I can't do that," Andrew said, shaking his head.

"But you just said—"

"The food is well prepared," he said, "but, unfortunately, it's too bland."

Bland.

It was the same word he'd used about her restaurant.

Julie's hands closed on the tablecloth. "'Bland'?" she repeated.

Andrew nodded. "As I said, it's fine. It's just... Frankly, it's wedding food."

"That's what this food is for," Julie had to point out. "A *wedding.*"

"Yes, but it's for my brother's wedding, and I'm sorry, this menu won't work. It's been done. There's nothing exciting here. There's no twist on any of the classic dishes, and there isn't anything innovative, either. This is my wedding gift to my brother and his fiancée. It needs to be special. But nothing about this menu makes it clear that their wedding is a really special occasion."

Julie thought the part where there would be a bride and groom saying "I do" in front of a few hundred people might be a clue as to the specialness of the occasion, but, of course, she wasn't going to say that. Besides, just then she was too busy remembering the first time Andrew Kyle had made those comments about her food. Remembering how much it had hurt.

About as much as it hurt right now, come to think of it.

"So what is it you want?" Julie asked. She very

carefully kept her voice level. Completely devoid of emotion.

Even so, Rose shot her a look before taking over the negotiations. "Yes, perhaps if you describe exactly what it is you do want, we will be better able to provide it."

Andrew smiled at them. He actually had the nerve to pull those gorgeous lips of his up at the corners as if nothing was wrong. "Something special. Something different. Something with a bit of imagination to it."

He focused his gaze on Julie and she refused to let her heart go pitter-patter, darn it.

"Something you couldn't cook in your sleep, Julie." Another smile. "This wedding is a big deal for our family and I *know* you can come up with something more innovative and special than what you've served me today."

Thank God, at least one of them knew it, Julie thought as Rose dove in to try to salvage the situation.

"Are you sure we can't—"

Andrew raised a hand to cut her off. "I'm sorry, but I'll need to see a completely revised menu before I can agree to sign off on anything."

"I see," Rose said. She didn't sound happy about it.

Julie didn't blame her, especially since right then she herself was undecided about her next move. Should she slip out the back door and make for the border, or stick pins in a doll with Andrew Kyle's "perfect" features on it—maybe adding a few new dimples while she was at it?

"Look," Andrew said, "I'd like to come back so that we can throw a few ideas around. Between Julie and myself, I suspect we can come up with something that's perfect for the wedding."

He'd just demolished her cooking for the second time

in a few short months, and he thought she would want him around?

"What a wonderful idea," Rose said before Julie could flat-out refuse to ever see Andrew Kyle again. "Our aim at The Rose Chalet is to make sure the day goes exactly the way the happy couple wants it. Julie would be happy to brainstorm menus with you, wouldn't you, Julie?"

Since the question was obviously rhetorical, Julie mumbled something that could be taken as a yes.

Rose stood. "Andrew, if you have a few more minutes, I'd like to take you for a walk around the Chalet to get a feel for the place. My full staff isn't here at the moment, but I'd like to get your opinion about a few other details."

Julie had never been so grateful for anything as when Andrew agreed to Rose's request. Ordinarily, with a guy like him, she would have watched him depart just because she couldn't *not* stare. Right now she simply wanted to make sure he was well and truly gone before she let out a sigh and slumped down in her seat.

What have I gotten myself into?

CHAPTER THREE

WHAT HAD HE gotten himself into?

The answer to that question was pretty obvious as Andrew followed Rose around the wedding venue. He'd just agreed to add supervising his brother's wedding planning to a schedule that already included taping a high-pressure TV show and working as a guest chef two nights a week at one of his friend's five-star restaurants.

All because he couldn't stand for food to be anything less than spectacular.

His family wouldn't have even noticed the difference. He would, though.

Andrew had always loved food and cooking, so much that he'd forcefully ignored enormous amounts of family pressure to attend law school the way his brother had. He had been, and still was, committed to the food industry. Which was why he couldn't stand by and watch food being prepared without that same commitment.

"Now this," Rose was saying, "is our rose garden. Some couples like to have their vows out here under the arch, but I think you were saying your brother and his bride are looking for an indoor ceremony?"

Andrew nodded. The garden was beautiful, but he'd spent some time talking to both Phil and Nancy before he'd agreed to help out. They might not have time to get here for all the wedding preparations, but they still knew what they wanted. However, Andrew couldn't help noticing how quickly they'd assumed *he'd* have time to spare.

"We'll arrange time for you to sit down with Phoebe Davis, our florist, and talk through the arrangements for that. Anne Farleigh, our dress designer, is already hard at work on a design based on the ideas Nancy sent over. Your future sister-in-law will be able to make the last fitting, won't she?"

Andrew spread his hands. "That's definitely one part of the wedding I don't have any input on."

His phone went off just as the gardener came over and gestured for Rose to quickly give her opinion on the new flower beds. Assuming Andrew was going to take the call, Rose excused herself and stepped away. Andrew thought he heard her say something to the gardener about not bothering her while she was with a client, at which point the gardener simply grinned and replied, "Don't worry, I won't get any dirt on you or your clients," before gesturing to the flower beds at the corner of the building.

Andrew looked down at the screen on his phone and saw that it was his assistant, Sandy, calling. Most likely she was calling to let him know about some of the final details about the TV episode they would tape later in the day.

His new show was doing away with most of the usual cooking show gimmicks. Instead Andrew cooked in front of a live studio audience. For a simple idea it could be complicated and the producer insisted that Andrew be consulted on every minor detail. His last question had concerned the arrangement of the salt and pepper containers—he wanted to make sure they didn't create lighting problems on the table.

For once Andrew let the call ring through to voice mail. Sandy might not look like a typical assistant to a top chef—and the producer had already made the mistake of expressing the opinion that twenty-five-year-olds with too many piercings couldn't possibly be real assistants—but Sandy had taken the comments in stride and had proved him wrong. She was extremely capable.

Besides, Andrew had another woman on his mind right then. Someone whose hair color looked completely natural, and someone who used bright colors on a dinner plate instead of on her head. Someone he'd just agreed to work with.

Julie Delgado.

He'd recognized her instantly. She wasn't exactly easy to forget. And it wasn't just that she was beautiful. In his line of work Andrew was more than used to being around beautiful women. He'd had his share of relationships with them, too. Generally they lasted until Andrew worked out that they were more interested in his celebrity status than in him, or until the women decided that there were better things in life than food.

Usually both.

There was something different about Julie. Andrew couldn't quite put his finger on it, but he knew she was definitely unlike the other women he had dated.

It had been there when he'd gone to review her restaurant. He'd taken one look into those deep brown eyes when she'd come out into the restaurant's dining room to check on his meal and it had almost, *almost,* been enough to make him change his mind about his review.

In the end, though, he'd had to behave with integrity.

But what was Julie doing *here?*

He'd heard that her restaurant had closed, but figured she'd pick up a spot in a great restaurant somewhere in the city. She certainly had the technical skills. Back when he'd run his own restaurants, Andrew would have been happy to offer her a spot in the kitchen.

In your kitchen? Or in your bed?

The truth was, Andrew silently admitted to himself, Julie Delgado sparked his interest in a way other women didn't.

Just then Rose returned and Andrew tried to turn his attention back to his brother's wedding. She gave him more details about the wedding, but Andrew was only half listening. He was too busy thinking about the wonderful darkness of Julie Delgado's eyes, the curve of her lips, the way she'd looked so stunning—even in clothes that had obviously been chosen more with the kitchen in mind than with impressing anyone.

Andrew had barely been able to take his eyes off her. Normally he would have asked her out in a heartbeat, yet things were, clearly, more complicated here.

"Tell me about Julie," Andrew said, playing things as cool as he could.

A worried look flashed across Rose's features. "I know the food wasn't quite what you were expecting, but I really think that if you give her a chance—"

"Her cooking skills are excellent," Andrew replied. "I like knowing about the people I work with. Has she been here long?"

"Just a few days." Rose kept moving as she talked. "Her aunt, Evie, used to run the catering for us but I'm afraid she had to retire due to poor health." Rose paused and, for a moment, she looked saddened by the thought.

"So this is the first wedding Julie will have catered?"

"Yes, but I assure you she comes to us well recommended. She used to own her own restaurant. Delgado's. I imagine you've probably heard of it, given what you do."

Andrew could tell that Rose not only wanted the wedding to go ahead without a hitch, but that she also cared about the people who worked for her. If she knew about what had happened with Julie's restaurant and his review, she might try to stop him and Julie from working together. But Andrew was too used to getting what he wanted to allow that to happen.

He and Julie would work together on his brother's wedding, and if Andrew judged it right, they might also be able to explore that spark that had been so obvious between them.

At the very least, he was going to get to the bottom of Julie's cooking. She had the technical skill. She obviously had the palate when it came to balancing flavors. She had a good knack for presentation and the ability to manage several dishes at once... All the individual ingredients necessary for her to be so much more as a chef.

Andrew knew as well as anyone that ingredients alone weren't enough. It was what someone did with them that truly mattered.

His phone rang again and this time Andrew excused himself to pick it up.

"Don't you pick up your phone anymore?" his assistant demanded.

"Did the lighting guys decide they needed my permission before they changed the shade of filter on the main spotlights again?" Andrew countered. "Come on, Sandy, you can handle that."

"Sure, I can handle that, no problem. But we really need you back at the studio."

"You know I'm dealing with my brother's wedding preparations. It's my wedding gift to him."

"And I still think you're crazy for agreeing to it. You could have just given him a vase and told Phil to take care of his own wedding. Or I could tell him for you. Because, frankly, you have enough to do right now without taking on extra projects."

Andrew couldn't help a small smile at his assistant's protective streak. "You know I could fire you, right?"

"Yay. Then someone else can have all those endless conversations with our producer about exactly why the frozen food he ordered for us wasn't good enough."

She had a point there. Andrew had to put his foot down somewhere, though. "Look, I don't need to be on set for the show until later this afternoon, so—"

"But that's what I'm trying to tell you," his assistant shot back. "The idiots have changed the schedule. They say they sent an email, but I never got it. Anyway, they wanted you on set twenty minutes ago."

Andrew normally wouldn't let the studio jerk him around like this, but if he wanted his new show to get off the ground on the right foot, he was going to have to cut his time at The Rose Chalet short.

"I'm sorry, but I've got to get going," he said to Rose as he pocketed his phone.

"You are planning to come back, aren't you?" Rose asked. "To go through the menu again and talk about the flowers? There's a lot to decide on."

Andrew thought about Julie Delgado once more. Cooking was so personal, so connected. The pressure of the kitchen was relentless, but there was also magic to it.

There was nothing like food for getting to know everything about people...and nothing like feeding someone—and being fed—for getting closer to someone.

"Yes," he said in answer to Rose's question. "I'm definitely planning to come back."

CHAPTER FOUR

JULIE CLEANED UP the dining room, carefully stacking the plates and putting them in the dishwasher, each movement precisely controlled. She was not going to end up breaking a plate on top of everything else that had happened this afternoon.

And she was definitely not going to wallow in thoughts about Andrew Kyle.

Admittedly, that was easier said than done. There were those dimples, for one thing. Not to mention the way he had just come in here and high-handedly dismissed Julie's best efforts as if they were nothing— exactly the same way he'd dismissed her restaurant. Julie knew her food was good and she had done a good job, too. Yet Andrew hadn't even bothered to come up with a better word than *bland* to describe everything.

Who did he think he was?

A successful celebrity chef, obviously, but other than that? Where did he get off, taking apart her carefully constructed menu in front of Rose? Now she would have to work twice as hard to convince her temporary boss that she was the right choice to be The Rose Chalet's permanent head chef.

Julie's best guess was that Andrew enjoyed the power. He could make or break careers. What an ego trip that had to be. Julie couldn't believe the casual way Andrew had suggested that he should come in and "help" her. In other words, stand over her and criticize everything she did. The nerve of the guy!

Unfortunately she knew his type only too well. Men who were too sure of themselves—utterly certain that all they had to do was to snap their fingers and women would come running. It was one of the main reasons Julie didn't date these days.

But to be completely honest, Julie had to admit that wasn't precisely the impression she'd gotten from Andrew while he was busy critiquing her wedding menu.

In truth, he'd seemed like a pretty nice guy. Serious about food, but not nasty. Or a jerk.

She took a few deep breaths. Yes, she reminded herself, people sometimes weren't what they seemed. Julie had learned that lesson more than once. No matter how *nice* Andrew Kyle might be, she wasn't going to make the mistake of trusting a man who had already played a major part in ruining her life.

"Hi, Julie."

Julie spun around and found Phoebe, The Rose Chalet's florist, looking as elegantly beautiful as ever in a dark dress and heels. Her hair was perfect in a way that made Julie—after a few hours in a hot kitchen—feel distinctly self-conscious about how frizzy hers must be.

Instead of replying with a simple hello, all she could manage was a heartfelt groan.

"Rough day?"

"Sorry," Julie said, "it's just this guy…"

She snapped her lips shut, knowing if Rose walked in and found her bad-mouthing the groom's brother, she'd be booted off the property.

Phoebe was a lot more laid-back about life than Rose was, but they were still at work. Besides, it seemed that she'd already said enough, because Phoebe reached out to put a reassuring hand on her arm.

"You shouldn't let some guy get you so upset," Phoebe said. "No man is worth that."

Julie knew that if Andrew was anyone else, if he didn't happen to be one of the greatest chefs in the city, and if she hadn't eaten a couple of the best meals ever in his restaurants, his complete dismissal of her food wouldn't hurt as much.

What a loser he must think she was. Not just because of her failed restaurant, but because she'd let him run roughshod over her food, not once, but twice!

I'm not a loser, she thought as she tossed a metal pan into the sink and it made a satisfyingly loud clanging noise. *But he doesn't know that, does he?*

Suddenly, Julie knew exactly why she'd been feeling so low since he'd left. It wasn't because she didn't think she was up to the task of preparing a great meal for his brother's wedding…but because she hadn't stood up for herself. In any way, shape or form.

It was one thing to be a loser with a failed restaurant.

It was another to be a coward, too.

Phoebe stared worriedly at her. "Julie?"

"I'm pretty much done here for today, but if Rose asks where I am, could you let her know I had a very important errand to run?"

"Of course I can," Phoebe responded, "but are you sure you're okay?"

Julie gave the only answer she could let herself believe. "I will be."

Yanking off her apron and grabbing her bag, she hurried out to the parking lot just in time to see Andrew climbing into a silver Porsche convertible and pulling out. She leaped into her aunt's car and set off after him.

On the open road, Julie would never have been able to keep up. After all, Andrew's car was a speedy, nimble sports car, while her aunt's old Volvo had been designed for family style driving, accommodating the maximum number of passengers and groceries.

Andrew wove between lanes on wider sections of road, darted in and out of traffic, ran through lights just as they were turning to red, and took corners in a way that would probably have gotten him arrested had there been any police around. Julie had to use all her driving skills just to keep up with him. The last thing she wanted was to get in an accident as she tailed him.

He turned a very tight corner. Refusing to be bested by him, she placed her hand firmly on the horn by way of a warning and drove through a couple of gaps in the traffic. Gaps that the average bike courier would have been hard pressed to get through. She made it through only because the drivers around her steered out of the way.

At this point, Julie could still see Andrew's car, but it was way off in the distance. So when his Porsche made another turn, she took her very next right, hoping a shortcut might just put her ahead of him. It certainly couldn't make anything worse.

Or maybe it could.

Julie slammed on her brakes, as did the cars coming toward her. She threw her aunt's car into Reverse as the other drivers started to blare their horns. She scooted lower behind the steering wheel, trying to make herself as inconspicuous as possible.

Who went and put a one-way street there?

That wasn't the important thing right then, though. Neither was getting out of there before things got any worse, or taking the time to hope that the ground would open up and swallow her.

The only thing that mattered was the fact that she could no longer see Andrew's car.

He was gone.

Any other day, Julie would have given up. But, she realized, there came a point when you had to keep doing the monumentally stupid thing, if only because, without some payoff at the end, it meant you were simply acting monumentally stupid for no reason.

That might be good enough for plenty of reality shows, but it wasn't good enough for her.

Driving more carefully, she headed in the direction she had seen Andrew go, hoping for some faint glimpse of the Porsche. Five minutes later she finally spotted what she was looking for: his fancy car was parked outside a large unattractive building that looked as if someone had just dumped a random load of concrete. On top of the building was a large sign that read Cuisine Channel Studios.

Julie drove into the lot, found the last available parking spot, then stepped out of her car. As she did so she could feel her nerves rising up. What exactly was she going to say once she got in there? If only she'd worked that out on her way over here rather than acting like a NASCAR driver hoping to arrive in one piece.

A security guard walked up and asked, "Do you need some help, ma'am?"

Julie decided to try the truth. "I'm here to see Andrew Kyle."

"Another one who didn't get the message about them starting the taping early, huh?" The security guard pointed toward the building. "I just saw him head inside a minute or two back. The studio's on the second floor."

Julie didn't bother trying to decipher what he meant by not getting the message about taping as she headed upstairs. Nobody tried to stop her, if only because everybody Julie passed seemed to be incredibly busy. Two men were arguing over a frighteningly tangled collection of wires. Others were running around with cups of coffee and stacks of papers clutched in their hands. Everyone looked terribly stressed out.

On a day like today, Julie felt as if she fit right in.

Was Andrew Kyle the center of all this? If so, it went a long way to explaining why he thought he could behave like an arrogant, pigheaded jerk.

With so many people running around on his behalf, he probably thought he could do anything he wanted.

Julie was certainly going to enjoy informing him otherwise…assuming she could find him, that is.

The entrance to the studios on the second floor was being guarded by a bulky stagehand who made Julie wait a couple of minutes before letting her in. The chaos outside had been bad enough, but this was, if anything, even worse. There was a kitchen set up in the middle of a small circle of cameras, wires and spotlights. Facing the stage kitchen was the audience. Every seat was full of excited, chattering foodies. The taping hadn't started, mostly because several harried staffers were still making final touches to the set.

In the middle of it all, exactly where Julie had known he would be, stood Andrew. He was leaning against one of the kitchen counters, deep in thought.

Julie started toward him but found her way barred by a young woman with fire-engine-red hair and multiple piercings. She was holding a clipboard.

"Sorry," the woman said in the tone of someone who'd had practically everyone in the room try her patience at some point that day, "we don't allow audience members on set. If you'll go back to your seat, please, there will be a quick meet-and-greet with Andrew after taping."

"I'm not an audience member. I'm Julie Delgado and I've been set up to do some cooking with Andrew, only—"

"Wait a minute, you're cooking with him?" The young woman looked puzzled as she rooted through the sheaf of papers attached to her clipboard, then shot a glare over at a gaggle of arguing stagehands that suggested they should probably be glad she didn't have any weaponry close at hand. "I can't believe the producer is trying to put something else in at this late stage. I've told them, we're not putting up with any more of this."

"No," Julie tried to explain. "It was all Andrew's idea. He—"

"*Andrew* put in a new segment? Without even mentioning it to me? Wait here, please, I need to have a little chat with him."

Julie was more than a little surprised when Andrew smiled and waved her over a minute later. As she headed toward him, she reminded herself to remain firm in the face of his dimples…and to ignore the fact that he seemed to be terrifically happy to see her. Why on earth would he be happy to see her?

Julie psyched herself up to let Andrew know in no uncertain terms that while she was committed to her work at The Rose Chalet, he couldn't walk all over her. But before she could say a word to him, a voice from somewhere outside that circle of oh-so-bright lights hollered, "Okay, everybody, let's go for a take!"

CHAPTER FIVE

BEFORE JULIE COULD protest that she shouldn't be on stage, Andrew was in full flow, talking to the nearest camera with the ease that came from doing television day in and day out.

"Hello and welcome to *Edgy Eats*. I'm Andrew Kyle and today I'm joined by local chef, Julie Delgado, who will be helping me prepare my take on the classic quiche."

She would? Since when?

Julie knew it was long past time to speak up, but when she looked around and saw that she was trapped in that broad circle of spotlights, the protest died on her suddenly dry lips.

"Classic recipes are great for cooking good food at home, but I've always believed it's important to do more than just repeat the same old things, to experiment with your food and make it your own. Don't you agree, Julie?"

Had he asked her that to try to throw her?

Deciding she wouldn't be that easily cowed, she countered, "I've always believed that classic recipes are classic for a reason."

Andrew laughed, turning slightly to address the studio audience. "I can see that I'm going to have my work cut out trying to convert Julie to my way of cooking." He gave her a look that couldn't be interpreted as anything but fond before turning back to the crowd. "What do you all say? Should we have a cook-off?"

As his challenging words got the inevitable burst of approval from an audience primed to respond with glee to whatever he said, Julie gritted her teeth. She'd come here to clear the air between them, and to stand up for herself while she was at it—not to get pulled into a battle of the kitchen with him. Not only was dragging her onto his show like this not playing fair, but it was just typical of a guy like him to do it without even asking.

Julie was tempted to walk off and leave him hanging there, if only to see what his precious audience would do then.

But she already knew what would happen. The audience would blame her. She would be the one who wouldn't go along with the "fun" and would end up being branded a "difficult character" that poor Andrew had to deal with. His show, meanwhile, would likely end up clipping along nicely without her, so it wouldn't actually achieve anything.

Except making Andrew think even less of her for backing away from his challenge.

No, Julie wasn't going to let him win like that. Instead she forced her best made-for-TV smile.

"Sure," she replied. "I'm up for the challenge."

Andrew looked extremely pleased that she'd gone along with it. Well, she'd see how pleased he was in a few minutes.

"We'll each make one quiche according to our own recipes and my viewers will get a good sense of the difference between the traditional recipe and a more modern take on it."

Without waiting for him to tell her to begin, Julie reached for the ingredients.

Quiche. Such a simple thing to make. Eggs, pastry crust, cheese, half-and-half, heavy cream and some simple filling ingredients like bacon and vegetables. It was all very easy. Far too easy for Andrew Kyle to ever do it that way, of course, which presumably explained why there were so many extra ingredients available on the kitchen bench. There was a full selection of herbs and spices and some unusual fruits and vegetables.

Julie concentrated on the recipe she knew. No distractions—that was the way.

Except…she should have known that Andrew wasn't going to let things be that simple.

"So, Julie," he said just as she was trying to remember how much nutmeg she liked to put in for flavor, "what is your approach going to be today?"

"I'm going to do it properly," Julie said. "Classic, time-tested recipes might not be very fashionable right now, but sometimes it is the best way to do things."

"It's not about what's fashionable," Andrew retorted, taking a handful of celeriac and mashing it up with some potatoes. "It's about the world of cooking moving forward. We can sit in the past or we can innovate."

"Again," she said in her calmest voice, "classic dishes *are* classics because people know good food when they taste it and they like to share those recipes with others."

Andrew smiled back at her and then over at the audience. "Wanting to make people happy with your food doesn't mean you have to close yourself off from experimentation, does it, Julie?"

She decided to ignore his way-too-pointed question so that she could concentrate on getting the consistency of her pastry just right. With any luck, Andrew would have to concentrate on explaining to the audience how he was putting together his ingredients and would forget about her for a while.

Sadly, though, it seemed he wasn't nearly done with her just yet.

"I know you owned your own restaurant, Julie. What do you think the most important thing is when it comes to cooking great food?"

Wow. He'd finally come out and said it: *he remembered her.*

Which meant that Julie had been right in her suspicions: this really was all just some sick, twisted game to him.

Working to keep her voice steady, she lifted her chin and met his gaze square-on. "I think it's about giving people food they actually want to eat. Too many chefs get carried away trying to prove how clever they are and end up forgetting about the people who are paying hard-earned money to eat what they create."

Andrew nodded as if he agreed with her, then said, "For me, it's all about passion."

Julie snorted. "I think I read about your latest *passion* in the gossip pages."

The audience laughed at her comeback. To her annoyance, he joined in good-naturedly. "What can I say? I'm a very passionate guy." He winked at the swooning audience. "However, just now I was talking about a passion for food. I want to be someone whose food is a reflection of me. I want the dishes I create to say something about me."

"Don't you have a publicist for that?"

That got another laugh from the audience, but before she could feel too smug about her comebacks, Andrew grinned and shrugged. "Sure I do. But I've always thought one taste of something I've made does a better job of selling my skills than a picture in a paper does."

Finally realizing she wasn't going to win a battle of words with the smooth-talking TV presenter, Julie bent back over her work. As she beat the eggs together, she was grateful it was a recipe that gave her the opportunity for a little mindless violence.

The trouble was, it wasn't going to be enough, no matter what she did. She could come out with the most flawless quiche ever made, and Andrew would probably declare it mediocre. Any audience member allowed a taste would undoubtedly side with him, too.

After all, there was no point in disagreeing with the gorgeous star.

So what then? Should she give up? Refuse to play this game any longer?

No, she quickly decided, that wouldn't work, either. She needed something else.

Julie looked over the ingredients set out on the counter. What would the quiche taste like with a little Tabasco sauce and a few unexpected spices to give it some extra dimensions of flavor?

She knew she shouldn't take the risk. She knew precisely what happened when she experimented. People complained. They threw it away uneaten.

And she ended up feeling terrible.

Mixing things up in the eleventh hour wasn't a risk she should take, period, let alone in front of a packed studio audience.

Except that, as Andrew told an anecdote about one of the kitchens he'd worked in and the audience lapped it up, Julie found herself reaching for several jars. She didn't have any measurements memorized, because she'd never put these ingredients into this recipe before. All she could do was smell and taste…and hope.

By the time Andrew came to the end of his story, the ingredients were in.

And the damage was done.

Andrew slid his own pie into the oven beside Julie's at almost the same moment.

"And…cut!" yelled the floor director.

Julie let out a breath. This was her chance to run away, to get out of the studio as fast as her legs could carry her. Especially given what she had just done with the recipe. If she ran off now maybe they wouldn't be able to use the footage, and she wouldn't be even more of a laughingstock in the chefs' community than she already was.

I thought you didn't want him to think you were a coward?

Julie knew her inner voice was right. She'd come to give him a piece of her mind and now she finally had the chance. But just as she moved toward him, Andrew's assistant, who finally introduced herself as Sandy, herded Julie into a folding chair and stood directly behind her as if personally responsible for making sure she didn't pull a runner.

While Andrew filmed a couple of segments in which he shared a few cooking tips, answered a handful of audience queries and generally played up to the camera, Julie couldn't take her eyes off him. It wasn't just that he was good-looking, though that was certainly part of it.

It was that he seemed to enjoy what he was doing so much.

He really did seem to genuinely love anything to do with food, whether it was showing the easy way to open up shellfish or mixing together an elaborate dessert from the ingredients set out on the table.

Passion.

Julie didn't want to use the word, given how much Andrew had made of it, but it was true. His passion for food and cooking came through in every word he spoke in front of the camera.

Finally it was time for her to head back in front of the cameras. As she took her spot beside Andrew, he turned his back to the audience and said, "I'm sorry to hear that your aunt was ill. I hope she's doing better now."

Julie blinked up at him in surprise. He knew about Aunt Evie? How?

The only way he could have known that was if he'd taken the time to ask Rose about Julie after the tasting. Why would Andrew ever go and do something like that?

Julie managed to stammer out something about her aunt being fine now and just needing to take things a little easier before the director yelled for cameras to roll again.

"I'm pleased to have Julie Delgado back with me for our friendly little cook-off segment," Andrew said to the audience before turning to open up the oven. "Earlier, we each created our idea of the perfect quiche. Now, you'll be able to see the results. Julie, you went for a more traditional option, didn't you?"

"Actually, I changed things up a little," Julie admitted, knowing that she had to give Andrew some warning before he tasted what she'd done to the basic recipe. "I put a few spices in. A little Tabasco sauce, too."

Andrew raised an eyebrow. "And here I thought I was the maverick cook." After the audience chuckled, he said, "It's time to taste them and see how things turned out. By the way, everyone, the full recipes will be available on our website."

They tried his recipe first and Julie had to admit it was phenomenal. Andrew had taken what should have been simple, home-cooked food and elevated it to something complex and delicious.

When it was her turn, Julie acted as if she was confidently taking a bite of her quiche. But, really, she was watching Andrew while he tasted, holding her breath as the moments ticked by, one after the other.

"This is great!" he declared. "Just perfect, Julie."

Utterly shocked, all she could do was stand there, staring at him in surprise. Amazingly, he was just as silent as she was, staring straight back at her for a moment.

Julie became suddenly aware of how close she was standing to Andrew…and how much closer she wanted to get. Fortunately he turned back to the camera just then.

She took another bite of her quiche. She had to admit, it *was* pretty good.

After the show wrapped, the chaos Julie had found when she'd first showed up immediately resumed. Andrew was pulled away by the producer and Sandy escorted her out to her car, saying something about how well everything had gone.

"There was real chemistry between the two of you. That's why it was such good TV, you know."

Yes, Julie thought as she got in her car, she knew only too well how good her and Andrew's chemistry was. So good, in fact, that she had completely forgotten to lay down the law with him.

CHAPTER SIX

THE NEXT DAY Rose immediately called Julie into her office. "I know it's short notice," Rose said, "but could you pull a sample menu together right away? Some really important prospective clients just called out of the blue and they are in a rush. It would really help me out. Tyce is already putting together some suggestions for music, and Anne sent over a selection of dress designs a few minutes ago."

Julie hadn't seen much of The Rose Chalet's resident DJ or dress designer, given that Tyce Smith did much of his mixing in his home recording studio and, according to Phoebe, Anne was a close friend of Rose's who seemed to enjoy more flexibility than anyone else who worked at the Chalet.

"Sure," Julie replied with a smile. "I'll just need to pick up some ingredients at the market."

If Rose wanted Julie to help out with another wedding, couldn't that easily become another wedding after that, and then another, until Julie slid right into a permanent position?

Just what she wanted. A safe, regular cooking position she could count on.

Not *bland,* no matter what Andrew said.

"When are they stopping by?"

"Not until four," Rose replied. "I know this is very

last minute, but, please, if you could make sure this is a good menu—"

"It will be fantastic," Julie promised, and she swore to herself that it would be.

With that in mind, she headed down to the local markets and delicatessens, looking for inspiration. Rose wanted something special for this wedding, and Julie wasn't going to let her down.

Every dish was going to be spectacular; a literal feast for the senses. If being on set yesterday with Andrew had proved one thing to her, it was that she *did* have the skills to cope with unexpected work on command. And the skills to do it well.

She was halfway through her shopping trip when she stopped by her favorite cheese shop. As she walked in she looked up and could not believe her eyes. Andrew was talking to a woman serving behind the counter.

Somehow, he even managed to make selecting cheese look incredibly sexy.

Julie quickly checked that thought. She hadn't let herself think about the brief moment of connection they'd had yesterday, and she wasn't going to start now.

But that vow became a lot harder when Andrew turned around and spotted her, treating her to a smile that could have lit up the entire store.

"Julie, what luck, seeing you here!"

It was all she could do to stifle a sigh of resignation. She'd been hoping her luck was about to change, but it seemed fate had other ideas.

Julie tried not to be nervous as his eyes scanned the items in her shopping basket. "I thought I might try one or two new things with a bride and groom Rose is wooing."

Andrew let out a short laugh. "I *knew* I'd convert

you. I can't wait to taste what you come up with. Are you free now?"

"Actually, Rose scheduled the menu tasting for the new clients this afternoon. It would be better if we shifted our meeting to tomorrow instead." *Or, preferably, to the fifth of never.*

She half expected Andrew to refuse, because he was the big star with the tight schedule, but all he said was an easy, "Tomorrow would be fine." She was momentarily mesmerized by his smile, just long enough for him to add, "But only if you agree to go out for lunch with me now."

"You want to have lunch with me?" As if thankful for the reminder, her stomach grumbled right on cue.

"Yes, lunch," he said, still smiling at her as if he found her adorable.

Julie frowned. She didn't do adorable. Not even for a gorgeous TV chef who made her stupid insides melt like butter.

"I don't have a lot of time."

Any other guy would have fled from her hard tone, but Andrew simply asked, "When are the clients coming around?"

She knew she was cornered even as she said, "Four o'clock."

"That will leave plenty of time for you to work some of the magic you showed yesterday," Andrew said with another one of those gorgeous grins. "And if you're worried about that boss of yours wondering where you are, I'll phone to tell her that this is an essential research lunch, and without it, I'm not going to be able to work with you anymore."

Julie's eyes widened. "Please don't do that. You

wouldn't, would you? Pull out of the wedding like that? She'd kill me."

Instead of answering her question, he simply said, "I'd really love for you to join me for lunch at *the Glass Square*. Say yes."

He dropped in the name as though it was nothing, rather than a restaurant with both a Michelin star and a waiting list that was so long most people couldn't ever hope to eat there. As for the prices... Julie didn't even want to contemplate how much a lunch for two would cost.

Not to mention the way his simply seductive "Say yes" had her heart pounding like a hard-rock drum beat.

"*The Glass Square?* Seriously?"

"Phillipe keeps telling me to drop in and I know he'd love to meet you." He gave her a smile that brought his dimples to the fore.

Julie wasn't sure which was more impressive— the fact that Andrew could talk about the head chef of such an important place so casually, or the fact that he wanted to take her to lunch there. Even so...

"Andrew," she said as she very reluctantly shook her head, "I—"

"I'm not taking no for an answer," Andrew warned before his expression softened. "I want to make up for dragging you onto the set of my show. One lunch at a nice restaurant is the least I can do."

Put like that, Julie couldn't say no, even if it wasn't quite the apology she really wanted for the terrible review he'd given her restaurant. Still, it would do. For now.

"That is very nice of you, but I took the bus to work this morning and I've got these groceries to deal with."

"No problem," Andrew replied. "I've got a cooler in my trunk."

Of course he has a cooler in his trunk. This man is ready for anything!

"Well, then, I guess we should get going," Julie said.

They stashed the cold groceries in the cooler and then, with the top down, they headed off to *the Glass Square.*

Andrew drove a tad more sedately than he had the day before, but even so he pushed the edge of the speed limit.

Yes, she thought as the wind whipped through her hair, Andrew Kyle was definitely a man who liked to push past limits.

He obviously hadn't phoned ahead and Julie knew anyone else would have been turned away at the door. Instead a rotund man in his fifties came out of the kitchen to greet Andrew with such enthusiasm that it spilled over into a bear hug for Julie. A moment later Phillipe clapped his hands and ordered the waitstaff to set up a table in the kitchen where Andrew and Julie could dine and watch him at work.

"Typical Phillipe," Andrew said softly. "A total showman. Especially in front of a beautiful woman."

Julie laughed at the idea of Andrew Kyle calling someone else a showman…and flushed at being called beautiful.

In the kitchen Phillipe opened a bottle of wine. Andrew pointed out that he was driving, but Julie was too bowled over by being in *the Glass Square* to possibly say no to the glass Phillipe handed her with a flourish.

"I'm almost thinking that you planned to get me a little tipsy," Julie whispered to Andrew, "if there was any way you *could* have planned it."

"Do you think it would work?" he whispered back, clearly enjoying teasing her.

Julie shook her head, enjoying his playfulness far too much. "I'm having one glass with lunch. That's it."

Andrew raised his eyebrows. "I see. There's still a way to go to get you to take risks."

Julie knew he was probably still teasing her, nonetheless she had to bite her lip to keep her sharp retort to herself.

While a part of her was glad his comment had reminded her to be on guard again, being in *the Glass Square*'s kitchen was too special to spoil with an argument. The kitchen, so much smaller than Delgado's had been, was hot and noisy, the air filled with shouted instructions as the staff chopped vegetables and flambéed desserts. To Julie, there was something so beautiful about it—an underlying level of chaos that belied that fact that everyone there knew exactly what they were supposed to be doing.

"Is this what it's like in your kitchen when you're not on TV?" Julie asked.

Andrew shook his head. "It's usually even more chaotic." He grinned. "At least when it's going well."

The first course arrived and Phillipe hovered behind them as they dove into wafer-thin layers of crisp, thinly sliced ham over crab and cinnamon cakes, all resting on a bed of mixed vegetables and served with a tarragon reduction.

At first it seemed to Julie that there were too many ingredients all vying for center stage, but somehow everything blended together perfectly. Phillipe seemed genuinely pleased when Julie said so, though not as pleased as he was when Andrew praised his creation.

The big man practically skipped off to start work on the main course.

"You seem to have a knack for making people happy," Julie said.

"Not quite everyone," Andrew replied with a deliberate look at her.

For a moment Julie's smile faltered. Unexpectedly, they were at a point already when it was best to just be honest. Even if it was painful.

"It's hard, doing your best, only to have someone say it isn't good enough."

"I know," Andrew replied. "It's just that I don't want to stand by and watch someone wasting their talent, Julie. You cooked phenomenally well on set yesterday. Why don't you cook like that all the time?"

"Because I know how much there is to lose if it goes wrong." She knew exactly what it was like to sink everything she had into her dream, to reach a goal she'd been aiming for her whole life, only to watch it explode like an over-risen soufflé. "More than you do."

As soon as she said the words, Julie regretted revealing herself to him like that, but Andrew wasn't looking at her with pity. He wasn't regarding her as he would a loser who didn't deserve to run a successful restaurant.

Instead the look in his eyes was gentle.

Almost as if he cared about her.

"I know you lost your restaurant," he said softly, so that no one but she could hear, "and I'm very sorry about that. But that's not all this is about, is it?"

Before she could respond, Phillipe presented them with a couple of delicate, savory soufflés and a lattice-work of crisped vegetables. Despite the intense discussion she and Andrew had been having, Julie thanked Phillipe profusely and, after he excused himself, she began sampling the incredible food in front of her. It was superb.

She was halfway through the entrée before she spoke again. "When I was a kid, all I wanted to do was cook. I'd cook anything for anyone. I'd gather up people around the neighborhood and I'd do all the stuff you seem to want me to do. I'd throw in crazy ingredients—"

"Like the hot sauce in your quiche. Which worked perfectly, by the way."

"—and they…" She sighed and admitted, "No one wanted to eat it. My parents came from Spain and they tried so hard to help me fit in. They stopped speaking Spanish when I was around. They even made sure I took what they thought was typical American food to school—yellow processed cheese in plastic wrappers on white bread with Oreo cookies for dessert. I don't know how many plates of artisanal food I cooked and threw away before I figured out that if I wanted to fit in, I had to stop being so experimental with my cooking and just give people the same food they were already used to eating."

She was shocked when Andrew's expression turned rueful. "My family are doctors and lawyers. People with *real jobs*. Trust me, I know what it's like to not fit in."

Unfortunately, before she could ask any more questions, Phillipe came by their table to ask, "How did you enjoy your meal?"

"It was one of the best I've ever had," Julie replied with a smile.

And not just because of the food. The company had been pretty nice, too.

Surprisingly nice.

Still, Julie realized after Phillipe hugged them both

again and then hurried back to the stove, all good things
had to come to an end. "Rose is going to be wondering
where I've gone, especially considering I need to put a
sample meal together by four o'clock." She shook her
head as she gestured at the busy kitchen. "Although,
frankly, I'm starting to wonder why I bother when nothing I cook can possibly come up to this standard."

"You aren't giving yourself enough credit," Andrew
said as he pushed his chair back and then, like a true
gentleman, helped her with hers. "Will you promise me
one thing before I take you back to The Rose Chalet?"

"That depends on what it is."

"Still so cautious, aren't you?"

"Around you?" She raised an eyebrow. "Definitely."

His mouth curved into a grin at her sassy response.
"Promise me that for this afternoon you won't be cautious. You've got good instincts, Julie. I have a feeling
if you follow them, you'll do really, really well."

CHAPTER SEVEN

ROSE WAS WAITING for Julie when Andrew walked in with her.

"Oh, Andrew, it's nice to see you again." Rose was clearly surprised to see the two of them together. "Have you and Julie had some time to work on revising your brother's menu?"

Andrew nodded. "We just finished conducting some research with a chef friend of mine. I hope you don't mind me stealing her away for an hour?"

What was it about him that made things go so easily? Julie wondered. In any case, she was glad when Rose smiled. She'd half expected Rose would fire her for coming back so late from the grocery store.

"No, it's no problem," Rose said. "I hope there isn't any more research to do today, however. Julie has some other clients to cook for, and they'll be arriving soon."

By way of an answer, Julie lifted her bags of groceries. "I have all the ingredients, so everything will go just great."

It felt good to be confident again and it also helped that she was actually starting to believe it. She had been inspired earlier that morning when she'd planned her menu, but after eating lunch at *the Glass Square,* Julie's head was fairly bursting with ideas.

Yesterday, on set with Andrew, she'd seen what she could do if she trusted her palate. Today, she was determined that Rose's new customers would have a wedding menu the likes of which the world had never seen.

"I've got to get back to the studio, anyway," he told them. "The producers love the idea of local chefs cooking alongside me so much that they now want me to do that as a regular thing."

He made no direct mention of Julie, but even so she tensed, waiting for Rose to pick up on their connection. Maybe she should have mentioned her impromptu appearance on his show, but there hadn't really been time to talk to Rose about it since then, had there?

Fortunately, Rose replied, "That sounds like fun," in a distracted way. "Sorry, I've got to run. There are so many things to get ready." She actually broke into a bit of a jog in her heels as she headed back inside.

Julie turned to Andrew. "Thank you for a really lovely lunch."

"It was my pleasure," Andrew said, and her breath actually hitched when he stared into her eyes. "I'm looking forward to seeing you again. Very soon."

This time Julie's breath simply stopped altogether. Finally, when Andrew had driven away and she remembered how to breathe again, she turned to go back to the kitchen and saw Rose talking with RJ.

Whatever the gardener said had her boss laughing out loud for a moment. Rose quickly recovered her composure, then hurried off to get back to work. The Rose Chalet's proprietor never seemed to slow down.

Julie got to work herself as she began writing out the menu and preparing the dishes that were taking shape in her head. The details weren't quite all there yet. It was almost as if her ideas were half-remembered tastes rather than the carefully planned recipes she normally stuck with.

It would be far safer to do something tried-and-true. Except that was what she'd tried with Andrew's brother's wedding menu, and look at how that had turned out.

Besides, today, the thought of doing things that way suddenly felt restrictive.

Instead, following her instincts, she tasted and smelled the dishes as she worked on them. Piece by piece, dish by dish, the food came together. Her first course would be squid, served with papaya segments. For the main course, traditional meats would be presented sushi style, relatively rare, and backed with delicately flavored rice wrapped in greens. The new approach was relatively simple, but one that would make a huge difference. As for the dessert, she would flambé pancakes at the table, enfolding them around a mixed berry and tart ice cream filling. This food would undoubtedly make a statement.

It was a lot of work to bring all the elements together and the time flew past. So when Rose put her head around the kitchen door to announce that their new clients—the soon-to-be O'Neils—had arrived, Julie hurriedly put the finishing touches to her handwritten menu.

"Something smells good," Rose said. "Will it all be ready on time?"

Julie nodded. She would nail this presentation today even if it killed her. "I'll have the three courses out in a few minutes. As Andrew suggested yesterday, it's better if I bring out everything all at once."

"Okay, if you think you can do it seamlessly then go for it."

That, of course, was the big downside to presenting things all at once. She had to plate up the first course, carve the trio of sushi-style meats, and remove the ice cream from the freezer. Julie could have used a few more pairs of arms.

But, somehow, she did it. She headed into the dining room with the plates carefully balanced, determined not to let the slightest slip ruin her perfect presentation.

This was going to be good. Better than good. This sample menu was going to be the one that convinced Rose she needed Julie permanently. Julie was certain of it.

Until she caught sight of the couple waiting in the dining room. Both were a little older than Julie had expected, and everything about them, from the cut of the future groom's suit to the neutral shade of the bride-to-be's lipstick, combined to create an impression that was conservative, even staid.

What had she done?

Sure, Julie had followed her heart, but looking at the O'Neils sent butterflies somersaulting in her stomach.

It was her childhood all over again, but with the added worry this time of losing a job she really needed.

No, she counseled herself, she needed to stay positive. She would remember what Andrew had said. *"Promise me that for this afternoon you won't be cautious. You've got good instincts, Julie."* Darn it, for the first time in a very long time, she was going to be confident about her food.

Still, that was easier said than done. The groom, whom Rose introduced as Stephen, fixed Julie with the expression of someone determined not to be impressed by anything, while the bride, Rebecca, was looking at the food coming out with hawklike suspicion.

"This is Julie, our chef," Rose said. "I'm sure you'll just love what she has come up with. She has assured me that it is going to be something special."

"It had better be," Stephen said. "For the money I'm paying—"

"Oh, hush now," Rebecca interrupted. "We all know how much you're paying. You tell us every few minutes. I just want everything to be perfect."

"Then maybe I should show you what I have in mind?" Julie said, putting the plates down on the table. She took out her menu and handed it to the couple, who pored over it for a few seconds. Their expressions soon told Julie everything she needed to know, and her heart hit her shoes with a messy splat.

"Does this say 'squid'?" Stephen asked.

"We don't like squid," Rebecca chimed in. "And what's this about the main course being done 'sushi style'? We don't want raw meat."

"Actually, if I could explain why I—"

"I don't see why you have to do all this fancy stuff at all," Stephen said, standing. "This is a wedding, not an excuse for you to try some crazy experiment." He turned to Rose. "Really, Ms. Martin, this was not what I expected from The Rose Chalet. If this is the best you can do, we will have to think about going elsewhere."

"I'm sure if you only try it—" Julie began, but the man fixed her with a stare.

"Try *that?* Why would I? Why would anyone? Rebecca and I know what we like, and that most definitely isn't it. Come on, Rebecca, we're leaving."

After Rose showed them out, for several seconds all Julie could do was stand there. Stunned. She stared at the uneaten food. All that work. Yet it hadn't been worth anything. All it was going to achieve was getting her fired.

Why had she let Andrew Kyle persuade her that doing something like this would be okay?

Rose came back after a minute or two, and she didn't shout, but she clearly wasn't happy. She sat at the table with Julie, the abandoned food hard to ignore.

"Julie, you told me that you were coming up with something great, not something that would have the clients threatening to take their business elsewhere."

"If they'd only *tried* the food, they might have loved it," Julie protested.

Julie had to give Rose some credit when she picked up a fork and tasted each dish.

"I can see you put a lot of work into these, Julie, but did you ever stop to think about whether they were right for the clients? I know Mr. Kyle said the food wasn't exciting enough yesterday, but now you've taken it too far in the other direction. And now I'm going to have to try very hard to convince them to give us another chance."

"I'm sorry," Julie said again, because it seemed to be the only thing to say.

"I know you are," Rose said, not unkindly. She sighed. "I took you on because your aunt said you would be the right replacement. I would hate for you to prove me wrong."

She left it at that, and Julie threw away the remainder of the food before washing up and heading back to her aunt's house.

Aunt Evie wasn't home, which meant she could storm around the house without having to answer the inevitable questions about what was wrong. Julie wasn't in the mood for people trying to comfort her.

So when the doorbell rang, after she'd finally settled on the couch to stew over her biggest failure to date, she hauled herself off the couch, stalked over to the door and threw it open.

Andrew Kyle stood there, trademark smile in place, looking as if he didn't have a care in the world.

"What are you doing here?" Julie demanded.

"You weren't at The Rose Chalet, so I had to track you down."

"How did you even do that?"

"My assistant Sandy is a fine detective when she wants to be." He finally seemed to notice her expression. "So, how did your food tasting go?"

Julie took a step back from sheer shock. First, that he'd come to see her so soon after they'd just had lunch together. Second, that he'd remembered about her tasting.

And, finally, at how *angry* she was.

"How did it go?" Julie repeated. "How did it *go?* They *hated* what I did."

"Whoa! What happened?"

Julie glared at him. "They wouldn't even taste my food before threatening to take their business elsewhere. Then they stormed out. That's what happened. And Rose is furious with me now. She was nice about it, but she didn't pull her punches. I don't think she'll be keeping me on much longer."

"Why not?"

"Because I listened to you, that's why!" Julie couldn't help raising her voice. How could Andrew not understand something so simple? "I followed my instincts, took risks…all those things you like so much. And what happened? It all went wrong. Rose even said it. It's not the right cooking for what I do."

Andrew shook his head. "Then do something else. Whose dreams do you want to follow? Yours or Rose's?"

"That's easy for *you* to say," Julie scoffed.

"You have so much talent, and you're wasting

it!" Andrew shot back, his own annoyance showing through.

"Like you know *anything* about my life!"

"I'm trying to know a lot more about your life, but you won't even take that risk, will you?"

"What are you talking about? Why would you be trying to—?"

Andrew kissed her, cutting off her question as his lips met hers full-on. The kiss was passionate, full of heat…and yet shockingly sweet all at the same time.

Before she let herself think about how wrong it was, Julie kissed him back, exploring his mouth with hers, losing herself in the moment. As their kiss went on and on, she ignored the warning bells in her head as long as she could.

Finally, though, the voice of reason made its way through. *What are you doing kissing Andrew Kyle as if you needed the air from his lungs to breathe?*

Julie made herself pull back. It had been, Julie had to admit, a great kiss. Like the man himself, the kiss had been confident and to the point, but just a little gentler than she had imagined.

And wrong, of course.

Utterly, totally, wrong.

"That was a mistake," she said. "A really big mistake."

"Julie—"

"Please, Andrew." She walked to the door and held it open for him.

Amazingly, he started to walk through it. But just before he crossed the threshold, he turned and held her gaze for several long beats.

"I'm not giving up on you, Julie. And neither should you."

CHAPTER EIGHT

"THANKS FOR AGREEING to help me, Aunt Evie," Julie said as she took the third layer of cake out of the oven and put it out on the side of her aunt's kitchen counter.

"It's no problem, honey," her aunt assured her, handing her a pastry bag full of frosting. "I know you haven't done many wedding cakes before."

"I haven't done *any* wedding cakes before," Julie corrected. "I really need to get this one right."

"But isn't this one just for the tasting?"

How could she explain why this cake was so important? Should she tell her aunt about everything that had happened with Andrew picking her food apart? Or how badly she needed to make things up to Rose after the fiasco with the O'Neils and their extreme reaction to squid and sushi-style meat?

But she knew she couldn't drop her problems onto Aunt Evie's lap, not when the stresses of the wedding business had already made her ill once before.

"I just want to make the best impression I can."

"I know you do. You've always worked so hard, honey. Too hard, sometimes."

While the cake was nothing more than a few simple ingredients mixed up right, decorating it was practically an art form—one that took extreme focus. Which proved to be a problem—a *big* problem—every time thoughts of Andrew's very unexpected kiss flashed into her mind.

"Julie?" Evie asked when she messed up a string of frosting for the third time. "Tell me what's wrong."

But Julie didn't want to think about what had happened the night before. Maybe if she buried it deep enough, she might just be able to forget how good Andrew's mouth had felt on hers.

"Nothing's wrong. I'm just not good at this."

Aunt Evie took the frosting tube out of her hands. "I'm not letting you do anything else to that poor cake until you tell me what has you making such a mess of the edges."

"I…I kissed this guy." Julie suddenly felt like a teenager again. "Actually, he kissed me and I kissed him back. And now I don't know what to do about it."

"Do you like him?"

Julie hesitated as Andrew's beautiful face swam into her thoughts once more.

"Let me rephrase that," her aunt continued with a smile. "You obviously can't run a line of frosting straight so, yes, you like him. Now, what's the problem?"

Julie shook her head. "I *shouldn't* like him. I should hate him. But things…"

"Aren't that simple?" Her aunt laughed softly. "They never are. My advice is to just get on with life and see where it takes you."

Fortunately her aunt left it at that and by the time they were done with the cake, Julie was fairly certain Rose would be pleased with it—enough, she hoped, to get them over the hump of the O'Neils.

Before she left for work, Julie put on far too much

makeup, then took most of it off again before changing into her normal work clothes.

When she arrived at The Rose Chalet, Phoebe was putting together a couple of small floral displays. The florist was dressed in a long blue-and-green dress that hugged her figure and Julie almost felt as if she were dressed in rags by comparison.

"Phoebe, those designs are incredible." She really hoped Andrew wouldn't pick away at her new friend's arrangements the same way he had at her food. "I didn't expect you to be here today, though."

Phoebe stopped what she was doing and turned to Julie with a smile.

"Rose suggested I should run the flowers by Mr. Kyle to check that I'm going in the right direction. So," Phoebe asked, "what's he like? I mean, I've seen him on TV, but who knows if celebrities are the same in real life."

Julie pushed back an odd sense of disappointment at not getting to see Andrew alone. How could that even be what she wanted after their kiss the night before and the way she'd asked him to leave?

"Andrew is—" She hastily shut down more thoughts of their kiss as she tried to think of a diplomatic way to put it. "He has a very clear idea of what he wants for his brother's wedding. *Very* clear."

"I see," Phoebe said, looking a little worried. "I heard that he was really picky when it came to the food. Sorry your first wedding here can't be an easier one."

This time it was even harder for Julie to be diplomatic. What she wanted to say was, *"You don't know the half of it."* The thing was, not only would she sound like a complete jerk, but she wasn't actually sure any of her preconceived notions about Andrew were true anymore.

"I'm sure you'll do fine with him," Julie said in what she hoped was a reassuring tone before turning her attention to unwrapping and assembling her cake.

"Wow, Julie, it's lovely. You must have gone to so much trouble. And all for a tasting."

Just then, Andrew arrived. Julie had barely been able to sleep after their kiss, but he looked annoyingly well rested. And confident.

Right in line with his *"I'm not giving up and neither should you"* parting comment.

Opting for an uber-professional tone that couldn't possibly give away their secret kiss to anyone who might be listening, Julie said, "Andrew, this is Phoebe, who'll be handling the flowers. Phoebe, meet Andrew."

"Hello, Phoebe," Andrew said, extending a hand. "That is a lovely dress. And, Julie, you're looking great as always."

The sudden compliment took Julie by surprise, but she tried not to show it as she led him through to the dining room. He made easy conversation with Phoebe, and the two seemed to hit it off, with Andrew telling her some anecdote about a minor starlet he used to cook for who was fanatical about having edible flowers on every dish.

Part of Julie wanted to reach out to Andrew and drag him back toward her; but she knew she couldn't have it both ways; pushing him away in one moment, pulling him in at another.

I am not jealous of how well they're getting along, Julie told herself. *Even if Phoebe is gorgeous today, and Andrew is...well, Andrew.*

The trouble was, it was hard to keep repeating that once they got into the dining room and Andrew caught sight of the flowers.

"Phoebe, this is wonderful. The arrangements you've put together will be perfect for the wedding. Thank you."

But instead of simply accepting the compliment, Phoebe said, "I know how important your brother's wedding is to you. I can change them if you'd like. It wouldn't be a problem at all."

Why was Phoebe fishing for compliments? She wasn't attracted to Andrew, was she?

Julie worked to quickly shut down that thought. Clearly the reason Phoebe couldn't believe Andrew might be complimentary about her arrangements was that she'd heard just how badly he'd ripped apart Julie's menu.

Which brought them to the cake.

Phoebe was already standing beside it, telling Andrew how much work Julie had put in. Meantime, Julie ignored that, focusing purely on Andrew as he circled it, examining it closely before cutting slices from each layer and trying them.

Come on, thought Julie, *how long does it take to have an opinion on a cake?*

Finally he turned to her and smiled a slow smile. One that brought both dimples to the fore.

"It's great, Julie. Really great. It tastes good, and the decoration must have taken you quite a while. I really like the idea of having the three different layers. It's inventive, while still being traditional."

Julie could feel herself glowing at his praise. She shouldn't care so much about what he thought, but the truth was, she did.

Phoebe offered to show Andrew out, but Julie practically shoved her out of the way. She waited until they were in the parking lot, away from prying eyes, before she said anything.

"Andrew, I—"

"Come to my place for dinner tonight, Julie."

"What?"

He took a scrap of paper out of his pocket, wrote an address on it and pressed it into her palm.

"Say you'll come. Please."

"Andrew, I...I don't know where I stand anymore," Julie admitted. "First I thought I hated you, and then I started to like you. But kissing you?" She shook her head. "I'm pretty certain I shouldn't have kissed you back."

"And I'm certain you should have." His eyes softened as he slid the back of his hand gently across her cheek. "It felt right to me, Julie. Are you going to tell me it didn't feel right to you, too?"

Oh, God, it had been so right that it was all she could do to keep from kissing Andrew again right then and there. But Julie knew she couldn't do that. Not in front of her workplace. And *definitely* not when he was still the man who'd held her future in his hands twice— once with her restaurant and now with The Rose Chalet.

Julie took a shaky step away from him and tried to still the butterflies twirling around in her belly.

"I don't think I'll be able to come over tonight, Andrew."

He started to reach out for her again. "Julie, I know this is difficult for you, but—"

"I can't, Andrew." She took another step back, rather than launching herself into his strong arms the way she so desperately wanted to. "I want to, but I just can't."

"Take a risk, Julie."

Julie shook her head at his softly worded urging.

"I'm glad you liked the cake," was all she could say. Julie watched him drive off a few moments later, his address still tucked into her hand.

CHAPTER NINE

"COME ON, ANDREW, how hard can it be to cook one meal?"

Andrew's father sat at the dining-room table, knife and fork already in hand, looking as if he might start banging them if the food didn't appear soon.

His father had gained a few pounds in his sixties, but he kept his hair dyed black, and his gaze was as steely as ever, perfect for reminding juries to take their jobs seriously.

Next to Andrew's father was his mother, who had stopped counting her age sometime after she hit forty. Between her fitness routines, plenty of days at the spa and the occasional plastic surgery, she didn't look that much over it, either.

Then there were Phil and Nancy. Phil took after their father, more heavily built than Andrew, with the same piercing stare. He dressed with the expensive elegance afforded a doctor with his own very successful practice. Nancy was blond and bubbly, but definitely no airhead. She had plenty of success in PR to prove it, too. Andrew watched as she leaned in to kiss her fiancé.

At least somebody's love life was going well.

"Come on, Andrew," Phil said a few moments later, "isn't dinner ready yet?"

"I'm just finishing the game hens now," Andrew said, taking the birds out of the oven and starting work with the carving knife. "You'll all just have to be patient a little while longer."

"Honestly," his father said, "I don't know why we can't just have steaks. Throw them on the grill for ten minutes and—bam!—they're done."

The answer to that was perfectly simple. Andrew flatly refused to serve steaks the way his father liked them, which was best described as "just this side of cremation."

Besides, steaks wouldn't have given Andrew the chance to show just what he could do with an oven. If putting up with a few complaints about the choice of food was what that took, then so be it.

His mother's brow barely wrinkled as she looked over the kitchen counter and said, "If you like, I could come give you a hand with—"

"It's fine, Mom," Andrew said quickly. "Our meal is nearly ready."

The sauce was bubbling away nicely, the potatoes were done, the vegetables were layered perfectly and all that remained was to get everything onto the plates. A family meal done with all the skill Andrew possessed, just to make it that little bit more special.

Family. Such a simple word in theory, such a world of difficulty in practice.

How many times had he invited his family over for meals like this? Dozens? And how often had they come? As often as their busy schedules allowed, certainly, but not nearly as often as Andrew would have liked. Invariably, his father would point out that he had a big case, or Phil and Nancy would be busy with either work or a night out with their friends. They'd either cancel altogether or suggest some other date, then not understand when Andrew pointed out that his constant rounds of show tapings and cooking didn't allow for many breaks in his schedule, either.

As he plated up the meal, they began to get into a discussion about some big trial his father had worked on. That was fine, but it also meant that any minute now...

"You know, Andrew," his father said, "my thoughts about legal work still stand. With all the work out there, we need everyone we can get. I just know you'd be a phenomenal lawyer if you'd only put your mind to it."

"I enjoy my career, Dad."

"Or you could go off to medical school. It's not too late, you know. You had the grades, so there's no reason why you couldn't eventually go into practice with your brother. Think what it would be like, two Kyles working side by side."

Well versed in years of tuning his father out at moments such as this, Andrew let his mind drift as he set out the plates. Of course, it would drift in only one direction.

Julie.

Had kissing her been a mistake? Andrew didn't want to think it had, but given her behavior at The Rose Chalet this afternoon, she didn't exactly seem to be warming to the idea of dating him.

Andrew's nature had always been to push for what he wanted, and out in the parking lot of the wedding venue, he'd wanted to kiss her again to show her exactly how good they could be together...and what she'd be missing out on if she refused to give in to it.

But if he'd done that, he knew Julie would have run from him, figuratively if not literally, and that would have been that.

Still, Andrew wasn't sure he could take much more waiting.

"Andrew," his mother said, interrupting his train of thought, "your father was making a serious suggestion. Medical school would be good for you."

Medical school would be a disaster for him, and Andrew had hoped that his family might see it by now. He wasn't a doctor, he was a chef. He had his own life, and he loved it.

"Son—" his father began, but at that moment the doorbell rang.

Eager to put off the inevitable argument a little longer, Andrew went for the door before anyone else could get up.

"Julie?"

The woman he hadn't been able to stop thinking about was standing on his doorstep looking absolutely stunning. She'd obviously gone home and changed, since she was now wearing a dark dress that did more to show off her gorgeous figure than her work clothes had.

Andrew's eyes lingered on her, appreciating every detail. Her makeup was just a fraction more than she wore during the day, too, he noted, while he caught the faintest scent of perfume standing this close to her.

He wanted to pull her into another kiss then and there. Instead he said, "I didn't think you were going to come."

"I almost didn't," Julie admitted. "I'm still not sure that—" She finally noticed they weren't alone. She lowered her voice to a whisper. "Andrew, who are these people?"

"My family," Andrew explained.

Julie's eyes widened and he knew that if he didn't think fast, she would be back out the door in a matter of seconds.

He put a hand lightly on her arm. "Please stay. I

haven't had the chance to cook for you yet. And I'm so glad you're here."

Julie hesitated for a second or two, but then she smiled faintly. "Only if I get to make scathing comments about your cooking, too."

Andrew guessed he deserved that. "If you think it deserves it, yes. Just as long as you stay long enough to taste it."

Another hesitation, but then Julie nodded. He reached out to take Julie's coat.

"I'd like you all to meet Julie Delgado," Andrew said as he introduced everyone. Knowing it was all going to come out soon, he said, "She's the chef who will be putting together the dinner at the wedding."

"Really?" Andrew's mother said. "Have you finalized the menu, then?"

Julie flushed lightly, but held her ground. "We're still working out the finer details. But I can promise you," she said with a smile at Phil and Nancy, "it's going to be absolutely perfect."

Andrew couldn't help noticing that no one asked her for details about being a chef at The Rose Chalet any more than they cared about the details of what he did for a living. It was almost nice to know it wasn't just him.

Almost.

Andrew set out another place for Julie and then served the meal. His father and brother ate the way they always had, shoveling down food with hardly enough time to taste it. Nancy and his mother both picked at their food, meaning that his mother was probably on another of her diets, while Nancy was probably determined not to gain so much as a pound in advance of the wedding.

Julie, meanwhile, ate with the gusto—and appreciation—that Andrew had loved in her when he'd taken her to *the Glass Square*. She shut her eyes for the first couple of mouthfuls, obviously savoring the full taste of everything Andrew had put on the plate.

"This is amazing." She looked up at Andrew. "Seriously, I think this is the best home-cooked meal I've ever had."

"Oh, don't encourage him," Phil told her. "At this rate, we'll never persuade him to give up this thing he has about cooking and get a real job."

His parents and Nancy all laughed along with that, but Julie just looked confused.

"What do you mean?" she asked.

"The boys have been trying to persuade Andrew to finally make the switch to medicine," his mother supplied. "If he doesn't do something soon, he'll be too late to reach the top of his profession."

Andrew saw Julie's frown deepen and he tried to signal to her that it was all perfectly normal behavior from his family and to just ignore it, but she was already saying, "He's already done that."

"Oh, you mean with the cooking?" his father said. "That doesn't help anyone."

Andrew's mother looked over at him. "I'm sorry, dear, but it has to be said. I know you're having a good time in the kitchen, but just think of all those people you could be helping if you went back to school. You could be doing something the world really *needs*."

Andrew bit back a sharp response, but Julie didn't bother.

"I was under the impression that the world needed to be fed." She looked over at Nancy and Phil. "Like at your wedding, for example. Andrew's going to a lot of trouble over it."

"And we're very grateful," Nancy replied.

"It's great," Phil agreed, "but a bit of cooking here and there can't take up that much time. It isn't brain surgery, after all."

"Are you kidding?" Julie looked at each of his family members with clear shock—and dismay—written on her pretty face. "Cooking, and cooking well, requires hours of work. It's not just putting together the food, but the planning takes a ton of time. And as for free time, Andrew has been running back and forth between sorting out your wedding arrangements and the taping for his new show, as well as putting in a couple of nights a week in a high-end restaurant with extremely exacting standards. I don't know if you can understand how much work that is, but I certainly wouldn't be able to juggle that much."

For a moment, just a moment, Phil looked a little ashamed. In Andrew's experience, he didn't look that way very often.

"Really, bro, Nancy and I are very happy you agreed to do this."

"It's my pleasure," Andrew said.

"Even so," his father began, "we do worry about you. Only because we care. What are you going to do when all this comes to an end?"

Julie shook her head with a smile that suggested to Andrew she would laugh if it wouldn't be too impolite. "I expect he'll invest the money he's made by being incredibly good at what he does and buy an island somewhere with the interest. Mr. Kyle, trust me, you don't have anything to worry about. In fact, you should be proud of your son. Particularly when he's just made you a meal that's better than anything you could get in the best restaurant."

Julie left it at that and, surprisingly, instead of blowing up at her for daring to speak to them like that, Andrew got the sense his family respected the way his beautiful guest had refused to back down.

Throughout the rest of the meal, Andrew couldn't keep his eyes off her. Nor could he help noticing the way the others took fresh bites from their plates, eating much more slowly, tasting it properly this time. He doubted it would last, but for now, at least, no one made any more comments about his chosen profession. Instead they made a few remarks about how good the food was.

A short while later they all stood to leave, but for once Andrew wasn't eager to get rid of them. Amazingly, his mother pulled him close and told him that he could do a lot worse—whether she was referring to his career or his dinner guest, Andrew wasn't sure. But he didn't care. He'd known the minute he'd first set eyes on Julie Delgado that she was an incredible woman.

"So," he said, turning to Julie when everyone else had gone, "would you like some dessert?"

CHAPTER TEN

"I DIDN'T THINK you'd come," Andrew said as Julie started to help with the dessert.

"*You* didn't think I would? Until I actually made it to the door, *I* wasn't too sure I would. I actually spent five minutes outside thinking I should just turn around, run for home and pretend you didn't exist."

Andrew smiled at her honesty. "I'm glad you didn't do that. And I'm glad you agreed to join my family for dinner."

"Me, too."

Together, they concocted a dessert that was part ice cream, part chocolate and a lot of random ingredients Andrew had in his refrigerator. There was no recipe. They barely even spoke as they worked together. Instead, the two of them simply threw things into a bowl and whipped them up into a sticky, gooey mess that had them both laughing as they finally scooped it into two bowls and attacked it with spoons.

"Well," Julie said as they ate, "your family is certainly… interesting."

"You mean the way they worry that I've made it to thirty-four without ever having a 'real' job?" Andrew smiled as he said it, but Julie could see the hurt in his eyes.

"We both know that isn't true," Julie said. "We both

know how hard you work. How difficult this job is. And how good you are at it."

Andrew's smile turned genuine then. "Now so do my parents and brother, thanks to you."

"They needed to hear it. From what I remember, you're a big fan of telling people what you think they need to hear, rather than what they want to hear."

Andrew winced slightly. "Julie—"

She shook her head. "Let's just eat our desserts, all right?"

They moved over to the couch. For another minute or two they continued to devour the crazy dessert they had created together, then Andrew laughed. "This dessert is a total mess, isn't it?"

"Are TV chefs allowed to admit that about their own creations?"

"Definitely. If you can't laugh at yourself doing TV, then you won't get very far. That and confidence are what get you through when everything goes wrong during a live taping."

"No one could ever say you have too little confidence," she teased, before adding, "I wish I had more, sometimes."

"You should be full of confidence, Julie. You're amazing. And not just because of your cooking skills. You're kind. You're funny. You're beautiful. You're—"

"Who are you, and what have you done with the real Andrew Kyle?" Julie joked, trying to lighten the mood a little. "Besides, you're not so bad-looking yourself. You know, for someone on TV."

It was true, too. Andrew looked great tonight.

Or maybe it was the fact that she could see so many more sides to him now. He wasn't just the TV star with the strong opinions about cooking. He was also a devoted brother, a busy chef and an excellent kisser.

Those extra facets shouldn't have made a difference in how he looked, but it seemed to Julie that they did, and he'd been pretty fantastic-looking to start with. It was just that now, he wasn't *just* a great-looking guy.

He was so much more than that.

"You have a little whipped cream…"

"Where?"

"Here," Andrew said, laughing, his finger snaking out to deposit a dollop of the stuff on Julie's cheek.

"Hey!"

She got him back with the current contents of her dessert spoon, and pretty soon, they were in a full-on food fight. Julie hadn't been in one of those since… ever, now that she thought about it.

It turned out they were lots of fun.

Or maybe it was just because of who she was having the food fight with.

She was still thinking that when Andrew kissed her. It was briefer than their first kiss, and more playful. Just a quick brush of lips, really, but it was enough to make Julie leap up off the couch, staring down at Andrew accusingly.

"What are you doing?"

"Kissing you," Andrew said unapologetically. "The way you were looking at me, I couldn't resist."

There was still a part of her that said he was completely wrong for her, and that he would only end up hurting her. Yet at the same time, there was another part of her that insisted she should dive back onto that couch and kiss Andrew until they were both covered in the dessert they'd just made.

That part of her reminded her just how glorious Andrew looked, even with a blob of cream decorating his features. Especially that way, in fact, because it gave her the opportunity to reach up and wipe it off. But when he carefully licked the mix off her fingers in a movement that made it clear exactly where things would end up going if she stayed, she knew she couldn't possibly control herself if they started kissing again. She would only end up wanting more than his kisses, more than just his body.

She'd want his heart, too.

In a matter of seconds Julie had her coat on and was heading for the door. Andrew didn't grab her arm, but he did touch it gently, turning her back toward him.

"Don't go."

"I have to," Julie insisted.

Andrew shook his head. "You don't *have* to. The question is do you *want* to?"

Yes.

No.

"What are you running away from?" Andrew asked softly.

"Being with you. Not being with you," Julie whispered, trying to put a little more distance between them. It was easier to think when he wasn't standing so close to her, but it was still not easy enough. "I don't know what I want."

"Can I tell you what *I* want, Julie?"

That brought a nervous laugh from her. "I would have thought that one was fairly obvious."

"I want you. And I don't just mean here, now, tonight, in my bed, if that's what's stopping you."

"I'm sure there are a few starlets who might say otherwise," Julie pointed out.

Was that what was stopping her? Andrew's repu

tion? Or was it just the fear of ending up like one of those other women, put aside after too brief a time when his attention flitted somewhere else?

Andrew seemed to sense her fear. "You aren't like them," he promised. "You aren't like them at all."

"I don't understand. What do you see in me?" If Andrew could have his pick of women, women who threw themselves at him, then why her? "Is it just the thrill of the chase?"

"There are thrills, and then there are roller-coaster rides," Andrew said.

She had to bite back a smile at his teasing tone. She shouldn't let him charm her.

"You really are different," he told her. "You just have to trust me on that."

Trust.

That was the problem. She wasn't sure she even trusted herself, let alone Andrew.

"I want to date you, Julie Delgado. I'm not going to pretend that I don't want to any longer. I'm not going to tiptoe around it, either. I like you. Really, really like you. And I think that you'd really like me, too, if you'd only let yourself."

Andrew stepped back. Julie hadn't realized that he'd been blocking the door until he moved.

"If you don't want me, just say it. Even if you don't want to take things further tonight, if things are moving too fast, say that. I've tried giving you space since we first kissed, but I can't do it anymore, Julie. I like you far too much for that, and I really want to see how far we could go together."

"I want that, too," Julie admitted, and as the words came out, she realized that she *did* want it. The only thing she didn't want was the pain that might come with it. "I just don't know if I should."

"You could go through life never taking risks," Andrew said, "but will that ever make you happy?"

He'd moved closer again, but he didn't touch her. If he had, that would have made her decision for her. She needed him so badly right then that if he'd only kiss her once more, Julie was sure she wouldn't say no.

But he didn't make things that easy, didn't take the choice from her. Instead he stood very still. Expectant. Gorgeous. But still.

Oh, why did he have to force her to be brave, tonight of all nights?

The sensible choice would be to turn around and walk away. This was Andrew Kyle, after all. He wasn't just the man who'd done so much to criticize her food, he was the brother of clients at The Rose Chalet. Taking things any further with him would almost certainly be a professional disaster for her. It would be the kind of risk Julie simply didn't take anymore.

But, oh, what if she did take that risk?

And what if being with Andrew was beyond her wildest dreams?

He'd asked her when had steering clear of risk ever made her happy. Well, right then, she couldn't think of a single time. Yes, Julie wanted Andrew—but more than that, she wanted to be happy.

She deserved this joy, didn't she? All she had to do was to let go, just once. To trust that things would work out okay.

Put like that, it was so simple. All she had to do was...

Julie pulled Andrew to her, pressing her lips to his.

She kissed him with all of her pent-up passion until he pulled back an inch.

"Does this mean you want to date?"

By way of an answer, Julie kissed him again. Andrew responded just as passionately this time, taking charge of the kiss, drawing the moment out in the most sinfully sweet way.

If their first kiss the night before had been good, this one was spectacular. It ended only as Julie pushed Andrew back toward the couch and they fell on it together, their lips meeting once more.

"Damn it," Andrew swore as their dessert spilled to cover most of his shirt.

"Oh, I don't know," Julie said. "It's going to be a good excuse to get that shirt off. And if any gets on you…maybe I can lick it off?"

Andrew's expression turned tender and his hands reached up to cup Julie's face. "You're sure?"

"Well, it was pretty tasty before."

"I mean about this. About us. I was serious before. If you want to just date first—if you want to put the bedroom on the back burner—you only have to say."

"I know," Julie said, reaching up to peel Andrew's hands away from her face and kissing each one in the middle of his palm as she did so. "And what I want right now is to be happy. With you."

Andrew laughed and lifted Julie easily, cradling her in his arms while his lips moved over her eyelids, her cheekbones, her throat. He carried her toward his bedroom and as the door swung shut behind them, Julie looked up into those deep dark eyes of his and kissed him again.

And this time, she didn't stop.

CHAPTER ELEVEN

JULIE WOKE THE next morning, a smile still on her lips, her skin still tingling, from her lovely—*and utterly delicious*—night with Andrew.

She'd wanted him, and she'd gone for him. Taking such a big risk had been scary, but thinking back to one or two of the more memorable moments from the night before, she knew it had been worth it.

Definitely worth it.

The only thing that would have made it better was if Andrew were still there to cuddle with on his large, oh-so-soft bed. She rolled over and hugged his pillow.

That was when she finally saw what time it was. *Uh-oh.* If she didn't hurry up, she was going to be late for work. Too bad it meant leaving behind the wonderful comfort of his big bed. Somehow, though, this morning, even that didn't bother her. How could it, when everything else seemed absolutely perfect?

Throwing back the covers, Julie hunted for her clothing. How had her bra managed to get *there?* Surprised to realize there was no bathroom off the master bedroom, she peeked her head into the kitchen to find Andrew working at the stove.

He caught sight of her and turned to say, "Good morning."

Suddenly conscious of how little of her clothing she

had managed to put back on, she pulled her dress across herself as best she could.

"Aren't we past that stage?" he asked with a gorgeous smile.

Knowing it was true, she stopped making such an effort with the pile of clothes and enjoyed the way his eyes lingered on her instead.

"Which way to the bathroom?"

"It's the only problem with a pre-war apartment like this," Andrew said as he used a spatula to point to a closed door off the living room. "It's right through there. Breakfast should be ready soon."

"I'm not sure I have time for breakfast."

Andrew shook his head. "There's *always* time for breakfast. At least if you hurry up in the shower. Although, I don't suppose—"

She couldn't stop the smile from stealing across her face. "You aren't about to suggest that you scrub my back, are you?"

Andrew grinned in a way that made it clear it was exactly what he had been about to suggest. "A man can hope."

"Hoping is fine," Julie said, "just so long as you don't think it's actually going to happen. Unless you want me to be late for work?"

"Spoilsport."

After piling her hair on top of her head and showering as quickly as she could, Julie realized there was no way she'd have time to go home to change before work. She was just going to have to find out whether the dress she'd worn the previous night—a dress designed for a nice dinner rather than a day at work behind a stove— was going to be suitable for cooking at The Rose Chalet. If Phoebe could get away with it, couldn't she?

By the time she was clean and dressed, there was a heavenly smell coming from the kitchen and Andrew was waiting for her. The appreciation in his eyes made her practically glow.

"What are you making?" Julie asked. "Prosciutto-wrapped eggs and French toast? An elaborate layering of fruits and homemade yogurt?"

"An omelet," Andrew answered.

He was still staring at her, but not with desire, though she knew there was probably plenty under the surface. No, his expression was gentler than that.

He looked content.

And as happy as she felt.

"Just an omelet?" she teased. "Why, Chef Kyle, what will the Michelin people think?"

Andrew laughed. "I won't tell them if you don't. Now come and sit down. I'm not letting you leave for work until you've cleaned your plate."

He was right, she needed to eat. And even if Julie had to get to work, she didn't really want to leave yet. Wanting to watch Andrew cook, she settled down at the edge of a counter to get a good view.

Julie didn't help this time. Making dessert together had been fun, and dinner the night before had really been for his family, since he hadn't known if she would show up.

This was the first time Andrew was cooking just for her.

Every movement he made was sure and deft, from cracking the eggs one-handed to mixing everything together with the sharp motions of a fork. He threw in a few pieces of bacon and roasted a couple of tomatoes, but there was nothing complex about it. Yet even before he was finished, she knew breakfast was going to be amazing.

He slid the steaming omelet in front of her and she took a bite. It was perfect.

Andrew had seasoned it as he'd cooked, let it firm up to just the right degree, and added just enough in the way of other ingredients to keep it from being bland. It was a confident take on what should have been such a straightforward dish, yet his cooking elevated it so that every bite Julie took as she attacked the finished product was heavenly.

"Have I told you how much I love watching you eat?" he said tenderly. He gave her a knowing smile. "Actually, I love watching you do almost anything."

The previous night in his arms had been fantastic. But this morning, just being here with him, eating together, teasing each other, was positively amazing.

"I enjoy watching you, too," she boldly replied.

"You *enjoy* watching me?" He laughed. "And here I was hoping for a much stronger word than *enjoy*." He raised one eyebrow and playfully said, "Soon I'll have you right where I want you."

This, Julie was sure, was a huge part of the secret of Andrew's success. Not simply technique. Not some magical understanding of flavor based on a superior palate. Not even the years of experience working in top restaurants.

Confidence.

It was the one ingredient that seemed to go with everything.

She could see it in everything he did, every move he made, every word out of his mouth. His confidence drew her—and everyone else's—eye as surely as those dimples of his did. It made his every move in the kitchen a joy to watch. And it made his food—Julie tasted her omelet and closed her eyes as the flavors worked their way across her tongue—absolutely delicious.

"It's good to see you smiling," he said.

"I have a lot to smile about." The kiss he gave her a moment later gave her even more reason to smile.

A few minutes later, though, as she was picking up her car keys to head to work and preparing to say good-bye, Andrew put his arms around her.

"You're being very quiet," he observed.

"I'm just thinking about things," she said, wanting to be completely honest with him.

"About us?"

"This morning," she said slowly, "things just seem so obvious. Maybe too obvious."

"There's no such thing as too obvious. Just trust yourself, Julie. Trust the way you feel."

If only she had that confidence, just for a little while. "I have to go."

"Are you sure?"

She nodded. "I'm already ten minutes late. Last night was wonderful. Really."

"I'll call you later, okay? And you know I'll show up at your aunt's place if you ignore me."

Things seemed so simple when she was in his arms, she thought as she drove to The Rose Chalet.

But were they really that simple?

CHAPTER TWELVE

"Wow, YOU LOOK really happy this morning." Julie looked up from her work in The Rose Chalet's kitchen to find Phoebe walking in. "You're practically whistling while you work. I'm pretty sure that isn't allowed, you know," Phoebe joked.

Julie hadn't realized her change in attitude was that obvious. Though to be fair, who wouldn't feel as great as she currently did after dinner—and breakfast—with Andrew Kyle?

"I know that look," Phoebe said with a mischievous note in her voice. She gave Julie a long look. "Who's the lucky guy?"

"Phoebe!" Julie squirmed with embarrassment, but she was dying to tell someone about how good she was feeling and who else was she going to talk it over with? Aunt Evie? Even if the older woman wasn't planning to go out with her friends tonight, there were some things you just didn't discuss with your aunt.

"How did you guess?" Julie asked.

"You're practically glowing, and you obviously haven't been home to change, because that dress is far too formal for work."

That was from a woman who was currently wearing a floral number that fell past her knees and looked as if it had come out of the 1950s. Julie raised an eyebrow, but Phoebe shrugged.

"This is retro-chic. *That,*" she said as she gestured to Julie's outfit, "is an impromptu sleepover. I know the difference. Now, are you going to tell me who it is, or am I going to have to guess?"

When Julie didn't answer immediately, Phoebe turned thoughtful, leaning her head on one hand while she ran through the possibilities and dismissed them.

"Let's see, it has to be someone you've been spending a lot of time with. Good-looking, obviously. Someone who—" Her eyes grew big. "Oh, my God, you didn't! Andrew Kyle?"

Not knowing what else to do, and frankly quite grateful to finally be able to tell someone, Julie nodded with a smile she couldn't possibly contain.

"Lucky you! He's gorgeous. How did it happen? Details, I demand details."

For a second or so, Julie blushed hot enough that she could probably have used her own face to heat a warming oven. Still, she had to talk this over with somebody or she would explode.

After a quick look around to ensure they were all alone, she gave a quick explanation of the highlights of her relationship with Andrew. Still, regardless of how encouraging Phoebe was about it, Julie knew not everyone would feel the same way.

"I'd really appreciate it if you didn't mention any of this to Rose. I'm pretty sure she wouldn't be very happy if she heard that I was involved with a client. Especially one I have a history with."

It wasn't that The Rose Chalet's owner was some fun-hating boss from hell, but Rose *was* running a business, and had to hope for the minimum amount of interpersonal complications between employees and clients.

"Don't worry, I won't say a word," Phoebe said, but

before Julie could get back to work, her friend put a hand on her arm. "I'm really happy for you, but with a guy like Andrew Kyle—"

"I know. Be careful," Julie said. "Thanks, Phoebe."

Phoebe headed out into the garden and Julie was just reaching for a baking pan when she turned and ran straight into Rose.

The owner of The Rose Chalet did not look happy. Actually, Julie quickly realized, it was more as though her face had shut down so that she didn't have to show what she really felt. It was, strangely, worse than if she had been shouting.

"Julie, I'd like to see you in my office, please." Rose walked off, not waiting for Julie.

Oh, God, she'd *obviously* overheard at least part of the conversation.

If talking to Phoebe had been like being back in high school, then this was like being summoned to the principal's office. It wasn't a question of whether Julie was in trouble.

It was simply a question of how much trouble.

Rose was sitting behind her desk by the time Julie caught up with her. It wasn't a neat desk. There were far too many pieces of paper scattered over it, all arranged in an order that presumably made sense to her boss, but wouldn't to anyone else.

Rose gestured to one of the client chairs in front of the desk. Julie hadn't sat there even when she'd been interviewing for the temporary job, because they'd done that in the kitchen. Things suddenly felt horribly formal.

"Please, sit down, Julie."

Julie sat. "Rose, I can explain this."

"I heard most of what you said to Phoebe," Rose said. She didn't raise her voice. She didn't even sound angry. If anything, she sounded disappointed. "You're dating Andrew Kyle?"

Julie hesitated, but then nodded. There wasn't much point in trying to deny it. "Yes."

"Do you know how complicated that makes things?"

"I'm sorry," Julie said, but a small spark of defiance leaped up in her. "To be fair, things were already pretty complicated between him and me."

"You mean because he gave you a bad review for your restaurant?" Rose looked at Julie pointedly. "One that you didn't mention to me after you learned he was the client's brother?"

Julie hung her head. She'd messed up. She knew she had. "I thought that if I told you about Andrew's review of my restaurant, then you wouldn't let me work on this wedding."

"So, instead, you lied to me."

"I didn't lie, exactly. I just didn't share all the details with me." Julie winced as she heard what she'd just said. "Not that it makes a difference, I know."

"It sounds like there were quite a few things you didn't tell me," Rose continued. "First there was the role Andrew played in the collapse of your restaurant, then you somehow ending up on TV with him during the taping of his new show—"

"That was an accident," Julie protested, although she suspected her comment wasn't helping her case.

"Then there's you kissing him a few days ago, you going to his house for dinner with his family, you spending the night with him... I don't know what to say to all this, Julie."

"I didn't plan any of this. I thought I could ignore Andrew's review." Julie squirmed in her seat. "I thought he and I could both be professional about it."

Rose pressed her lips together, obviously not saying the first thing that came into her head. "Yes, professional would have been good," she said after a second or two, "but that's clearly not how things have worked out."

Julie nodded. "I'm sorry about this. Really." She briefly wondered exactly how many times one person could say sorry in a day. Although, the truth was she would apologize as many times as she needed to, just so long as she got to keep her—

"Julie, I'm going to have to let you go."

—job.

"Let me go?" For a second she could barely take the words in. "You're firing me?"

Rose nodded. "I don't have a choice."

"But the Kyle wedding…"

"I'll have to find someone else to do it. Look, I'll be happy to offer you a reference. The food I tasted was good. It's just all the rest of it that's a problem."

Julie brought her hands up to her face. She could feel the beginnings of tears in her eyes, but she was determined not to cry. Not here, not like this.

"But I—"

To Julie's surprise, Rose got up and moved around the desk. Briefly, Julie wondered if the other woman was going to throw her out physically. That would be the perfect ending to her day.

Instead Rose did something even more surprising. She put a comforting hand on Julie's shoulder. "I know it's hard, but I think this is the best thing. When you have time to think about it, you might even agree. I need someone here who can commit to doing this job long-term, and I think you've never really been that interested in it, Julie."

"That's not true," Julie tried to argue, but Rose stopped her.

"You had your own restaurant. Working here, putting on food for weddings, was always going to be second best. Even Andrew said that your heart didn't seem to be in it back at the tasting."

How, Julie wondered, had things fallen apart so quickly, from a perfect morning to a miserable afternoon? What would Evie say when Julie told her that she'd managed to lose the job her aunt had more or less handed to her?

"I'm not going to make you work out the rest of the day," Rose said, "and I want you to know that this isn't anything personal. I just don't think that you're a good fit for The Rose Chalet. I'm sorry. Obviously you'll be paid for the work you've done so far."

Julie nodded and stood. She had to get out of Rose's office before she broke down and cried. She mumbled something about being grateful for the opportunity and made it as far as the parking lot before she stopped, the reality of it finally sinking in.

She'd been fired.

The only job she'd been able to get after the demise of her restaurant was gone, just like that...all because she'd been stupid enough to get tangled up with Andrew Kyle.

CHAPTER THIRTEEN

KNOWING SHE SHOULDN'T get behind the wheel of a car right then, Julie walked back to her aunt's house with her breath coming short and her gut clenching. She didn't even try to catch the bus home, passing it in a daze as she tried to make some sense of everything that had just happened.

Her phone rang as the first drops of rain started to fall. The thought of actually having to talk to someone was too much to bear. But she couldn't resist checking the message. What if it was Rose calling to say she'd reconsidered?

Phoebe's voice rang out on voice mail. "I just heard what happened and that you won't be working here anymore." Her new friend paused as if she only just realized that had come out wrong. "I hope you're okay. I'm so sorry. I shouldn't have started asking about Andrew. I shouldn't have even gone near that whole conversation. I feel so bad about everything. Please let me know you're all right when you get the chance."

Julie hesitated, finger poised over the call button. She didn't blame Phoebe for anything. She even thought it was sweet of her to check in. But she still couldn't face the thought of talking. Especially not to tell someone she was all right.

She wasn't all right. She was a long, *long* way from that.

Tucking the phone into her pocket, Julie continued

LUCY KEVIN   101

down the sidewalk, not bothering to dodge the puddles that had started to form. All she wanted was to curl up on the sofa and pretend for a little while that none of it mattered. Even though it mattered so very much.

Julie walked past a food truck at the end of her block and kept going without even pausing to wonder what it served. Just the thought of food made her stomach knot.

By the time Julie got to Aunt Evie's place, the rain had worked its way through her clothes. Oh, how Julie wished her aunt was home, rather than out with her friends. She would hug her and tell her that everything would be all right, even if it was a lie.

Then again, considering all the work Evie had put into cooking for the wedding venue and then recommending Julie for the job, only to have her lose it after three days... What a mess. Would her aunt be angry? Disappointed? The stress of trying to keep up with multiple weddings had been bad for the older woman's health. What would this news do to her?

Julie went to her room, picking up the small notebook she had originally intended to write recipes in, but which sat, largely blank, in one of her drawers. She pulled out a piece of paper tucked in between the cover and the first page and unfolded it, rereading the familiar words of Andrew's review.

Delgado's Restaurant: 2 stars out of 5.

Why had she printed out the review and put it there? She could hardly remember now. Maybe she'd thought to use it as a spur to action, a source of inspiration. Maybe she'd wanted it as a reminder of how easily things could go wrong. All Julie had known at the time was that she needed to keep a copy; that she wasn't going to let the couple of brief paragraphs that had ruined her life simply float off into the electronic ether.

To survive and do well, restaurants must offer more than bland food....

That passion for food didn't come across at Delgado's.

She'd had visions of one day being able to force Andrew Kyle to eat his words. Julie smiled grimly at that as she read the piece over again, her eyes skimming the words that she could have recited from memory.

Judging by the many empty seats in the dining room, it appears as if other customers likely felt the same way.

Such simple phrases, but they had done so much damage. When she got to the end of the review, she went back to the beginning to read it again.

Perhaps in future, the owner will couple her obvious skills with a more imaginative menu....

Strangely, two things jumped out at her from that sentence for the very first time. *Obvious skills* was an actual compliment. And *future...* Well, it seemed to imply that Andrew thought she had one.

She didn't know how long she'd sat there, with the world closed in around her and Andrew's old words in front of her. It would be easier to tell herself that, once again, her life had gone from almost being okay to falling apart the moment he had appeared.

But she couldn't lie to herself about his motives. He hadn't been trying to hurt her, hadn't been deliberately trying to rip her life to shreds.

It was simply that he couldn't understand that the way he threw himself at the world simply didn't work for everyone else. He acted on instinct and never thought about the consequences, because there never *were* any consequences for him.

Yet, for Julie, life seemed to be nothing but consequences. Rotten ones.

She knew she was wallowing and forced herself to put the review back in the notebook, though by then, it didn't make much difference. The words were still playing on repeat in her head.

A minute later Julie stood under the jets of the shower, turning the water as hot as she could bear and squeezing her eyes shut. It didn't make any difference. She could still see Andrew's final pronouncement on her restaurant—*unmemorable*—in her mind's eye, as if it had been typed into her brain in indelible ink.

She opened her eyes again to find that she was on the floor of the shower, her arms wrapped around her knees, hugging them close. As much as she wanted to deny it, Delgado's had been heading downhill for months before it closed. The two-star review was just the last nail in the coffin. And last night with Andrew, this morning's breakfast and sweet kisses…it had been her choice to stay. Her choice to take that risk.

Her choice to try for happiness.

In the end, Julie was left with one simple truth: she was the one responsible for messing up her own life. Not Andrew.

Out on the bathroom counter, her phone started ringing again. She ignored it, sitting in the shower until the water ran cold. It didn't achieve much—it certainly didn't get rid of *unmemorable* circling in her head—but by the time she dried off, at least she could think a little again. She changed into a combination of jeans and a dark sweater before checking her phone.

Missed Call: Andrew Kyle.

Julie couldn't possibly call him back. Even if she didn't blame him for all that had happened, she wasn't sure she could be around him, either.

Not after she'd found out the hard way that the risk simply wasn't worth it.

A quick stab of hunger told Julie how late it was getting even before she looked at her watch. She wasn't deluded enough to think that a mess on this scale would look any better after some food, but starving herself wouldn't achieve anything. However, for the first time ever, Julie simply couldn't face cooking. Even when the restaurant went under, there had been something soothing about picking out a recipe and following it.

Julie thought back to the food truck she'd passed on the way home. Would it still be there? She found an old umbrella and huddled under it as she walked down the empty sidewalk.

Fortunately the truck was still there, being run by a man in his fifties, whose apron had the obligatory grease stains and whose hair had long since been able to cover the full surface of his skull.

He beamed as Julie approached. "A customer! I was beginning to think that the rain had chased you all off. What can I get you?"

The menu was a relatively simple one. Steak sandwiches, chicken sandwiches, sausages, burgers, fries. It was exactly the comfort food Julie needed right then. She ordered a chicken sandwich. Her original intention had been to take it back to the house, but she stayed outside by the truck instead. Better to be out in the drizzling rain than all alone with her misery.

For his part, the truck owner, whose name turned out to be Frank, was happy to have her there. He told her he hadn't had any customers since the rain started. He hadn't moved locations because it would be raining just as hard anywhere else. All part of the marvelous life of the traveling food vendor, as he cheerfully put it. When a couple of new customers showed up despite the rain, Frank declared Julie to be a good-luck charm.

"That's pretty much the opposite of what I am right now," Julie informed him.

That was when she noticed the small help wanted sign stuck to the side of the truck. Part of her dismissed the thought immediately. Even The Rose Chalet had been a step down for her. Something like this was so many steps down that it might as well be a ladder. She'd owned her own restaurant. She shouldn't even *think* about something like—

"What kind of help do you want?" Julie asked before she could stop herself.

The truth was that she was currently jobless, and unlikely to get anything else. Besides, given everything that had happened, did she really think that she deserved anything better?

"Oh, I'm looking for a general helper," Frank said. "Washing up. Some fry cooking. Do you know someone who'd be interested?"

Julie knew she ought to say no. Andrew would have been angry with her for doing anything else. Even Aunt Evie would have told her that she was selling herself short.

Right then though, Julie just needed something real. Something solid. Something she knew she could do and do well.

"Yes," she said quickly, before she could change her mind. "Me."

CHAPTER FOURTEEN

"Cut! Get ready for the basic skills section."

After the cameras were turned off, Andrew shook the hand of the local chef he was cooking with—whose name he frankly couldn't remember—and moved off to the side of the set. He checked his phone as discretely as he could.

Nothing. No texts, no emails, no phone messages.

Just like the last three times he'd checked.

He put his phone away as Sandy brought over a couple of women in their early twenties who proclaimed themselves his biggest fans and asked if they could get a photo with him. For the first time in a long time, Andrew had to force himself to go through with the whole being-gracious-with-the-fans thing. He stood between the two of them while Sandy took their picture. One of them slipped a piece of paper into his hand and when Andrew looked, he found that it had a phone number written on it.

Sandy escorted the two young women off the set and then returned to speak with Andrew. She arrived just as he was throwing the telephone number away.

"What's up with you today?"

"Leave it alone, Sandy. In fact, why don't you go find something useful to do? Go get me a coffee, or something."

She simply raised an eyebrow and crossed her arms over her chest.

"I'm sorry," he said immediately, knowing he was behaving like the worst boss on the planet. "I'm just a bit—"

"Pigheaded? Idiotic? Monumentally—"

"I could still fire you, you know."

Sandy rolled her eyes. "So are you going to tell your long-suffering assistant what's wrong, or do I have to guess?"

Andrew smiled at that. It was about the first time he'd smiled all day, except while on camera, but that didn't count.

"It's that chef down at The Rose Chalet, isn't it? The one you're so gooey-eyed over."

"Sandy, I'm a full-grown man. I don't get gooey-eyed."

Another eye roll came his way. "You've been checking your cell phone more often than a teenage girl praying the star quarterback will call her again after their hour together in the backseat of his car."

He hadn't realized that it was that obvious. It was embarrassing. Sandy had hit the nail on the head: he was acting like a jilted teenager.

Why *hadn't* Julie called? He'd thought things were going great. The night they'd spent together had been amazing, but it was more than that. The morning after—that had been the really surprising part. They'd solidified their connection then. He'd been sure of it.

Yet here they were again with Julie ignoring his messages. It was as bad as it had been after they'd kissed for the first time. Worse, actually. Avoiding him after their kiss had been nerves, a bump in the road.

Whereas this silence felt more like a full-on retreat.

"Why don't you go see her?" Sandy asked. "Talk things through. Isn't that what the magazines always say? Besides, that would be so much better than getting drunk and having a meaningless fling with someone on the rebound."

Sandy was right. Talking things over with Julie had worked before and, besides, he probably needed to go down to The Rose Chalet anyway.

Not that he needed any excuses. Andrew had told Julie the last time they'd seen one another that if she didn't return his calls, he *would be* coming to get answers.

"You know, Sandy, sometimes you have good ideas."

"Finally, what I've been waiting so long to hear," she said in a sarcastic voice. "Hey, while you're at it, tell her that the producers are planning the season finale. They want her in on it, boss."

Andrew drove like a madman over to The Rose Chalet, but Julie wasn't there. Rose wasn't in, either. The only person Andrew could find was Phoebe, the florist.

"Have you seen Julie?"

"She doesn't work here anymore, thanks to you."

"What—fired? Thanks to *me?*"

"Who else do you think got her fired?"

He ran his hand through his hair, already planning to tell Rose he'd cancel the wedding if she didn't take Julie back. "She hasn't been answering my calls. I didn't know."

The florist's eyes narrowed. "Look, I get that this is what always happens to relationships, but Julie is my friend and I hate knowing she's hurt over this. Over *you.*"

"Tell me where she is, Phoebe. I need to talk to her."

"I don't know. But I think you should just leave her alone and let her get on with her life."

Why hadn't she told him any of this? What reason could Rose have had to fire her? He didn't know the answers to either of those questions, but he was going to find out.

He sped across town to Julie's house, only to have her aunt tell him, "Oh, she's gone off to work but she should be back later this evening," as if everything was perfectly fine.

"But I've just been to the—" Andrew realized that he was starting to raise his voice. He never did that. Never. "Please let Julie know I was here to see her. That I'd like to talk to her."

He got out of there as quickly as he could, trying to work out what was going on when even Evie didn't seem to know Julie had been fired.

He wasn't sure how he found Julie a few minutes later, except that perhaps he would have spotted her anywhere, simply because she mattered so much to him… and he wanted to talk to her so badly.

But he certainly would never have thought to look for her in a food truck like the one parked at the end of the block.

He pulled into the first spot he could find, ignoring the fact that it was a no parking zone. Julie was serving a customer a burger, and it was all Andrew could do to keep from pushing the guy out of the way.

"Julie, what are you doing in a place like this? And why haven't you answered any of my messages? Phoebe told me what happened. I'm going to tell Rose we're going to cancel the wedding unless she—"

"No!"

The force of the word took Andrew by surprise even

as he continued. "Why have you been avoiding me? Why didn't you call to give me the news about your job? You promised you wouldn't pull away like this."

"And you told me everything would be all right if I only trusted you." She shook her head. "I'm sorry I didn't return your calls. I'm sorry I didn't tell you about losing my job at The Rose Chalet. But you should go. I don't want to lose this job over you, too."

"Julie," he said gently, "I get that what's happened has been pretty rough, but if you'll just come out of there and talk to me—"

She shook her head. "I can't. I just…can't anymore. Please, we tried things your way before, but now I need to try them my way."

"And what exactly is your way?" he demanded, all gentleness disappearing in the face of his frustration. "Not calling? Not speaking to me? Not letting me know when you're hurting?"

Didn't she care that it hurt him, too, not hearing from her like that? Being cut off as though he didn't matter to her at all?

"We were good together," he reminded her. "You were happy."

"For one night. And one morning." She looked away. "It cost me too much. Everything I'd worked for."

He could hardly believe that. And, God, he hated the way her voice was so calm. Almost lifeless. "So you're going to let getting fired from one little job ruin everything we might have? You aren't even going to take that tiny risk to be happy?"

"Why should I?" she demanded, her voice finally rising again. "Every risk I take, there's something waiting around the corner to squash me. I know you don't understand, that you will never understand, but that's just part of the reason I haven't been calling." She sighed and shook her head. "I don't want to fight."

She sounded more sad than angry, and that was enough to send Andrew's emotions spiraling the same way. He stood there for several seconds, staring at her standing in the food truck, a stained white apron covering her jeans and T-shirt.

"At least let me help you out of here."

Julie was shaking her head before he'd even finished the sentence. "No, please. I don't want any more of your help."

Andrew winced. He forced himself to try to deliver the next piece of information the way he would if he had just run into an old friend.

"The producers of my show want you back on," he informed her.

"Andrew—"

"They liked having you on the show, and now they want you as part of their live grand cook-off. Come on, Julie. You know you deserve that much."

She shrugged. "I know as well as anyone that people don't get what they deserve."

"So you're not going to do it?" Somehow that made him angrier than all the rest of it put together. "One or two things go wrong—"

"Not one or two things," she pointed out. "Pretty much everything."

"—and now you won't even take what could be a great chance for you? I don't understand you, Julie. I just don't."

She went back to her grill for a moment, flipping a few pieces of chicken and a hot dog. To his eye, it all looked far too easy.

"Maybe you don't have to understand it," she said.

"But the important thing is that I do, and I can't go on your show again."

"Am I supposed to believe that this is enough for you?" he said, gesturing to the food truck.

She shrugged again. "It's going to have to be. At least for now. I didn't try to make things work out this way." She was looking at him again, and the pain on her face was obvious. "I'm sorry that I've hurt you. I'm sorry I can't do the show. I'm sorry I can't be the person you want me to be."

He shook his head. "I can't accept your apology. I *won't* accept it. You say you're sorry, but you're still giving up on what we could have. On what we *did* have. What good is an apology without—?"

Without you.

He didn't say the words, but they hung in the air anyway.

"I'm sorry," Julie said again.

Andrew knew he wasn't going to get anything more out of her. But her explanation wasn't enough. It wasn't nearly enough.

He would have turned everything upside down for her without even hesitating…but she was still too frightened to admit how she truly felt about him. She likely wouldn't take the risk of opening her heart after the bruising it had taken with all her work-related problems.

And it seemed pretty damn clear that she never would.

He stalked to his car without a backward glance, threw it into gear and set off for the studio. *He was,* he told himself, *better off without Julie Delgado.*

If only he actually believed it.

CHAPTER FIFTEEN

"HERE YOU GO, Betty." Julie handed over a grilled tuna-and-egg-salad sandwich. "We'll see you again tomorrow, I hope?"

"Oh, no. I couldn't possibly eat here two days in a row."

Julie smiled to herself. That was what the woman had said the past three days running. She served the next customer, while Frank conducted a conversation with an elderly man over whose baseball team was going to win that season. Without being asked, Julie put together Alvin's order and passed it over to him.

"You're looking good today, Alvin. Does this mean things are going well with Ethel?"

While he filled her in on his elderly wife, Julie grilled up several orders during their long and winding conversation. After Alvin left, Frank said, "You know, you really shouldn't talk to the customers for so long, Julie."

She laughed out loud at that, if only because every time Frank said it, he would immediately spend a good ten minutes talking to the next customer to come along.

"I'll stop when you do."

He spread his hands. "This is my own personal soap opera. I can't stop now." He paused for a second or two. "Julie, could I ask you something?"

That sounded a little ominous. "I guess so."

"What are you doing working in a job like this? I pay you less than minimum wage, you haven't gone home before dark once this week, and you obviously know how to cook well enough that you could get a job somewhere else if you wanted it. Why stay here?"

"I'm happy here." She was surprised to find that, for once, things really were that simple. "Besides, what would you do without me now that you've got a bunch of new customers?"

He acknowledged her comment with a nod before saying, "Even so, I worry."

She smiled at the man she'd really come to enjoy working with. "There's nothing to worry about."

"At the very least, I'm going to give you a raise, because that way I get to feel better about completely exploiting you." He looked a little sheepish. "As soon as I can afford it, anyway."

"Sounds great, Frank."

For all that her boss liked to talk with his customers about their lives, he hadn't asked too many questions about how Julie's was faring. Likely because it had been painfully obvious that she needed space—especially after the debacle with Andrew a few days ago.

Telling her aunt about her new job hadn't been easy, though the hardest part had been plucking up the courage. When Julie had finally done it, Aunt Evie had hugged her and told Julie that she was sure things would work out. Her aunt had popped by the truck the next day and she and Frank had gotten on like two old friends. They had both spent a fair bit of time talking in low tones about Julie's cooking skills and her menu ideas. Finally, in good fun, she'd had to remind them that she could hear them perfectly.

Then right after the lunch rush, five days, three hours

and forty-eight minutes after Andrew had walked away from the food truck, and out of her life, Julie's phone rang. It was Sandy, Andrew's assistant.

Julie took the call out behind the truck. "Hello?"

"Hi, Julie. I'm Andrew Kyle's assistant and I'm phoning to ask whether you'd given any thought to appearing in our cook-off on the finale of *Edgy Eats?*"

"I—" Momentarily flustered, Julie couldn't stop herself from asking, "How is Andrew?"

"Why don't you ask him yourself?" The harsh tone reminded Julie just how protective Andrew's assistant was toward her boss. "Look," the woman said with a sigh that sounded slightly sympathetic, "I get that things have been kind of weird between you two, but I really need to know, do you want to be on the program or not?"

"I'll have to think about it." Julie said goodbye and, putting her phone in the pocket of her apron, got back to work.

An hour later the producer of the *Edgy Eats* called to try to convince her to appear on the show. She gave him the same answer she had given Sandy—she would have to think about it.

Of course, Andrew was the only one who didn't call to talk to her about being on the show again. It hurt, but she told herself it was better that way. This was what she'd asked for, after all. To be left alone. She could hardly complain, could she? Even though most nights Julie still found herself thinking about him. When Aunt Evie had carefully turned off his show on TV, Julie had turned it back on and told her that it was okay.

Apart from her feelings for Andrew, and the fact that she hadn't stopped wanting him for one single second since she'd sent him away from the food truck, amazingly, everything else did feel okay.

Working on the truck meant there wasn't much pressure. Occasionally people would ask how they managed to get the food there tasting so good, and Frank would always reply that it was just good, simple food to feed hungry people.

More and more, Julie was starting to see that he was right. There wasn't any pressure on her to be staggeringly different and precise. Nor were there any real "rules." People were only too happy to try the things she put together, even when they were just that little bit different. Without any pressure, and with her new boss happy to let her cook how she liked, she could simply relax and cook good food.

After all the years of trying to fit herself into one kitchen after another, she was amazed to realize she could finally be herself.

"Hey, Frank," a muscular young guy who worked on a local construction site asked, "what's in this hot dog?"

"Why?" Frank asked. "Is there a problem?"

"No, no problem. It's good. Really good. Reminds me of the way my grandmother used to make sausages from scratch when I was a kid."

"It's Julie's special recipe," Frank said with enough obvious pride to make Julie smile.

She had many more recipes for food like that stored away in her brain. Like the tomato sauce she'd thrown together for the meatball sandwiches today. With a few extra spices she had turned plain old tomato sauce into something special.

But even though Julie had found herself smiling on the way to work today for the first time in a long while, she knew there were things bubbling on her back burner that she needed to deal with.

Soon.

She took a deep breath and wiped her hands off on her apron.

Not soon, but right now.

AFTER FRANK GRACIOUSLY agreed to give Julie an hour off, she quickly pulled some food together and headed for The Rose Chalet. Rose, Phoebe and RJ were all in the main dining hall, discussing where to put a gazebo. At least, Rose was discussing it. Phoebe was tactfully trying to point out there might be a better spot for it. RJ seemed to be ignoring the pair of them and wanted to fit it in the one place where it wouldn't fall down.

Julie briefly smiled at the way they all worked together.

"Hi, everyone."

"Julie! What are you doing here?" Phoebe hugged her as she said it.

To Julie's surprise, so did Rose. "Hi, Julie. Is everything going okay with you?"

A few days ago Julie wouldn't have been able to nod. Today, despite her nerves, she was smiling as she hefted the hamper she'd packed up at the truck. "I brought food. I know you're all too busy here to remember to eat lunch half the time." When Rose eyed the basket slightly suspiciously, Julie laughed. "Don't worry, this isn't some ploy to get my old job back. I have a job, and I'm really enjoying it. This is… It just felt right to come and say hello."

And it really did feel right, especially when they opened up the hamper and started to eat. RJ devoured a couple of chicken sandwiches before starting work on a hot dog. Phoebe made her way through a full plate of blue cheese French fries before she even looked around to see if anyone else wanted some. Even Rose tried a meatball.

"This is good," she said, then looked at the other two as they finished up their meals. "Just remember that that gazebo has to be set up today. Julie, why don't you come through to my office and we can talk?"

The only memories she had of Rose's office were of getting fired, but right then, that didn't matter as much anymore. She took one of the client chairs and, to her surprise, Rose took the other rather than sitting behind her desk.

"I'm glad you're okay," Rose said. "When I let you go, I could see how upset you were."

"It was rough, but I understand why you had to do it. Really."

"With the upcoming wedding, and everything that had happened, I didn't really have much of a choice," Rose explained. "I probably overreacted a bit, but when I heard that you had spent the night with Andrew, I couldn't see what else to do."

Julie nodded. "As I said, I get it. I didn't come by to blame you for that."

"I'm still not quite sure why you did come by," Rose admitted. "Don't get me wrong, it's nice that you brought us lunch and it's good to see you again, but why are you here?"

"I came by to apologize. Not to get my job back, but because I like you and respect you and hope we can be friends. I know I messed things up with the O'Neil wedding—all those problems with the squid and raw meat—and all the complications with Andrew and his brother's wedding…"

"I've worked with the same crew here for so long that I haven't had to train someone new for a while now. You've helped me a lot by making me realize that I need to pay much better attention to my new employees in the future to help them succeed. Was there something we could have done to make things easier for you?"

Julie shook her head. "I think most of it was inevitable. I'd been kidding myself about a lot of things ever since my restaurant fell apart. Even before that. I'd convinced myself that Andrew's harsh two-star review was the only reason my restaurant failed. But it wasn't. *I* messed up. I let the pressure of trying to run a place like that squash me into the person I thought I needed to be in order to run it successfully."

And then, instead of taking responsibility for her own life, she'd blamed all her problems on Andrew.

But now that she'd accepted that those things were *her* fault—and that changing the bad decisions she'd made in the past wasn't out of her hands—she'd finally begun to feel the seeds of true confidence sprout and blossom inside her.

"Once I got to The Rose Chalet," she continued explaining to Rose, "I piled on even more pressure, trying to be perfect, trying to be the cook I thought you wanted."

"Why do I get the feeling that I should be the one apologizing?" Rose asked.

"No," Julie said, "that's not what I mean. Yes, there were times when you were so busy with things that there wasn't really anyone to go to for help but, honestly, I don't think I would have asked for help anyway. I was always trying to be perfect, just like Aunt Evie had been. The trouble is perfection... Well, it just isn't me."

"How is Evie?"

Julie smiled. "She's good. Better than that, these days. In fact, when I left work just now, she was plotting behind my back with my new boss to get me to take better care of myself."

"You didn't say before. What are you doing now?"

On the way over here, Julie hadn't been sure whether she would answer that question after imagining how this conversation might go. After all, it would probably seem to Rose like such a step down from her old job. Now, though, Julie knew it didn't make a difference. After all, what Rose thought didn't matter.

"I'm working on a food truck," Julie said. "General cooking. Simple stuff really. I'm happy."

She expected a look of pity, or at least sympathy from Rose. Instead her ex-boss smiled.

"Sometimes that's the most important thing." Rose looked wistful for a moment. "Happiness."

"Only sometimes?"

Instead of answering Julie's question, Rose deftly transitioned into an update regarding the Kyle wedding. Evidently, Andrew and Rose were still discussing how to deal with the food, since Rose didn't think that she'd be able to get another cook in quickly enough. She hoped Andrew would be able to persuade one of his friends from the culinary world to take it on, though obviously, that wasn't ideal. Julie apologized again for making things difficult as she left, then met up with Phoebe on the way out.

"So," the florist demanded, "how did it go? Did you get your old job back?"

Julie laughed. "That wasn't what I came for, Phoebe. It really wasn't."

"That's too bad. I miss having you around here." She raised an eyebrow. "I probably shouldn't ask, but what about you and Andrew? I take it he's history after getting you into trouble?"

"The situation with Andrew is…" Julie paused. "Complicated."

Once Phoebe assured her they would definitely be going for a girls' night soon, Julie left. She stood in the parking lot of The Rose Chalet and took a long breath.

She had needed to settle things with Rose, to let her know how she felt. To let her know why things had happened. There had been a closure that Julie hadn't even known she was seeking. She stood with the sun on her face for several seconds, knowing she had to stop stalling.

Julie had dealt with things at The Rose Chalet, but there was still something much bigger to deal with.

Could she do it?

Even that morning, Julie might have said no, but now, things felt different. And as she fished out her cell phone from a pocket, she suddenly felt as if there was nothing too big for her to face.

Which was a good thing, considering she wasn't at all sure her plan would work.

She might have left this too late. Her chance might already be gone. And even if it wasn't, it was not going to be easy…and it would take a lot of courage.

Along with tremendous belief in herself.

Julie smiled as she thought of Andrew saying, *"You've got good instincts, Julie. If you follow them, I predict you'll do really, really well."*

Looking down at the screen on her cell phone, Julie scrolled through numbers until she found the one for Andrew's producer.

"Hi," she said. "This is Julie Delgado. Is your offer still open?"

CHAPTER SIXTEEN

"ALL RIGHT, PEOPLE," Andrew's producer told the group on the set of *Edgy Eats*. "I know this is the last show, and we're all excited, but can we please try to get it in the can before we start the party?"

Andrew had found it hard to get excited about much of anything this past week, ever since his failed trip to see Julie at the food truck.

He'd been so sure things would work out. So sure that she'd finally come to see what a great couple they could be. Yet here he was, back to square one. Further back than that, actually, because there didn't seem to be much hope of ever getting through to her.

From what he'd heard through the grapevine, Julie was enjoying her new life. Even if it was nowhere close to being what Andrew had imagined for her, it seemed she was finally cooking in a way that made her happy.

He knew he should be glad...but how could he be happy about anything when she didn't want him?

"Excuse me, Andrew."

He looked around to see a woman, obviously one of the audience members, who had somehow managed to get onto the main set.

"I know I'm probably pushing my luck just coming up to you like this, but I was wondering, after you're finished here, if you would like to go get a—"

Fortunately, Sandy came running over just then

and interrupted them. "We need you to take your seat, ma'am, right away. Thank you."

As the woman left, leaving Andrew with one more longing glance, he asked, "Are Phil and Nancy here yet? What about my mother and father? You sent the tickets, right?"

"I not only sent them, I couriered them over personally," Sandy said. "Trust me, they got them. But—"

"There isn't any sign of them," he finished for her.

"I'm afraid not. Sorry, boss."

"It's not your fault." It was his, for thinking that his family might actually come in the first place. Oh, if he phoned them, they would probably have excuses about how busy they were. And they were. It was just that once, just once, it would have been nice if he'd been important enough for them to break into their busy schedules. Simply because he was family and family was supposed to count for something.

Fortunately there wasn't much more he had to do to get through the rest of the day. Finish shooting the finale—where he had to stand around looking good while six of the city's cooks tried to outdo each other— and then...

What? What would he do then?

He briefly thought of Julie and shook his head. She'd made it perfectly clear about what she wanted. She'd made it even more clear about what she *didn't* want. So why was he still thinking of hanging around, begging for scraps?

Better to get away. From her, from his family, from everything.

On his hiatus he could fly off to France and make his way around the restaurants there. Heck, he could even buy a cottage in the Loire Valley and stay there until the next season of shows started. He could do whatever he wanted.

He'd have to come back for the wedding, of course, but that could just be a quick pit stop in San Francisco before he headed off again.

Sandy touched his arm lightly. "Are you okay, boss?"

"Fine," Andrew lied. If you couldn't lie to your own assistant, who could you lie to? "You're still planning to start that production company, right?"

His assistant nodded, but she looked a little worried. Obviously the start-up fund wasn't quite where she wanted it to be. Well, he could take care of that easily enough. It would be good to do something nice for her before he left town.

"You're sure you're okay?" she asked again. "You don't seem like yourself."

He shrugged. "Are we ready to get cooking?"

"Pretty much."

Good. The sooner they were done, the sooner he could get away. He wouldn't even have to pack. He could be on a flight within a couple of hours of the end of shooting. That thought made it a little easier to smile his trademark smile as he stepped out into the middle of the set kitchen.

"Hello and welcome to *Edgy Eats*. For our final show of the season, we have a special treat for you. Several people who have been cooking with me this season graciously agreed to come back for our grand finale. To make it extra special, they're going to be cooking not just for me, but for a panel of critics taken from San Francisco's food press and restaurant world. Please welcome our judges."

Lanie reported on food happenings for the Cuisine Channel, and had the bubbly good looks that came with the territory. Geraldine was a local chef with a reputation for an abrupt tone and an unsmiling face to match. Steve was a restaurant critic for one of the local newspapers who, given the size of his paunch, obviously enjoyed his work.

Andrew had met them before, but didn't know any of them well. Now, though, he had to smile and pretend they were best friends. That was TV for you.

"The rules today are simple," he told the audience. "Our cooks will produce four courses for our judges. An amuse-bouche to give us a little taste of their cooking style, a first course, an entrée and a dessert. They can use any ingredients they wish and I, for one, am looking forward to a real taste revelation or two."

"I certainly hope so," Lanie agreed.

"Though, obviously, the standards achieved are vitally important, too," Steve put in.

Geraldine nodded. "I was told the chefs are among the finest cooks who have been on your show, so I will be expecting high standards from all of them."

And no doubt taking the opportunity to turn the knife if they weren't up to it.

Still, the contestants presumably knew what they were getting themselves into. Which reminded him...

"Shall we welcome our contestants?" Andrew asked the audience, waiting until their enthusiastic response died down a little before continuing. He had the names on the teleprompter, just to make sure nothing could go wrong. "Please give a big welcome to Mitchel Crane, Antonio Summers, Elaine Neilson, Gregory Brown, Natasha Smith and...Julie Delgado?"

Andrew couldn't keep the surprise out of his voice at seeing Julie's name on the screen. He fully expected the director to yell "Cut" and explain it was all some big mistake—that they had added her name when they'd still been trying to get her on the show, and then forgotten to remove it from the list.

But there she was, walking over to her workstation with the others, all the ingredients for her chosen dishes in a box…and looking so beautiful that he could hardly believe his eyes.

Somehow, Andrew managed to get back to the job at hand, wishing them all good luck then starting the big timer for the cook-off. Knowing he couldn't very well go over and have a talk with Julie about their relationship while they were live on air, he had to wander among the contestants instead, asking them what they were planning, and what they'd been up to since the last time they'd been on the show.

He found this hard going with the first contestants, mostly because his attention wasn't focused on them. It was hard to keep up one half of a conversation about how someone had expanded their café or had dramatically improved their approach to fine dining when it took every last ounce of his effort not to stare at the woman he'd fallen head over heels for.

He tried to tell himself not to be such a fool, and reminded himself what had happened last time, but it didn't make any difference.

Because he was in love with her and nothing else mattered.

Finally, *finally,* he was standing beside her. Lord, how he hated speaking to her as a presenter…rather than as the man who loved her.

"Julie, it's great to see you back here."

She smiled at him, so sweetly that his chest tightened. "It's good to be back here, Andrew."

"And what have you been doing since we last saw you?"

"Oh, all kinds of things. You're probably going to ask me about my menu now, right?"

No, he wanted to ask much more important questions. *Why are you here? Can you see how much I love you? Will you love me back?* The trouble was, being on live TV meant that he had to play his part.

"What is on your menu today, Julie?"

"I'll tell you when I've worked it out." Her eyes twinkled, matching her wide smile. "Don't tell the judges, but I'm making it up as I go."

Andrew's eyes widened at that. He waited for the live audience's laughter to fade. "That's quite a risk to take."

"Yes," she said, nodding serenely, "it is. But I once had a very wise person tell me that if I trusted my instincts, everything would work out fine." She paused. "It took me a while to understand, but I've finally decided that friend was right."

He wanted to pull her into his arms. He wanted to kiss her. He wanted to tell her how much he respected her. How much he adored her.

Somehow, Andrew pulled himself away from Julie and moved back to the judges. None of whom had liked what she had just said.

"It seems a little silly not to have a plan," Lanie said.

"Silly?" Geraldine echoed. "It's idiotic. I'll be surprised if there's anything worthwhile on her plate as a result."

A few of the audience booed, obviously knowing who the bad guy was on this panel. Andrew felt like joining in. He couldn't, though. He was supposed to be impartial to give all the contestants a fair chance. Which meant that all he could do was stand there and make small talk with the contestants and judges while the chefs raced against the clock.

Normally he wouldn't have minded doing that. He liked watching people cook. It said so much about them.

Now, though, he spent his time glancing at Julie, trying to work out what she'd meant by finally being willing to take risks. Was she simply talking about cooking?

Or was she also talking about being with him?

"It looks like time's up," Steve the restaurant critic pointed out. Andrew glanced at the clock and saw that it was.

"Time to put your knives and spatulas down, folks," Andrew said, sliding back into host mode. "We're going to judge this course-by-course, tasting everybody's food in turn. I don't get a vote on our winner, so those bribes you all paid me earlier are wasted, I'm afraid." Another laugh on cue from the audience. "But I am going to taste and offer comments, since this is my show, after all. Who wants to bring over their amuse-bouche first?"

Andrew was proud of Julie when she stepped forward, bringing with her a plate full of what appeared to be tiny meatballs, each covered in an individual sauce.

"Meatballs?" Geraldine said with obvious distain.

"With a few extra ingredients," Julie replied with a smile.

The judges tasted first. Lanie said that they were nice, but that they seemed a bit too simple for a TV cook-off. Steve questioned whether she had a prayer of keeping up with the fine dining from the other contestants, and suggested that more of a plan might have avoided the problem.

Geraldine put it more bluntly. "It's fast food, and we expected more on a show like this. It's awful."

None of their comments left Andrew with high hopes

as he bit down on one of the meatballs. His taste buds identified two kinds of meat: beef and chicken, while there were hints of subtly blended spices mixed in, and the sauce… Well, the sauce was something else entirely. Something amazing. The ingredients seemed to fight for space in it before joining forces to blow his taste buds apart, in the best possible way.

"I don't understand what you're all talking about," he said. "This is great."

"Thankfully, some of us *know* what we're talking about," Geraldine snapped. That earned her more boos that died down only when the rest of the cooks came forward one by one. They'd prepared the inevitable fine-dining combinations, and Andrew had to admit that several of them tasted very good, but to his mind they weren't in Julie's league for originality. For *passion*. But, naturally, the judges disagreed.

It was the same story with the first course. Some of the other contestants did elaborate on things that were exactly the same dishes Andrew could have eaten in any upscale restaurant in the area. Their first courses were all something that aspired to *the Glass Square* aesthetic.

Julie, on the other hand, served up what seemed like a simple tortilla wrap, until she explained that it included a mixture of pork, Thai-style spices, Oriental vegetables and lime. The judges couldn't get past the tortilla outer shell.

"Are you trying to make fun of this whole process?" Geraldine demanded.

Andrew tasted it. He didn't bother to hold back his smile. "It's perfect." The audience broke into spontaneous applause while Geraldine glared at him.

Julie's main course was a hot dog. Except that it was a venison hot dog, stuffed with herbs, homemade spiced bread, and served with celeriac fries and a combination of sauces that had absolutely nothing to do with ketchup and mustard.

Geraldine described it as, "Simply awful. The worst so far."

Even Lanie was a little less forgiving. "I'm sorry," she said, "but this is really an unexpected combination for a hot dog. You're a long way behind the others now, Julie."

Steve nodded. "Frankly, your dessert is going to have to be the best thing anyone has ever tasted just to give you a chance. I just don't see it."

Andrew laughed.

"What's so funny?" Geraldine demanded.

"Frankly, I just can't see how three people can be so wrong. This isn't just a hot dog." One by one, he went through the elements in it, ignoring the judges, facing the audience. "What I'm trying to say," he explained, "is that this is easily one of the most delicious hot dogs anyone has ever produced."

Julie's dessert was a big concoction of chocolate, cream and whatever else had been lying around. Normally even Andrew would have dismissed it, but he couldn't this time.

Because he recognized it. She had perfectly recreated the dessert they'd come up with together the night she had spent with him.

"Awful," Geraldine declared again.

"It is a mess," Lanie said.

Steve shook his head. "It looks like you ran out of time and threw everything on the counter into a bowl."

But for Andrew, there couldn't have been a more perfect finish to the meal. The first three dishes had been Julie through and through, a perfect mix of simple and complicated. Basic, working-man's food that had been reinvented with interesting flavors and textures. Each dish had been a risk, but each had come straight from her heart, as well.

And her dessert? Well, that was such a clear and direct message that Andrew wanted to yell "Cut" just so that he could rush over and kiss Julie.

God, how he loved her. Now, he just had to wait long enough for everyone to leave so that he could... Oh, who cared if they were on live TV?

Andrew strode across the stage, pulled Julie into his arms and, in front of the studio audience and crew, he kissed her.

CHAPTER SEVENTEEN

THE JUDGES DELIBERATED. Andrew finally let Julie go so he could stand with the other contestants as they waited for the verdict. As she waited with everyone else, Julie knew her face held a special well-kissed glow that every woman in the room had to be envious of.

"In third place," Lanie said, "we have Mitchel Crane."

He stepped forward to applause from the audience. Julie joined in politely, but her eyes were on Andrew—he barely even pretended to play his part as the gracious host. He was too busy staring right back at her, that gorgeous smile—along with the heat in his dark eyes—sending shivers through her.

"In second place, Natasha Smith."

More applause. But Julie couldn't stop thinking about their beautiful unexpected kiss. What did it mean? Was it enough? Was she ready for—?

No, she wasn't going to go down that road again. She was going to stop questioning the magic between her and Andrew once and for all.

What mattered was right here, right now. She loved him and she couldn't see any way that was ever going to change.

Especially when he had believed in her even before she had believed in herself.

"And our series winner for the grand finale of *Edgy Eats* cook-off is…"

The judges dragged it out, of course. That was more or less obligatory, designed to ratchet up the tension according to the TV show handbook. Julie didn't worry one bit about who the winner was going to be. After the comments from the judges, there was only one way it was going to go.

"Elaine Neilson!"

That was it. She didn't even land in the top three. In fact, given the nasty look that Geraldine gave her, she was very definitely in last place.

There was a time when that would have mattered to Julie. Not today, though.

Not when the only person in the room who mattered was looking at her as though she were personally responsible for the rising and setting of the sun.

Julie took her turn congratulating the winner, then waited as patiently as she could at the side of the stage while Andrew wrapped up the show. He hurried through his lines at a speed that was just barely intelligible. Fortunately the director didn't call him on it, though that might have had something to do with the way Sandy was speaking to him very firmly through her headset.

"Cut!" yelled the floor director. "That's a wrap for the show and the series, folks."

The crew and the audience all cheered. One of the camera crew cracked open the beer, and even the producers seemed happy to join in the party. It had been a successful series and everyone was feeling good about it. Pretty soon, the place looked less like a TV studio than the middle of a house party.

Julie couldn't have cared less about any of it as Andrew moved beside her and gathered her into his arms.

"I love you," he said. "I'm not going to hide that anymore, Julie."

"I love you, too. So much."

Before they could seal it with a kiss, they were interrupted by the approach of Geraldine and Lanie from the judging panel. Geraldine looked at them and sniffed. "So that's how you got into a contest like this. By sleeping with the host."

A day or two ago a comment like that would have had Julie cringing and letting go of Andrew. Now, she just held him closer. "Absolutely. In fact, I'm pretty sure that there was only a contest at all because Andrew was trying to seduce me."

He pressed a kiss to her temple. "Not just a great cook, but brilliant, too."

"But...but that's—"

Julie raised an eyebrow at the nasty woman. "What's wrong? Jealous?"

"Jealous? Of you? Some of us are real chefs, producing real food, with real quality."

Julie shrugged. "I'll settle for producing good food people want to eat—as long as I'm doing it my way."

"And that's why you'll never amount to anything," Geraldine snapped back.

Andrew raised an eyebrow. "As opposed to being a fine-dining chef who can't quite make the grade? I've seen some of the reviews for your cooking, Geraldine."

The chef stalked off, muttering to herself. Lanie, the Cuisine Channel presenter, waited a moment or two longer before talking with them. "For what it's worth, I'm sorry I had to be harsh. I think I maybe got a bit carried away. Oh, and by the way, you are right about one thing. I am."

"You are what?" Julie asked, not quite understanding.

"Just a tiny bit jealous that you landed the best-looking man in the food industry." She smiled at them both. "Good luck."

Julie laughed as the other woman headed off, leaving her and Andrew as the calm center of the party chaos going on around them. Sooner or later, they would have to move out of each other's arms, but not yet.

Not for a while, she hoped.

"So what happens next?" Julie asked after a minute or two.

"Well, we could always head back to my place," Andrew suggested. "And then I could make good on my promise to seduce you."

"You know what I mean," Julie said, laughing as she stood on her tiptoes to brush her lips against Andrew's neck. "Though, I'll admit, your idea does sound nice. Very, very nice."

He buried his face in her hair for a long moment before saying in a low voice, "I was thinking of spending some time in France, but now I think I might just stay in San Francisco."

"You'd better," she warned him. "Though a vacation would definitely be fun at some point, working our way through offbeat, hidden restaurants over there."

"A woman after my own heart."

Julie didn't know many men who would have been excited about her idea, but then, Andrew wasn't most men. Not even close.

Suddenly she wondered about how easy it would be to put his previous idea into action and get them back to his place. Although, the truth was that the best part of it all was knowing they could stay here, enjoy the party, and still be there for one another afterward.

Because neither of them was going anywhere this time. They were a team from now on.

Julie was surprised when several people came up to ask her about the dishes she'd made in the cook-off. One woman, around Aunt Evie's age, said, "It's nice to see that real food, when it's done right, can keep up with all that showy stuff."

Everyone seemed to like the idea of Julie's "real food" even as they acknowledged that the way she'd done it had been unique and entirely personal. In fact, one of the producers even came up to her and Andrew, introducing himself as Rick.

"Hello, Julie," he said. "A few of us were just discussing the show. Everyone in the audience seemed to be really excited about your performance today."

"They've been very kind," she said.

Rick shook his head. "They're never kind. Trust me. They do know what they want, though. You're a natural in front of the camera."

"I don't know about that."

"You are," Andrew assured her. "And you're a natural in the kitchen, too."

Rick got right to the point. "We still have a few gaps in our schedule, and we'd like you to consider putting your unique spin and personality into a new show."

Julie took a moment to translate his TV-speak. "You want to work with me for more than just a cook-off?"

"Yes, and we're hoping you'll see what a great opportunity this is for you to increase your exposure, get some great ratings, and maybe move on from there to other shows, or even opening another restaurant. The same things everyone who appears on this channel wants."

He was right. Anyone who cooked for a living would be leaping at the chance to have their own cooking show—except that Julie had tried for perfect before...

and she wasn't sure whether she was ready for that kind of pressure again.

"What exactly would be involved?"

"A few weeks of taping. We like to record multiple episodes each day to minimize the disruption to our performers' busy lives."

Beside her, Andrew snorted. "And to keep costs down, Rick. Let's not forget that part."

"And that, too," the producer said unashamedly. "Then you'd be involved with a bit of promotion and possibly some spin-off things."

"It's a lot while it's going on," Andrew said, "but he's right. It could be a great opportunity for you. It's just a question of what you want, Julie."

Which begged the question: What did she want?

One answer to that was obvious. She wanted Andrew.

Yet, he of all people would be able to work around her TV schedule, so that wouldn't stop her. So what was it that was making her back off even as she recognized what a great opportunity it could be? It wasn't that fear of taking a risk again, was it?

She smiled as she realized her reluctance stemmed from something else entirely.

At the moment, working on the food truck, she was free. She could do what she liked, she had a boss who let her work her way, and she had customers who loved what she did.

She was happy.

Did she really want to trade that for a life of being told where to stand and what to say, just because it was what other people thought she ought to want? She could see the opportunity it represented, and she might very well take it, but not if it was going to mess with that freedom.

"So, what do you say?" Rick pushed. "If it's the money, then I can assure you—"

"Can I get back to you?" Julie asked, cutting him off. "This is all very quick and I want to make sure that I can fit it all in the way I want…if I agree to do it, that is."

The producer's smile froze ever so slightly. "Sure, just don't take too long thinking about it. We might not wait, you know."

Andrew shook his head. "Yes, you will, and you know it, Rick. Julie's worth waiting for."

The producer drifted off and Andrew took Julie's hand in his, twining their fingers together gently. It was such a simple gesture but, standing together in the middle of all those people enjoying themselves, it made her feel as though they were the only people in the world.

He leaned close to her, which only reinforced the effect. "Whatever you decide to do, we'll do it together," he promised.

"I know," she said, and then, "I wish your family had been here for you today. I know being with me isn't the same as having your real family around, but—"

Andrew silenced her with another kiss. "No. It's better. Because with you, I know that you aren't here because of some halfhearted sense of duty. You're with me because you want to be. I thought I was the one giving my brother a gift by helping put the wedding menu together. Little did I know I was the one getting the best wedding gift of all. *You*."

Their lips touched again, a sweet kiss of true love. "Of course," he said softly against her mouth, "being family means you get invited to family weddings. Will you come with me? Something tells me I'm going to need the backup."

Julie hugged him tightly to her. "I'd love to."

He beamed at her before saying, "The only problem left is that I've still got to figure out what we're going to do for the catering." He shook his head. "Because I am *not* cooking at my brother's wedding."

"Don't worry. You won't have to. I've got a plan." Julie smiled up at the man she loved. "You know how I'm so gung ho about food trucks?"

Andrew smiled back as he quickly caught on. "What a great idea. There are some really great ones in the city." He pressed a soft kiss to her lips, then said, "Why don't the two of us get out of here and start doing some delicious research?"

EPILOGUE

As THE FLORIST at The Rose Chalet, Phoebe Davis's job on the day of a wedding was always multilayered. She kept an eye on the floral arrangements and changed out blooms if they began to wilt. But she was also happy to lend a hand serving food and drinks, or to root through Anne's sewing kit if the bride or bridesmaids' dresses needed a touch-up. She would even help Tyce with the sound check of his equipment.

For the Kyle wedding, though, things were a little different. For one thing, there was no need to help serve dinner because everyone was serving themselves from one of the food trucks that had been parked around the edge of the property. Idly, Phoebe wondered which had been harder, talking the owners of the food trucks into spending their day working at a wedding venue, or talking the owner of The Rose Chalet, Rose Martin, into letting it happen.

Rose had been the tougher sell, Phoebe decided, noting that she was currently watching over the proceedings like a hawk.

She followed Rose's gaze out to the dance floor where Andrew Kyle and Julie Delgado were dancing— and laughing—together. Phoebe was happy for her friend. After all, who wouldn't want to date a gorgeous guy like Andrew? She wished Julie all the luck in the world.

It was just... Phoebe couldn't help the slight twinge of cynicism she felt at seeing them pressed so close together out there on the dance floor.

No, not cynicism.

Realism.

If true love was real and couples stayed together forever, that would be great. But that wasn't how things actually worked out.

Phoebe shook her head slightly, only too aware that as the florist for so many weddings she shouldn't think like that. She knew most people thought florists were hopeless romantics, all obsessed with the thought of true love and finding Mr. Right who would bring her roses every day for the rest of her life.

But all she needed to do was to look at the facts. However happily the bride and groom looked at each other on their wedding day, the statistics were clear: it was a fifty-fifty shot whether they would still be married just three years later. Believing that you'd found true love was as crazy as being certain the lottery ticket you'd just bought was going to be the big winner.

You could be as certain as you wanted; but it didn't change the facts.

Not that Phoebe would ever express such thoughts to her friends at The Rose Chalet—or, God forbid, to Rose herself.

Phoebe picked a white rose out of one of her own displays and let the scent of it drift over her. Forget Mr. Right. What was wrong with Mr. Right Now? How about being honest with herself and having a little fun?

Relationships were like the flower she held. Right now it was beautiful. Perfect. Pristine. With an incredibly beautiful scent.

But in a day or two, it would wilt and end up on one of RJ's compost heaps.

To Phoebe's mind, people who thought they would be the exception as far as the longevity of their relationship was concerned were simply deluding themselves, however much they believed otherwise.

"Would you like to dance?"

Phoebe turned to see to see a man with broad shoulders and handsome, square-jawed good looks. He reminded her a little of someone, though she couldn't quite place who.

"I'm Patrick," he said with a slightly crooked smile that did funny things to her insides.

As she'd just pointed out to herself, why bother with Mr. Right when Mr. Right Now was standing in front of her, gorgeous, available, and asking her to dance? A little short-term distraction was just what she needed.

"It's a shame to have great live music like this and not have the prettiest woman in the room dancing."

He didn't wait for Phoebe to reply, but instead twirled her into his arms. And such nicely muscular arms they were.

Yes, this was exactly the kind of guy she could have a fun fling with, especially since he seemed to be as willing to act on impulse as she was. Guys like him always understood how the game was played and, fortunately, didn't go around asking for more than they were willing to give.

"You still haven't told me your name," Patrick pointed out. "Or should I just go on calling you the prettiest girl in the room?"

It had possibilities, but still, she smiled up at him. "Phoebe. And I'm fairly sure you're supposed to say that the bride is the best-looking woman in the room."

Her voice wasn't usually this breathless. Then again, she didn't often see such available, good-looking men at a Rose Chalet wedding…much less dance with them.

"She does look good, but every woman looks beautiful on her wedding day."

Uh-oh.

"You like weddings?" Phoebe asked.

"Who doesn't? Two people making that commitment to one another is so important. We should celebrate it more often."

Oh, wonderful. Mr. Gorgeous was a romantic. Of all the guys in the room, she had to attract the one with hearts in his eyes.

When they ended the dance in front of RJ, Phoebe finally put two and two together. No wonder Patrick looked so familiar.

"You're brothers, aren't you?"

RJ grinned. "Yes, but he's the brains of the family."

"I'm in town doing the designs for a new house," Patrick explained with a smile.

But Phoebe didn't feel like smiling back. Not when she now knew that Patrick wasn't just a weekend wedding guest. He was someone who was going to be in town for however long his building project lasted.

Phoebe quickly made an excuse about needing to check the flowers. She wasn't sure if either of them believed her. The only thing she was absolutely, positively, sure of was that she had just spent the past few minutes dancing with the worst possible guy for her. Thank God, she hadn't been foolish enough to chat him up and arrange to go on a date with him.

She was definitely not looking for any kind of commitment.

But as she walked away she felt the intensity of his

dark gaze on her from across the room. A shiver worked its way up her spine and told her resistance might not be quite so easy this time.

* * * * *

Turn the page to read THE WEDDING DANCE featuring everyone's favorite wedding florist, Phoebe Davis.
Enjoy this next story in the wonderfully romantic ROSE CHALET series by Lucy Kevin.

THE WEDDING DANCE

CHAPTER ONE

PHOEBE DAVIS MADE her way around The Rose Chalet's main hall, helping to tidy away the remains of the previous day's wedding. It had been a gorgeous affair and Andrew Kyle, brother to the groom and defacto wedding wrangler, had been very happy with the way everything had turned out. Now the flowers in particular, while so spectacular on the day of the wedding, were a bit of a mess and Phoebe had her work cut out. Case in point: the white roses that were part of the table arrangements were wilting, some already dead. She collected the stems in a garbage bag, being careful not to prick herself on the thorns.

RJ, The Rose Chalet's general handyman and gardener, was working to disassemble the indoor gazebo, his shirtsleeves rolled up to the elbows as he lifted a heavy piece of wood. Rose Martin, the Chalet's owner, was helping him, her deep red hair tied back out of the way. Every so often RJ would "borrow" the tool that Rose was using and then put it back slightly out of reach. All this led to at least three mock threats from Rose to fire him that morning.

"You wouldn't fire me," RJ shot back. "At least not with so much still to do."

And not, Phoebe added in the privacy of her head, *when that would mean getting rid of one of the best-looking guys here.*

Not that RJ was the only good-looking man on the premises. Tyce Smith, who handled the music for the weddings, was a handsome guy, too. Right now he was busy packing up his amplifiers and winding up the cables. He looked a bit of a wreck this morning, even by his standards. Normally he wore a couple days' stubble along with artfully disorganized hair, but today his imperfect look needed help.

"The rock-and-roll lifestyle getting to you, Tyce?" Phoebe joked.

Tyce shrugged, his black T-shirt exposing a few of the tattoos on his upper arms. "What can I say? Some of us know how to party."

"And some of us know how to handle the mornings after," Phoebe shot back with a playful smile.

"You must not be having enough fun. I'll show you how it's really done sometime."

Phoebe simply laughed at his invitation. All the employees at The Rose Chalet knew that relationships with coworkers were off-limits. Besides, she'd never looked at either RJ or Tyce in that way. Rose had hired another new temporary caterer none of them had met yet, but Phoebe knew better than to ever mix work and play.

"Would you two focus please?" Rose said to Phoebe and Tyce, but it was clear from her fond tone that she was enjoying their banter. "RJ has to get out of here soon to go look over the site for the house Donovan and I are building, and the architect will be here any minute."

"Everything's going to be fine, Rose," RJ said.

"I hope so," Rose said. "It's just that the house...well, it's such a big deal for me." She flushed. "I mean, for us. For Donovan and me." She turned to smile at RJ. "I'm really glad you agreed to help with the landscaping."

"Sure, no problem," RJ said, but from the way his entire body language changed at the mention of Rose's fiancé it looked, to Phoebe's eyes, as if there *was* a problem for RJ. And a big one at that.

Phoebe continued to pick up and discard the wilted flowers. Every time she did this, she couldn't help but think that there was so much waste for an event that, statistically, would likely not last.

Still, she knew just how lucky she was to get to work with flowers every day. She'd loved gardens and blooms ever since she was a child playing in the soil at her mother's feet. When she'd seen the job listing for a full-time florist at The Rose Chalet, she'd known it was an opportunity she couldn't pass up. Not only was it a fantastic job, but she absolutely loved working with Rose, Tyce, RJ and Anne Farleigh, who made wedding dresses for the Chalet's brides. Week in and week out they all worked together to put on the perfect San Francisco weddings.

"Actually," Rose said, "while most of us are here, I'd like to go through the arrangements for our next wedding."

"Is there anything to go over?" Tyce asked from where he was packing up a microphone stand. "It's just the Three-Peat. We all know what we're going to be doing at least one more time."

Marge Banning, the Three-Peat, was heiress to a fortune founded on vitamin pills. She was also the woman who single-handedly confirmed everything Phoebe believed to be true about marriage.

Marge's upcoming ceremony was her third wedding at The Rose Chalet. The previous two had been big occasions, and they had been identical, using the same flowers, the same cake, even the same dress.

As for the marriages themselves, neither had lasted a year.

"Now, Tyce," Rose said in a tone of gentle rebuke, "you know I don't like you using that term for Marge. She has as much right to a special, unique wedding as any of our other customers."

"But she never *wants* a unique wedding," Tyce pointed out. "She always wants exactly the same thing."

"I have photos of the arrangements," Phoebe said, "so I can repeat them, but won't she want something new this time?"

Rose shook her head. "I've already had this conversation with her. Apparently she loved everything so much last time she wants it *exactly* the same again."

"She obviously likes the wedding part of things," Tyce said with a conspiratorial smile across at Phoebe. "It's just finding the right man for it that's proving to be a problem."

"Tyce," Rose said, but the warning was halfhearted. "Who knows, maybe this one *will* be right for her. I'm sure we all wish her every happiness, don't we?"

Sure, Phoebe wished Marge Banning luck. She'd need it. The whole idea that there was a "right man" out there waiting for you was crazy. As if life ever worked like that. And while you were waiting for him to come along, you missed out on actually living your life. Of course, Phoebe had more sense than to say any of that in front of Rose.

"Look," Rose said, "why not think of this as a relatively easy week? Anne will be taking a vacation week since Marge plans to use the same dress as last time." Rose smiled at them all and admitted, "With trying to finalize the plans for the house on top of everything else, I could do with an easy week myself."

Turning to RJ she said, "I wish I could go with you to look over landscaping options at the building site, but I've got back-to-back meetings all afternoon. And, speaking of the building site, shouldn't your brother be here soon?"

Memories of dancing with RJ's brother swept through Phoebe just as Patrick Knight himself came through the doors to The Rose Chalet's main room, looking every bit as good as he had the previous evening. His dark hair was neatly combed back and a faint dark shadow covered square-jawed good looks. He was wearing a casual shirt-and-slacks combination similar to the one he'd been wearing last night, minus the jacket. She couldn't help staring at him for a moment or two and, for one intense moment, he stared back.

"Hello, Phoebe. It's great to see you again."

"Hi," she replied awkwardly, trying to think of an excuse to get out of there and away from temptation.

Unfortunately the perfect excuse didn't spring to mind. How could it when her brain was too busy replaying every second of how natural, how exciting, it had been to be in Patrick's arms at last night's wedding?

She couldn't forget their conversation while out on the dance floor, either....

"Every woman looks beautiful on her wedding day," he'd said.

When she'd asked, *"You like weddings?"* he'd immediately replied, *"Who doesn't? Two people making that commitment to one another is so important. We should celebrate it more often."*

Patrick might have been great to dance with, and it might have been fun to take things further had he not been RJ's brother, but Phoebe wasn't going to waste her time with some romantic who would always want more than she was willing to give. Especially not when the inevitable breakup would make things hard for her to continue working here—the whole mixing-work-and-play issue would end up front and center.

Fortunately, Rose pulled Patrick's attention away from Phoebe as she started talking over plans for the new house. Rose sounded almost girlishly excited as she said, "I can't believe that Donovan and I are actually doing this."

Nor could Phoebe. The idea of doing something so utterly permanent as building a house with someone made Phoebe's stomach cramp. But if Rose wanted to go and do it, there wasn't a lot Phoebe could do to stop her. Just as she hadn't done anything to stop Julie Delgado from running off into happily-ever-after land with Andrew Kyle.

All Phoebe could do was be there when things inevitably fell apart. She wished that wouldn't happen, of course. If any two people deserved to beat the odds, it was Julie and Rose. Phoebe was still cleaning up the dead flowers as Rose confirmed with Patrick, "You don't need me at the site today, do you?"

"No," Patrick said. "RJ and I will take the day to run through various landscaping options, which I will then present to you and Dr. McIntyre."

"Great." Rose's relief at not having her busy workday interrupted was palpable. "Thanks so much for taking care of everything."

"You ready to head out?" Patrick said to his brother.

"Actually," RJ replied, "I was thinking that it might be better if Phoebe went instead of me."

"'Phoebe'?" Rose repeated, clearly confused by RJ's sudden change of heart.

"Me?" Phoebe asked.

"Sure," RJ said. "You know as much about flowers as I do, more probably, so you're the perfect person to walk over the building site and come up with ideas. You know she'll do a great job, Rose."

"But I thought you were going to do it," Rose said.

RJ shrugged, gesturing to the remains of the gazebo. "I can't leave this. It could, potentially, fall down and hurt someone."

Tyce edged over to Phoebe and whispered, "Is it just me or is that the lamest excuse ever?"

"You haven't heard mine yet," she whispered back while Rose was busy looking over the half-dismantled gazebo.

"I guess you're right, RJ," Rose finally said. "The gazebo should come down today so we don't run into any problems."

"Exactly," RJ agreed. "Plus I still have a complete recreation of Tara from *Gone With the Wind* to fit together for Marge Banning's wedding. Like you said, just because it's the woman's third wedding, doesn't mean we shouldn't do it right." RJ nodded to where Phoebe stood. "Phoebe will do a much better job of putting together general ideas for the garden than I could, and I'm sure she'd be happy to help. Right, Phoebe?"

Rose looked over at her. "Would you mind? I know it's a lot to ask, but you only need to go up to the site with Patrick while he surveys it, take a look around, and work out what the contractors should do with the gardens. It's easy, really."

Correction, thought Phoebe. *Two out of those three things are easy.*

Spending the day that close to Patrick Knight would be anything but.

The trouble was, Phoebe didn't have an excuse to not

go that was even half as good as RJ's. The dead roses pricked her fingers through the garbage composting bag as she clutched it tightly. She was just about to remind Rose about all the cleanup she had to do when RJ beat her to the punch.

"Don't worry about picking up the rest of the roses and flower arrangements," RJ told her. "I'll clean them up after taking the gazebo down."

Phoebe looked over at Patrick who was watching the conversation with a bemused expression on his face. If it was a purely professional trip, how bad could it really be? And Rose was both her employer and her friend. Could Phoebe really say no? No, she couldn't, especially since Rose was virtually pleading, and she almost never did that.

"Sure, Rose," Phoebe finally said with a smile. "I'd love to help you out."

CHAPTER TWO

PATRICK WASN'T SURE why his brother hadn't wanted to come along to the site as they'd planned, but every time he glanced over at the passenger seat of his SUV and saw Phoebe sitting there, he was glad RJ had stayed behind.

As Patrick drove, he found his gaze drifting over to Phoebe again and again. She had been beautiful the previous night at the wedding, but in more casual clothes she was stunning. Her figure was great, her pretty features were exquisite, and he could easily imagine kissing those full lips. Very easily...and with great pleasure.

"So where is Rose's property, exactly?" Phoebe asked, breaking Patrick out of that very distracting line of thinking.

"The plot's in the Sea Cliff district," he said. "It's not much of a drive."

Which was a pity. He could have driven beside her for the rest of the day quite happily. Unfortunately she would probably notice if he took a few detours.

"Sea Cliff is an impressive neighborhood," Phoebe commented. "Donovan and Rose must really be investing in this." She shook her head. "I'm still a little bit shocked at how easily your brother roped me into this."

"I'm glad he did."

He could have sworn Phoebe stiffened before saying, "Why don't you tell me more about the site?"

The deflection was obvious, but Patrick went along with it. For now. "It's a great spot. There's a good view, plenty of space for a garden, too. It's going to be a fun one to work on. Lots of possibilities."

"You sound like you really enjoy your job."

Patrick shifted gears going down the hill. "It's an easy job to enjoy. I get to build places that will make people happy and that will be lived in for years to come."

"Seems to me most architects want to leave their stamp on the world. Don't you?"

Patrick shook his head. "I do that kind of thing when the client wants it. I've done it before, but I mostly prefer to create spaces people can enjoy."

That was always the challenge, to figure out exactly what would make people happy. What, he wondered, would Phoebe enjoy? What kind of date would she love? Houses were personal things—you had to get to know the people involved if you wanted to have any chance of giving them a space to live and grow in. Patrick liked to think that dates were pretty much the same.

What would it be for Phoebe? Dinner and dancing? Patrick liked to be more original than that, but that very originality had let him down a few times in the past. Women who would have been perfectly happy at a nice restaurant generally didn't react well to men who suggested hang gliding as a first date. Only, what did those first-date dinners ever achieve? They got two people into a situation where they might be willing to sleep with one another afterward, but they were always so busy playing the game that they never really got to know one another any deeper than that.

He couldn't see the point. He wanted to know a lot more about Phoebe than that. He was *attracted* to her a lot more than that. Yet maybe the classic option was the best one in this case. She was as elegant as one of those flowers she arranged so deftly, so maybe she was the kind of woman who would expect a restaurant.

Patrick wasn't about to risk letting the obvious attraction between them slip away just because a normal first date wasn't his idea of a great time. Besides, he'd already danced with Phoebe once, and the memories of how good it was to hold her in his arms were still fresh.

They turned into the Sea Cliff district and Phoebe marveled at the location of the plot, saying, "You weren't kidding about the view, were you?"

He couldn't take his eyes off her as she looked out at the ocean with wonder in her eyes. He'd wanted to date her from the first moment he'd seen her working at the wedding the night before.

Hopefully, she felt the same way.

ROSE AND DONOVAN'S plot had enough space for a huge house and garden, along with a view Phoebe doubted anyone could ever get tired of. Although in her experience, didn't people always find ways to get tired of everything sooner or later?

"Phoebe, could you hold this for me?" Patrick passed her a striped ranging pole.

"Oh, so *that's* why you needed me to come out here with you," Phoebe said, smiling, even as she stepped into some soft, damp dirt. She really wasn't wearing the right shoes for a muddy building site. "Where do you want me?"

The answer to that turned out to be lots of different places.

With Phoebe leaning against the pole while Patrick took measurements, they covered most of the property.

It wasn't exactly how she'd imagined spending her day, but it was interesting to see the planning that went into building a place like this.

As they worked, Patrick asked her questions about her opinions on the landscaping options. "Do you think we should put ice plant on the side of the site to stabilize the slope to the ocean?"

Phoebe shook her head. "It's such an aggressive species that it grows over the delicate native flowers. Besides, the roots aren't deep enough to really stabilize the soil…and I suspect the neighbors won't be too pleased with a cascading wall of ice plant."

"Well, I wouldn't want to scare off a delicate flower," Patrick murmured as he looked around at the site. "Should I plan for putting all the garden space at the front of the house, rather than on the ocean side to protect the plants from the sea air?"

"As long as we stick to local varieties, it shouldn't be a problem. San Francisco flowers tend not to be quite as delicate as they look."

Patrick nodded, his gaze holding hers a beat too long. "Good to know," he said, but even as he turned his focus back to the job at hand, she couldn't seem to get her heart to settle down to a normal rhythm around him.

He was in his element as he discussed layouts and possibilities, options for changing the basic plan and where the gardens could go. Even as she struggled to keep up in her heels, she had to admit that it was nice to be around someone who was so passionate about what he did.

"What do you think about putting some Pacific Coast irises in here?" she suggested, pointing to an area that looked perfect for them.

Patrick hesitated. After a second or two Phoebe figured out why. Laughing, she said, "You haven't got a clue which plants I mean, have you?"

"Honestly?" Patrick admitted, "I don't know much about plants, apart from the very common ones."

"You really are the black sheep of the family, aren't you?" she teased. "All those generations of landscapers, including your brother, and you go off to build houses instead."

"How did you know I keep a close eye out for relatives waiting to ambush me with wheelbarrows?" They both laughed, but then Patrick said, "Seriously, though, they've been great about my breaking with family tradition to create buildings instead of gardens."

She couldn't look away from his strong hands as Patrick packed up his surveying equipment. Were they done already? It seemed as if they'd hardly been there any time at all, and Phoebe had really enjoyed spending the day with Patrick.

More than she could remember enjoying herself with a man in a very long time.

"I helped out a bit as a kid," Patrick continued, "but the garden just wasn't quite the place where I felt I fit, you know?"

Phoebe gestured at the nearby houses. "And this is where you fit in?"

He nodded. "I love to create things. To build something out of nothing."

"So what had you turning your focus to homes?" Phoebe asked as Patrick led the way back to the car and put his gear in the trunk.

"I've done a few big offices and public buildings," he told her, "but I wanted to build things that would have more of an impact on peoples' day-to-day lives."

When was the last time she'd met a man this modest?

She knew firsthand he'd won an award for "changing the face of the modern city landscape" because she'd given in to curiosity and had looked him up on the internet after returning home from The Rose Chalet the night before.

All because of one sweet slow dance she couldn't stop thinking about.

"Everyone thought I was crazy," Patrick admitted. "They told me that family homes were what you did when you couldn't get work doing 'real' architecture. But residential architecture was what felt right for me."

"It sounds like you go a lot by what feels right, don't you?"

"All the time," he agreed. "If you never take risks, you never get any rewards worth having." His gaze had gone from easy to intense in an instant and Phoebe's heart pounded in response to his nearness.

"So now you go around designing houses as a favor to your brother?" Phoebe joked, trying to lighten the mood between them.

"Actually," Patrick said, "I was going to ask you about that. Do RJ and Rose get along well?"

She thought about the way her boss and RJ sometimes seemed as if they were flirting with one another, despite the fact that Rose was engaged to someone else.

"Yes, they get along. Why do you ask?"

"I actually heard about this project from Donovan. He contacted me after he'd read a piece in *Architecture Magazine* that talked about my ideas about bringing modern technology to family homes. And we went from there. I didn't even know he knew RJ until he happened to mention The Rose Chalet."

Phoebe thought RJ would have been only too happy to help his brother by suggesting him as architect for the new house. Then again, maybe he'd assumed that The Rose Chalet's owner had everything under control. Rose generally did, after all.

"What is the next step for you in planning for the house?" she asked, curious now after seeing what went into the initial architectural planning stages.

She could tell he was pleased by her interest as he replied, "I'll spend some time speaking with Rose and Donovan to get a better idea of what kind of couple they are. For instance," he explained, "are they going to be the kind of couple who spend all their time in the kitchen cooking together? If so, I'll shift the focus of the house so that the kitchen is the central space. Or are they the kind of couple who like to cuddle up together on the sofa watching Sunday football? Will they spend a lot of time hosting friends or business associates? Are they going to want their own spaces in the home, or do they do everything together?"

Phoebe found herself suddenly imagining a home with a large atrium filled with plants. A home with a nice, warm living room that was the hub of everything, a smaller kitchen because they'd eat out a lot, and a big bedroom because they'd be spending a lot of time there. They'd probably need a study, too, so that Patrick could have a home office to fill up with blueprints and scale models while he—

Hold on. Why was she thinking about Patrick like that?

And why was it still so darn easy to picture him coming out to the sun-filled atrium bearing coffee while she carefully teased exotic flowers into growing the way she wanted them?

She was still trying to deal with those very unexpected visions when Patrick said, "I'm glad you came to help with the initial survey of the land, Phoebe. I'd love to take you to dinner. Would you join me?"

PHOEBE LOOKED STARTLED by his question, her cheeks flushing beautifully. "You want to go out on a date with me?"

"I enjoyed dancing with you last night, Phoebe, and I'm enjoying being with you now even more."

She took a step back from him, shaking her head as she said, "Last night, dancing… It was a mistake."

"A mistake?" He frowned, wondering why she was suddenly so skittish around him after they'd been working together so well for hours. "It definitely didn't feel like a mistake at the time."

He thought he saw momentary indecision move across her face before she tamped it down and the light that had been in her eyes all day dimmed slightly.

"I don't think that we're right for one another, Patrick. Not when we seem to want two very different things out of life."

He had to know. "What is it you want out of life?"

"That's a serious question for two people who barely know one another."

"I've already suggested trying to get to know you better over dinner, remember?"

For a moment or two it didn't seem as if Phoebe would answer. Finally she shrugged. "What does anyone want? To be happy. To enjoy life and to love what you're doing."

"From what I've seen, you do love your job, don't you?"

She nodded. "It's good. I've always loved flowers. Working at The Rose Chalet means I get to do more than just produce endless bouquets for guys trying to make up for missing an anniversary or something else they did wrong."

He felt as if a window into Phoebe's heart had just been flung open. "Do you really think that's the only reason people give each other flowers?" he asked softly.

"It's the usual one."

"I've never given anyone flowers as an apology," he told her. "Have you ever received them that way?"

She shook her head. "I've never received flowers from anyone. I guess people think I've already got enough of them with my job."

That seemed sad to Patrick. If any woman deserved flowers and if any woman would appreciate them, it would be Phoebe. And she of all people ought to see that gesture as more than just a way to make up for mistakes.

"What does it matter, anyway?" she asked, breaking the sudden silence. "Like I said, all I want is to be happy, and I am. I have friends and a career I love at The Rose Chalet. Why would I want to complicate that?"

Patrick could think of all kinds of reasons, but he simply said, "Maybe one day you'll want more than that."

"Maybe." But it was obvious from Phoebe's reply that she didn't believe it, which was quickly confirmed when she said, "Don't hold your breath."

Common sense told him that he should leave it there, but there were times when common sense had to take a backseat to feelings.

"I'm never going to talk you around to the joys of romance, am I?"

She shook her head firmly. "I think that's one area where we're just going to have to agree to disagree."

"Well, I think we've certainly got the disagreeing part down."

She laughed at his assessment. "I guess we have."

"So, how about if we go on disagreeing over dinner?"

Phoebe rolled her eyes. "You aren't going to let it go, are you?"

"No," he said, working up a smile for the beautiful woman in front of him, even though he was as serious as he'd ever been. "I'm not." Although the truth was, one more *no* and he was going to have to let it go—for the time being. "One dinner, Phoebe, as a thank-you for your help today. What do you say?"

Patrick had always believed in the power of hard work and dedication, but that didn't mean he discounted luck. On the contrary, it had smiled down on him many times in his life…but none better than the moment when Phoebe finally smiled and said, "Let's eat."

CHAPTER THREE

"ARE YOU SURE I shouldn't stop by my place to change first?" she asked. "I have mud on my shoes. Lots of mud."

"I don't think anyone will mind a little dirt," Patrick replied, having just gotten off the phone with the restaurant to confirm their arrival in a few minutes. "Besides, you look great."

Phoebe smiled, both at the compliment and the thought that, wherever they were going, it wasn't so serious that they had to dress up for it. She loved dressing up, but at the same time she hated stuffy dates.

She knew she should be putting maximum distance between herself and Patrick. Especially given that from the moment she'd met him, crazy thoughts had been flitting through her usually practical brain one after the other.

She couldn't deny that he was a gorgeous guy, with whom she had great chemistry. Most important of all, there was a built-in ending to things: as soon as he finished the house he'd be heading back to Chicago.

Which meant neither of them could possibly make the mistake of getting in too deep.

With those rationalizations firmly in place, she wondered, Why not allow herself a little fun?

"So where are we going?" she asked.

Patrick grinned at her. "Don't you like surprises?"

"I like *some* surprises," Phoebe said. "To be honest, though, with most guys, the surprise is generally something horrible."

"How horrible?" he asked.

"One guy I met collected antique dolls. They all sat on his shelves and stared at me. I couldn't get out of there fast enough."

Patrick laughed out loud. "You'll be glad to hear I don't have anything like that hidden away."

"People always have *something* hidden away," Phoebe found herself saying, even though she knew she was revealing far too much. She'd just vowed to herself to keep things light and easy. Which was exactly what she needed to do, starting now. "The same way you're hiding the name of the restaurant from me now," she said with a smile.

"I'll tell you if you really want to know."

"No," she said, forcing herself to sit back and relax against the leather seat. "You're right, surprises can be fun." Although she couldn't think of the last time any man had bothered to give her a good one.

As they drove through the city, she silently ran through the list of restaurants she knew. She'd done the first-date thing so many times that by now she could tell a lot about a man by the kind of place he chose for the first date. Some went for the fanciest place they could afford, trying to impress her. A few others went for smaller places. Either way, she always came prepared with enough cash to split the check.

They seemed to be heading for a spot out by the Bay and Phoebe wondered if it was some new place that had sprung up. They parked near a small green space with great views out over the water, where a number of tables had been set out for people to eat al fresco style.

"What is this?"

Patrick grinned, looking so utterly gorgeous that her heart actually skipped a beat for the first time ever.

"I heard about the Nomadic Caterer when I was planning my trip to San Francisco. It sounded like a great idea—a restaurant that moves to wherever the owner feels like putting it for the evening. I've wanted to try it since I arrived in San Francisco. I just needed the right person to go with."

The right person to go with him to a restaurant that never stayed in one place for too long and was always moving on to the next, better, spot? Yes, that definitely sounded like her. She was glad Patrick seemed to see it, too.

It also explained why he wasn't too bothered by the mud on her shoes. Dining out in the open like this meant it was casual and, besides, there was only so much mud you could avoid.

The outdoor restaurant looked almost magical—the space was decked out with lights, and every table was positioned to have the best possible view of the Golden Gate Bridge.

"I have got to tell my friend Julie about this," Phoebe said as they went over to take their reserved seats. "It's just the kind of thing she'd love."

Patrick raised an eyebrow. "The question is whether it's the kind of thing you love."

"I think I can probably put up with it for the evening," she said, smiling at him.

They took a moment to order, Phoebe starting with a salad and Patrick choosing the soup. The young man hurried off with their first-course orders, while Phoebe looked around at the spot the Nomadic Caterer had chosen for that night.

There were flower beds not far from the tables; blue periwinkles and red poppies. "Early friendship and pleasure," Phoebe murmured aloud.

Patrick gave her a questioning look. "What was that about friendship and pleasure?"

"Oh, it's just 'language of flowers' stuff." Phoebe glanced away briefly when she saw how intent Patrick's gaze was. "It goes with the territory, when you're a florist. I suppose it's a bit old fashioned now, but it's nice to be able to put together a bouquet now and again that has more to it than just a few pretty colors shoved together."

"Somehow, I doubt that you have ever 'shoved together' an arrangement," Patrick said as their first course arrived. "If all flowers have meanings, does that mean that you match people to their flowers when you prepare the bouquets for their weddings?"

"Like an undertaker sizing them up for a coffin," Phoebe said without thinking. But that was what it *was* like, wasn't it? "Honestly, though, most of the time it's just the flowers they like best. Mostly roses and orchids, although I do try to slip a few other things in here and there to make it unique."

"What flower would you use to sum yourself up?"

She was surprised by the depth of his question. "You realize I could just make up anything here, right? Remember that I've just spent the day explaining flowers to you."

"True." He leaned forward slightly. "I'm willing to risk it."

If they were playing that game, what should she say? The orchid, for beauty and refinement? That would probably make Patrick smile, and he'd already proved several times that evening that he had a gorgeous smile. Maybe one of the roses?

But, for some reason, she couldn't give him the off-hand, meaningless answer.

"Probably the pasque flower." It was the symbol sent to show that a lover had no claim on her. Yes, perfect.

When Patrick looked blank for a moment or two, Phoebe winced theatrically before saying, "Are you sure you aren't adopted?"

"RJ wonders that occasionally, too," he said, and then, "tell me about the flower."

Why hadn't she just given him the playful answer? It was what she normally did with men, after all.

Unfortunately it seemed Patrick wasn't like any other man she'd been with.

"It blooms in spring and is a lovely light purple color." But that wasn't really what he was asking, was it? "Some people," she continued softly, "think it symbolizes freedom."

Fortunately, just then, the waiter came back to clear their plates and take the rest of their order. Afterward, she was careful to steer the conversation clear of anything that had to do with her. Men, in her experience, loved to talk about themselves.

"So, how long does it usually take to build a home?"

"It can take months," Patrick said, "but I'm not actually there for most of it. I take a few weeks to draw up the plans and then I fly in to deal with any big issues the contractors have."

"So you drift from place to place, always on the road, never settling down?"

Phoebe quite liked that image. Particularly since it meant whatever brief fling she and Patrick were going to have wouldn't hurt either of them. They'd both just move on naturally, and that would be that.

"I suppose so," he said, "though I like to think of

it as doing what I can to help out as many couples as possible with their dream homes. Plus, I always know my family will be there for me whenever I need to be brought back down to earth. They've always provided me with a sense of rootedness."

"You know," she said as their steaks arrived and they dug into the perfectly prepared meat, "this is the first dinner date in a long time that I've actually enjoyed."

"It's been pretty fun from this side of the table, too," he said with a look that made it clear exactly how much fun it had been.

She could practically feel his appreciation brushing across her skin. Still, she wanted to take the time to enjoy the rest of the date, rather than rushing Patrick home with her. There would be time enough for that. One of the best things about these brief flings was that they were *intense.*

"You know, Patrick, there's one thing I don't get."

"What's that?" he asked.

"Well, you build homes for couples, and you're obviously deeply into marriage, commitment and the rest of it. Yet you're here with me, rather than at home with a wife. Why hasn't some lucky girl snapped you up?"

Patrick grinned. "Lucky, huh?"

Phoebe barely held back a snort of laughter. "Now you're fishing for compliments. And avoiding the question. Come on, if you're so into the joys of marriage, why isn't there a wedding ring on your finger already?"

"Maybe I just haven't met the right girl yet." Patrick shot her a pointed look, full of humor and something else, something bigger than she wanted to consider. "Though I'm not ruling you out just yet."

Phoebe flinched so hard she almost knocked her

plate off the table; her enjoyment of the evening quickly fading away.

How could he? The evening had been heading toward being a lot of fun for both of them, the start of exactly the kind of casual fling she preferred. Now though…no.

She couldn't stay.

She reached into her bag for her cell phone and pressed the button for the app that made it ring. It had come in handy on previous dates when she'd wanted to leave before the guy was ready to let her go, but she hadn't thought she'd need to pull that with Patrick.

Or, rather, she had hoped she wouldn't need to use it with him.

"I'm sorry, I need to take this call," she told him after it rang, then put the phone to her ear. "Mom? What is it? Where are you?" She nodded, then said, "Hold tight, I'll be right there."

"Is everything okay?" Patrick asked when she put her phone back into her bag.

"Not really." At least that part was the truth. "That was my mother. She's unexpectedly in town." She pushed her seat back and stood. "I didn't get all the details, but I have to go."

Patrick stood, too. "Well, at least let me—"

"No, it's fine," she said quickly even though it was anything but that. Needing to get out of there as quickly as she could, she said, "You should finish dinner. And enjoy this view. Everything tasted great. Thanks, Patrick." The words tumbled out one after the other before she hurried away.

CHAPTER FOUR

PATRICK PULLED INTO RJ's driveway, pausing to call Phoebe again. He wanted to make sure that she was okay after the abrupt way she'd left dinner, but she wasn't answering his calls. He'd circled the block around the park several times with his car to see if he could take her home, but there hadn't been any sign of her.

She'd looked so nervous—and guilty—right before she'd left that he couldn't help but wonder if the whole thing about her mother had been an excuse. Had he been wrong to come on so strong? To not only take her to dinner tonight…but to also make it clear that he was looking for more from her?

Yet Patrick knew he couldn't really have done anything else. He wasn't about to lie to Phoebe. He couldn't act as though one night together would be good enough. He wasn't that guy.

He would never be that guy.

RJ was sitting on the sofa watching the start of the football game. "You've been gone awhile. Was there a problem at the site?"

Patrick took the beer his brother offered. "No problems, everything went great." With the property, anyway.

He tried to get into the match-up between the San Francisco 49ers and the Chicago Bears, but it was hard to concentrate on anything but Phoebe. Especially when he couldn't stop thinking about how soft, how sweet, her mouth had looked as she'd told him about the language of flowers. It was all too easy to imagine what her lips would taste like pressed against his.

Not that he'd get the chance at this rate.

"Are you kidding?" RJ yelled at the screen. "That ref is blind!"

Patrick was glad to be able to laugh at something. "You're just upset because my team is winning."

"Your team?" his brother demanded. "A little thing like moving to the other side of the country and suddenly you've switched teams?"

"At least when they're winning."

"Traitor."

They made it through to halftime, with RJ cursing every mistake the home team made and Patrick making a point of cheering for the Bears as loudly as possible. After all, if you couldn't revel in the sporting misfortune of your sibling's favorite team, what could you do? For a little while it was like being kids again crowded into their parents' old home with everyone sitting in front of the TV watching whatever big game was on.

At halftime RJ asked, "Was Phoebe upset with me? I should have warned her that I might need her to step in to take a look at the landscaping for Rose and Donovan's property."

Patrick caught his brother's slight twitch when he mentioned the eminent plastic surgeon's name. "No, she wasn't upset, although we both were surprised you'd decided you couldn't help."

RJ shrugged. "I had a lot to do this afternoon."

Patrick was pretty sure his brother could have had his work done at The Rose Chalet in no time flat if he'd needed to. Not to mention the fact that the owner, Rose, seemed perfectly happy to let him off the hook for a few hours to take a look at her property.

But rather than giving Patrick the chance to ask any further questions, RJ got up off the couch to grab a new bag of chips from the kitchen. "You hungry?" he said as a clear subject changer. "I could throw some burgers on the grill."

"No, I ate. I took Phoebe out to dinner."

His brother raised an eyebrow. "Just as a thank-you for helping out, right?"

Patrick frowned, even though that was precisely the reason he'd given Phoebe to try to convince her to spend the evening with him. "No. More as a date."

"A date?"

"Why are you so surprised?" Patrick asked a little more hotly than he needed to.

"It's not you. It's just that Phoebe's not exactly a relationship kind of girl."

"What is that supposed to mean?" Patrick demanded, immediately taking offense at his brother's offhand judgment. "I thought Phoebe was your friend."

"Take it easy."

"So you can keep insulting her? I don't think so."

RJ shook his head. "I'm not insulting her. All I'm saying is that Phoebe isn't the settling-down type. Just... don't expect too much, okay?"

"Are you actually telling me you've never been tempted to ask Phoebe out on a date yourself?"

RJ looked shocked by his question. "What? No. No way."

"Oh, come on. I know that our taste in women isn't all that different. You must have thought about it."

RJ shook his head. "That's not how things work at The Rose Chalet."

"Why?" Patrick asked. "Have you all taken vows of celibacy?"

His brother smiled. "No, I'm pretty sure that wasn't in our employment contract. It's just that we've all been working together so long that we think of one another more like family than anything."

"Really?" Patrick asked before he could stop himself. "What about Rose, then?"

RJ looked at him sharply. "Especially Rose."

Patrick suddenly realized why RJ hadn't wanted to work on Rose and Donovan's house plans. At least one thing was coming clear tonight.

"Are we going to sit here arguing," RJ asked, "or are we going to watch the second half?"

Patrick took the second beer his brother handed him and forced himself to sit back and watch Chicago claim their victory, though there wasn't a lot of pleasure in it by then.

How could RJ think that Phoebe wasn't ever going to respond to a guy who was looking for more than a one-night stand? And even if that really was the case, did it matter?

Patrick already knew he couldn't give up on the chance to be with her just because she put up walls around herself to keep other people out. He would just have to find a way past them. Then he would build what lay between them slowly and carefully, until it was something that could really last.

Fortunately, he thought with his first real smile since she'd walked out on him at dinner, if there was one thing he was good at, it was building things that lasted.

CHAPTER FIVE

PHOEBE PAID THE taxi driver, then began to make her way up the stairs of her apartment building. All she wanted was to get to the other side of her front door so that she could shut out a world where guys like Patrick Knight thought it was perfectly acceptable to start talking about marriage on a first date.

First and last date.

There was no way she was ever going near Patrick again romantically. He might be gorgeous and fun to be around, but there were plenty of guys like him out there.

Well, maybe not *quite* as good-looking or as easy to be with as Patrick, but at least they wouldn't go around demanding more than Phoebe was willing to give.

She turned a corner and almost walked into a neighbor; a guy she had seen coming out of an apartment downstairs a couple of times. "I'm glad I ran into you," he said. "I've been meaning to introduce myself." He held out his hand. "I'm Jack. My girlfriend and I live in 1F."

"Phoebe." She shook his hand. "It's nice to meet you."

She was already starting up the stairs when he said, "Listen, we're planning to throw a party in a few weeks to celebrate getting engaged and we thought it would be nice to invite everyone from the building. We figured it was a good excuse to finally meet the neighbors. We'd love to see you there."

"Congratulations," she said, and then, "I often work weekends, but once you know the date, let me know and I'll check to see if I can make it." She hoped she wasn't being too rude for not prolonging the conversation, but all she could concentrate on just then was a long bath and vegging out in front of the TV with a glass of wine.

But, for some reason, the combination of engagement parties and her day looking at Rose's property with Patrick, had her needing to push back a strange longing for a house and garden of her own to putter in.

Didn't all her friends with houses and yards always tell her how lucky she was not to have to deal with the upkeep a house demanded? And didn't they always marvel at how she managed to live virtually clutter free?

Phoebe had never seen much point in weighing herself down with stuff, with two exceptions. The first was the collection of clothes that had long since outgrown the available closet space and now occupied stylish racks stationed along the side wall. The other came in the form of the potted plants dotting every surface. She loved the fact that plants didn't demand anything beyond a little water and some light to grow in.

All in all, Phoebe's apartment was the perfect space for her to remind herself why she didn't need anyone making things—

"Hi, sweetie."

—difficult.

"Mom?"

Phoebe thought back to the excuse she'd given Patrick. One little white lie about her mother being at her apartment needing help, and now here she was, probably let in by the super if Phoebe had to make a guess.

Even by karma's standards, that was quick.

Angela Davis was in her fifties and people tended to say that if women ended up looking like their mothers, Phoebe was going to be very lucky indeed. Her mother exuded a sense of elegance, from the tips of her manicured nails to her perfectly applied makeup. But a few cracks showed in the facade—the smudges in her mother's eye makeup, and the suitcase perched next to the sofa, pushed back slightly so that Phoebe wouldn't have seen it immediately if she hadn't been looking for it.

"Hello, honey. It's so good to see you."

Her mother enveloped her in a hug that immediately took Phoebe back to being five years old and sitting in the warmth of her mother's lap, enveloped in the floral scent Estée Lauder had created out of tuberose and gardenia.

"You, too, Mom," she said, already counting down the seconds until—

"So you're still in this place," her mother said as she pulled back and looked around dismissively. "You have a good job, Phoebe. You could do so much better for yourself than this."

"I *like* my apartment, Mom."

"Really?" her mother asked as if that couldn't possibly be in the realm of possibility. "But if you had a house, instead, then you might have civilized things like a spare room for your mother to stay in when she comes over. In fact, if you had bought when the market was at its lowest—"

"Then I'd be stuck with a huge debt that would tie me down."

But Phoebe's mother wasn't listening. Instead she

was moving to run her fingers over the leaf of a flourishing pink flowering bromeliad in the corner of the room.

That particular love was one thing they had in common. About the only thing, it seemed sometimes. Which was why Phoebe knew her mother hadn't just dropped by for a visit. After all, they'd been through this enough times by now, hadn't they?

She hated to see her mother's face fall and her shoulders hunch as she dropped the leaf from her fingertips and sat back on the couch.

"David left me."

Phoebe's chest clenched. It was so difficult seeing her mother like this. Phoebe never knew what to say… and when she did, she never felt as if it was the right thing or what her mother wanted to hear.

She sat next to her mother and took her hand. "He left you, just like that?"

"He said he wanted to be *happy*." Her mother was tearing up now and Phoebe reached for the box of tissues on the end table. "I thought we were happy. We had just celebrated our one-year anniversary."

A year was practically a lifetime based on the standards of her mother's relationships. Why anyone would invest so much of themselves in something so brief, Phoebe didn't know. She just knew that her mother kept on doing it and every time it went wrong—*every single time*. She would end up here, and they would have the same conversation they'd had so many times before.

Her mother was struggling hard not to cry, which meant that any minute now she was going to try to distract herself from her emotions by—

"You know, honey, if you are going to live in an apartment, you could at least make it look a bit nicer.

Especially with so many great furnishing stores here in San Francisco."

Phoebe pulled her hand back from her mother's. "I like my apartment." She gestured to the kitchen window. "Look at how well the orchids are doing in this light."

"The flowers look good," her mother agreed, "but the rest of it…"

Phoebe stood. She loved her mother, of course she did, but on the days when she showed up needing somewhere to stay after a bad breakup, it could sometimes be quite hard to remember all the reasons why.

"I'll go get some sheets and things to make up the couch as a bed. You can take my room."

"Thank you, honey. It won't be for too long, I promise."

After helping her with the sheets, her mother sat on the couch and gave her the look Phoebe dreaded as she patted the seat next to her. "Are you dating anyone?"

Phoebe felt her cheeks grow hot as she shook her head. "No."

But she could be, couldn't she? If she hadn't freaked out over dinner, she could still be out on a lovely date with Patrick…and he might even be kissing her by now.

Oh, the thought of being kissed by that sinfully gorgeous mouth.

"Make sure you don't end up like me, Phoebe," her mother said in a hollow voice. "That's why I worry about you so much. I know you think you have all the time in the world but, trust me, the years move past you faster and faster every year. You don't want to end up alone." Her mother paused a beat before asking, "Do you hear anything from your father these days, Phoebe?"

Beyond frustrated with how her night had gone, Phoebe barely held it in check as she said, "Mom, can we once, just *once,* not do this?"

"Not do what?"

Her mother actually looked surprised by Phoebe's question. Could she really not remember the way things always went when she broke up with someone?

Then again, maybe she couldn't. Maybe that was what let her keep going around and around, making the same mistakes. It would explain a lot, but the trouble was that Phoebe *could* remember. She could remember far too well.

"You're going to ask how Dad's doing, if he's seeing anyone, and if he ever talks about you anymore. Then you'll go over the whole divorce and—"

"I was married to him, Phoebe. That creates a connection that lasts forever, even if the marriage doesn't."

Phoebe knew she should leave the room before she said anything she might end up regretting. "It's been a long day, Mom. I'm sorry, but I'm really tired and dirty. I'm going to take a bath and then tuck myself into bed on the couch."

Frankly, she thought as she sank into a tub of steaming water a few minutes later, the only good thing to come out of the evening was that her mother's latest breakup had made it very, very clear how smart she'd been to stop Patrick in his romantic tracks.

She picked up the soap and washcloth and began to clean the dirt from her hands and feet. But no matter how hard she scrubbed, she couldn't clear away the unwanted longings within her. Longings not just for a house and garden…but for a man to share them with. A man who would love her unconditionally.

A man she could trust.

A man who made her heart pound too fast as he held her in his arms.

A man who looked and sounded an awful lot like Patrick Knight.

CHAPTER SIX

PHOEBE GOT TO work early the next morning and found
RJ in the main room of The Rose Chalet working to put
up a facade based on Tara from *Gone With the Wind*.
Marge Banning wanted them to turn the whole of The
Rose Chalet into a reconstruction of the old plantation
house. Phoebe had never been able to understand why
Marge Banning had opted to recreate *Gone With the
Wind* for her big day, especially given that the story
ended with Scarlett not getting the man she wanted.

"Is everything going to plan?" Phoebe asked RJ. The
supporting frame was almost all up, but she could see
there was still plenty of work to be done.

"It'll take a while, but I'll get there just like last
time."

That was one good thing about the Three-Peat's wedding plans. They already knew exactly what would work
and what wouldn't, so it was mostly just a question of
trying to replicate what they had done last time.

"By the way, there are a few gladiolas that have just
bloomed." He grinned. "Do you think you can persuade
Marge Banning to try something new?"

"Of course I have to try," Phoebe said. "Though I'll
probably have better luck trying to stop the tide coming in. Besides, I suspect Rose will kill me if I convince
Marge to change her wedding plans."

RJ frowned at the mention of their boss's name and

returned to work. Phoebe moved away before he could remember to ask her about Rose and Donovan's landscaping plans.

Talking about the house would mean talking about Patrick. And after the way things had ended last night, it would be more than a little awkward to discuss one brother with another.

Hadn't she known better than to say yes to dinner with RJ's brother? She'd known it would cause problems when things went wrong.

Thankfully though, for the moment at least, RJ seemed no more inclined than Phoebe to talk about the house or what she thought about his brother.

She headed out into the gardens of the Chalet, looking around to see which flowers were available. That was one of the best things about working where she did. The Rose Chalet gave her the garden she could never have living in an apartment. Between this garden, the small greenhouse hidden at the rear of the wedding venue, and her contacts in San Francisco's flower markets, she could generally find what she wanted when it came to wedding flowers.

If only men were that easy.

Phoebe forced the thought away as she checked on the gladiolas. They were, as RJ had said, perfectly in bloom. Phoebe cut one carefully, taking a moment to savor the scent.

Gladiolas symbolized love at first sight.

There was, she told herself firmly, absolutely no reason for that thought to make her chest twinge as she set out to go see Rose in the other corner of the garden.

Her boss was going over a couple of papers as she sat at a table in the sunlight. Since even Rose couldn't find that much to organize in Marge Banning's repeat wedding, Phoebe guessed she was working on either her new house or on her own personal wedding plans.

Rose looked up with a smile as she approached. "Oh, Phoebe, I'm glad you're here. I've been wanting to thank you again for going to check out the property with Patrick. It really means a lot to me that you took the day to work with him on it."

"It was my pleasure," Phoebe said.

As the lone non-romantic in the business, she'd learned to put on a good face with Rose, and she definitely didn't want her boss thinking there was any funny business going on with RJ's brother. Especially after what had happened not long ago with Julie, their former in-house caterer, and her new boyfriend.

"I was hoping I could ask you for another favor. There are just such a lot of things to consider with the house and Donovan asked me if I could get away from work for a few hours today. Would you mind holding down the fort when Marge comes in to go over any last-minute details?"

"Sure, I'm happy to do whatever you need me to do."

"Great." Rose handed her Marge's wedding information binder. "Oh…and, Phoebe?"

"Yes?"

"The gladiolas are beautiful, but don't try changing the bouquets."

Phoebe couldn't help but laugh out loud as Rose walked away. Even when her boss was busy with other things, she still seemed to have eyes in the back of her head. Just as Phoebe's own mother always had.

Before she had time to dwell on what her mother might be getting up to, alone in the apartment all day, with no one to entertain her, Marge Banning showed up in a Lexus hybrid, looking as excited as she had the first time she'd gotten married at the Chalet.

She smiled at Phoebe with genuine warmth. "It's great to see you again, Phoebe."

"You, too, Marge. Rose was called away, so it's just us today." She looked behind Marge. "Unless you brought the lucky guy with you?"

"You know I don't like to have them around for this part," Marge said with a wave of her hand. "They'd only go around suggesting things, and a girl's wedding... Well, it should be all hers, don't you think?"

Fortunately, Phoebe knew an answer wasn't expected. "Should we head inside now so that you can check out the displays?"

"I'd like that," Marge said. The sound of hammering came from the main room and she happily clasped her hands together. "Is Tara going up?"

Phoebe nodded. "Everything will be ready in plenty of time for your wedding. I promise."

"I know it will be," Marge said. "I've seen the finished product, but I haven't had the chance to see Tara being built. Could we go inside and take a look?"

As Phoebe walked with Marge into the Chalet's main hall, they discussed a few timing issues for the ceremony. RJ was still hammering away and Tyce was there, too, moving his sound system into the right spot while occasionally stopping to make notes.

And then Patrick unexpectedly walked in, carrying a stack of lumber over one shoulder, and Phoebe's heart immediately started racing.

This explained how RJ had been able to get so much done. He was getting help from his brother. Patrick wasn't wearing a shirt while he worked, leaving Phoebe to stare at the lean, well-defined muscles of his chest. It took her a second or two before she could snap out of it.

"My friend at the flower market says the roses will be in perfect bloom for your wedding day," she told Marge in a voice that was far too loud.

"That's wonderful, Phoebe," Marge said.

But even though she sounded happy about it, and despite Rose's warning to stick with the plan, Phoebe couldn't help at least trying to suggest something else.

"Are you sure you don't want me to come up with something new for this wedding? There are so many other flowers in bloom this time of year, truly lovely ones."

"I'm sure there are," the other woman said, "but the arrangements you made last time were perfect." As if she could tell Phoebe was disappointed, she added, "You know what they say, don't you? Third time's the charm!" Marge looked past her and Phoebe followed her gaze to where Patrick was still working shirtless. "Though a girl can't help but think about making it a fourth time for a man who looks like that."

Architects were supposed to sit at desks all day, drawing things, thought Phoebe. They should not have bodies like *that*.

"Hello, Phoebe, Ms. Banning," Tyce said as he moved past them to rig up the sound system on the other side of the wall.

Phoebe forced her gaze from Patrick to Tyce. The Rose Chalet's music director was definitely handsome, but he never made Phoebe's stomach do somersaults.

"Oh, come on, Tyce," Marge said. "We must surely know one another well enough that you can call me Marge now."

He raised his eyebrows and gave her his patented

heartbreaker look. "In that case, it's very nice to see you again, Marge."

"Mmm," Marge said softly as she watched him walk from the room. "It's a wonder you manage to get anything done around here with so many good-looking men around. And it's even more of a wonder that you don't have a ring on your finger."

"Married?" Phoebe choked. "I'm not even dating anyone."

"You must have the self-control of a saint." Marge smiled a smile that said a lot about how she had acquired three husbands. Well, almost three. "That or you just haven't noticed the way the gorgeous one with his shirt off is staring at you."

Phoebe glanced around quickly, but by that point Patrick wasn't looking at her anymore. Was the whole world conspiring to try to get them together?

And the idea of Marge Banning giving her advice on love and marriage...

"Marge, can I ask you something?" When the woman nodded, Phoebe took a breath and asked the question she'd been wanting an answer for since Marge's second wedding. Even if it meant Rose might kill her, she had to know. "Why do you do this?"

"Do what?" Marge asked, cocking her head to the side.

"The weddings. Going through it all again and again, the same way every time. Especially if it didn't work the last two times."

Unexpectedly, Marge smiled. "I do it the same way because the details don't really matter, and I like them like this. All you really need is a man, a woman and that feeling."

"What feeling?"

Marge put a hand over Phoebe's. "Trust me, you'll know it when you feel it."

That was the kind of romantic nonsense she would normally have scoffed at, yet she couldn't speak her mind when it was a client saying it to her.

Although, at present, there was another much more important reason why she didn't say anything...a reason that had a lot to do with what she felt every time she glanced at Patrick.

Were the butterflies flying around and around in her stomach at the thought of being in Patrick's arms what Marge meant?

And if so, had she just been hit by Marge's "feeling"?

CHAPTER SEVEN

PATRICK HEFTED HIS length of lumber, fitted it into place on the side of the elaborate structure taking shape in The Rose Chalet's main room. He held it steady while his brother hammered it into place. He tried to concentrate on the job at hand, looking at what he was doing rather than staring at Phoebe…but it was far from easy. She looked stunning today. Simply stunning.

Just as always.

Patrick didn't care to make a secret of how he felt about her, but if one little joke could send her running off, what would openly staring at her do? Better to at least pretend to be focused on helping RJ, even if Patrick had been the one to volunteer to do it, simply to have the chance of seeing Phoebe again.

If she wouldn't take his calls, what other option did he have if he wanted to see her?

"You'd better move your thumb out of the way," RJ said, "unless you want it to become part of the Chalet's new look." His brother made a pointed sound. "Are you listening, Patrick?"

Patrick managed to hold focus long enough to help get the next few pieces of wood attached. He'd always enjoyed building projects but, as an architect, he rarely had a chance to do hard physical labor. As much as he loved his job, there was something about sweating over putting something together with his own hands that could never be replaced. It was why he was so active—hiking and swimming and boating whenever he had the chance.

"Thanks for your help, but I can get the rest," RJ said. "Why don't you go take a shower out in the back?"

Patrick followed RJ's directions around to the rear of the building. He took his time using the shower, trying and failing to stop himself from imagining what it would be like if Phoebe were there with him. Patrick had to turn the tap completely cold before finally stepping out and getting dressed again.

He knew he could have gotten together with her for one night. But one night—a quick, sexy *fling*—wasn't what he wanted. He didn't just want to get to know her body better.

He wanted to learn the secrets of her heart, too.

Patrick made his way back to The Rose Chalet's main room, hoping the client had left so that he could get a chance to speak with Phoebe. But even though the bride-to-be was no longer in the room, the woman he couldn't get out of his head was standing there, in the middle of a conversation with the music director.

"Are you going to be dancing at Marge's wedding the way you did at the last one, Phoebe?" Tyce was asking her.

"Why," Phoebe asked, a flirtatious lilt to her voice, "are you planning on joining me, Tyce?"

"Is that an invitation?"

She laughed and said, "You know, Tyce, that sound system of yours just keeps getting bigger. Does any of it actually do anything or is it all just there to compensate for something?"

"Agree to dance with me and you'll find out."

"So I'll never know the answer, then?" she said before leaving the room and heading for the garden.

Beside Patrick, RJ smiled as he reached for a drill. "See what I mean? One big, happy family."

Really? It didn't feel like the kind of family banter Patrick was used to. No, what he had just witnessed was more like straightforward flirting.

A burst of jealousy ran through Patrick and heat flashed along his skin. Phoebe deserved more than flirting with some guy she worked with. She deserved a man who could sweep her off her feet. She deserved romance.

Real romance.

Forever rather than a string of meaningless one-night stands.

"Hey," RJ said, "if you're heading back out to Rose's property, could you pick up a few things at the nursery for our volunteer project tomorrow?"

Along with a couple dozen other people, RJ and Patrick had volunteered to do some upkeep in Golden Gate Park's overgrown areas. It was just the sort of thing their family had done together when they were kids.

Just like that, Patrick was hit with an idea for a date that could be a whole lot more fun than sitting around in a restaurant making small talk until he said the wrong thing. Knowing there was no time like the present, he made his way over to where Phoebe was clipping a few roses from the garden.

"Hello, Phoebe."

Her cheeks were flushed as she looked up at him. Would he ever get used to how beautiful she was?

"Hi, Patrick." She bit her lip. "I'm sorry I had to leave so suddenly last night. Good thing my building manager had already let my mother in by the time I got home."

He worked to mask his surprise that her mother's arrival hadn't just been an excuse. Still, Patrick had the feeling that she'd been only too happy to leave the outdoor restaurant—and *him*—last evening.

"Is she doing okay?"

"I hope so. Her latest relationship didn't work out and—" She cut herself off and ran a hand through her hair before forcing a smile onto her face. "I began to write up some ideas for Rose's landscaping plans last night. I'll try to get them to you in a couple of days, if that's all right?"

"That's fine, thanks," he said, not wanting to talk business with her right now. "RJ's volunteer gardening group is landscaping part of Golden Gate Park and I was wondering if you'd like to come help out tomorrow."

That wary look was back in her eyes. "So this would be you and me—"

"And about thirty other people," he said quickly. "It's a worthwhile project, and we could really use your skills. Having someone who really knows what she's doing with plants could make all the difference."

Phoebe hesitated and he resisted the urge to push her any harder to get her to agree. Doing that would just give her more of a reason to back away.

On impulse, he reached down to pick up a lone gladiola that was lying on the grass between them and handed it to her.

"I hope to see you there."

CHAPTER EIGHT

PHOEBE STOOD IN front of the mirror in her bedroom, trying to pick out the right thing to wear for the gardening project. She wanted to look good, but she needed something different from her regular work clothes. Working on a few well-maintained flower beds at the Chalet and hacking through overgrown shrubs to reclaim an untamed section of parkland were two very different things.

Of course, it shouldn't matter how she looked today now that Patrick seemed to have finally gotten her "let's just be friends" message. After all, no one in the history of the world had ever recommended a day of hard manual labor as a technique of seduction. It was about the least romantic idea for a date that Phoebe could think of. And maybe that was the point. Maybe this was Patrick's way of making it clear that he could work with her without romance intruding on everything. Maybe he really did want to be buddies with her the way his brother was.

As she pushed back the disappointment at the thought of only being "buddies" with Patrick, at least it made picking out clothes a little easier. Jeans and a dark sweater wouldn't show too much dirt. After putting on some boots, she checked her watch and saw that she'd have to hurry if she wanted to make it to the park on time. Just as she was gathering her tote and keys she heard a familiar voice.

"Where are you going?" her mom asked. "I've come over to visit, and I've barely seen you."

"A—" Phoebe paused, trying to find the right word for what Patrick was to her "—friend from work asked me to help out with a volunteer gardening project."

"Gardening? That sounds lovely."

Her mother looked so hopeful for a moment and it was such a nice change from the lost, forlorn expression that had been all but etched into her face since the previous night, that Phoebe suddenly found herself saying, "Mom, how would you like to come out with me today?"

"Are you sure?"

"Absolutely. I don't think it's healthy for you to sit around here in my apartment all day. You should be out doing things. Having fun."

"I don't know..." her mother began.

But Phoebe wasn't about to give her the chance to come up with an excuse. Instead she pulled her mother up by the hand. "You'll enjoy it. I promise."

Angela probably would, too. Her mother enjoyed gardening almost as much as Phoebe. She would just make a point of keeping her away from the more back-breaking parts of the landscaping project.

"I guess it would be nice to do something together," her mother admitted. She looked around at Phoebe's apartment. "And to get out of this place. Really, dear, maybe we should spend the afternoon visiting Realtors or—"

"Come on, Mom." And with that, they locked up the apartment and headed down to the parking garage.

Phoebe had already put a few basic supplies in the

trunk of her car, so they didn't need to do anything beyond driving over to Golden Gate Park. Her mother was quite subdued as Phoebe drove, but at least she wasn't talking about how badly the men in her life had let her down.

Not wanting her mother to be too surprised by the work that awaited them, Phoebe said, "We're actually going to be spending the afternoon helping a local gardening group clear some of Golden Gate Park."

"We're going to be pulling up weeds?" Her mother sighed. "Well, I suppose that's all right."

"I remember when I was little, you'd take me around the garden," Phoebe said, "showing me which were plants and which were weeds. I had my own watering can, but you'd only let me help with the planting if I was very careful."

"That watering can was nearly as big as you were, but you'd take it everywhere." Her mother sounded lost in the past. "As I recall, I had to stop you watering the cat. You wanted to see if that would make it grow."

Seeing the reflection of her mother's features in the windshield, Phoebe caught the barest hint of a smile. Thank God.

Phoebe parked the car then went around to the trunk. She'd brought gardening gloves, trowels and a few other things she normally used to keep The Rose Chalet's flowers looking their best for the upcoming weddings. Thankfully, she had a spare pair of gloves to lend her mother, though, to Phoebe's surprise, she turned that offer away.

"If I'm going to be elbow deep in dirt," her mother said, "I might as well do it properly and get some dirt under my fingernails."

There were groups of people working to weed flower

beds and trim back trees. Other teams were building retaining walls to prevent erosion on the banks of the elevated ground. Work was also being done to thin out some of the wilder scrub. Everyone seemed to be working in an organized way, but there didn't seem to be much indication as to who was in charge of the organizing. There was a small tent set up over to one side, but that was obviously intended for the volunteers to relax in after they were done working. There was no sign of a group leader over there, either.

It was only when she looked over the gardens for a second time that Phoebe spotted Patrick helping with one of the low retaining walls. It made sense that he wasn't anywhere near the plants.

She headed over with her mom in tow. "Hi, Patrick. This is my mother, Angela."

"It's nice to meet you," Patrick said.

"You, too, Patrick."

Her mother looked from him to Phoebe then raised her eyebrows, which Phoebe prayed he didn't notice as she asked, "Where do you want us?" Although, with the way Patrick's muscles stood out against his shirt, Phoebe couldn't make up her mind whether it would be better to work next to him or as far away as possible.

He smiled at her; that gorgeous smile that turned her insides to goo every time. "Let me check with RJ to see who needs extra help the most. I'll be back in a minute."

Phoebe watched him leave. So did her mother.

Angela gave Phoebe a pointed look. "I'm suddenly starting to understand why coming out here to help was such a big deal for you."

Phoebe frowned. "It's not a big deal. I'm just here to volunteer."

"Oh, come on, honey. I'm your mother. I know you

better than anybody. It's obvious that you like him. And why wouldn't you?" Angela added with an appreciative sigh. "He's gorgeous."

Phoebe thought briefly about arguing, but there didn't seem to be much point. Lately, no one seemed to believe that she wasn't interested in Patrick. Why should her mother be any different?

CHAPTER NINE

"PHOEBE'S JUST ARRIVED," Patrick informed his brother, "and she brought her mother, Angela. Where do you want them?"

"The flower garden," RJ said. "If anyone can make sense of the mess in there, Phoebe can. Unless you think she's needed somewhere else?"

"No, I think that makes sense for the two of them. Does that old palm tree stump next to the flower garden still need digging up?"

RJ looked at him with obvious surprise. "Are you offering to do it? I was thinking of leaving that one. It's going to be backbreaking work, you know."

Patrick shrugged. "You've got it under control here, so I might as well handle that."

Although his brother clearly thought he was nuts, he said, "If you're offering, that would help a lot. Thanks."

No, Patrick thought, he should be thanking his brother for a tailor-made excuse to spend the afternoon just yards away from Phoebe.

When he went back to them and relayed RJ's assignments, Phoebe looked surprisingly happy at the amount of manual labor she'd just been given. Her mother looked less enthusiastic, especially when they reached the gardens, which were every bit as bad as RJ had suggested.

"It's like a jungle in here," Phoebe said.

"Yes," Angela agreed. "We won't exactly be wandering around with a watering can, will we?" her mother said, clearly taken aback.

Patrick watched Phoebe pull back her shoulder blades and stare down the unruly garden. "Well, at least we'll know we made a difference today." She smiled at him. "Thanks for showing us what we're doing. I guess you'd better get back to the walls."

"You won't be getting rid of me that easily, I'm afraid," Patrick said. He nodded to the old tree stump in the middle of the garden. It was gnarled and dark with age, obviously rock-solid. "That's my project for the afternoon."

"Oh, boy," Angela said. "Those things have roots like iron."

Patrick could barely take his eyes off Phoebe to reply to her mother. "I've often heard it said that nothing worth doing comes easy."

"Yes, well, occasionally you put in all that work and still get nothing out of it," Phoebe pointed out, but then stopped and glanced across at her mother. "We should probably let Patrick get to work, Mom. It looks like he has a lot to do, and so do we."

What Phoebe said was true. First, he had to dig around the stump, find the roots and remove them with an ax before chopping down the remaining stump to a movable size. Even then, he'd probably need RJ's help with the final removal. The sooner he got started on it, the sooner he'd be finished, so he went and fetched a shovel.

By the time he got back with his tools, Phoebe and her mother had already set to work putting the garden into some kind of order. Phoebe worked her way methodically along the rows, separating the weeds from those plants that could still be salvaged. She worked with a straightforward determination that Patrick greatly admired.

He set to work on getting the stump out, and it was every bit as hard as both RJ and Phoebe's mother had predicted it would be. Pretty soon, sweat was pouring from him as he worked his way around the roots. But it was all worth it because he not only got to watch Phoebe working with her mother, he was also close enough to hear them chatting.

"I'd forgotten what hard work this was," Phoebe's mother said. "Are you *sure* we used to enjoy it that much?"

Phoebe laughed. "Oh, yes," she said in a deadpan voice, "we *loved* it."

Only, instead of laughing with her, Phoebe's mother picked up a plant her daughter had put into the compost heap and stuck it back in the ground.

"Those aren't weeds, honey. They're perfectly good gardenias."

"I know, but they're dying." Phoebe removed the plant again. "It's better to get them out now and get it over with, so that there's room for something to really flourish."

Her mother's face fell. "Maybe all they need is a little loving attention, rather than being tossed in the nearest trash container." Her mother took the trowel from Phoebe's hand. "And it would be better if you held it like this."

Phoebe pressed her lips together. Patrick was almost certain she was counting to ten before speaking. Just as he sometimes had to do with difficult clients.

"You know I do this for a living, right, Mom?"

Phoebe said in a voice so soft that Patrick more read her lips than heard the words.

"That doesn't mean that you know everything, dear. Besides, maybe if you spent a little less time working and a little more time getting out to meet some suitable young men, then you would spend your days off doing something other than more gardening."

Patrick clenched his teeth at the idea of Phoebe meeting any "suitable young men." She'd already met one, thank you very much.

"I've told you before," Phoebe said in a voice that was a whole lot more relaxed than it should have been. "I like my life, Mom."

Patrick had to admire her self-control. It seemed clear to him that her mother wasn't trying to be unpleasant, but that surely couldn't make it any easier for Phoebe. If this was something that she had to deal with on a regular basis then no wonder she was careful about letting people in.

Looking at the pair of them, he could guess an awful lot about Phoebe's childhood with a mother who was often disappointed and broken up by the loss of the men in her life. But instead of that sudden insight making Patrick want to back off, he only admired Phoebe more. And it only made him believe all the more strongly that if anyone deserved some real romance in her life it was Phoebe.

Patrick wasn't sure how he was going to do it yet—the walls Phoebe had set up around herself seemed as solid as the tree stump he was working on—but he was determined to get through to her. Besides, he'd always thrived on challenges.

When Patrick finally looked up from his hard work he was amazed by the transformation of the garden under Phoebe's hands. He could hardly believe it was the same overgrown wilderness they had started with.

Looking back at the remains of the stump, he considered calling over his brother for help. But then he had a better idea.

"Phoebe, Angela, would you give me a hand with this?"

"Sure," Phoebe said as she and her mother headed over to help. "What do you need?"

There were so many possible answers to that question, starting with a simple *You* and going from there. For now though, Patrick settled for pointing to the remains of the tree.

"I'd love some help getting this into the wheelbarrow."

Phoebe didn't hesitate. So many of the women he'd been out with would have hated the idea of doing hard manual labor. Most wouldn't have stayed for an hour, but she was only too happy to help at one side of the stump while Patrick got the other. Even Angela didn't balk for too long, and he suddenly realized where Phoebe got her strength. Angela wasn't an easy woman, perhaps, but in the end she was a survivor.

Between the three of them, they managed to lift what was left of the tree stump into the wheelbarrow. As Patrick wheeled it away, he stole a glance back and saw Phoebe smiling over at her mother. It was obvious how much Angela mattered to her, but then, that had been obvious all afternoon.

And what a lucky woman Angela was, to be loved by Phoebe.

CHAPTER TEN

BY THE END of the day, Phoebe was so exhausted that she felt as if she could sleep for a week. Looking around and seeing the difference she and her mother had made to the flower garden made it easy to realize it had been worth the effort.

"So," Patrick asked, coming back from getting rid of the last of the tree stump, "did you have fun today?"

Phoebe was surprised to find that she had. It had been fun spending the afternoon doing something worthwhile, even if it had taken a lot of effort.

Maybe *because* it had taken so much effort.

"I did," she said with a small smile, suddenly feeling shy around Patrick.

"How about you, Angela?"

"Just as long as I don't have to do it all over again tomorrow," her mother replied, but she was smiling, too.

Phoebe hadn't seen many smiles from her mom since she'd shown up at her apartment. Clearly, an afternoon out in the fresh air had done her some good. That, or time around Patrick.

She had been impressed with the way Patrick had persuaded her mother to help, coaxing her into assisting with the remains of the tree. He'd made a real effort, but he hadn't intruded. It would have been easy to make things worse for her mom.

"RJ tells me there's a small party for the volunteers

over by the tent. It would be great if you could both come after putting in so much effort today."

"We'd love to, wouldn't we, Phoebe?" her mother said before Phoebe could make up an excuse to leave.

Knowing there wasn't much of a chance of stopping her mother now, she settled for putting away her gardening gear in the car before she headed over to the tent. Patrick did the same, walking over to his brother's waiting truck with the ax and the shovel he'd been using.

"Will she be okay?" he asked.

"Oh, she'll be fine," she said, even though the truth was her mother had never been able to hold her liquor... which was made worse by the fact that she thought she could.

Knowing it wouldn't look good if she sprinted over to check on her mother, Phoebe briskly walked across the lawn, glad for her hiking boots. In the tent the volunteers were enjoying themselves with BBQ chicken and drinks from a couple of large coolers.

RJ intercepted them. "Thanks for coming out today. You've made a real difference to that flower garden."

"It wasn't just me," Phoebe said, looking past RJ to see if she could spot her mother.

"Your mom seems great, by the way."

Phoebe tried to smile. "She is great, thanks. Have you seen her?"

RJ turned to look for Angela. "She was just here a second ago. Is everything okay?"

What could she do but nod? "Sure."

"Why don't you relax and have something to eat?" he said and before she knew it she found herself eating a BBQ chicken sandwich while caught up in a conversation with a couple who were in the middle of landscaping their own garden and had heard she was a plant expert.

"What kinds of flowers would you recommend for a deer-tolerant yard?" the woman asked. "We keep trying things that people have recommended, but they don't always do that well."

"Honestly, the best advice I can give you is to take a look in your neighbors' gardens. Nine times out of ten, what works has as much to do with the soil and the general location as anything else."

A few minutes later she spotted Patrick at the entrance to the tent, waving her over. "Sorry," she said, "I think I'm needed."

She hurried over to Patrick, who looked worried. "What's wrong?"

"I've found your mother."

"It's bad?"

Patrick didn't reply immediately. "I think you should come and look."

He led the way outside, around to the back of the marquee. There, Phoebe's mother was sitting on the grass, a bottle of champagne in her hand. It was nearly empty. She looked up as they approached.

"There you are. I thought you'd run off, Patrick."

"I just went to get Phoebe, Angela."

"I wouldn't have blamed you if you had left me here," she continued. "Men are always running off on me. It's like there's something wrong with me."

"No, there isn't," Patrick said as they got closer. Very gently, he took the champagne bottle out of her hand and put it aside.

Phoebe moved to kneel beside her mother, who looked more stricken by the second. "What kind of example am I…am I—" she paused for a moment, as though trying to remember the word *"—setting?"*

Phoebe hooked an arm under her mother's. "Let's get you home."

"I don't have a home anymore. Not since me and your father split up." She was now crying.

"Here," Patrick said, "let me."

He lifted her mother easily, carrying her over to Phoebe's car and helping her into the backseat before sliding into the passenger seat.

"What are you doing?" Phoebe asked.

"You'll need help getting her to your apartment."

She didn't bother to argue with him. Not when the thought of trying to carry her mother up the long flight of stairs made Phoebe a hundred times more tired than she already was.

"Thanks," she said at last, and started to drive.

When they reached her apartment, Patrick helped her mother out of the car, wrapping her arm around his shoulders to support her.

"I've made such a mess of things," her mother murmured as they got to the door and Phoebe unlocked it.

Knowing Angela wouldn't remember their conversation in the morning, Phoebe murmured something comforting as she tried to help her inside, but in the end Patrick just picked her mother up completely.

"Nice apartment," he said with a nod to the flowers and plants occupying every surface. "Where should I take Angela?"

"Right through here." She led the way to her bedroom, trying not to think about how differently this might have gone with Patrick the other night if it had been just the two of them.

Patrick laid her mother down on her bed and Angela

crooned, "It's been years since a strong young man carried me to bed."

Phoebe winced. Apparently her mother was determined to be as embarrassing as possible tonight.

Angela immediately curled an arm around the extra pillow and held on tight to it. "I love you, Cally."

"I love you, too, Mom."

As she headed back out into the living room with Patrick, he admired the flowers again before saying, "You obviously believe in bringing your work home with you." He paused. "'Cally'?"

She'd been hoping Patrick wouldn't pick up on that. She should have known better. He noticed everything.

Especially the things she didn't want anyone to see.

"It's my middle name."

"Phoebe Cally Davis?"

Phoebe moved over to the sofa and sat next to the pile of folded sheets. She might as well get comfortable. It was where she was going to be spending the night again, after all.

"It's short for Caladenia. It's a type of orchid."

Patrick sat next to her, and Phoebe wasn't sure how she felt about having him that close.

No, that was a lie. She was very sure how she felt about him being so close.

Far too good for her peace of mind.

"Caladenia," he repeated, and she loved the way it sounded when he said it. "It's a very beautiful name. You got your love of flowers from your mother, didn't you?"

Phoebe nodded, swallowing hard at the lump in her throat that had grown bigger and bigger as he became kinder and kinder. "She loves orchids. The Caladenia orchid is her favorite. When I was a kid, she used to try to grow them, because she said they were the most beautiful of all the orchids. The most precious."

It was the same thing she'd always said about Phoebe. *You're my beautiful, precious little girl, Cally.*

"It's one of the things she used to let me help with, but it never worked that well."

"You have such a green thumb that I take it the flower is hard to grow?"

"Almost impossible. The roots are too easily displaced. You have to care for it more than almost any other flower."

Why was she fighting back tears? She never cried. *Never.*

"The crazy thing is, regardless of how much time you put in, it still dies after a couple of years."

"It must be a very beautiful flower for people to want to put in all that work," Patrick said softly. "A small miracle."

Phoebe nodded. "It is."

The one time they'd been able to get one to grow, her mother had said just that same thing. *It's a miracle, sweetie. Right here in front of us. Let's appreciate every second of its bloom.*

Oh, God. She *was* going to cry.

No. She couldn't. Not now. Not tonight.

And definitely not in front of Patrick.

"There are other beautiful flowers out there," she made herself say. "Why put in all that effort waiting for a miracle when the odds are it probably won't happen?"

"Because sometimes the rewards are worth the risk," Patrick said so gently, so sweetly, she almost felt as if the words were more of a caress than anything else. "Even if the odds aren't great, they're still so much better than if we never take a risk at all."

He was silent for a few seconds after that, and Phoebe half expected him to lean across and kiss her. To finally make the move that she was sure he had wanted to make all day.

Yet, Patrick didn't close that gap. Instead he stood.

"I'm glad we got your mother back safely. And I hope you enjoyed the day in the park. Good night, Phoebe."

He left, then, shutting the door behind him, leaving Phoebe to stare after him, trying to make sense of her very confusing feelings for Patrick Knight.

CHAPTER ELEVEN

PHOEBE WOKE TO the sound of her phone ringing. What time was it? And what was she doing on her couch?

It took a moment for the memories of the previous day to seep in. At the same time her phone kept ringing, leaving her scrambling to locate it. She finally found it under one of the cushions on the couch. How exactly it had gotten there she didn't know.

The number on the screen was for Lisa Harding, a local florist Phoebe occasionally ran into down at the flower market. They often met for coffee to catch up on flower-business gossip. Lisa had even helped to source a couple of unusual blooms for Phoebe. She had some friends who liked to grow the rarer species in their greenhouses.

"Hi, Phoebe. I've just had an order in for a bouquet, and I thought I should probably let you know."

Phoebe frowned slightly. "Why?"

"It's to be sent to your address." Before Phoebe could push past her surprise to respond in any way, the other woman said, "It's one of my best arrangements."

Phoebe's heart fluttered with something that felt too much like hope. Moving over to the small kitchen area of her apartment she tucked the phone under her ear and started making coffee, a strong brew that would help her wake up and get her head back on straight. The morning would definitely look better after coffee, and her mother would undoubtedly need it, too.

Patrick knew *exactly* how she felt about flower deliveries. So why had he done this?

Phoebe took a deep breath, then let it out slowly before asking, "Do you mind if I come by your shop in a bit?"

"Sure, but don't you even want to know who ordered it?"

"I can guess."

There was silence on the other end of the line and Phoebe figured her friend was confused by her reaction to the news. And rightly so. Most people loved getting flowers. Phoebe might have, too.

If only they didn't mean what she was afraid they meant.

"Lisa," she asked before they disconnected, "if you wouldn't mind, could you not start on it until I get there?"

Phoebe had been so sure the other day that Patrick understood how they stood. That he'd finally decided just to be a good friend to her. The whole day yesterday had been about as far from a date as it was possible to get. Then, when he'd helped to bring her mother in, and he'd had an opportunity for a kiss that no guy would have ever passed up...he just left. And now he was sending her flowers?

Phoebe quickly showered and dressed without waking her mother, leaving her a note saying she was heading in to work. Then Phoebe set out for Lisa's flower shop. It was a tiny place wedged between a small boutique and a store selling furniture. The shop had a small front room tastefully put together with a few flower arrangements next to a couple of awards. Bouquets from

Lisa didn't come cheap, which made it all the more worrying that Patrick had ordered one for her.

Lisa smiled as Phoebe came in. "Actually, I'm glad you're here since I've been wondering about the message on the card."

Her friend hunted behind the counter for a moment then handed Phoebe a card that read, "It's not every day I get to carry a woman home. I hope you're feeling better."

Relief and disappointment warred with each other as she told her friend, "These flowers aren't for me. They're for my mother."

She was glad that Patrick intended to send flowers to her mother rather than her; it was incredibly sweet of him. Not a lot of guys would do that. And yet, for a moment Phoebe had almost felt as if he was going to push past her walls, no matter what, by giving *her* a bouquet of flowers, whether she wanted them or not.

"Lisa, would it be all right with you if I put this one together?"

"Sure, why not? I have the original order and the design sheets are here somewhere. Everything you need is through the back."

The back room of the shop was quite a bit larger than the front room, consisting of an office table off to the side, a big table in the middle and boxes of flowers stacked neatly around the walls. There were spools of ribbons, pieces of cane and myriad other decorations that might be needed as part of an arrangement.

Phoebe put the plans for the bouquet down on the table and looked through them. It had been a while since she had worked from someone else's plan, but Lisa took extremely detailed notes when taking down an order, so that made things easy.

"'Orchids,'" Phoebe read aloud, heading over to the boxes. Lisa had drawn a diagram, with suggestions of colors. Of course Patrick had opted for orchids, given that they were her mother's favorite flower.

She laid out the orchids she'd chosen on the table, going back for the other elements of the bouquet one by one as she started to piece it together. As she did so, she thought about the way her mother had always had an orchid blooming in the house when Phoebe was a child. Angela had been so beautiful then. So happy. Of course, her mother hadn't actually changed that much since those days. When she was happy, at least, she was still an incredibly beautiful woman.

As Phoebe assembled the arrangement Patrick had ordered, she had to admit it was breathtaking. For a man who didn't know much about flowers, he had done a good job of picking out the perfect elements for it. Phoebe wove them together, a stray memory coming to her of the way her mother had taken the time to weave her hair into elaborate braids and intricate knots when she was a teenager.

She took a step back when she finished with the bouquet, the reds, yellows and whites of the orchids leaping out at her. For once, it didn't matter that it would wilt in a couple of days. It was enough that, for the moment at least, Patrick had made a gesture that would undoubtedly bring a smile back to her mother's face.

Phoebe took the bouquet out to Lisa to show her. The florist looked at it admiringly before saying, "It's a good one, isn't it? And it's for your mother? Now, whatever did she do to deserve that?"

"I think Patrick wants to cheer her up. She's been a bit upset." She smiled at her friend. "Thanks for letting me put the bouquet together. I'll let you take care of the delivery."

It had been a strangely cathartic experience.

"You know, Phoebe," Lisa said in that voice people used to offer advice they knew you didn't want to hear. "If it were me, I'd hold on to a man who did something like this, who cared enough about you to care about your family, too."

Lisa's words played on repeat in Phoebe's head as she drove to The Rose Chalet.

CHAPTER TWELVE

ARRIVING FOR HIS meeting with Rose and Donovan, Patrick realized The Rose Chalet was the quietest he'd ever seen it. He looked around for Phoebe's car, but there was no sign of it. Had she stayed home to take care of her mother?

Donovan McIntyre's Porsche was instantly recognizable, however, which meant that the plastic surgeon was probably looking at his watch and thinking about the clients Patrick was keeping him from.

He collected the roll of plans from the passenger seat and headed inside the Chalet where he found his brother installing a spotlight. "Are you going to need a hand with anything when I'm done?"

RJ shook his head, frowning as he looked in the direction of Rose's office. "Did you know Rose built this place so people could have somewhere small and intimate for their weddings?"

"Rose is a very impressive woman," Patrick said to his brother, wondering as he did so if they had both been hit with some sort of Knight brother curse of falling for women who didn't want anything to do with them.

RJ's jaw flexed. "Yes, she is." He turned back to the spotlight. "You should probably get to your meeting."

Rose was in the office, sitting at the side of her desk, her deep red hair tied back. Donovan was sitting in her usual seat, behind the desk, wearing a suit Patrick knew cost a fortune.

Patrick had to admit they looked great together, and he couldn't help but wonder how he and Phoebe would look as a couple. He was dragged out of that thought as Donovan's bronzed features rearranged themselves into a smile as he said, "Let's get the ball rolling."

Rose's smile was much wider than her husband-to-be's. "Good morning, Patrick. Are those the plans?"

Patrick began to unroll them on the office table, stopping halfway to move aside a vase of flowers so that he could spread the plans all the way out. Had Phoebe put together the arrangement? And, if so, what had she been thinking about as she did so?

They were lovely—a spray of purple flowers against a background of white roses—and Patrick wished he knew more about the "language of flowers" if only for the possibility of a glimpse into Phoebe's emotions. For her, he would memorize an encyclopedia of flowers and their meanings.

Donovan cleared his throat and Patrick worked to refocus as he went over the preliminary drawings with them. "This will be the entrance hall opening into the living room with access through to the kitchen area here. It's designed so that the spaces aren't cut off from one another." He paused to give his clients time to look over the drawings.

"Hmm…" Donovan mused, looking over the plans. "Four bedrooms seems like too many."

"Four bedrooms is fairly standard for a family home."

What kind of home might he have with Phoebe if she let him into her life? Looking down at the plans, Patrick started to mentally redraw them, adjusting lines and reassigning rooms, and even adding an atrium, which he'd always liked in a house. It was so easy to see how their dream home would work.

As before, Donovan interrupted his thoughts. "Rose and I are both very busy people. If we don't have children, we won't need the extra rooms." Not seeing the stricken look on Rose's face at his mention of not having children, Donovan continued, "I think we should move the office upstairs and join it with what would have been one of the bedrooms to create a large study and library."

Patrick had done this enough times to know how to carefully say, "That space would certainly work as a library. But it wouldn't be a very cozy room."

Donovan frowned. "We're not going for cozy. Are we, Rose?"

Rose paused for several beats before finally saying, "A large library would be lovely."

Patrick looked from Donovan to Rose, on the verge of suggesting a compromise when the office door opened and RJ came in.

"Sorry to interrupt," RJ said. "There's a problem with the lights, Rose."

"Can't it wait?" Donovan asked him in a tone that wasn't entirely friendly.

"There seems to be some issue with the sequencing. I won't be able to get the rest of the rig up until we've worked out how we want to deal with it."

"I'm sorry," Rose said as she stood. "Can we finish with the plans in a few minutes once the lighting situation is back under control?"

Donovan stood. "I only had this brief window to meet today. I've got to get back to the clinic." He shook

Patrick's hand, kissed Rose on the cheek and nodded slightly to RJ as he took his leave.

Rose and RJ were just heading out to deal with whatever had become so pressing with the lights that were "no problem" a short while earlier, when Phoebe walked in.

"Rose, could I—?"

Suddenly realizing Patrick was in the room, her cheeks flushed and her question fell away. He was glad to have a moment to drink in her incredible beauty.

"I'm sorry, Phoebe," Rose said. "Can you hold that thought for a few minutes while I help RJ sort out the lighting?"

Phoebe looked more than a little nervous now that it was just the two of them in Rose's office. He wanted her to be comfortable enough around him to want to spend time with him but, right now, nerves were good, too.

Women didn't flush like that around men without a reason.

"How's your mother doing?"

"She's a lot tougher than she looks," Phoebe said. "I'm sure she's already up and about, watering and talking to my plants."

He loved her small smile as she reached over, adjusting a few of the flowers in the vase on Rose's desk.

"Thanks for helping me get her home. I'm not sure I could have done it alone. And thanks, too, for inviting me to work at the park. It was a lot of fun."

Patrick had to grin at having found a woman who thought being knee-deep in cow manure was a good time.

"What could be more fun than backbreaking work?"

"Says the man who single-handedly tackled a tree stump," she teased back.

"But I wasn't single-handed," Patrick pointed out. "I had you and Angela to help me out."

"The flowers you sent her are beautiful, incidentally," Phoebe said softly. "Just what she's always loved."

"I hope she liked them."

Her cheeks flushed again and he was *this close* to pulling her against him for a kiss when she said, "Actually, as a thank-you, I would love it if you—" She broke off, her eyes widening at her slip. "I mean, we would love it if you came over to dinner tonight."

"I'd love to have dinner with you and your mother."

"Great. Will seven o'clock work?"

He nodded, very careful not to say, "It's a date." Because if there was one phrase that would undoubtedly ruin things, that was it. Instead he settled for a nod.

Phoebe was quick to leave rather than stay and chat with him, but she had invited him to dinner. Okay, so her mother would be there, too, but in some ways that actually felt closer than the alternative. Anyone could do the traditional first-date dinner, and Patrick guessed that Phoebe had done it more than a few times, but how many men had she invited back to her apartment for dinner with her family?

That was definitely something to think about.

Then again, he couldn't stop thinking about Phoebe if he wanted to.

CHAPTER THIRTEEN

"MOM, IF YOU'RE feeling up to it, I would love some help with dinner," Phoebe called out from her kitchen.

An hour ago, when Phoebe had come home and seen that the bedroom door was still closed, she'd been happy enough to leave Angela be while she got started on dinner. She'd settled on pasta with meatballs and home-made sauce. It wasn't hugely imaginative, but Phoebe was well aware what years of cooking for one had done to her culinary skills.

No answer had come from the bedroom, and she had assumed her mother must be taking a nap. When the pasta sauce chose that moment to bubble up and spray all over her, Phoebe looked down at her splattered clothes and realized she'd need to quickly change before checking on her mother—just in case Patrick arrived early.

Thanks to the racks of clothes taking up space between the plants, Phoebe only had to walk a few yards across the apartment to slip on a dark dress dotted with bright lilies that she'd owned for ages but had never found an excuse to wear. Not that spending an evening with Patrick should be an excuse for *anything,* Phoebe reminded herself, and then she hesitated. She didn't want him thinking that she'd dressed up just for him. Maybe she should change into something more casual before he—

The chime of the doorbell cut off her indecision. She hurried over to get the door, looking back briefly to the flowers she'd put on the apartment's biggest table, so that Patrick could see how much her mother appreciated the gift. Even though it seemed that Angela hadn't been out of bed long enough to spend much time looking at them.

Patrick looked gorgeous as he stood in her hallway. He handed her a potted iris bulb. In the language of flowers, iris meant *friends, hope,* and *faith.* If he had taken the time to look it up, and she was sure he had, which sentiment did he mean exactly?

"I would have brought wine, but I wasn't sure whether that would be a good idea."

"Good call," Phoebe said, glad that she didn't have to sidestep the issue of her mother for the very first time ever on a date. "Come in."

"You're looking great tonight."

She felt as if she could bask in the glow of his appreciation forever…which was what had her backing away from him instead.

"I'm just going to go check on Mom. Could you keep an eye on the pasta sauce for a minute?"

Phoebe went over to her bedroom door and knocked. "Patrick's here for dinner."

When there was no answer again, she pushed open the door, more than a little worried now. If anything had happened to her mother while she was at work, she'd never forgive—

The room was neat. Too neat. On top of the newly made bed, there was a note. Phoebe sat on the edge of the bed and picked it up, recognizing the elegant swirls of her mother's handwriting.

Cally,
I'm sorry about yesterday. I know I must have
embarrassed you in front of your friend. There's
good news, though. David called me and we
talked. I think there might still be a chance with
him. By the time you read this I'll probably be
back in Sacramento. Please don't worry about
me. Everything is going to be fine. I can feel it.
Love always and my best to Patrick if you see him
again—which I hope you will!
Love, Mom

Phoebe read the whole thing through again, just to make sure it wasn't all some huge joke. It felt as if it should be but, at the same time, she knew it was exactly what her mother would do—and exactly the way she would do it. She stared at the note for several more seconds before putting it down and heading back to the kitchen.

Without a word, she took out a couple of plates and served up the pasta. "Looks like it's just the two of us tonight," she said to Patrick as she carried the plates over to the table and set them down.

"Is your mother still not feeling well?"

"She's fine." She tried to smile, but couldn't manage it. "She's gone."

"Gone?"

Phoebe nodded. "She left me a note telling me she's going to try to work things out with David after all."

She found a bottle of wine, poured two glasses, then sat at the table with Patrick, who was very quiet as he watched her carefully. She picked up her fork and tried to force herself to take a bite, but it was another thing she couldn't manage just then.

"Phoebe—"

The way he said her name was too gentle, too kind.

Hating the tears that were springing to her eyes, she said, "I just hate the way she keeps making the same mistakes. She went running back to him the moment he snapped his fingers."

"Maybe she thinks it's her best chance of being happy," Patrick suggested.

"Being happy?"

Phoebe got up, moving away from the table. The flowers Patrick had sent her mother were still there, still beautiful, despite everything. Flowers had always been that for her, she suddenly realized; a balm to her soul no matter what else was happening. No matter how she was hurting. As a child, when her mother and father had split up, she'd spent hours in the garden. Planting. Growing.

Healing.

"I wish that were the case. She'll go back to him, and then six months or a year down the line, things will fall apart again and she'll be hurt by it."

"And you'll be hurt by seeing her like that again, won't you?" Patrick added, moving to stand beside her. He put his hands on her shoulders, turning her gently to face him.

In that moment it occurred to her just how close he was.

"I think Angela is being very brave."

"You aren't the one who has to deal with her every time a relationship falls apart."

"No, that's true. It's bad for you, Phoebe, I know. But it must be worse for her. And yet she's still willing to take that risk. It's a hard thing, putting yourself out there for someone else."

Phoebe wanted to argue with that, but she couldn't think of a good comeback. She was too busy staring at Patrick, drinking in the feel of his strong hands on her shoulders, tracing every line of his features.

She wasn't sure which of them began the kiss, but it was Patrick who took control of it. He kissed the way she had dreamed he would, with a sense of strength behind every movement of his mouth on hers. It wasn't the intensity of it that made Phoebe catch her breath. It was the intimacy of his kiss as he held her in his strong, warm arms.

She pressed closer to him, tight against his body, kissing him back with all the fire she'd been trying to douse for days. Her hands moved to his shirt. She wasn't sure of much right then, but she was sure that she needed this from him.

"Come through to the bedroom," Phoebe whispered, but Patrick stepped back, holding her at arm's length. "I'd like nothing more right now than to be with you, Phoebe, but I want more than that."

Phoebe hesitated. Why did he have to break the mood like this?

She bent her head over to the side to place a kiss on the inside of his wrist. "Can't we just enjoy the moment? If I want you and you want me..."

"That's the trouble, Phoebe," Patrick said as he threaded his fingers through hers. "I do want you. *All* of you. And until you'll agree to give me more than just one night, I can't." He leaned in and kissed her gently one last time. "I just can't."

He slowly slid his fingers from hers, then headed for the door. By the time Phoebe had recovered enough from that second kiss, and realized how perfect it had felt to have her hand in his—by the time she could think straight—he was already shutting the door behind him.

CHAPTER FOURTEEN

IT WAS AMAZING how empty Phoebe's apartment felt the next morning. Her mother hadn't been there long, but the place suddenly seemed too quiet without her. Phoebe watered the plants before leaving. It was her day off from the Chalet, and she'd thought she'd be spending it with her mother.

Feeling a little at loose ends, Phoebe headed out of her apartment and almost ran into Jack, the neighbor she'd met on the stairs the other day, accompanied by a woman who had to be his fiancée.

"Oh, hello," he said, smiling. "Nicky, this is Phoebe Davis, our upstairs neighbor." The woman with him was petite and pretty, with spiked blond hair and blue eyes.

"I've been looking forward to meeting you," Nicky said, offering her hand. "Do you think you'll be able to come to our party? It will be the last Friday night of the month."

"I'd love that," Phoebe found herself saying, surprised to realize just how much she meant it. For so long, she'd kept herself apart from her neighbors. Now, she wondered, what were her reasons for insisting on making her apartment feel so temporary?

Watching the happy couple walk away, hand in hand, Phoebe's thoughts slid to Patrick and the way he'd held her hand when he told her he wanted more than just one night of passion. He'd looked so good, had kissed so well. If she closed her eyes she could remember every moment of that kiss as if it were still happening. Phoebe bit her lip at that memory, savoring it as she got into her car.

If only he'd wanted to go further, everything would have been so simple. So straightforward.

She turned her relationship with Patrick around in her head for the hundredth time. They'd only known each other a few days—admittedly an intense few days—but even so, could he really have been asking for some kind of commitment from her? Especially when he was due to go back to Chicago as soon as he was done with Rose and Donovan's house?

Phoebe impulsively decided to head for Golden Gate Park to see how things were looking in the garden. She parked by a swing set full of children and mothers, and something twanged in her stomach as she remembered the freedom of swinging way up high, with her mother behind her to help her soar.

Feeling the sun on her face, she headed over to the garden patch they'd all worked so hard on. It wasn't yet perfect. Not all the flowers were out in full bloom, and there were still gaps where they'd had to re-seed spots of it. Still, the whole place looked a lot better than it had when they'd started.

She, her mother and Patrick had done that. Phoebe looked at the space where the old tree stump had been. It was bare, but they'd filled the hole with fresh soil, planted plenty of seeds, and already Phoebe could see a few hints of shoots trying to rise through the recently cleared earth. She gently made sure that the soil around them would support them and went back to the car to get a bottle of water to pour around their roots.

If only making things grow with people was as easy, as straightforward.

Phoebe's thoughts circled back to Patrick once more. She'd been so careful until last night to keep a distance between them, yet right now all she knew was that she missed him...and wished he was here with her now to enjoy the garden.

He was far too unrealistic about romance, but did that really matter when Phoebe, at least, knew better? Since every relationship had a built-in cutoff point, surely it couldn't hurt if she started dating Patrick with her eyes open, knowing that it wouldn't last. Could it?

The answer to that came in the form of a memory, not of their kiss this time, or of how sweet and lovely it had been to hold his hand, but of dancing with Patrick at the Kyle wedding.

He had held her close and she'd felt so safe, so warm, in the circle of his arms.

She knelt to tuck soil back around a new root that had pulled loose and as she did so, she could practically hear Patrick saying, *If you never take risks, you never get any rewards worth having.*

Wiping her hands clean, Phoebe got out her phone and punched in his number. "Hi, Patrick. Any chance I can steal you away from your work for a few hours?"

"You do realize I wouldn't ever normally end up blind-folded this early on a date?" Phoebe said, and then flushed slightly as she realized exactly what she'd implied.

Thankfully, Patrick simply laughed. "Then I'm obviously a very lucky guy. Left a bit from there, and don't swing too hard."

She adjusted her stance ever so slightly, swung the

putter in her hands, and tapped the space in front of her where she hoped the golf ball was sitting. She felt the club connect, followed a few seconds later by a dull *thunk*.

"It's in!" Patrick said.

Phoebe felt his hands brush her face as he pulled off her blindfold, and her skin tingled with electricity for a moment. She passed the miniature windmill to the hole beyond.

Sure enough, her ball was sitting in it.

"I did it. With your brilliant guidance." She couldn't help smiling at that. She stole a glance over at Patrick and caught him staring at her. "You know, one has to wonder about a man who thinks up blindfolded miniature golf as a date."

"What do you have to wonder?"

Phoebe cocked her head to one side. "Oh, I wonder all kinds of things when it comes to you."

That was true, though she already had the answers to some questions, such as how he'd kiss. Which was why she stole one from him right then and there.

"I was going to take you somewhere fun today, but now you've managed twice to surprise me. I'm definitely going to have to come up with something to top this."

Patrick grinned. "If you think you can?"

Phoebe simply smiled back, her mind already whirring with the possibilities.

PATRICK WAS A little surprised when they headed for Golden Gate Park a couple of days later. But even though they'd just been there together to work on the garden, he quickly realized there were things he hadn't seen. A good dozen of them, in fact.

"I bet you don't get many bison in Chicago," Phoebe

said with a look that made it clear she'd guessed exactly what he'd been thinking up to that point.

"Not in the middle of a city park, no." Patrick admitted, "I'm impressed. I'm going to have to think of something good to top this one."

Phoebe smiled. "Good luck."

The enclosure was huge, yet it still seemed barely big enough for some of the creatures within. Their shaggy fur moved in the breeze as they slumbered, or shifted around as they hurried from one part of their home to another. Patrick and Phoebe watched the huge creatures from the sidewalk. When Patrick's hand brushed hers, Phoebe didn't pull away, and he allowed himself the pleasure of sliding their hands together.

"INDOOR SKYDIVING?" she asked a few days later.

"Why not?" Patrick replied as if they were about to do the most normal thing in the world.

With anyone else, she would have quickly listed a half dozen reasons why this was not a good idea—from the baggy and shapeless jumpsuits, to the fact that they were currently being blown around by a huge fan and might be bounced almost anywhere.

But a few minutes later, as she was tossed around by the air currents, she was glad she didn't seem able to say no to Patrick…because she was enjoying herself more than she had ever believed possible.

There was something utterly exhilarating about the air rushing past as she balanced in the upward flow. And it was strangely relaxing to have to give in and go along with that flow.

Patrick turned out to be pretty good at it, too, floating there opposite her almost perfectly still in the airstream. Somehow, Phoebe noted, he managed to look good even in a skydiving suit.

He even reached out a couple of times to stop Phoebe drifting off out of that flow. They were just small touches, but just as it always was when they touched, there was something powerfully electric about their moments of contact.

PATRICK HAD BEEN more than a little surprised when Phoebe took him to a cathedral the following evening just as the sun was setting. It didn't seem like the kind of place for a date, somehow. Yet when they went inside Grace Cathedral and he saw the labyrinth marked out on the floor, he understood.

There was peace here. Along with joy.

And boundless love for everyone.

"I read about this on one of the tourist sites for the city," he told her. "But it's even more spectacular than they said it would be."

Phoebe looked pleased by his appreciation for the cathedral and the gardens. "It seemed like a good place to come."

"You've done this before?"

She shook her head. "You know how when you live somewhere, you always tell yourself that you'll do these things, but you never actually get around to them?"

"Ah, so I'm just the excuse," Patrick said as they began to make their way along the path of the labyrinth.

Phoebe grinned at him and said, "A very good-looking excuse, though," before turning her focus back to the path of stone, with Patrick following close enough behind to take her hand in his.

PHOEBE HAD BEEN wondering what Patrick would do to top their last outing. A few days later they sat next to the Bay's wave organ, eating tortillas while the collection of wave-powered pipes around them droned and groaned, whispered and whistled. Phoebe had to give him the credit he deserved. It was yet another place she had never gotten around to visiting, and another experience that was all the better for spending it with Patrick.

If every day could be like the ones they'd shared recently, she might almost see how people could fall in love. It was just as well that Patrick was in town for a strictly limited time, or she might be in trouble. Even looking at him there with the sunset in the background was enough to make her chest clench with longing.

An idea came to her, and she took hold of Patrick's arm. "Come on," she said.

"Where are we going?"

"You've supplied the dinner. I think it's only fair that I supply the movie. How's your singing voice?"

"My singing voice?"

Phoebe grinned at his confused expression. "You'll see."

PATRICK DID HIS best to join in as a couple hundred people sang the words to the *Sound of Music* in the Castro theater. It was by far the strangest experience he'd shared with Phoebe so far, and yet there was something immensely fun about joining in on a chorus with a group of complete strangers.

The theater was crowded, which meant Phoebe was next to him, so close that she was leaning against his chest, her hair soft against his upper arm.

Patrick savored their physical closeness, but he wanted more than that. So much more.

Phoebe was amazing. How many other women would have gone so far off the beaten path on a date?

Not many, and certainly none as wholeheartedly as the beautiful woman beside him.

When the movie ended and they spilled out into the street with the rest of the movie-goers, he was caught almost completely off guard when Phoebe said, "I've never had as much fun as I do with you."

"It's the same for me," he agreed. And it was true. Every moment he spent with Phoebe was perfect.

"Come back to my place," Phoebe said, so low that she barely breathed it.

"You're sure?" Patrick said carefully, even though there was nothing he wanted more.

Phoebe knew what he wanted, that he wasn't just after a quick fling...and he knew she wouldn't ask him unless she was feeling the same way.

Her answer was another sweet kiss that rocked through him, head-to-toe.

THEY MADE IT back to her apartment with the anticipation in the car hard to ignore. It was nearly impossible to sit still in the passenger seat when all she wanted to do was to reach out and touch him. To start to unbutton his shirt...

It was obvious that Patrick felt the same way, given the way he kept looking across at her, practically undressing her with his eyes. She didn't want to think too hard about the decision she was making, didn't want to face the fact that this wasn't just another one-night stand that didn't mean anything.

Hand in hand, they made it up the stairs with only a couple of pauses to kiss one another passionately, pressed against the rail and then the wall.

"I'm pretty sure," Phoebe said as she unlocked her

front door, "that tradition says that I should pretend I'm inviting you in for coffee at this point."

Patrick opened the door, pulled her inside, then pushed it shut. "I think," he said as he bent to kiss her again, "we've already proved we're the kind of couple who don't do traditional dates."

A LONG WHILE later Phoebe lay on her side, the covers of her bed drawn up around them both, drifting on the edge of sleep with a blissful smile. She could feel Patrick beside her, his strong muscles pressed firmly against her back as he held her close.

She'd never done this before. Never taken a man to her house, never made love to him with more than just her body, and certainly had never been perfectly happy to drift off to sleep beside him, letting him stay the night.

Yet with Patrick, it felt so simple. So obvious.

Phoebe felt so happy. Not just basking in the afterglow of what had been a frankly amazing couple of hours, but genuinely, truly happy.

Briefly, she wondered if this was how people felt when they were in love.

Patrick's fingertips brushed her hair aside and his lips moved in to kiss her just below her ear. He pulled her closer then settled in behind her to sleep. Utterly content for the first time in her life, she was drifting off to sleep when his softly spoken words landed straight in the center of her heart.

"I love you."

CHAPTER FIFTEEN

PHOEBE WOKE TO the sound of someone cooking in her kitchen.

Patrick.

She put on a T-shirt and jeans and headed into the kitchen just as he was serving up a huge plate of pancakes, which he had sculpted into the shape of a skyscraper. Trust an architect to do that.

Trust Patrick to do that.

He turned as she entered the room and smiled. "You're awake. Perfect. I made breakfast."

"I can see that." Phoebe happily sat and claimed some of the small mountain of pancakes for herself. "Did you have to come up with blueprints for a stack that high?"

"It's my signature architectural achievement," Patrick assured her as he joined her at the table and picked off some of the remaining pancakes. "Buildings will come and go, but people will always remember my refinements in the field of pancake engineering."

Phoebe laughed at that. She couldn't *not* laugh. She hadn't forgotten what he'd said just as she'd fallen asleep, but right then it was hard not to simply bask in what promised to be a wonderful morning.

She knew that most people who said "I love you" didn't hang around for long, but Patrick *definitely* wasn't most people.

And the most amazing thing of all was that just the sight of him sitting in her kitchen, his hair rumpled from sleep, dark bristles across his jaw as he smiled at her with an adoring look in his eyes, was almost enough to make Phoebe want to blurt "I love you" right back at him.

"How did you sleep last night?" he asked.

"Great," Phoebe replied with a smile she couldn't contain. "Better than great. This is nice, too. Really nice."

And it was true. When she thought back to the previous night, she couldn't feel anything but happiness. And having breakfast with him now, she found herself wishing that even this moment would never end. Wishing that every morning could be like this.

Patrick understood her, the real her, not the version of Phoebe Davis that she often felt she needed to put on to make others happy. And with all that he'd done for her mother, he already knew her better than anyone else ever had. Even her friends didn't truly comprehend how things were with her mother.

And now, she had a great breakfast, memories of a great night, and a wonderful guy who had already proved that he wasn't the kind to run away.

Yes, it definitely seemed safe to relax and enjoy the moment.

Finally.

Just then, Patrick's phone buzzed and he frowned briefly as he read the message before putting it back into his pocket. "I can't believe it's been two weeks already," he was saying when his phone buzzed again.

Phoebe felt everything go still inside her at his mention of the time since they'd met; the same amount of time that he'd been planning on spending in San Francisco before he left for Chicago again. For so long she'd celebrated that "end date" to their relationship…but now she realized she'd spent the past week with Patrick trying to forget it.

So when his phone went off a third time, Phoebe knew she had to ask, "Is something wrong?"

"No, it's nothing that can't be dealt with," Patrick assured her. "There are just a few complications with the job I have lined up after Rose and Donovan's house. I'll take care of it later today."

Tension knotted Phoebe's stomach and she put down her latest forkful of pancake, untouched.

"What job?"

"It's for a newly married couple up in Chicago," Patrick said lightly as though it wasn't a big deal. "They're very nice, but I suspect they're also going to be a couple who have a hard time settling on what they want. They want me to fly out to take care of a few things. Honestly, it could be one of those jobs that takes forever. My assistant is texting me with the information for a flight back later today, actually. I shouldn't need to be there long, just for a few—"

Phoebe couldn't listen to any more. She pushed her plate away and stood, stepping back from the table.

"Phoebe, what is it?"

She could feel the corners of her eyes stinging with the start of tears. But she wasn't going to cry. Not over a man. Not when she'd known how things would end all along.

So then why did it feel as though she was heading straight for a dangerous tailspin?

Patrick rose, began to move toward her. "Phoebe, just tell me what's—"

"You're leaving for Chicago," she said in a wooden

tone. "You're going to be there 'practically forever.' You're *leaving*." She tried to keep her expression as blank as possible. She wasn't going to show him how much this part hurt.

"It's the twenty-first century, Phoebe," he said gently but firmly. "They have these amazing things called airplanes that mean I can travel back and forth from San Francisco to Chicago as often as I want to."

"Yes, but you won't want to come back," Phoebe said. "At first, maybe, you will, when everything is fresh and new. But then, eventually, you'll get caught up in whatever it is you're doing next. You'll forget all about our *fling*."

She could see how much she was hurting Patrick with that word.... Just as much as he'd hurt her by saying "I love you" and then planned his immediate escape.

"This isn't a fling, Phoebe. Not even close. Not to me, and, I thought, not for you, either. Especially after yesterday—"

"How could you have said those words to me?" Her bleak question was barely above a whisper. "How could you?"

And how could she have been stupid enough to believe it, even for five minutes?

He reached for her, but she took a step back before he could make contact. Still, he said, "I told you I love you because I do, Phoebe."

He waited for her to reply, but there was a huge lump in her throat and it was taking all her self-control not to break down sobbing...or, worse, to ask him to hold her tight again, the way he had last night.

When his arms came around her, she didn't have the strength to push him away.

"From that first moment we danced, sweetheart, my

heart has been yours." He brushed his thumb across her cheek and she realized there was wetness there. "I didn't tell you how I felt as a way to try to force you to say you feel the same way. I wouldn't do that to you, you know I wouldn't. But I can't keep holding inside what I feel for you any longer."

Phoebe had never been so confused, so torn in two, between what she wanted and her long-held beliefs about life...and love.

"What if," he whispered in her ear, "the walls you've put up to protect yourself are only keeping out the very people who want to love you?"

"We've only known each other two weeks," she protested as she forced herself to step out of his arms. "We hardly know anything about each other."

"You know that I love you. That's all you really need to know, Phoebe. Everything else is just...details." Patrick shook his head, and it broke her heart to see the strong man she'd fallen for, despite herself, looking so miserable. "I've tried to change your mind, but I can't. You're too strong for that. The only one who can change your mind is you."

As he headed for the door every cell in her body wanted to pull him back to her. He was halfway out the door when he turned back to face her.

"Have you ever thought about why you chose to be a florist for weddings, Phoebe?"

She was surprised enough by his strange question to reply, "It was a good job."

"But it could have been so much more than that, couldn't it?"

It was the last thing he said before he closed the door behind him...and walked out of her life.

CHAPTER SIXTEEN

ANGELA'S HOUSE WAS a big space with great views out over Sacramento, and it was filled with expensive furnishings. When she arrived home, looking much happier than she had been when she'd been staying with Phoebe, she let out a small squeak, surprised by her unexpected visitor.

"Phoebe?"

"David let me in," Phoebe said, her voice breaking on the final word. She'd told herself a hundred times during the drive from San Francisco to Sacramento that she wasn't going to cry over some guy.

Only, Patrick wasn't just *some guy*.

This was exactly the kind of emotion she'd worked so hard to keep from feeling. She'd seen this pain so many times in her mother, and her girlfriends, and now it was bubbling away inside her as she struggled to manage it.

But she couldn't stop it. Not this time, not when the full pain of breaking up with Patrick was sweeping over her like a tidal wave.

All these years she'd told herself she didn't need anyone.

What a huge lie that had been.

Because when push came to shove, Phoebe had realized she didn't want to be alone. And then the memories of how loving her mother had been with her when she was a child came back to her in a rush, and it had seemed so obvious: If she just went to her mother, everything would be all right, wouldn't it?

"Oh, honey, what happened?" Her mother sat beside her, putting an arm around her shoulders.

Phoebe had always been the one comforting her mother, not the other way around. Now, though, she let her mother hold her while she began to cry.

"You drove here like this?" her mother asked.

Phoebe nodded, not trusting herself to speak. She could barely remember the trip now. She'd made it, somehow.

And the important thing was that she wasn't alone.

"All right, Cally," her mother said. "Whatever it is that's wrong, I'm here for you and you can stay with David and me as long as you need to. You haven't eaten, have you?"

Phoebe shook her head.

Angela tucked a blanket around Phoebe's lap and dried her tears with the backs of her hands. Just as she had when Phoebe was younger. "I'm going to make us both something to eat."

Over the past few years Phoebe had been the one in the kitchen putting together a meal for her mother, grasping for a way to try to cheer her up. And yet, everything was backward today as she sat there on her mother's couch, trying to find some way through the knotted maze of pain tangled inside her, but failing utterly.

"Here," her mother said a short while later, putting a plate of pasta down in front of her. "Eat. It will do you good."

Phoebe shook her head. "I'm not sure I can, Mom. I feel…"

How did she feel? How could she explain what it felt

like, when the sheer heartache throbbing inside her was indescribable?

"I know," her mother said.

Phoebe had the vague thought that it must be one of the reasons why she had come running to Sacramento. Her mother was the one person on the planet who would understand the raw anguish that came from losing Patrick, even if Phoebe didn't fully understand it herself yet.

"Eat," her mother insisted. "You've always said it would make me feel better. And you were always right. Trust me, it *will* make you feel better."

The meal her mother made her didn't do anything to make the hurt go away, but the simplicity and normality of it seemed to ground her a little, helped her to think about something other than just how badly things had ended with Patrick. Not only how badly *she'd* ended them…but what he'd said about her needing to be the one to change her mind about love if things were ever going to work between them.

"Can you tell me what happened now?" her mother asked. "Is this about Patrick?"

"We decided to start dating…and then we split up."

Her mother took her hand. "It's all right, Cally. I'm here for you now. Just tell me everything and together we'll work through it, I promise."

"We spent a lot of time together over the past two weeks. And then, yesterday, we went on the most amazing date. It was incredible." She took a shaky breath before saying, "He made me breakfast, Mom. No one's ever done that before. He even said—"

Oh, God, it was hard to say the words aloud. Even though she'd replayed them over and over, saying them a thousand times in her head.

"He said he loved me."

"Oh, Cally, honey. If he loves you and you lo—"

Phoebe had to cut her mother off before she could actually say it. "But then, he started talking about going back to Chicago for a long-term project. And we argued." Phoebe bit her lip, remembering the things she'd said, the way she'd thrown the word *fling* at him. "It all went wrong, Mom, and now…now it just feels so bad."

"It's going to be okay, I promise."

Phoebe shook her head. How could her mother say that when it felt as though nothing would ever be right again?

"It will be," her mother insisted. "You'll get him back, and things will be fine again, you'll see. Just look at David and me. When I was at your apartment, I never would have thought that things would work out, but now… Well, our relationship isn't perfect yet, but we're working on it."

"You think that I'm going to get back together with Patrick after being with him once made me feel like this?"

"I know it hurts right now, but just think of how happy you were when you were together. You could be like that again."

"I could be like *this* again," Phoebe insisted, moving away from her mother on the couch. "If I get back together with Patrick, then I'm just setting myself up for even worse heartbreak later."

Her mother reached out for her, but Phoebe moved back again. "You don't know that, honey. He seems like a lovely young man. I don't think he'd just abandon you."

"You didn't think Dad would walk out, either, and look what happened there."

Phoebe saw the hurt look on her mother's face and she realized that she'd gone too far. Again. Just as she had with Patrick.

"Neither one of us has all the answers," her mother pointed out in a gentle voice. They sat there for several seconds before her mother shook her head and said, "You know, honey, sometimes I think I'm never going to understand you."

"Funny," Phoebe said, even though she definitely didn't find it the least bit humorous, "I was just thinking the same thing."

How could they both be so different? How could her mother keep insisting that happiness was just the next man away? Those seemed like questions to which Phoebe would never have the answers. Yet she knew one thing: relationships hurt no matter how you felt about them.

"I'm sorry, Mom," she said at last. "I shouldn't have brought up Dad."

"Well," her mother said softly, "I've never been the best of role models when it comes to relationships, have I?"

Perhaps she hadn't, but Phoebe finally understood that love didn't follow a strict list of rules and regulations.

It happened whether you wanted it or not.

"You did your best," Phoebe said.

"We both still got hurt, though, didn't we?"

Phoebe was only starting to realize that sometimes you couldn't help hurting people, even when you didn't want to. Even when you cared about them.

Especially when you cared about them.

"I'm sorry," she said again.

"I know. So am I." Her mother put an arm around

her. "You see, making up with someone isn't all that bad, is it?"

Phoebe shook her head. Her mother was one thing, but Patrick was another. Her mother was family. She had a feeling it wouldn't be quite as easy with Patrick.

He wasn't tied to her by blood, so what was to stop him walking away the way her father had? The way so many of the men her mother had dated had?

Yet wasn't there something almost brave about that? Just as Patrick had once said, *Sometimes the rewards are worth the risk. And even if the odds aren't great, they're still so much better than if we never take a risk at all.*

Patrick had been perfectly honest with her from the start about the way he felt and his belief that love was something to be cherished. It had seemed like such a foolish way to look at life, but now she finally understood that the alternatives weren't much better.

Phoebe looked up, gazing out her mother's window at the city lights in the distance. It was getting dark, but for a moment or two, it seemed as if she could see things more clearly than she had for a long time. She impulsively hugged her mother.

"Thanks, Mom."

"For what?"

"For everything. For being there for me whenever I've needed you. For teaching me to love beauty and to cherish it."

"You're welcome, honey," her mother said. Phoebe thought she heard something catch in her mother's voice as she said it. "Are you going to stay tonight?"

"Thanks, but I need to get back home."

"You're sure?"

Phoebe nodded. "There's something I have to do."

CHAPTER SEVENTEEN

BY THE TIME Phoebe arrived at The Rose Chalet early the next morning, things were well under way for Marge Banning's wedding that evening. RJ was setting out furniture. Tyce was running through a last-minute sound check—though Phoebe didn't recall much punk being on Marge Banning's set list last time around. Rose was bustling around, fetching the linen for the tables, rushing over to the kitchen to make sure that the food was going well, and looking as if she was absolutely convinced that the whole thing was going to fall apart at any second. In other words, she was behaving exactly as she normally did on the morning of a wedding.

"Where were you yesterday?" Rose asked when Phoebe walked in. "I thought you'd be here in the afternoon getting ready. Did you get my text messages?"

Phoebe was too tired to come up with a good answer to that. "Sacramento."

"Sacramento? What were you doing in Sacramento? Are you okay? You look like you've been up all night."

"I have." Which was probably not the best thing to admit to her boss. Even if it was Rose. She was no longer able to maintain the separation between her work and her personal life. Frankly, she wasn't sure that she wanted to anymore.

She expected Rose to read her the riot act. Instead

her boss simply put a hand on her arm. "I hope everything's okay."

Phoebe felt those darn tears spring back up. She swallowed hard. "I hope it will be, too." She forced a trembling smile. "I've got a lot of work to do on the arrangements. Because Marge deserves the best wedding ever, don't you think?"

Surprise gave way to a smile on Rose's face. "Yes," the other woman said, "she definitely does."

Phoebe headed off to her workroom, where the flowers were waiting for her thanks to RJ and her suppliers. She put her laptop down on the workbench, determined to concentrate on her centerpieces, but her heart wasn't in it. Not when she still hadn't managed to make any headway on the plan she'd made yesterday on the drive home. After she'd returned home from her mother's house, she'd spent hours making calls and sending out dozens of email queries to locate what she was looking for. But she hadn't found it yet. Even her friend Lisa hadn't been able to help.

I'm sorry, Phoebe, Lisa had said, *can't we substitute something else?*

"No," Phoebe had insisted, "there's a message in that particular flower."

Turning away from the flowers in her Chalet workroom, Phoebe opened up her laptop and started scouring the internet for florists she hadn't approached yet. Although at this point, even if she could find the flower, could anyone possibly deliver it on time?

Finally she located a man named Brian. On the phone he said, "I'm sure someone mentioned something to me about them recently. The trouble is I'm not sure if I can remember who exactly it was."

"This is really important, and you're the first glimmer of hope I've had so far," she told him. "Please, if you could try your hardest to remember, it would mean so much to me."

"I've got your number, so if I think of it, I promise to let you know."

"Thank you. Thank you so much." Phoebe put the phone down and looked up just as Rose walked into the room with RJ.

"Phoebe, I just wanted to check to make sure you had everything— Oh, my God. You've barely even *started*. What have you been doing?" Rose was clearly working hard to keep it together in the face of all the work Phoebe obviously hadn't done on the centerpieces.

"What's going on with you?" Frustration morphed to worry on Rose's face. "I've never seen you like this. You've always been so reliable. So steady. If something's wrong, you can tell me."

But Phoebe didn't know how she could possibly explain about what had happened with Patrick. Not with RJ right there behind Rose. Besides, she knew what everyone thought of her.

Phoebe, who didn't have relationships.

Phoebe, who never let herself be hurt by anyone or anything.

And why did everyone think that? Because she'd worked very hard to make it true.

Except that right now it wasn't.

"How about if I help out with the arrangements?" RJ suggested. "Tyce can take care of any issues with Tara. It'll be nice to see him do something other than strum that guitar of his on the day of a wedding." He turned to Rose and added, "Phoebe covered for me when it came to the work on your house. The least I can do is help her out today."

Rose finally nodded, although she clearly looked reluctant to leave Phoebe in such a state. "Just let me know if you need anything today, okay? Anything at all."

Phoebe had to swallow past the lump in her throat. "Okay. Thanks, Rose."

Her boss hurried out, leaving Phoebe alone with RJ. He started picking out the flowers, looking them over.

"Do you have a design I can follow?"

She nodded and passed it over silently, not daring to speak. Not when all she wanted was to ask him how Patrick was doing since he'd returned to Chicago.

"So," RJ asked, "is this about what happened with Patrick?"

Her mouth opened in shock. "You know about that?"

"Of course I know. He's my brother. Even if he doesn't tell me everything, I still know how he felt about you."

She hesitated before asking, "And you're still helping me? I mean, shouldn't you hate me?"

"Of course not, Phoebe." He shot a glance toward the door Rose had walked out through. "The truth is, we don't always get what we want, and no one can force two people to be happy together."

She didn't know what to say to that, not when Patrick was the one she should be talking to about this, not his brother. Fortunately, RJ seemed to understand because he changed the subject.

"We'd better get going with these arrangements, shouldn't we? At this rate, it will be a miracle if everything is ready in time for the wedding."

Miracles. They seemed to need a lot of them at the moment. It was definitely what they'd need to get the arrangements for the wedding finished on time. And a miracle was almost certainly what it would take to fix things with Patrick after the way they'd argued. Unfortunately, as for the miracle of finding what she was looking for, the odds on that seemed to be getting longer by the second.

The hours passed by in a blur as she and RJ worked as fast as their fingers would let them. And then, suddenly, her phone rang, causing her to drop a handful of roses onto the floor.

She recognized the number, because it was the last one she'd called before Rose and RJ had walked in. She picked it up in breathless anticipation.

"Brian?"

"Hello, Phoebe. I think I have just remembered where to find what you were looking for. Actually, it's slightly embarrassing that I didn't realize where I'd seen them before now. My sister grows them. Only, she doesn't sell them, so I'm not sure if it's really any help to you. I guess that's why it slipped my mind."

On any other day Phoebe might have left it there and kept looking, but today... Well, if today wasn't a day for taking chances, then when was?

"Could you give me her number? And if I can convince her to say yes, could you deal with the delivery side of things right away?"

"I guess so, though I really must warn you that the odds of Jane handing over one of her precious blooms aren't good."

"I'd like to try anyway," Phoebe told him before hanging up then dialing the number she'd just been given. She introduced herself to the woman who answered and explained exactly what it was she wanted.

"I'm sorry," Jane said on the other end of the phone, "but my brother's right. I'm not a florist, and if I sell you one, then hundreds of other people will want them. Soon, I won't have much of a garden left."

"Please," Phoebe said, offering the woman the bulk of the contents of her last paycheck, enough that RJ's eyes widened from across the workbench.

"Please, I can't take your money. Especially not that much," Jane said. "They really aren't for sale. You sound like a perfectly nice young woman, but I'm not here to fill flower orders for your customers."

"This isn't for one of my customers," Phoebe pleaded. "This is for me. Please, I'm running out of options, and this is the only way to make things right with a man that I—" She took a deep breath, feeling RJ's eyes on her. "That I love."

The other woman sighed. "If you had said anything else, anything other than this flower being about love…" She paused, then said, "Let's call it fifty dollars, just to cover my brother's trouble."

"I can have the flower?" Phoebe felt hope finally spring to life inside her, light breaking through the darkness, at last. "Oh, thank you. Thank you so much."

"You're welcome. Good luck with that man of yours. I hope he's worth it."

Phoebe had never been more sure of anything in her life. "Oh, he is."

CHAPTER EIGHTEEN

PATRICK'S OFFICE WAS on the seventeenth floor of a building that he had helped to design, giving him a view of the Chicago skyline that was hard to match, as well as an address that attracted high-end clients. The office itself was spacious and open, with models of previous buildings placed strategically around the room on stands. His desk sat in the middle of the room and was big enough for Patrick to work on blueprints by hand. His laptop was there, along with his desk phone and the papers relating to his upcoming project.

He was walking a slow circuit around the office, making his way around the models he'd built, looking for inspiration. Lord knew he needed it considering he hadn't been able to start work on the changes he needed to put in place for his new clients' house. It should have been a simple matter of moving a couple of rooms, but he couldn't quite find the balance of the space.

What, he wondered every few minutes, was Phoebe doing? She'd be working on the flowers for Marge Banning's wedding by now, wouldn't she?

Patrick could easily picture her sorting through the blooms with a deft touch, frowning just slightly as she concentrated on making it as beautiful, and meaningful, a display as anyone could. Tyce and RJ would be there, too, all three of them joking around to lighten the mood despite the pressure to put on another perfect wedding at The Rose Chalet.

For what had to be the hundredth time, Patrick pulled his phone out of his pocket and scanned through the address book for Phoebe's name... But his finger stopped short of making the call.

She'd been so clear that they were over.

And that she didn't want anything else from him.

Patrick put the phone down, even though his instincts said that he shouldn't, that he should phone her...and that he shouldn't give up until she realized how good they were together.

Only, the unassailable truth was that a relationship took two people. However much he wanted what they could have had, it only worked if Phoebe wanted it, as well. That thought was frustrating enough that Patrick barely realized he had a stack of papers crushed in his fist moments before he destroyed them.

He forced himself to turn back to figuring out a way to make his new clients' requirements work. He'd done it plenty of times before. It was just a case of focusing in on the kind of couple they were.

And what about the kind of couple you and Phoebe would have made?

Patrick tried with all his might to ignore that thought. But, again and again, every time he tried to start work on the plans, all that came to mind were visions of Phoebe.

Playing miniature golf blindfolded.

Leading him through the labyrinth at Grace Cathedral.

Kissing him for the very first time.

Her softness as she lay against him when he'd told her that he loved her.

And then the way she'd all but kicked him out of her apartment the next morning as soon as he'd mentioned needing to work on a long-distance project.

Knowing he had to think about something else if he was ever going to get any work done, he moved over to the window and looked out at Chicago. With any luck the sight of the city would inspire him. It generally did, even if it was occasionally just by reminding him of what he'd done before. After all, he'd been part of the architectural team on several of the newer buildings he could see from his office.

He let his gaze drift along the city's skyline, determined to come up with an answer this time. Briefly his eyes flicked down to take in a restaurant just across the street from his office; a fancy French place that even he'd had trouble getting into. Patrick winced as he remembered that date. The woman he'd been with had been nice enough, but the whole occasion had been so stilted and formal that they'd never gotten to know a thing about one another. That relationship hadn't lasted long.

Patrick shifted his gaze to where Wrigley Field sat farther away, but was easily visible from so high up. That date had been even more disastrous. He had met her at an architectural awards show. It had just seemed so obvious at the time that they should date, since they were about the same age, working in the same field, and at least a little attracted to one another at the awards. Patrick had surprised her with two tickets to a Cubs game. It turned out that she didn't like baseball, or any sports at all, come to that. She hadn't liked nachos, or any of the other snacks that had seemed like such an essential part of the experience to Patrick. She'd even spent most of the game complaining that in a world that valued architects, they should be allowed to pull down places like this and redesign them "properly." They hadn't gone on a second date.

More memories of dating disasters came back to haunt him one by one. There had been the one where he had suggested indoor rock climbing and his date had pulled out. And then another where it had been obvious from the moment they'd sat together at a restaurant that they simply weren't right for one another. There had been others where things had started all right, then simply petered out. Where the woman he'd been dating had seemed nice enough, but they simply hadn't clicked well enough to want to go to the next level.

Whereas, in the short time he'd been with Phoebe, Patrick had gotten closer to her than to anyone else before. She loved doing crazy, offbeat things as much as he did. She was smart, and strong, and caring enough that she'd been able to cope with her mother and the demands of her job at the Chalet.

If only she hadn't built up all those walls around herself to keep people out, they could...

A knock came at his office door. He went over to open it and found a man in his fifties holding a long, slender box.

"Mr. Knight?"

"Yes, that's me."

"Oh, good," the man said, sounding incredibly relieved. "If you wouldn't mind signing to say that you received this, I'd be very thankful."

He pulled out a small notepad from his jacket pocket and Patrick signed as he looked at the box, trying to work out what might be inside the plain white container.

"Do you know what this is?"

"I'm sorry, but the young lady asked me not to say

anything. I *can* tell you that she went to a great deal of trouble over this, though. My sister normally doesn't let anyone have her... Well, that would spoil the surprise, wouldn't it? I suppose that there has to be some code of confidentiality for florists."

Florists? That word was enough that Patrick almost ripped the box open there and then.

"Enjoy," the man said, turning and leaving Patrick holding the box as he walked away.

Patrick placed the box carefully on his desk, not caring if it smudged the plans beneath. He opened it slowly. There was a single flower within.

It was electric-blue above a slender stem, with four petals spread out in a semicircle around the front of the flower and a fifth standing straight. The heart of the flower curled over in a mixture of yellow, darker purple and a deep red-brown. The overall effect was that of fragile beauty, nearly translucent when Patrick held the flower up to the light coming through the window.

There was no note, just the flower, and he knew Phoebe was using the language of flowers to tell him something very important. Praying it was what he thought it was, first he had to rule out what it wasn't.

He'd looked up the meaning for the pasque flower and knew what it meant, and that it wasn't good. He went over to his computer, searching for images of flowers. He typed in *pasque flower* and when he saw the purple petal in the first picture that popped up on his screen, a moment of physical pain shot through him.

But when he took a breath and looked at it more closely, however, he could see it simply wasn't the same as the flower that sat on his desk. Next to the flower Phoebe had sent him, the pasque flower seemed ordinary and not nearly so beautiful.

Patrick hardly dared to type the next words in, praying harder with every letter that appeared on his computer monitor. He sent the new search off, and held his breath for the fraction of a second it took to come back with an answer.

He reached out to lift the flower Phoebe had sent and held it next to the image on his screen, looking from one to the other, wanting to be sure.

Only when he was absolutely certain that he had found the right flower, did he stand again, walking over to the window holding Phoebe's flower.

A Caladenia orchid.

Cally.

It was every bit as beautiful as Phoebe had said it was…and it was in full bloom.

Which meant miracles really did happen.

CHAPTER NINETEEN

NOTHING.

How could there be nothing?

Phoebe stared at her phone accusingly, praying for it to ring. But it remained still and cold in her hand, the way it had the previous nineteen times she had checked it.

"We're ready for the bouquet," Rose called out.

Phoebe put the phone away. If Patrick was going to phone, he would have done it by now. She knew he'd received the flower, because Brian had called with the news of his successful delivery just as he was leaving Patrick's building.

Looking up, Phoebe realized Marge Banning was standing a couple of feet away in her wedding dress. She looked amazing… Like a woman in love whose every dream was coming true.

Phoebe carefully picked up the bouquet she'd put together for Marge. Roses, exactly the same as last time, yet today they looked fresh and bright. They went perfectly with the wedding dress and, if Phoebe didn't know better, she would have sworn that Anne had secretly made some changes to it. Today, it looked truly perfect on Marge.

As Phoebe handed her the bouquet she said, "You look beautiful."

Marge was normally a good-looking woman, but

today she shone with happiness, and that only made her more beautiful. Phoebe had never before believed that brides could be *radiant* but tonight that was the only word to describe her.

"Thank you," Marge said softly. "It's amazing what being in love will do for you."

"Good luck," Phoebe said.

"You know what?" Marge said with a smile that only made her look more radiant. "I don't think luck is going to come into it this time."

On the other side of the doors to The Rose Chalet's main room, Tyce and the string quartet he was directing struck up the "Wedding March."

Phoebe concentrated on pinning the ribbon from the bouquet to the dress. "There," she said to Marge. "Perfect."

The other woman studied her for a second or two. "You know, Phoebe, there's something different about you today."

Phoebe felt those darn tears she'd had so much trouble with lately rise up again and she shook her head. "There is," she admitted, "but today is about you, not me. Are you ready to go in?"

For the first time Marge actually looked a little nervous. Phoebe put a hand on her shoulder, searching for the right thing to say. Fortunately it didn't take long to find it.

"Third time's the charm, remember?"

She opened the door for Marge, giving them both a clear view down the aisle to where RJ's re-creation of Tara stood. Phoebe had to admit it was impressive today with the guests gathered around. The flower arrangements at the end of each row and on the tables were stunning, even if RJ had put together at least half of them in the end. The guests all looked as if they were enjoying themselves, even though most of them had been to the first two weddings, as well.

The groom waiting on the deck was a good-looking man, distinguished and fit. But right then, his looks weren't what mattered.

All that mattered was the way he looked back at Marge standing there, and the way she looked at him.

With pure love.

They both looked so nervous and so happy as Marge made her way down the aisle. Phoebe knew that she ought to be feeling cynical about their chances, given Marge's track record, but she couldn't. Not this time.

Not now that she knew what it felt like to be head over heels in love.

"You're braver than I am, Marge," she whispered.

And luckier, apparently, because there were still no messages or texts on her phone, on silent now so she wouldn't interrupt the ceremony.

Usually she disappeared at this point and went back to clean up her work. It was the best way to avoid as much of the wedding as possible. But today she found that she wanted to watch, wanted to be a part of two people making vows of *forever* to each other.

All at once Patrick's parting question came back to her. *"Have you ever thought about why you chose to be a florist for weddings, Phoebe?"*

Oh, my God, she thought as she stumbled back from the doorway and braced herself against the wall. Patrick, amazingly, knew her so well that he'd figured her out long before she had.

All these years she'd rationalized being a romantic cynic at The Rose Chalet by telling herself the job had been better paying, with better hours, than most florist jobs. And there was the added bonus of not being tied down by running her own shop.

But now—finally—she realized what the real reason was.

Phoebe had taken the job at The Rose Chalet because she'd been secretly hoping the day would come when she could find a reason to believe in love.

It had taken a long time, but she'd finally found that reason...in Patrick Knight. If only she'd realized it before it was too late.

Oh, God, she prayed, maybe it wasn't too late.

As Marge and her groom began to say their simple vows, Phoebe remembered a very wise bride telling her that when you had found the right man, the actual details weren't important. Love was all that mattered.

Tears streamed down Phoebe's face as Marge and her new husband kissed. She never cried at weddings. But then, she never normally cried. But today was different.

Out on the small stage at the side, Tyce started up the music again, and Phoebe gently slid the doors closed. In a minute or two, she would have to help with the reception, but for now it was all she could do to try to dry her tears.

She was surprised when a hand touched her shoulder. "Would you like to dance?"

Phoebe turned and saw Patrick standing close, looking at her with an impossibly sweet, heartfelt expression that wasn't hard to read. After all, she'd seen it on two different faces just a moment ago.

He was also holding a primrose.

I Can't Live Without You.

Eternal Love.

Both were the commonly accepted meanings for a primrose in the language of flowers.

At first she was so stunned she simply didn't know what to do. And then, at long last, she did.

She kissed him, with all the love in her heart.

"Is that a yes?" he asked when they finally broke apart from one another.

"Patrick, I…" Phoebe began.

He put a finger to her lips. "I know. You don't have to say it. You don't have to say anything at all, sweetheart."

"I *want* to say it," Phoebe said, pressing close to him. "It scares me, and it's hard, but I want to say it." She stared into his eyes, not wanting to hide anything from him anymore. "I love you. I've loved you from the start and I'm sorry I pushed you away. I shouldn't have."

He gently brushed her tears away. "But then you wouldn't have been you, and it's *you* I'm in love with, Phoebe. All of you. I know you're scared, but can't you see how strong you are? How brave you've always been?"

"I want to be brave. For you. And for myself, too."

Patrick held out the half-crushed Caladenia orchid to her and when she took it from him with a teary, "Thank you for giving me my first flower," he kissed her again before spinning her around in his arms. Together, they swayed to the sound of the music coming through from the other room.

Phoebe thought back to what it had been like dancing with Patrick the first time they had met. It had been wonderful… But this was better. So much better.

Back then he had been just a particularly attractive stranger suitable for a quick fling.

Now he was so much more: he was the man she loved. For all that being in love was strange and frightening, it was also wonderful.

Absolutely wonderful.

Phoebe pressed closer to him, wrapping her arms around his neck as they gave up any pretense of dancing. Instead they simply held one another.

"Are we going to start making plans for the future?"

Patrick placed a gentle kiss on her forehead. "Later. And trust me, Phoebe, there will be a later."

He pulled her aside just as the doors opened, letting people spill out as he held her close behind the door, where no one could notice them.

Phoebe took a breath and pulled them out into the open.

She didn't mind if people saw them.

She *wanted* people to see them.

Marge Banning went past, arm in arm with her new husband. She saw Phoebe with Patrick, paused for a brief moment and then smiled a wide, knowing smile. Phoebe grinned back and held on to Patrick a little tighter.

"I'm going to have to go help with the reception in a minute," she whispered, though she made no move to let go.

"I know," he said. But he didn't let go, either. "Tell me, Phoebe, do you believe in miracles yet?"

"I believe in us."

"That's close enough."

Phoebe nodded. Yes, it was.

EPILOGUE

TYCE SMITH TAPPED away on his laptop, making a few last-minute changes to the playlist for the wedding reception currently under way at The Rose Chalet. He looked over at the dance floor. Marge Banning looked great, twirling around the room with her new husband, who clearly knew exactly how lucky he was, if the smile on his face was anything to go by. All the other dancers looked as if they were having a good time, too. That was one thing Tyce always prided himself on: he could always get people out onto the dance floor.

So far, he'd had a busy day. First there had been that business of taking over the final Tara details from RJ so that RJ could help Phoebe. Tyce grinned as he saw her dancing with Patrick Knight.

It looked as if he wouldn't be able to flirt with Phoebe anymore. He hoped the new permanent caterer Rose had hired would be pretty...and single.

On top of RJ's duties, Tyce had had the string quartet to manage. He'd written out parts for a new viola player who was filling in, and then made sure that the set list was properly arranged. Not to mention having to quickly rewire one of the speakers on his amplifiers. All in all, he'd been so busy that he'd barely been able to enjoy the party. And he *always* enjoyed the party. He had a reputation to uphold, after all.

He looked out over the reception again and saw that

Marge was done dancing and was waving him over. What could the beautiful bride want with him?

He picked his way through the dancers with ease. He'd had lots of practice in the clubs. "Hi, Marge. I hope you're having a good time."

"I'm the happiest I've ever been. Everything is perfect."

"You do realize that today is a sad one for all of us single men, don't you?" Tyce gave her his saddest expression, which got a brief laugh from the vitamin heiress.

"It's just as well I planned ahead then, isn't it?" she said, taking his arm. "Come here, let me introduce you to my bridesmaids. They're all my nieces." Marge winced theatrically. "I'm still not used to the idea of being old enough to have nieces, let alone grown-up ones. Please flatter me by saying I don't look it."

"Will your new husband be angry if I say that you're the most beautiful woman in the room?"

"Not since we know you say that to all the women."

Marge's bridesmaids had congregated in one corner of the room forming, thanks to the theme for the wedding, a cluster of blue taffeta.

"Now, girls," she said, "there's someone I'd like you all to meet."

Tyce found himself being scrutinized. Marge's nieces obviously liked what they saw, because they moved forward slightly, obviously eager to say hello. Well, all except the one at the end of the line who was hanging back a little. Who could blame her, when Marge was clearly in a mood to set him up with one of them?

For the next few minutes Tyce smiled and made jokes with niece after niece. There was Annette and Georgia and…? He couldn't remember all their names.

"So, Tyce," Marge asked after she'd introduced him to a few of her bridesmaids, "what do you think of my nieces so far?"

"They're all very lovely," Tyce said automatically. The truth was that any one of them might have been good to go on a date with sometime, but he half suspected that giving one of them his number would only spark a feeding frenzy. And it would be difficult to make a quick getaway with so many wedding guests in his way.

"Now, Tyce," Marge said, "I just have one more niece to introduce you to. Don't hide at the back there, dear."

Marge stepped forward, taking the woman's arm and bringing her forward firmly.

"I'm afraid this niece is strictly off-limits, Tyce. She's getting married here herself four months from now."

Tyce thought he remembered Rose saying something about Marge being responsible for nearly a quarter of the Chalet's income, what with her own weddings, as well as those of her friends and family. He readied his best smile. He was prepared to say something about how he hoped that her upcoming wedding would go as well as this one.

Then he finally caught sight of the final niece's face.

He stopped, frozen to the spot, unable to say anything. For what seemed like an eternity, he couldn't do anything except stare into the deep green eyes in front of him. Eyes he remembered perfectly.

Eyes he had *never* thought he would see again.

* * * *

Turn the page to read THE WEDDING SONG,
featuring everyone's favorite DJ, Tyce Smith.
Enjoy this next story in the wonderfully romantic
ROSE CHALET series by Lucy Kevin.

THE WEDDING SONG

CHAPTER ONE

THE RECEPTION FOR the wedding at The Rose Chalet was in full swing, but Whitney Banning wasn't dancing yet. For the moment she was leaving the dancing to Aunt Marge, who was whirling around the floor with her new husband.

Her aunt looked especially beautiful and Whitney hoped Marge would finally find the happiness she deserved with her third husband in as many years. Besides, Whitney thought as she looked down at the blue taffeta bridesmaid dress she was wearing, she really didn't think a fourth *Gone With the Wind* themed wedding was a good idea. If for no other reason than the fact that no one—absolutely, positively, *no one*—looked good in blue taffeta.

The music stopped and Marge caught her eye, then made her way over to where Whitney was standing.

"Are you enjoying yourself?"

Whitney hugged her aunt. "Of course I am. I'm just sorry Kenneth couldn't be here." Her fiancé had been in Hong Kong for the past couple of weeks on business and would likely be away for another dozen weeks at least. "A text was waiting for me this morning, asking me to tell you 'Congratulations' on his behalf."

"I'll look forward to the four of us raising a toast together when he returns home," Marge said with a smile.

She put her arms around her niece. "I'm so glad you could be here today, honey."

The business of managing the Banning empire had kept her away from Marge's first two weddings. Whitney had been determined to make it this time, though. She wasn't about to miss her aunt's wedding three times running.

Even with bridesmaids' dresses like this one.

Marge glanced over to where another of the bridesmaids was dancing, her artfully braided hair flying free as she did so. "Annette seems to be having a good time."

"Annette always does," Whitney said, her affectionate smile laced with mild exasperation. Her cousin looked enough like her that they could have been sisters, but that was where their similarities ended. Somehow Annette always managed to dodge the business duties that kept Whitney so busy.

"You always were the sensible one," Marge said. "Just, don't be too sensible today."

"In *this* dress?"

Her aunt smiled at that. "It's a very lovely dress, as I'm sure half the men in the room would agree if you weren't already engaged to Kenneth. Speaking of men, I've found someone absolutely perfect for Annette. Or maybe Georgia."

"You know how they feel about your attempts at matchmaking," Whitney reminded her aunt. "I think you're just looking for an excuse for another wedding."

Marge laughed. "Am I that transparent?"

"Yes," Whitney said, but she was laughing as she said it.

"Today has been wonderful," Marge said as she tucked her arm into Whitney's. "Just think, in four months it will be you walking down the aisle with Kenneth. Your wedding is going to be so lovely."

Every time someone mentioned her upcoming wedding, Whitney was taken by surprise. Even in the middle of Marge's wedding, it had been hard to picture herself standing in front of friends and family with Kenneth, waiting to be pronounced husband and wife.

Pushing away a twinge of uncertainty at the hard-to-form vision, Whitney followed her aunt's gaze over to the string quartet that had just finished playing the score of *Gone With the Wind*. A tall, broad-shouldered man shook their hands as they put down their instruments, then he walked over to a laptop at a corner of the stage. He hit a few keys, starting up a pulsing beat clearly intended to move the party into a higher gear.

Half hidden from view, Whitney caught a few glimpses of spiky dark hair and a tattoo curling just below the man's rolled-up sleeves.

"Excuse me for a minute," Marge said as she headed toward the stage.

A strange buzzing moved up Whitney's spine. There was something familiar about The Rose Chalet's music director. She took a few steps to the side to try to get a better look at him, but Annette blocked her view as she danced over, hips swaying in time to the beat.

"Now *this* is more like it. Come on, Whit, let's dance." Annette gestured to the other wedding guests. "There are lots of good-looking men here you could grab for a song or two."

"I have Kenneth," Whitney pointed out patiently. There wasn't any point in being offended by Annette's suggestion.

"That shouldn't stop you from dancing." Annette looked over at the stage where Marge was talking animatedly with the music director. "Mmm. Aunt Marge has taste. I wonder if she's planning to bring him over for an introduction."

"Probably. She said something about having found the perfect guy for—"

Whitney's words dried up on her tongue as her aunt moved aside enough for her to get a clear view of the man's face.

Oh, God. It couldn't be him.

It just *couldn't*.

"She was talking about what?" Annette demanded, but all Whitney could do was blink and stare, then blink and stare some more. "Come on, Whit. You aren't thinking about something boring like business, are you? You should be telling me more about gorgeous guys."

No, she wasn't thinking about business at all, actually.

Instead she was completely fixated on the most gorgeous guy she'd ever seen.

The most gorgeous man she'd ever kissed.

Tyce Smith was every bit as good-looking as he'd been the last time she'd seen him. More so, if anything. Women were actually turning to stare at him, openmouthed, as he walked across the room with Aunt Marge.

Straight toward her.

She hadn't seen him at the ceremony, likely because he was busy setting everything up for the reception. If only she'd arrived here early enough to check in on things in the reception hall, she might have caught a glimpse of him…and figured out an exit strategy before now.

Her heart pounding in time to the driving beat of the

music, she said, "Annette, I need to leave. Can you tell Marge that I'm sorry, but—"

"Oh, no," Annette said with a shake of her head as she put her arm around Whitney's shoulders and held her in place. "This is Marge's big day. Well," she amended, "it's her third big day, and I am absolutely not going to let you run out of the party just to go to work on some boring presentation." Whitney was surprised by the firm set of her cousin's chin as she said, "And I'm definitely not covering for you if you do."

Shooting a panicked glance toward Marge and her companion, Whitney worked to slide herself free of her cousin's grip. "What about all the times I've covered for you?"

Annette looked uncharacteristically serious. "Not going to happen. You weren't here for the past two weddings, and look what happened."

Whitney stood there speechless. "You are *not* trying to pin Marge's two divorces on me, are you?"

Annette shrugged. "All I know is you weren't there and I've ended up having to wear this ugly dress *three* times. For all we know, you might be the good-luck charm she was missing at the first two weddings."

Her cousin thought Whitney was good luck?

On the contrary, she had the worst luck of anyone in the room.

Feeling her heart pound and her palms grow sweaty, she still couldn't believe she was finally coming face-to-face with the man who had haunted her dreams for so long. Not to mention the fact that the timing was utterly, completely, rotten.

Maybe if they had met each other again two or three years ago, it wouldn't be such a disaster. But she was engaged to be married in four months.

Here, at The Rose Chalet.

Where Tyce worked.

As she watched him move closer with her aunt's arm tucked into his side, Whitney wondered how it was that after planning three weddings at the Chalet, her aunt hadn't mentioned him once.

Whitney knew she should be poised for flight, to tear free from Annette's grip and make a run for the door. The problem was, she couldn't take her eyes off his muscular body and square jaw, and she couldn't get her feet to move, either.

How could she leave now when she'd longed for this moment—for the chance to see Tyce one more time, to touch his hand, to stare into his beautiful eyes—for so long? To give it up would tear her in two.

A moment later Tyce was stepping around Annette, and Whitney was finally able to look up at him. As she drank in the depths of his dark eyes, the strength of his beautifully masculine features, he sent so many different feelings spinning around inside her.

Excitement.

Fear.

And pure, sensual attraction.

"I'm afraid this niece is strictly off-limits, Tyce. She's getting married here herself four months from now," Marge said with an affectionate smile. "The Banning business empire would fall apart without her," she added.

For a second or two it was hard to think of anything to say at all as her heart leaped even faster in her chest and her breathing quickened. It was little comfort knowing that Tyce seemed to have the same problem. He stood there staring as if he couldn't believe it was actually her.

Whitney recovered first, but then she'd had a few extra minutes to process her shock at seeing him again.

"Hello, Tyce."

"Hello, Whitney."

There was so much layered into the way they were looking at each other, and the four words they'd said to one another, that Whitney was amazed her aunt couldn't see or hear it.

Tyce reached out a hand for her. "Would you like to dance?"

Whitney's heart skipped a beat at how beautiful his smile still was, and how familiar it was, even after so many years.

She knew she ought to say no, that she should leave the past in the past where it belonged. Yet now that she was faced with all the emotions, hopes and dreams that welled up at seeing Tyce again, Whitney didn't have even the slightest chance of doing anything but putting her hand into his…and saying, "I'd love to."

CHAPTER TWO

ELECTRICITY JUMPED ALONG Whitney's skin as his strong fingers curled around hers as he led her onto the dance floor.

"You shouldn't have asked me to dance, Tyce."

He gazed down at her, so exquisitely handsome, so real, so *there,* that Whitney felt her stomach flipping over just looking at him. He had such a magnetic presence. Slow dancing with her, he was as attention-grabbing as a rock star walking onstage in a stadium.

"Are you telling me that you don't want to dance?"

Unable to lie, Whitney said, "You should have picked one of my cousins to dance with instead. Annette would have loved it."

"I don't want to dance with them, Whitney. You're the only one I want to hold."

Oh, God. He shouldn't be saying that. Not now. Not when she had a fiancé.

She should have been pushing out of his arms and walking away, but it was simply impossible. With his arms wrapped around her as they danced to a slow song, she couldn't help but breathe in his scent, masculine and clean. All these years she'd remembered that scent; the memory of it coming back to her on the edge of her dreams far too often.

"You're beautiful," he murmured against her hair.

"So beautiful, I can hardly believe you're here. Finally, with me again."

Every cell in her body—and her heart—responded to his sweet words. Other men had told her she was beautiful, but it had never mattered this much.

And that was just the problem. Tyce mattered too much, even after just sixty seconds in his arms. Another sixty and she'd be forgetting everything. Her family, her job, her fiancé and the future she already had planned.

A future that didn't include Tyce.

Steeling her voice to be crisp, she said, "We can't do this, Tyce. Things have changed since the last time we saw each other. It's been a long time."

"Trust me," he replied softly, "I know exactly how long it's been." He pulled her a little closer and her body betrayed her by melting against his strong, hard muscles. "It's been much, much too long."

Five years.

Five years since they'd last been this close to one another.

Five years since she'd felt the heat of his skin touching hers, the strength of his arms around her.

Five years from the one night they'd spent together in San Francisco.

And yet as Tyce led their dance, his arms strong and gentle all at once, Whitney could still remember every moment of it as if it had been yesterday.

Five years ago…

"WHITNEY," ANNETTE SAID, tugging at her arm, "come on. The headliner will be on in a minute!"

"I just need some air," Whitney said. "I won't be long."

Annette paused, obviously caught between wanting

to get back inside the club and feeling that she should stick with her cousin. But when Whitney waved her away and said, "Don't worry, I'll come back inside soon," it was all the encouragement Annette needed to plunge back into the crowd of people in the club.

Whitney pushed out of the fire door at the side of the club and stepped into an alley, illuminated with lights strung between the brick walls. The barest hint of fog was coming in from San Francisco Bay and Whitney slipped her arms into her coat as the catchy melody of the last song performed by the opening act, a band called *T5*, ran on repeat in her head.

Neither she nor Annette had heard of *T5* and her cousin had initially suggested they get to the club late to just catch the headliner. But considering this was Whitney's last big night out before having to formally take over her father's responsibilities in the family business, she had insisted on coming early so that she wouldn't miss out on even a minute of freedom.

She was more than glad that she'd heard the opener play. *T5* had been electric. More to the point, the singer had been incredible. He was gorgeous, but she'd been struck by more than just his good looks.

He'd sung with such passion. Such conviction. On the rock numbers, he'd totally taken over the stage. On the slower ballads, it had been as if he'd been singing just for her.

She smiled at that fanciful thought, sure that every girl in the room had felt that same way.

Suddenly, Whitney heard a whimper from behind some garbage cans a little farther up the alley. She'd once planned to go to veterinary college and had majored in animal science at the University of California, Davis, so she knew how to work with animals. She hoped this one wasn't too hurt or too scared to let her close.

She stepped around the garbage cans and found the dog. Its fur was matted in a way that made it clear it had been outside for a while, and she guessed it was part terrier. It wasn't wearing a collar, and when it trembled and backed away from Whitney, she could see that it was limping to try to keep weight off its left front paw.

"Oh, you poor thing," Whitney said. The dog looked up at her and then yipped. Fortunately it wasn't growling, which meant she might be able to assess the injuries. "I hope you'll let me help you."

The poor little dog was obviously hurt, not to mention starving and filthy. "I just need to find something to bandage your paw with and then we'll find you something to eat."

The dog's ears perked up a bit as if it understood exactly what she'd just said.

"Do you need help with something?"

Whitney immediately knew who had joined them. After all, she'd just spent the past hour listening to that marvelous low voice.

Turning to look over her shoulder, she watched the lead singer of *T5* move closer to her. She couldn't help but be struck by the fact that he looked even better now than he had out on the stage.

"Hi, I'm Tyce. I was in the band that just played."

"I'm Whitney."

"And who's this?" Tyce asked, concern darkening his eyes as he looked down at the ragged little dog.

"I found him in the alley," Whitney told him. "He's obviously a stray, and he's hurt his paw. I was just going to head inside to see if the club has a first-aid kit."

"I'll do it. He obviously feels safe with you, so you should stay with him."

Tyce wasn't just gorgeous, he was sweet, too, she thought as he headed back inside the club.

Less than five minutes later he came back with a bowl of water in one hand and what looked like broken-up hamburger in the other. He also had a roll of bandages tucked into his belt.

He slowly went down on one knee in front of the little dog, then held out bits of meat on a flat hand. The scruffy-looking mutt sniffed at them for a second or two, then flinched and started shaking.

Whitney's heart broke in two as she wondered what had happened to the dog before she'd found it.

"It's okay," she said softly, hoping he'd understand her. "Nothing bad is going to happen to you again. I promise."

She took the meat from Tyce and held it out in her palm. This time the dog cautiously ate the food. When he had eaten it all and had lapped up some of the water, she gently put her hand on top of the dog's head and stroked it.

At first the terrier shook at her touch. "Didn't I promise you I wasn't going to hurt you?" she whispered to him. "I'm simply going to bandage up your paw now."

She could feel Tyce's eyes on her and despite the cool air she felt warm all over. Maybe he thought she was strange for talking to the dog, but she'd always had such a strong connection with animals.

The perfect assistant, Tyce passed the bandages to Whitney. She lifted the little dog's paw, wrapping it as carefully as she could. He cringed again, but didn't pull his paw away.

"Good boy," she murmured as he stilled to let her wind the bandage slowly around his leg.

When Whitney was done, she looked up into Tyce's eyes and her breath caught in her throat at the way he was gazing at her.

"You knew exactly what you were doing, didn't you? He really trusted you."

"I took a few animal science classes at UC Davis, but it's not like I'm a vet or anything." Feeling suddenly shy at his compliment, she changed the subject by saying, "Do you know anyone who could take in a very sweet little dog? I wish I could take him home with me, but I can't."

Her new building had a strict no-animal policy. She thought it was a silly rule, but the location had been perfect for getting to the office with a minimum of traffic delays. Besides, with her new responsibilities at work, she wasn't going to have much free time anymore. She couldn't stand the thought of leaving a dog all alone in her apartment while she put in long hours at the office.

Tyce slowly reached out his arms for the dog. The terrier sniffed his hands for several moments before suddenly leaning into the singer's arms.

Tyce picked him up. "Actually, I think I do," he said with a slow grin.

Oh, my, weren't they a cute pair? The gorgeous rocker with the mangy mutt tucked under his arm.

Still she had to say, "That's very sweet of you, but a dog needs a stable home, not someone living on the road."

"My life's a lot more stable than you'd think," he informed her with the same sexy grin. "So, how about you let me take you for a drink to celebrate my new dog? Or," he said, looking at the terrier who was already snuggling into his strong arms, "perhaps we should go for a walk instead."

Whitney didn't know anything about Tyce besides the fact that he was a great singer...and had a major soft spot for dogs in need.

Well, she thought as she also grinned, that was enough information to go for a walk, wasn't it?

Pushing aside the unwelcome thought that a guy like Tyce wouldn't fit into her corporate life at all, she said, "I'd love to go for a walk with you."

After she texted Annette to let her know about the change of plans, they headed off. As they walked, Tyce ran his hand over his new dog's fur, gently untangling it with his long, strong-looking fingers.

"Do you know what you're going to name him?" she asked.

Tyce stared down at the dog for a moment. "I think he looks like a Milo."

"That's a perfect name." Whitney reached out and Milo immediately burrowed his head beneath her palm. "Hello, Milo. You really are adorable, aren't you?"

"Clearly, he feels the same way about you," Tyce said. "So, how long until you're officially a vet?"

"I've dreamed of being one since I was just a little girl," she said, then shook her head. "But I'm going to be taking over a new position in my family's business soon. Tomorrow, actually."

Tyce frowned. "Will you still be able to pursue your dreams?"

She took a deep breath, working to center herself before saying, "Maybe. One day." Not wanting to ruin what had turned out to be an exceptional evening so far, she said, "Let me guess, your dream is to play packed stadiums while people chant your name?"

"Actually," Tyce said as he stared out at San Francisco Bay, the water a dark purple, "my dream is a lot simpler than that. I just want to write a perfect song one day. And I want someone to really be moved by it."

They kept talking, and walking, until Whitney completely forgot about both Annette and the club. It felt as if the night was just beginning....

WHITNEY CAME BACK out of her memories in a rush, with Tyce still holding her tightly as they danced at The Rose Chalet. When she was in his arms again, it was so easy to feel as if everything was the same as it had been that night five years ago.

But so much had changed since then. Too much for her to be standing here dancing with Tyce.

Too much for this moment to ever be more than a brief encounter.

She wasn't the same girl she'd been five years ago. And her life had changed to the point where the feelings she was having for Tyce were horribly inappropriate.

"I'm getting married here in four months," she reminded Tyce.

Tyce's muscles tensed against hers as she spoke. A tension that was matched by her own.

He lifted her hand to look at her engagement ring before saying, "Tell me about your fiancé. Does he make you laugh? Does he make you happy? And tell me why he isn't here with you tonight. Because if I were your fiancé, I wouldn't want to risk some other guy coming in and stealing you away."

Whitney froze in his arms. She couldn't do this. She *shouldn't* do this.

"Whitney?"

Knowing nothing she said tonight could change the

past—or change a future that was already set in stone—
she did the only thing she could.

She turned and fled the dance floor, not stopping
until she was completely clear of The Rose Chalet.

CHAPTER THREE

TYCE SMITH COULDN'T make up his mind whether the worst part of the morning after was getting over having a little too much fun the night before, or helping to clean up The Rose Chalet grounds after a wedding.

He packed up his amps before pitching in with the others on cleanup. Everyone was there but Phoebe Davis, who hadn't resurfaced since disappearing with RJ's brother, Patrick Knight, after Marge's wedding.

Rose Martin, the Chalet's owner, was dressed in jeans and a sweater today, rather than one of her well-tailored suits. RJ, the Chalet's handyman/gardener, had just started taking apart the reconstruction of Tara that he'd built for Marge Banning's wedding. Even the Chalet's dress designer, Anne Farleigh, had showed up, which was something of a surprise. Normally, the blond-haired, blue-eyed designer came and went at hours that only made sense to her. Her wedding gowns were so spectacular that Rose rarely, if ever, complained about her strange work schedule.

Tyce picked up a wilted rose and pricked himself hard, wincing. He couldn't concentrate on anything but Whitney.

She'd been so beautiful yesterday. So perfect. And there had definitely been chemistry between them.

For Tyce, it had felt as if the intervening five years

hadn't happened at all. If only she hadn't run out like that…

Yet she had, and Tyce knew he ought to leave things alone. Not only was Whitney getting married in the fall, she was getting married at the Chalet. Rose would kill him if she thought he was trying to steal away one of their brides, and Tyce seriously doubted that telling his boss about his amazing night with Whitney five years ago would do anything to help.

Yes, leaving Whitney alone was the smart thing to do. The right thing to do.

So then, if leaving things alone was so *smart* and *right,* what explanation was there for the way fate had stepped in, bringing Whitney into his life not once, but twice?

And how could he possibly ignore the fact that Whitney had been with him every second since their dance? In his head. In his heart. In his dreams when he'd finally fallen into a restless sleep.

"I've got to switch out some of this gear at my place," Tyce said, hefting his guitar and pedal board. "I won't be long."

Rose frowned. "Is this just a ploy to abandon us in the middle of the hard work?"

"Would I do that?"

Rose raised an eyebrow. "Yes."

"You've still got us," Anne pointed out to Rose. "Hasn't she, RJ?"

Tyce couldn't help but notice that the look RJ gave Rose lingered just a little too long. "Yes," his friend said to their boss, "you have me."

"I won't be long," Tyce promised before he headed over to his van and loaded it with his gear.

Last night, after he'd made a pathetic excuse to

Marge about Whitney rushing off to take an important call, he'd gone into the kitchen and pulled out his phone to look up Whitney Banning on the internet. What a difference a last name made. Tyce had quickly learned that she was vice president of operations for Banning Wellness Corporation and that she worked downtown in their office complex.

He drove through the city, cutting through the traffic to get to her office as quickly as possible. He parked across the street from the tall building and was just heading for the large gold-trimmed glass doors when Whitney stepped out into the sunlight.

Even in a charcoal-gray business suit she was beautiful.

Beyond beautiful.

Her expression was both intelligent and focused as she spoke into her cell phone, gesturing with her hand to make a point to her wireless audience.

It was so different from the way she'd talked to Milo in the alley that night they'd met, when she'd been so gentle, so soft. And yet he could still see that gentleness, that softness, in every move of her hands, in the purse of her full lips as she smiled at something her caller said.

She had just slipped the phone back into her bag when he got to her.

"Whitney."

"Tyce?" He saw a flash of pure joy sparkle in her eyes before she tamped it down. "What are you doing here?"

"You ran off so fast last night, we didn't get much of a chance to talk."

"We don't have anything to talk about."

"Are you sure about that?" Tyce asked. "After our

dance last night you really don't think there's anything to say? Ten minutes, that's all I'm asking." *For now.*

Whitney paused, and as he waited for her to make a decision about whether she would allow herself to talk to him, Tyce was worried she might shut him down. Completely.

Forever.

"All right," she said at last. "Ten minutes. But this is my only chance for a break today, so I'll need to get some food."

He hated to see her like this, so tense, so rushed. "This was the job you were starting five years ago, wasn't it?" he asked as they made their way down the street.

"Yes." Her answer was clipped, but even in that one short word he could hear the strain in her voice.

"What about veterinary school?"

Her mouth tightened, her lips pressing against each other for a moment before she said, "Maybe one day."

But Tyce could easily hear the *maybe not* that was far closer to the truth.

Hating the way she seemed to have tossed aside her dreams so casually, he said, "So that's it, you've given up on the life you always wanted for yourself?"

"I'm helping to run my family's business. I'm making decisions that have an impact on thousands of people's lives. Besides," Whitney shot back, looking him square in the eye, "have you written that perfect song of yours yet? Or are you too busy with your job at The Rose Chalet?"

When she turned to walk away, he reached for her hand and said, "That's nowhere near ten minutes."

Whitney looked down at her fingers linked in his,

a beautiful flush spreading across her cheeks. "You're really going to keep me here for every second of it?"

Tyce worked to get a grip on his emotions, but he couldn't stop himself from saying, "I'll do whatever I have to for one more second with you."

"Tyce," she said softly as she slipped her fingers from his, "you can't—"

"Please. Just give me five more minutes."

She bit her lip as she made her decision. "Okay. Five more. What do you need to talk to me about?"

Tyce had rarely ever felt nervous. Big stages and audiences had never fazed him. But this moment with Whitney was so much harder.

And so much more important.

"Your wedding."

Her eyes widened. Then narrowed. "We already talked about that last night. Besides, it doesn't have anything to do with you."

"Tell me about the guy you're marrying."

It killed him to ask, but he needed to see if her eyes lit up when she talked about her fiancé. He needed to see if she really loved the guy…or if marrying was just another family duty she felt she needed to fulfill.

"Kenneth," she said quickly. "His name is Kenneth. He's a very nice man and he's going to be a really great husband."

Relief flooded every cell in Tyce's body. Because she definitely didn't say the guy's name like a woman desperately in love.

"You don't really want to marry him, do you?"

"My God!" she exclaimed. "How can you even *say* that?" Whitney demanded. "You don't know anything about him."

"No, but I know you, Whitney."

"One night," she reminded him. "That's all you and I had together. Whereas Kenneth and I have been friends practically forever. We even work together."

His chest clenched at the thought of another man kissing her, slipping a ring on her finger. Especially a man she didn't love.

Whitney deserved real love… Not a pleasant marriage to a friend that almost sounded like a business deal.

"I've seen a lot of couples get married over the past five years," he said softly. "I know what real love looks like and I know when people are getting married for all the wrong reasons."

"The wrong reasons?"

Her expression was somewhere between shock and anger. But she wasn't walking away yet and he prayed that meant he still had a chance.

"It's only four months until your wedding and neither of you has been into the Chalet to check it out and plan the big party to kick off your future together. As far as I know, there haven't been any talks about the dress, the food or the music. When couples are really eager to marry, we have to find ways to slow them down and remain patient until the big day."

"You don't know anything about my relationship," she told him in a low voice. "For your information, Kenneth has more important things to take care of than wedding details. He isn't exactly going to fly over from China to pick out the color of our napkins or to decide between salmon and chicken."

With every angry word, she moved closer to him. One of the hardest things he'd ever had to do was to not reach for her, not pull her against him…not kiss her the way he'd dreamed of kissing her again for so long.

He'd known this wouldn't be easy; had known Whitney was too strong to let him convince her so easily to give him a chance. But fate wasn't going to visit them a third time.

Which meant he had to make this one count.

"I'm sure he's a nice guy, because I can't see you ever going out with some loser. But are you really telling me that what you feel for him is as intense as what we both felt that one night?" He paused before laying himself completely bare. "Are you telling me that your feelings for him are anywhere near what the two of us are feeling right now?"

"Tyce—"

He reached for her then, simply unable to stop himself from touching her face. "Look me in the eye and tell me that you don't feel the same. Tell me that you don't still feel what's between us as intensely as you did that night five years ago when you were in my arms. Do *that* and I'll go."

Whitney's eyes were locked on his and she took a deep, shaky breath as she contemplated her answer. And then, suddenly, she looked past his shoulder.

Her eyes went wide as she saw where he'd just taken her. "The Happy Pig hot dog stand," she exclaimed. "I haven't been here in years. Not since—"

She blinked up at him and five years fell away.

Five years ago, after walking hand in hand for hours...

"A HOT DOG STAND?" Whitney said. "Tyce, I can't. I'm a vegetarian."

Tyce smiled, still holding Milo in his arms. "So am I. Luckily, it's a vegetarian hot dog stand."

"There are vegetarian hot dog stands?"

"There sure are," he said, gesturing to the Happy Pig. Even late at night there was a line. But then, the place did make the best hot dogs in the city, vegetarian or not.

"So, which one should I have?" Whitney asked him.

Tyce cocked his head to the side. "Let's ask Milo, here."

"You're serious?"

"Why not?" Tyce asked.

"I've never met a guy who'll actually talk to his animals. I mean, I used to talk to my family's cat all the time, but most people don't get that."

Tyce smiled and then stroked Milo's head. "Ah, well, Milo here says you can't trust anything a *cat* has to say."

That got a laugh from her, but it wasn't just laughter that Tyce wanted right then. He looked down at the small dog in his arms.

"What's that, Milo?" he said. "You think I should do what? Yes, I think you're right."

"What did he say?" Whitney asked.

Tyce answered her by leaning in, with Milo pressed between them, and kissing her. It was a soft kiss. A tender kiss.

He kept kissing her while she stood there in shock… And then, when she finally kissed him back with a passion to match his, he kissed her some more, not stopping until the guy running the hot dog stand coughed pointedly and asked if they were going to order anything now that he'd served everyone in front of them.

They fell back from one another, laughing.

TYCE COULD SEE that Whitney remembered the incredible kiss they'd shared standing in front of the Happy Pig hot dog stand just as well as he did. Her half-closed eyes and the faint smile that worked its way across her lips were dead giveaways.

He leaned in toward her, just a little, and for a second Whitney leaned in, too. Tyce could practically feel the space between them shrinking and knew that, any moment, their lips would meet.

Suddenly, Whitney's eyes opened wide and she took a step back from him.

"No, I can't. I *can't,* Tyce."

"Are you telling me that you don't want this?"

Whitney hesitated just a fraction of a second too long before saying, "All we shared was one night. That's all it was."

"Whitney—"

She looked at the Happy Pig hot dog stand and even though he could see how much she wanted to eat one of their hot dogs—and how much she wanted to kiss him, too—she shook her head.

"Your ten minutes are up," she told him.

And then she turned and walked away.

CHAPTER FOUR

RETURNING TO THE Rose Chalet as promised, Tyce found the main room still needed a lot of clean-up work. There were tables to be put away, his cables still needed to be wound up, and most of the flowers were still in place.

RJ called out, "Hey, Tyce, can you give me a hand?"

Knowing hard physical work was exactly what he needed right now to burn off some steam, Tyce grabbed tools from the toolbox and set to work ripping apart Tara.

"Whoa, take it easy," RJ said as Tyce yanked off a large section. "We might need to put it back together someday."

"Nope," Tyce said. "I think Marge is actually going to stay married to this husband. Which means we've seen the last of Tara." From what he'd learned today, the Banning women were better at sticking with their men than he'd given them credit for.

"Well," RJ said, "someone else might want it. That niece of hers, maybe."

Tyce gripped the hammer even harder as he slammed it into a beam. If he'd been at home, he would have turned his amplifier up as far as it could go, added plenty of distortion, and played hard rock until his neighbors complained. Heavy manual labor was a good substitute, though.

He and RJ made a good team, especially when RJ

got into the spirit of things and attacked the wood just as much as Tyce did. By the time they were done, they had both worked up a sweat.

RJ nodded to him. "Thanks."

Tyce should be the one thanking his friend. There was something profoundly satisfying about being able to look at something he'd done with his own hands, even if it was a demolition job.

"Tyce, there you are." He turned to see Rose standing there watching them.

"Would you look at the two of you?" she said with a smile that made it clear she was trying not to laugh. "Sweaty and covered in wood shavings. I don't know whether I should be keeping customers away or charging them an entry fee." Tyce caught the way her eyes flicked to RJ again, and she flushed before saying, "This feels like the end of an era. I don't think we'll be getting another *Gone With the Wind* wedding for a while."

"We're all hoping Marge won't be back, aren't we?" RJ said.

"I always wanted the Chalet to be about love working out," Rose agreed. "It looks like Marge has finally gotten her happily-ever-after."

It was obvious to Tyce that they were all glad Marge had finally found someone who made her happy. Now if only her niece didn't do so many crazy things to *his* feelings.

And if only Whitney would let him make her happy.

"Did you need me for something?" Tyce asked Rose.

"I've been running a client through the last few things for his big day and he has a special request for you. It would be great if you could come and meet with him for a few minutes to discuss the situation."

"Let me just clean up a bit and put my shirt back on."

A handful of minutes later, Rose introduced them.

"Tyce, this is Hugh Washburn." The middle-aged man had a pleasant, open face. "He and his fiancée, Theresa, will be getting married here a couple of weeks from now. When they came in a few months before to meet with the rest of the group, you were away for the day."

After they shook hands Tyce said, "Rose said that you had a special request. Is it about a particular song?"

"I've decided I'd like something special for Theresa as a surprise at the wedding. It's why I came without her today. We've both always loved music, so I was hoping that you might be able to write a song in her honor for the occasion."

Tyce couldn't believe the day he was having. First Whitney had walked away from him—yet again—and now he was being asked to write a song.

A love song.

Biting back the "No" that threatened to jump off his tongue, he diplomatically said, "I could certainly do a new arrangement of an existing song by changing the lyrics."

The client frowned, looking over at Rose. "I thought you said that we'd be able to choose whatever custom elements we wanted for the day?"

"Of course you can," Rose said. "Tyce, Mr. Washburn would like you to write an original song for his bride."

"I understand that," Tyce said, knowing he had to spin this carefully. "I'm just thinking about the end result. With a reworking, you're absolutely sure of what you're getting ahead of time, especially if you pick a song that you know your fiancée already loves. That way, it will have her at the heart of it."

"So you're saying that a rearrangement offers the best chance of a good result?"

"Yes," he said. He shot his most reassuring smile the client's way. "You will still be making an incredibly personal gesture, and Theresa will still be a part of the song, but you will also be showing her just how well you know her musical tastes by picking out the song that she loves most in the world. When you think about it like that, it's actually almost *more* romantic." He hoped that last bit wasn't overkill as Rose shot daggers at him with her eyes.

"Yes, I guess so," Mr. Washburn said, sounding a little more convinced. "And there aren't many other places that would be able to arrange swans at the wedding. Well, I think we've covered everything else, and I'll be back with Theresa to work out the final details on her dress. I'll email you soon with the song choice."

"Wonderful," Rose said, shaking Mr. Washburn's hand before showing him out.

Tyce started to head back to the main hall to help RJ finish up, but Rose caught up with him halfway there.

"Tyce—"

"You're about to ask me if I'll reconsider writing this song, aren't you?"

"You can see the client isn't happy about it, and we didn't build The Rose Chalet's reputation by giving customers *almost* what they wanted."

"I know," Tyce said, "but he seemed happy enough by the time he left."

"Maybe," she admitted, "but I don't understand why you won't at least try to write a song."

He really liked Rose, felt that she was more of a

friend than just a boss. Still, he couldn't help a flash of annoyance at her comment. "If Anne told you what she thought was the best way to go about a dress design, or Phoebe explained that she had a better idea for a floral display, you'd accept it, wouldn't you?"

"Yes, I would. But I'd want to know they'd given it their best shot first. That they weren't just settling for second best."

"I am giving it my best shot."

"Easy, Tyce," Rose said in a gentle voice. "I was just hoping that whatever's stopping you from doing this, it might be something we can talk through."

He felt his shoulders slump, the weight of the bad day—and the sleepless night—dragging him down. "It's been a long time since I've written a song."

Five years.

Rose looked as if she was waiting for him to say more, and he was afraid she might press him further. Instead she simply said, "Please promise me you'll at least try."

Tyce nodded reluctantly. "I'll let you know if I can make it work. Otherwise, assume we'll be reworking her favorite song."

"Thank you, Tyce." Rose gave him a small smile and put her hand on his arm. "You know I've always trusted you to do your best by our clients. I still do." With that, she turned and headed to her office.

With her vote of confidence ringing through his head, Tyce went out to the parking lot and dug his guitar out of the trunk where he'd left it. He sat on the hood of his car, guitar in hand, because he knew as well as anyone that the way to get inspiration to show up was to just start playing. The longer he tried to build up to it, the harder it would be.

He tried strumming his way through a simple three-chord progression to see if any inspiration would bite. Nothing. Not so much as a glimmer of a lyric. He tried running through a few riffs instead, but they were tired old standbys. There wasn't the faintest hint of anything original coming through.

Then again, had he really expected anything else?

He hadn't written anything original since that night with Whitney five years ago. He'd started to write a song the morning after, but he'd broken it off after the four-bar introduction because there hadn't seemed to be any point. He could still play those four bars without thinking about them, and as he finger-picked, the notes rang out.

He repeated the four bars a few times but he just didn't know what came next.

Not without Whitney.

Five years ago, just moments after their first kiss...

TYCE HADN'T BEEN looking for love, or for a partner, or for a woman to share the rest of his life with. He was a young musician with the world at his feet; it was all waiting to be explored. Waiting to be conquered.

But what he and Whitney had just shared had been every symphony, every ballad, every single one of his favorite songs all wrapped up into one sweet, perfect kiss.

He and Whitney would do that conquering, that exploring together. He didn't know how he knew it, only that after a few hours with her every piece of his heart—and every part of his soul—knew it to be true.

They took their vegetarian hot dogs and walked to a bench that looked out over the Bay. For the first time since they'd met, they didn't speak. As they enjoyed their meal, with Milo sleeping at their feet, the silence was a perfect one.

The first rays of light were beginning to rise up through the darkness, casting an incredible glow over the water, but Tyce could barely take his eyes off Whitney's beautiful face.

Their hot dogs and sodas long finished, she turned to smile at him. "Do I have mustard on my face?"

She didn't, but it was more fun to pretend that she did as he gently ran a finger along the corner of her mouth. "Right here."

Whitney reached up for his hand and held it against her cheek. "Tyce, I—"

Her cell phone rang loudly, jarring both of them. Her hand slid from his. "Sorry. It must be Annette making sure I'm okay. I should get it."

But when she pulled the phone out of her pocket he could see the word *Dad* on the screen, along with a picture of a nice-looking, middle-aged man.

She frowned and put it up to her ear. "Dad? Is everything okay?"

The early morning was quiet enough that Tyce was able to hear the other side of the conversation, even though he didn't want to eavesdrop.

"I'm fine, honey. Just calling to wish you luck before your first day in my—" Her father broke off with a laugh. *"Well, it's your office now, isn't it?"*

Tyce could feel Whitney tense up beside him, one muscle at a time. She'd been so relaxed, had looked so happy over the past few hours as they'd walked and talked…and kissed.

But now her mouth was pinched and her eyes were shadowed as she said, "Thanks, Dad. It's going to be—"

She couldn't seem to find the word for a moment. "Great. Don't worry about anything at the company. I'll make you proud, I promise."

"Your mother and I are already so proud of you. We never expected you to want to take over my position. It's the best gift you could give us, honey."

She swallowed hard. "I love you, Dad."

"We love you, too. Be sure to call to let us know how your first day goes, or if you have questions about anything at all."

As she put the phone down on her lap, Tyce was struck by the sense that, in one short phone call, he'd lost the woman he'd just found. Her previously vibrant energy was muted now, as if the fog had moved from covering the Bay to enveloping her instead.

"I need to go get ready for work."

No. He didn't want her to go. Especially not like this; not when it felt as though the bond they'd created was threatening to snap apart.

"It's early, still," he said as he reached for her hand. "Stay a little while longer."

But instead of linking her fingers with his the way they'd been for so much of the night, she brought her hand in closer to her body.

"Tonight has been—" She looked at him and everything she felt was in her eyes. The passion, the longing… and the sudden sadness. "It's been amazing, Tyce. And I'm so glad we met. But—"

He didn't think, he just put his hands in her hair and kissed her again. He would do anything he needed if it would keep her from listing all the reasons why they couldn't be together.

After a split second of surprise, she kissed him back

just as passionately. And yet, when they finally pulled apart, she looked sadder than ever.

"You're wonderful," she told him, "but I can't be in a relationship right now."

"Why not?"

"I owe it to my family to give one hundred percent of myself to the business. This was my last night out before taking over for my father. I can't let him down. Thank you for making it more special than I could have ever hoped it would be."

Didn't she hear herself? The way she made it sound as if she was walking into a prison cell, locking the door behind her and tossing the key out of reach?

"It doesn't have to just be one night, Whitney." He could see she didn't like the way he was pushing her, but how could he let her go? "At least give me your number."

He held his breath as she pressed her lips together and looked away from him. Finally she gave him the numbers he so desperately wanted.

She reached for his hand. "You're amazing, Tyce. I can't wait to hear your songs on the radio."

It sounded as if she was saying goodbye. But when she leaned over to press one more soft kiss to his lips, he lost track of everything but her scent, the taste of her, the sweet pleasure of knowing he'd found the woman of his dreams.

When she suddenly stood and quickly walked away, he knew she didn't want him to follow her. She obviously needed to focus on her job today. And he would let her do that, because he respected her.

But she also needed to know that he wasn't giving up…and that he would be waiting for her when she was ready to date him.

Pulling his phone out of his pocket, he dialed her number, surprised when she didn't pick up and her voice mail came on.

But it wasn't Whitney's voice speaking in his ear.

"Hello. You've reached the San Francisco SPCA. Our business hours are 8:00 a.m. to 5:00 p.m., Monday through Saturday."

He woke Milo as he jumped up off the bench and scanned the Bay front for Whitney.

But she was gone.

That was when he saw it—the sticker on the side of the bench where they'd been sitting, with the SPCA logo and phone number.

She'd left him with no last name, no phone number…and no way to find her.

FOR THE PAST five years, Tyce hadn't been able to write anything worth listening to. He'd tried putting a few things together, and they'd come out by the numbers—so awful that he hadn't even bothered letting the rest of his band hear them. Worse, without that buzz of writing new songs and hearing people respond to them, everything else about life in the band had seemed pointless. Other *T5* members had written a few things, and they'd played the old songs, but getting up onstage hadn't been the same. So he'd quit before his friends could throw him out for doing such a halfhearted job as lead singer.

Now he noodled aimlessly up and down the guitar neck as he thought about the way The Rose Chalet job had come along right after he'd left the band. Since then, Tyce occasionally filled in with other bands. The combination was a good one, giving him a regular paycheck along with a few moments up onstage every now and again.

What more did he need?

Tyce hit the guitar strings hard, discord ringing out. The Rose Chalet was fine, but he wasn't kidding anyone. Not even himself.

He needed more. So much more. He needed his creative soul to be fulfilled.

And he needed his heart to be made whole.

Whitney had been right. She might have settled for second best by going into the family business, but he'd done exactly the same. He'd settled for a nice, easy, comfortable job rather than putting himself out there to go after his dream.

Tyce loved the friends he had at The Rose Chalet. He loved being able to make a living with music.

But it wasn't the same as writing the perfect song.

And it never would be.

CHAPTER FIVE

"I CAN'T BELIEVE he'd accuse me of not following my dreams," Whitney said as she got ready for work.

On the bed behind her, Clementine, a black-and-white tabby cat, stretched out and yawned.

"I know," Whitney said as she put on her suit jacket. "I shouldn't be making such a big deal about what he said. It's just… How can he say that about me when he's hiding away at a wedding venue?"

Clementine sat up, staring at Whitney until she stroked the cat's ears.

"Okay, so maybe I wanted to be a veterinarian when I was a kid, but what does that have to do with my life now?"

Her cat mewed in response.

"If I left the business, who would take over? Annette?" Whitney laughed at that thought, but there was little humor in it. "Come on, let's get you some breakfast before I go."

Clementine leaped down off the bed, brushing against Whitney's legs as they headed to the kitchen. One day, she'd manage to get to work without being covered in cat hairs.

"You'd probably like it if my cousin were in charge. You always ignore me when she's in the house."

That was just how cats were. The person who gave them food and disposed of the dead mice they brought in was never as much fun as the person who made a total fuss over them. On top of that, Clementine recognized a kindred free spirit when she saw one. After all, wasn't it true that cats did exactly what they liked, slept through about half the day, and expected you to put up with them simply because they happened to be gorgeous? Clementine and Annette were a perfect match.

Not that Whitney wanted Clementine any other way. Annette, either, for that matter.

Clementine finished her breakfast, then followed Whitney around as she hunted for her keys. She'd hated that first apartment five years ago where she hadn't been able to have a pet, and as soon as the lease had run out she'd found this cute little place just outside the city but close enough to the office that she could justify the short commute. There was a small kitchen, a cozy living room, a master bedroom and a home office.

She paused in the middle of the living room and looked around at the small space. "I guess when Kenneth and I get married we'll have to look for a bigger place, won't we?"

Funny, she and Kenneth had never discussed where they'd live after the wedding. They obviously needed to talk about their plans for the future and whether they'd move into one of their homes or get a different one together.

But she didn't need to talk to him to know they needed a new wedding venue.

Clementine raised a paw and started to lick it, but her eyes were on her owner.

"Don't look at me like that. You know I can't have the wedding at The Rose Chalet. Not with Tyce there. It wouldn't be fair to Kenneth."

And she was going to be fair to Kenneth, regardless of what it took.

After all, he was the man she was going to marry.

Kenneth was the perfect choice in so many ways. They'd known each other forever. They'd been friends at school. He was good-looking and funny, and they'd worked together in the business for years. After a couple of years of dating, everyone had assumed they would get married. One day they had ended up at a jewelry store and she'd walked out with a diamond on her left hand.

Come to think of it, had he ever officially proposed?

Surely that was something she should be able to remember instantly. But she was tired.

And more than a little shaken up from seeing Tyce again.

In any case, if keeping everything on course meant changing the wedding venue, then that was what Whitney was going to do.

She called her secretary, leaving a message to say that she was going to be coming in a little late.

On the way to the Chalet she stopped at *the Last Bean,* her favorite coffee shop. The morning never really started for her until she'd had her first cup of their coffee. She'd bought their beans to grind at home, but it never tasted quite right when she made it for herself.

"Hi, Janet," Whitney said as she went in. "Could I have the usual, please?"

"Sure. One coffee and one morning bun coming up. You're here a little earlier than normal. Big day?"

"Just something I have to do before work."

A few minutes later she was walking through The Rose Chalet's beautiful gardens. Even the small pond was surrounded by delicate flowers.

"I missed you, too."

Whitney hadn't heard Tyce approach, but at the sound of his low, mesmerizing voice, she spun to face him. He was standing just a few feet away, wearing jeans and a dark T-shirt.

She wanted so badly to put her arms around him again and kiss him.

All the more reason to get this over and done with.

"Tyce, I don't want another fight." *Or to do something shocking and wrong, like kissing you while I'm engaged to another man.*

"I don't want to fight, either. But I do want to tell you that you were right."

She stared at him in surprise. "I was?"

"Yes. I did give up my dreams of writing that perfect song. And I don't have any right to call you out for working in the family business. Not if it's what you think is right."

For a second or two she simply didn't know what to say. "Tyce, I…"

"You're not actually here to see me, are you?"

He looked so sad, she wanted to reach for him.

Tightly gripping her purse in one hand and her coffee cup in the other, she finally said, "I'm looking for Rose."

Although the truth was much more complicated than that, wasn't it? Because somewhere deep down, despite all her protestations to the contrary, hadn't she been hoping to see Tyce one more time?

"Rose has been busy trying to get everything together for a house she's building with her fiancé and she will be coming in a little late today. Maybe I can help," he offered. "What did you need to talk to her about?"

Oh, boy, this was awkward. Canceling on Rose was

one thing. Saying the words to Tyce was another thing entirely.

But she still had to do it. To be fair to Kenneth.

"I need to pull out of The Rose Chalet as a wedding venue." Hating how shaky her voice was, she took a deep breath before adding, "I can't spend the next four months trying to plan the wedding with you around constantly, Tyce. I just can't."

He moved closer to her. "You shouldn't be afraid of what you feel."

"I'm getting *married*." Her unspoken *to someone else* floated in the air between them.

"Don't change the venue, Whitney."

"What else can I do?"

"It's about what *I* can do," Tyce replied, moving closer still. "I'll tell Rose I can't work this wedding. I'll find you another music director. A great one."

Whitney shook her head. "I still don't think it's a good idea, Tyce."

"You get to keep your dream wedding venue and the others don't suffer because of me. It's a good solution."

They were so close now that they were almost touching. Whitney looked up into his eyes and could see how important this was to him. She could see a lot more than that, too. His desire for her was so clear she would have to be blind to miss it.

Or maybe it was just the reflection of her own desire for him. It would be so easy to move that last little bit closer...

A loud crash rang out from behind them, coupled with the sound of a bird in distress and a male voice swearing.

Whitney whipped around to see a swan stuck in the netting around a rosebush, its head caught fast. The huge bird thrashed in terror, perilously close to the rose's thorns.

She dropped her bag and coffee cup on the lawn and ran over to the swan. Taking off her jacket, she threw it over the bird, wrapping her arms around it to try to stop it struggling. The bird was so agitated that it might have knocked her down if Tyce hadn't been right there beside her, helping her to hold it still.

"What happened, RJ?" Tyce asked the man in the overalls who had come running after the bird.

RJ shook his head. "I don't know. One minute the swan was fine, the next it spooked and took off straight toward the roses." He pulled a phone out of his pocket. "If you two can keep it steady for a little while longer, I'll call a vet."

Whitney, fearing that they wouldn't have time for a vet to arrive, immediately went to work on the netting, but as she did, the swan became frenzied, thrashing whenever she got close to its head.

Knowing the poor thing was obviously terrified, she tore the netting around its neck the best she could without getting bitten. Finally she and Tyce were able to at least move the swan away from the rosebush. Amazingly, it didn't seem to be too badly scratched.

"I need a pair of small scissors," Whitney told RJ after he'd arranged for an emergency visit from a mobile veterinarian. "We've got to cut this netting free before the swan gets so tangled it starts to choke."

The bird was still struggling, but Tyce had a good grip on it. Gradually it seemed to sense that Whitney was trying to help. It had stopped fighting her once RJ returned with the scissors.

As delicately as she could, she snipped the netting away.

RJ knelt beside them. "Is it going to be okay?"

"I think so," Whitney said. "I can't see any marks from the netting, or any serious scratches. I think this is one very lucky bird. In any case, we'll know more once the vet gets here."

"I've got it now," RJ told Whitney. "Sorry to drag you into an emergency like this. I promise we'll make it up to you by pulling out all the stops with your wedding in a few months' time."

A shiver went down her spine at the thought of walking down the aisle with Kenneth…and from the darkness of Tyce's eyes on her as he obviously envisioned the same thing.

Whitney excused herself to wash up and had just finished cleaning up when the vet arrived.

"So this is the patient?" she asked. "I don't see that many swans. You—" she pointed to RJ "—stay and hold it. You other two, I'm sure you're worried, but if you could give us a little space?"

Whitney moved back with Tyce by her side as they watched the vet carefully check out the bird.

"That was intense." Her hands were still shaking a bit but she suspected that was more from exhilaration than anything else.

"It was, but it seemed like you knew exactly what to do," Tyce said. "Just like you did with Milo." Tyce picked up her bag and handed it to her, before taking the spilled coffee cup and carrying it to a nearby garbage can.

When he returned to Whitney's side she was watching the vet examine the bird with clear, precise movements to ensure it was okay. The woman dabbed disinfectant on the worst of the scratches and slowly extended each of the swan's wings to check for damage.

Whitney fought back a fierce longing to be in charge of the bird again.

Tyce moved up close to her shoulder. "Are you really going to try to tell me that your family wouldn't want that for you? That they wouldn't see the way your eyes light up when you work with animals?"

Whitney swallowed. The truth was that they loved her and wanted the best for her... And yet that didn't change the obligation she had to them.

It was a relief when her secretary, Olivia, called.

"Sorry, Whitney, but we need you in the office. There's an emergency. We've just learned the East Coast deal is about to fall through."

Just as she'd been about to explain to Tyce, her family—and their business—needed her.

"I'll be right there."

CHAPTER SIX

Tyce sat in his apartment, his work guitar across his knees. The apartment wasn't large, but it was enough for him and Milo, with old, comfortable furniture and space to store his recording gear. Milo was in his basket in the corner, half asleep this morning. Tyce's other guitar, the road-battered and scarred Telecaster copy he'd put together from parts, sat on a stand in a corner of the room, next to a small table containing both a pile of sheet music and an empty cup of coffee. Compared to the guitar on his lap, the remade Telecaster was an ugly old thing. It had pickups that didn't match, gouges in the wood where he'd rerouted it to take a third pickup, and a bare wood finish. The only reason he didn't sell it was because he doubted anyone would want to buy it.

Well, maybe that wasn't the *only* reason. There were plenty of good memories with it. He'd played it so many nights on the road, in front of so many audiences, it was more like an old friend than anything.

He'd been playing it the night he'd met Whitney.

"I'd hoped she would have called me by now," Tyce said to Milo.

The dog looked up from his basket, opening his eyes sleepily.

"Yeah, I know she doesn't actually have my number, but she could have looked it up. Or come to The Rose Chalet again."

It had been a hectic week at the Chalet. The Washburn wedding had gone off without a hitch. Fortunately. After letting Rose know he wasn't able to write an original song, he'd managed to get the reworked song together in plenty of time to serenade the bride. The swans had been in good form and everyone had gone away from the wedding happy.

In spite of all the work he'd been doing, he still thought about Whitney. All the time.

Especially their almost-kiss at the Chalet.

When Milo whined, Tyce put his guitar away and grabbed the leash. "Come on, let's go out."

Tyce was about to drop his half-drunk cup of coffee into the sink when his thoughts flashed back to the cup Whitney had dropped when she'd moved to rescue the swan.

"I know just the place we can go for our walk," Tyce announced. "It's not that far, and you'll probably really like it."

Milo's head tilted to one side, one ear flopping down over an eye.

"I'm pretty sure they'll find a water bowl for you. You know how you love a good water bowl, don't you?"

Milo looked at him, those big brown eyes boring into him. For a dog, his expression was eloquent.

"Things are easier for dogs. Trust me on that."

That just earned him another look, this time with Milo's tongue lolling out.

"When was the last time you ran into a girl you hadn't been able to find for five years, only to discover she's planning to marry some other guy who isn't even here treating her right?"

Milo yapped.

"Exactly. Never." He hooked up Milo's leash. "Let's go."

Tyce led the dog down from his apartment to the street. Milo looked a lot healthier than he had the first night he'd met Whitney, but there was still something fundamentally unkempt about him, no matter how well Tyce groomed him.

He smiled slightly at that thought and ran a hand through the unpredictable spikes of his hair. What was it they said about dogs and their owners ending up looking the same?

They set off in the direction of the Last Bean. It was the name of the coffee shop that had been on the side of Whitney's coffee cup.

Milo hurried along beside him, and it was only when the small dog broke into a jog that Tyce realized just how much he was hurrying to get there.

"Sorry, little guy," he said as Milo gave him a reproachful look. "I don't want to risk missing her."

He slowed down slightly to let Milo keep up and noticed the way the morning traffic stopped and started all around them as people made their way to their nine-to-five office jobs.

Tyce had never planned on having a "regular" job. He'd always assumed he'd be an artist, a musician and songwriter.

Of course, he still got to play music at The Rose Chalet. And the friends he had there were great. But wasn't he still going in every day, knowing exactly what he would be doing for his monthly paycheck?

Milo pulled at his leash and Tyce looked up to see Whitney sitting in the sun at one of the coffee shop's outdoor tables. She was dressed for work in another suit, this one a dark navy that set off her coloring beautifully.

When Whitney spotted him, she looked uncertain as

to whether she should smile at him or not. Fortunately, when the dog ran over to her with an excited bark, she no longer bothered to hold back her grin.

"Oh, sure," Tyce said softly. "Steal the show completely."

Whitney stroked Milo's fur while the dog licked her hand excitedly. "It's been a long time since I last saw you, hasn't it, Milo?"

The dog barked.

"You obviously remember me, though."

Tyce smiled at that. "You aren't exactly easy to forget."

"How has he been?" she asked. "I still wish I could have taken him home with me."

"Milo has been great. I always loved knowing that he was my link to you," Tyce said honestly. He sat opposite Whitney. "Though from the looks of it, he could have done with seeing more of you." He paused, just for a moment. "He isn't the only one."

"Is that why you're here?"

Tyce raised an eyebrow. "Milo heard that this place had great water bowls. I couldn't keep him away, could I?"

That got a laugh from her. Too soon, she grew serious again. "Tyce," she began, "I'm not going to deny that there is definitely something between us. But you can't expect to fit into my life as though nothing has happened in between. I've got a family I love that I need to support and a business to run. I like you," she said softly, "but—"

He couldn't let her get to the "but." Not if it meant she'd be walking away again.

"I won't push you, Whitney. Not today, I promise. But I'd love it if we could talk. Just talk, that's all we'll do."

Whitney looked momentarily uncomfortable. "Actually, I'm meeting someone here."

"Did Kenneth come back early?" Tyce asked, feeling as if he'd just been kicked in the gut.

Before she could reply, a kid in his early teens, with the same dark hair and green eyes as Whitney, headed over to the table. He had the gawky, unfinished look most kids had around that age, but Tyce guessed that he was probably one of the kids who got plenty of attention from the girls at his school. He was carrying a guitar case.

"Sorry I'm late," he said.

"Sebastian, I'd like you to meet Tyce. Tyce, this is my brother."

Tyce hadn't known she had a brother. Had he been at Marge's weddings? Then again, once he'd spotted Whitney, he really hadn't paid attention to anybody else.

Part of him wanted the opportunity to spend more time alone with Whitney, but part of him recognized this as a chance to show Whitney he wasn't a threat to the life she'd built up, and that he could fit in with her family.

"Hi, Sebastian. It's good to meet you."

"You, too. Is that your dog?"

"His name is Milo." The dog quivered with happiness while Sebastian stroked his ears.

"What are you playing?" Tyce asked with a nod to the guitar case.

Sebastian opened the case and the guitar within wasn't bad. In fact, there had been times in his life when Tyce would have happily traded most of what he owned to be able to play an instrument that good.

"Whitney bought it for me."

"I figured if you were going to play, it should be on a decent guitar."

"You made a good choice," Tyce said. "That's a serious instrument." Sebastian seemed pleased by that. "Are you planning on becoming a musician professionally?"

The teenager shook his head. "No way. This is just a hobby for me. Kind of the way Whitney is with animals."

Tyce couldn't let that *hobby* comment go. "Do you know how I got Milo?"

"Tyce…" Whitney began.

Sebastian looked between the two of them. "How?"

"I found Whitney tending to a stray, hurt dog outside a gig I was playing. It was Milo, and she bandaged him up and got him to trust her. How many people would have done that?"

"Not many, I guess," Sebastian admitted.

"Your sister knew exactly what to do. And last week, a swan at the venue where I play at got caught in garden netting. I would have just waited for the vet, or hurt the bird by approaching it wrong. But, thanks to Whitney, we managed to get the swan out of the netting in one piece. She has a real talent with animals and would be an amazing veterinarian."

Sebastian looked over to where Whitney was petting Milo, her head lowered so no one could see her face. "I guess you're right. I never really saw it that way."

Finally, Whitney looked up at Tyce, giving Milo the opportunity to finally visit the water bowl. Tyce couldn't quite decipher the look, but there was definitely gratitude in there along with something that looked like affection she wasn't trying to hide anymore.

"Tyce was in a band," Whitney suddenly told her brother. "That's why he knows about guitars."

Sebastian's eyes went wide. "Were you guys famous?"

Tyce shook his head. "We got close, but never quite made the big time."

Still, he had plenty of stories from the old days to impress a young would-be guitarist.

He started with the time his guitarist and his keyboard player had made a bet over who could talk the venue owners into doing the craziest things, segued straight into the story about having to pretend that an entire rock set was meant to be acoustic after all his amps failed, and went on from there to mention a few of the bands they'd shared stages with at festivals.

"No way," Sebastian said after a while. "You didn't really end up jamming with *those* guys when they were in town. I mean, that would have been right before…"

"Right before the bass player made a run for the border. Trust me, if I'd known then what I know now about the hundred-mile-an-hour chase, I would never have accepted a ride home from the guy. They sure could play, though."

Whitney gave her watch a brief glance. "I'm about to be late for work. You're due in class, too, Sebastian."

She stood, ruffling Milo's fur once more. "It was good seeing you again, Milo." She looked at Tyce, her eyes warmer than they'd been in a long time. "You, too, Tyce."

"Yeah," Sebastian said, "it was good meeting you."

Brother and sister exited together, leaving Tyce with too many things left unsaid.

Beside him, Milo whined and lay down.

"I don't know what you're complaining about. At

least she touched you." Maybe, Tyce thought as he went back over the past few minutes in his head, he should have pressed Whitney harder before her brother had showed up by telling her flat-out how he felt.

At the very least, he definitely should just have kissed her.

CHAPTER SEVEN

WHITNEY'S OFFICE WAS at the top of the Banning Building, giving her both plenty of space to work in and an excellent view out over the city. Annette was there, having come into the office for once. Her cousin was on the board of directors, but rarely spent much time on site.

"I heard you needed someone to pose for the new catalogs," Annette said.

Whitney made a noncommittal sound. She wasn't thinking about her cousin; she was looking out the window at the city, wondering where Tyce was.

Was he starting his day at The Rose Chalet?

And was he thinking of her, too?

"What if I did it?" Annette asked.

Until this morning Whitney had been able to pretend that she could keep a lid on things, but it *so* wasn't true. Right then, it was all she could do to keep from remembering the moment after they'd helped rescue the swan together, when they'd been so close. When they'd nearly...

"Are you listening to me?" Annette demanded.

"Of course I am," Whitney replied as she turned away from the window. "It would be good to have you doing more in the business."

"I'm not sure about that," Annette said. "Most of it's pretty boring."

"Sometimes we have to do the boring stuff, too."

Annette made a face as Whitney went back to her desk. "No thanks. I'll leave those parts to you."

"I get the feeling that posing for the catalog will be plenty of work," Whitney pointed out. "Especially since the first thing you'll need to do is convince our art department that you're the right person for it."

"You could—"

Whitney held up a hand. "Go convince them yourself. That is, if you really want it bad enough."

Annette looked at her for a few seconds. "You're in a really bad mood today. What is it? Missing Kenneth?"

Whitney sighed. "Just go talk to the art department."

When Annette left a few seconds later, Whitney turned back to the window.

Missing Kenneth?

Her cousin couldn't have been more wrong if she'd tried.

Instead of thinking about Kenneth, Whitney's mind drifted back to that moment at The Rose Chalet, comparing it with memories from five years back, so that instead of having to pull apart, she could see herself and Tyce kissing. She could feel every movement of his mouth against hers—

"Stop it," she ordered herself, and opened a file at random, hoping that work, any work, would be enough to distract her from the images going around and around in her head.

Ten minutes later, when she'd read the first page half a dozen times, Whitney knew it wasn't going to be that easy. Her every thought led back to Tyce; from the observation that he probably didn't have to deal with this kind of paperwork, to the memory of how good he'd been with her brother down at the coffee shop.

And, of course, every thought about Tyce led back

to that moment at the Chalet when he had nearly kissed her.

And when she had nearly kissed him right back.

"Stop it," she ordered her imagination. "You're getting married to Kenneth. This isn't fair to him."

Kenneth didn't deserve this. She should be fantasizing about him, not Tyce. She should be thinking about Kenneth every minute he was away, and looking forward to the moment he got back, not dreaming of someone else who made her heart race every time she thought about him.

Kenneth didn't make her heart race like that, but so what? This…this thing with Tyce, it wasn't real.

It *couldn't* be real.

Whitney closed the file and sighed.

Kenneth was a great guy. He was handsome, kind, hardworking. He'd make a good husband. But had he ever actually made her feel the way Tyce did every time he looked at her? Like there were goose bumps rising on her skin with every glance, every touch?

And had she ever imagined forever with him the way she couldn't help doing with Tyce?

Whitney knew the answers to each of the questions; had known them for most of the past week, actually. It was why she'd kept away from The Rose Chalet. Not only because she was far too tempted to fall into Tyce's arms, but because just looking at him made the truth of her feelings for Kenneth far too obvious.

Whitney took a deep breath and forced herself to say it aloud. "I don't love Kenneth."

There, she'd said it. It hadn't been nearly as hard as she'd worried it would be. She said it again, with more certainty this time.

"I *don't* love Kenneth."

He would, as she'd just pointed out to herself, make someone a great husband.

Just not her.

Oh, God, was she actually saying that she couldn't marry him?

She immediately imagined the reactions of everyone around her. Her parents would think she was insane for breaking up with such a great guy. Aunt Marge would be upset at the thought of another wedding at The Rose Chalet collapsing. Her family and friends all loved Kenneth and thought he was perfect for her. They'd said it so many times. It was, she was starting to suspect, the reason that she'd agreed to wear his engagement ring. With everyone around her commenting on what a great couple they were, it had seemed so natural to believe it herself without giving it much thought.

It was, she suddenly understood, a terrible reason to marry someone.

"Don't just sit there," she said aloud. No matter how difficult it would be to see things through to where they needed to be, it was time to finally be brave. "Do it."

Dialing Kenneth's number by heart, she was glad when he picked up after three rings.

"Hello?" The voice on the end of the line sounded sleepy and she belatedly realized she must have woken him up just after he'd gone to bed. "Whitney, is that you?"

"Hi, Kenneth."

She realized they sounded like two old friends rather than two people desperately in love who were planning on spending the rest of their lives together.

Just as Tyce had said.

"What's wrong?" Kenneth asked.

Stalling for a moment to try to get her equilibrium

back, she asked, "How do you know that something's wrong?"

"You wouldn't have phoned me at this time of night otherwise."

He didn't point out that Whitney hadn't exactly been calling every day to say how much she missed him or to catch up on their time apart. An entire week could go by between their conversations. Or more.

"Is there a problem with the contracts I sent over?" he asked, sounding much more awake now.

"No, it's not that." She hated stalling, but Kenneth was a good guy. She didn't want to hurt him any more than she needed to. "It's about the wedding."

"Actually, I've been meaning to talk to you about the wedding, too. I've just been… Putting it off, I guess." She heard him take a deep breath before saying, "You're a wonderful person, Whitney. You're smart, you're beautiful, you're funny and you've been one of my closest friends for as long as I can remember. But—"

"I don't want to marry you," Whitney said.

There was a pause and then Whitney could hear Kenneth's sigh of relief across the phone line.

"You have no idea how relieved that makes me feel."

"Actually, I think I have a pretty good idea," Whitney pointed out, shocked that they were actually laughing together over this strange conversation.

After a few minutes of reassuring each other that they were still going to be good friends, he asked, "Would you like me to take care of telling people that the engagement is off?"

Even in the aftermath of their broken engagement, she couldn't ask for a better friend. One she only felt the warmth of friendship for, rather than the white-hot passion of true love.

"How about if you tell your relatives and I'll handle mine? Just try not to make me sound utterly coldhearted when you do it, okay?" she teased.

"That won't be easy," Kenneth said in a tone that was mock serious. "I mean, you did call me up at midnight to break off our engagement."

They both laughed again.

"I'm so glad we're still friends," Whitney told her ex-fiancé.

"Me, too," Kenneth said. "And now that I don't have to rush back for the wedding, I may extend my time in China. I'll see you in a few months, Whitney. I'm glad you called."

As she put the phone down, she could hardly believe the way the past few minutes had gone. Turning around to stare out the window again, she waited a little while to let the whole marvelous mess of their breakup sink in.

CHAPTER EIGHT

TYCE ROLLED INTO work on time, ready for the big debriefing that followed every wedding.

"Good morning, Tyce." Phoebe looked as beautiful as ever in her elegantly customized dress, with her dark hair tied back.

"Things are still going well with you and Patrick, I take it?"

Phoebe's smile widened. "Not well. Perfect." In the flirtatious way they'd always had between them, she teased, "Why? Are you jealous?"

He was, but not because he wanted Phoebe for himself. It was because he wanted what she had with Patrick for himself and Whitney.

He forced a smile, determined to keep up the appearance of everything being the same as usual as he said, "Obviously."

Phoebe reached out to touch his arm. "Is everything okay, Tyce?"

"I'm fine," he said, knowing it was a bad sign if he couldn't keep up the facade of happiness. "Come on, Rose is going to start hollering for us soon."

"Actually, the last I saw her, Rose was busy staring at all the scuff marks on the dance floor and wondering if there's time to replace it." Phoebe stepped in front of him. "So you have plenty of time to tell me what's going on if you want to."

Tyce shook his head. "Maybe some other time."

Even if he were the kind of guy to talk about his emotions, he couldn't tell anyone at the Chalet about Whitney. Not if he wanted to keep his job.

They headed through to the main room where Rose was indeed staring at the floor, adding items to her inevitable post-wedding list. RJ was applying varnish to a small section of floor he must have stripped back to prove to Rose that fixing up the wedding venue's dance floor wasn't going to be a complete nightmare. Tyce could practically see her blood pressure reducing as RJ worked.

Anne was there, too, wearing a dress with fabric that shifted and changed as the light came in through the windows. Like so many of Anne's designs, it seemed to be so much more than the sum of its parts. Tyce couldn't claim to be the world's biggest fashion expert, but right then, with Anne staring out into the sunlight, she looked like a fairy princess.

"Hi, Tyce. Hi, Phoebe." She hugged each of them. "It was a wonderful wedding, wasn't it? The swans were beautiful, the bride looked lovely, and having a special song done for the two of them was so romantic."

Not wanting to talk about the song, he told her, "The dress was lovely."

She beamed at him. "Thank you."

Rose turned and saw that they were all gathered.

"Why don't we get started? Let's do a quick recap of the Washburn wedding before we look at the upcoming events on the calendar."

The five of them gathered around. They'd done this so many times that it was a comfortable ritual, more of a family than a bunch of coworkers.

"Now, I want to start by thanking all of you for doing

a great job, as always. The wedding went really well," Rose said. She checked something off on her list as she said it. Tyce tried to look over her shoulder to see if she actually had "Say the wedding went well" written down, but he couldn't quite see. It would be such a Rose thing to do. "The Washburns were very pleased. All that's left to take care of is returning the swans."

"I took them back this morning," RJ said.

"Thank you," Rose said with a warm smile. "I don't know what I'd do without you some days. There's still a bit of cleanup to do, and, RJ, you were saying that it would take a few days to refinish the floor?"

"It shouldn't be a problem," the handyman said, though Tyce wasn't so sure. It looked like a big job to him. RJ was obviously determined to get it done for Rose, though. He'd always been there for their boss.

"I'm talking to Julie about the possibility of her and Andrew handling our catering on a long-term basis. Since the caterer I hired after Julie didn't work out, having to scout out a different company for each wedding is getting tricky." Rose paused to consult her list again before continuing. "The other news is that we've had our last Banning wedding here for a while."

"What?"

Everyone turned to stare at Tyce's outburst. He gestured for Rose to continue.

She frowned before saying, "Whitney Banning phoned me earlier to say that she was going to have to cancel hers."

"She isn't going to a new venue, is she?" Anne asked.

"No," Rose said. "The wedding is off completely. We will be returning most of the deposit she left with us as a gesture of goodwill. We don't actually have to do it, but I'd like to, so if you could all let me have a list of anything you've already spent in preparations, then— Tyce, where are you going?"

"Sorry," Tyce said, heading for the door as fast as he could. "There's something I have to do."

"Tyce!"

He hurried out before Rose could say anything more. He didn't think she would fire him, but right then, he didn't care. Some things were simply more important than a job.

He'd wasted far too much time already; he wasn't about to waste any more. After five years, another few minutes or hours shouldn't make any difference, but they felt like the most important minutes in the world.

Amazingly, there was a spot to park outside the coffee shop. Tyce took it, hopping out and checking the time. Yes, if he was very, very lucky...

He was. A quick glance through the coffee shop window revealed Whitney standing at the counter, ordering her regular morning coffee. She looked radiant this morning, happier than he'd seen her at any point in the past few days.

He strode up to her and looked deep into her beautiful, surprised, eyes.

"You canceled your wedding."

Four simple words, but there was so much behind them. How much he'd hoped for this moment. How perfect she looked standing there. How he wanted her right then more than anything else in the world.

"Tyce—"

If he couldn't express everything in words, he could at least *show* Whitney how he felt.

So he cupped her face in his hands and he kissed her the way he'd wanted to on the morning the swan escaped.

The way he'd wanted to for every moment of the past five years.

It could so easily have been disappointing. It could so easily have failed to live up to his memories of their previous kiss. Yet from the moment that his lips touched Whitney's, she kissed him back with pure, sweet passion. He continued to kiss her every bit as fiercely, as hungrily, wanting to relearn every last inch of her lips.

But then, Whitney pulled back from the kiss, far too soon.

Not just from the kiss, but from him, too.

"No, Tyce," she said, her eyes wide and shocked, her skin flushed. "I…I can't."

Tyce moved forward to brush a hand down across her cheek. "You canceled the wedding. You're free to do whatever you want now, Whitney."

She took hold of his hand, moving it away from her skin. "Tyce, I can't. I just can't."

For the first time since he'd spotted her through the window, Whitney didn't look happy. She took another step away from him. This time Tyce didn't close the distance. The last thing he wanted was to upset her.

"Why not?" he asked. "And don't try telling me that you aren't attracted to me, because you know I won't believe it. Not after a kiss like that."

"The kiss was good," Whitney admitted in a soft voice that only he could hear, looking slightly embarrassed as she said it, as if she wasn't sure that she should admit quite how good it had been. "The kiss was *great*. But it isn't that simple."

"It's exactly that simple," Tyce countered. "What do you want, Whitney? Just say it, and whatever it is, we'll make it happen. Together." But the look in her eyes had him asking, "I am what you want, aren't I?"

"I don't know what I want right now, Tyce," Whitney said. "I know how good I feel every time I'm around you, but I'm not ready to jump headfirst into a relationship the day after breaking things off with Kenneth. I haven't even told my family yet. I need time to work out, for once, exactly what it is that *I* want." Whitney turned toward the door. "I need to go now, Tyce. I have to get back to work."

It was an excuse, and they both knew it. Tyce wanted to reach out and stop her. Wanted to kiss her again so that she saw how great they could be. His hands clenched with the effort of not doing it, but he didn't reach for her to pull her against him.

Because he loved her.

And right then, it looked as though loving her meant letting her walk away again.

CHAPTER NINE

TYCE PLAYED A scale on his guitar, bent the top note, then slid down the neck to repeat the riff. Milo blinked up at him from where he was lying beside the amplifier in the living room, one ear up, the other flopping to the side.

"Yes, I know," Tyce said. "It's not really a song, but it's better than nothing, isn't it?"

He went into a quick legato sequence and Milo put his head under his paws. His dog had a point. Tyce had started off well, but now his guitar playing had descended into aimless noodling. Just the same tired licks coming from his fingers, with no input from either his brain or his heart. He'd thought there was a glimmer of melody there, but he'd gone after it too quickly and the result was a mess.

Tyce forced himself to rein it in and settle into a simple four-bar sequence. It was only when he'd been through it a couple of times that he realized he'd unconsciously gone back to the song he'd started to write all those years ago.

"I can't give up on Whitney, Milo."

The dog looked up from under his paws, looking hopeful at the sound of her name.

Tyce reached down to ruffle the dog's fur. "I want to see her even more than you do, if you can believe it. But she wants space, and I have to respect that. I just have to hope that if I give her a little time, she'll come around to seeing how good we'd be together."

Milo barked as Tyce started rooting through a stack of sheet music. Waiting was the right thing to do, even if it was hard, but he did need something to take his mind off thoughts of Whitney. He'd hoped working on the musical arrangements for The Rose Chalet's next wedding would help with that for a while.

Unfortunately there wasn't much to do. Another wedding spent directing the same parts for the same musicians. He must have worked at least a hundred weddings with the string quartet over the years. The only difference in the routine was that they'd acquired a new viola player recently. The previous one had just taken a position with the San Francisco Philharmonic. Tyce couldn't blame him. Moving on to bigger and better things is what musicians did.

Most of them, anyway. Tyce could still remember what it had been like in the early days. The bands he'd been in had broken up and reformed, swapped drummers and fought over bass players, splintered and reformed under a dozen different names. Being so passionate about music made every band a strange and fragile thing; perfect one night then gone the next, always reaching for that special blend of ability and chemistry.

Chemistry? It was more like alchemy with some of the bands he'd been in, but occasionally, just occasionally, the results were too good to ignore. Just like the way he and Whitney were together.

Pure heat. Perfect chemistry. And gravity that pulled them together every single time they were near to one another.

What would that younger version of himself think

of Tyce's life now? Working the same wedding gig for years, occasionally guesting with another band to fill in for one of their players.

He'd probably think this "mature" Tyce was nuts. But then, he'd never cared about financial security when he was younger.

He'd still been convinced that he could write songs, too.

Tyce turned his focus back to his guitar again, working to find the faint melody playing in the back of his mind. If he could only get it out through his fingers and onto the strings.

A beautiful picture of Whitney smiling, her cheeks flushed, her eyes bright and intelligent, swam into his mind again, making him pause. He hated having to work so patiently around the edges of their relationship, when what he really wanted was to dive straight into the heart of their feelings for each other.

But he'd tried that before; had tried to force everything in place. And where had it gotten him?

No songs.

And no girl.

Maybe, he started to think, it would be better in the end if he didn't try to force it…and just let every note play out as the one that was meant to be there.

Tyce slid his guitar onto the stand and reached for Milo's leash. "How about if I take you for a walk? It has to be better than sitting around here."

The dog yapped his approval and they'd almost made it to the door when Tyce's phone went off.

"Hi, Tyce. This is Sebastian. Whitney's brother. I found your number online. I hope it's okay that I'm calling."

"Hi, Sebastian." Praying Whitney wasn't in trouble, Tyce asked, "What can I do for you?"

Her brother was silent for a long moment. Too long for Tyce's peace of mind, before the teenager said, "It's kind of embarrassing."

Relief flooded through Tyce. It didn't sound as if it had anything to do with Whitney.

"Sure, no problem. I've been in some pretty embarrassing situations. What's up?"

"Well, I've got this talent show coming up at school and the thing is…" He paused before saying in a rush, "I've never actually been onstage before."

Tyce could still remember the first time he went onstage. He'd been so nervous the guitar had shaken in his hands as if there was an earthquake rolling through the theater.

"Been there, too," he told Whitney's brother. "How can I help out?"

"Whitney said that the band you were in was really good," Sebastian said. "Maybe you could give me some tips? I really don't want to mess this up. Not with everyone watching."

Tyce thought for a minute. It would be easy to give Sebastian a few basic suggestions over the phone, but that didn't feel like enough. After all, this was Whitney's brother. Besides, it was good to see at least one member of the Banning family going after their dreams.

"We can do better than that," he said. "You've been to The Rose Chalet for one of Marge's weddings?"

"Sure. Three times."

"Meet me over there, and bring your guitar."

Tyce grabbed his guitar. On impulse, he chose his beat-up one, rather than the one he usually used for work. Milo looked up at him, then back down at the leash.

"Sorry about your walk," Tyce said. "Don't worry, though, you're coming, too."

Once he'd loaded up his gear, he drove over to the Chalet with Milo. The little dog didn't usually come with him to work, even though Rose clearly adored him. There was usually enough chaos on site without adding an excited dog underfoot. The Chalet was closed and empty tonight, but Tyce had a key for late-night rehearsals with the wedding bands.

Whitney's younger brother was trying to look casual as he stood by the Chalet's front door with his guitar case in his hand, because, obviously, looking excited about things wasn't cool. Still, Tyce could see the nerves.

"Hi, Sebastian. Come on inside."

"I know you're probably too busy to hang out for too long…" the kid began.

Tyce shook his head and said, "I'm always up for jamming with another musician."

"Thanks." Sebastian crouched to stroke Milo's head, and the dog gave his hand a big slobbery slurp. "Yuck."

"It's the first rule of show business," Tyce said with a smile. "Never work with animals." He ignored Milo's affronted look. "Tonight is all about getting experience playing onstage when there's no one around, so you don't have to worry about the simple things."

"I'm not worried."

"Sure you're not," Tyce said as he unlocked the door. "I once had a bass player who was so blinded by the glare from the lights that he walked off the front of the stage." He laughed. "His playing didn't get a whole lot worse, to be honest."

Sebastian was laughing as they went through to the main hall, carefully keeping off the floor RJ had just revarnished.

"It's important to make sure that everything is working before you start," Tyce said as they set up the amplifiers. "I've had gigs where we were too rushed to sound check and the gear broke down just as we went onstage."

Sebastian nodded, obviously taking it all in. He pointed to Tyce's instrument. "That's a cool guitar."

Tyce slipped the battered and heavily customized old Telecaster over his neck. "It's all I could afford to put together back when I was gigging. I don't play it much these days."

"Why not?"

"It's not the kind of guitar people expect when they come for a wedding. It wouldn't look right."

"I bet you've been through a lot with that guitar," Sebastian pointed out. "And if it's right for you, why use something else?"

Tyce shrugged and plugged the old thing in. He had to admit, it sounded a lot sweeter than he remembered.

Turning his focus back to Sebastian's show, he said, "The best thing you can do for yourself and your audience is just to enjoy the show you're putting on. The people in the crowd want you to succeed, because they want to be entertained. If you look like you're having fun, it's easier for *them* to have fun. Go ahead, plug in and play. Pretend you're out on your school's stage and everyone you want to play for is in the audience."

Sebastian started to play, and although the first few bars were tentative and shaky, he quickly relaxed.

Tyce was glad to see that the teenager had talent. He quickly fell in to providing the rhythm parts, stopping Sebastian here and there to give advice.

"Don't be too focused on making sure your technique is perfect," he suggested at one point. "Impressing people is fine, but what they'll remember are the songs that move them."

"How do I do that?" Sebastian asked.

"Back when I was writing songs, it was always about tapping into emotion. If I could pin down what I wanted to get across and really open up a part of myself, there was always a much better chance of connecting with the audience. Not," he felt compelled to add, "that I've written anything in a long time." Which then brought him to asking, "How's Whitney doing?"

"Good," Sebastian said as he bent back over his guitar. Almost as a second thought he said, "Even though she canceled her wedding."

"So…" Tyce said slowly, knowing he shouldn't be mining her little brother for information, but unable to stop himself. "I guess she's told everyone by now, huh?"

Sebastian shook his head. "No, she's weird about that stuff. Like Mom and Dad would ever be upset with her."

Tyce frowned. Why hadn't she told her parents?

But he knew when it was time to back off, so he went back to showing Sebastian the basics of how to use the stage to get feedback through his guitar, and talked with him through the brief talent show set list.

"Close with your best song."

"Close with it?" Sebastian was clearly surprised. "Shouldn't I start with it instead?"

Tyce shook his head. "It's the one people will remember most."

Sebastian swallowed hard. "What if I still don't feel like I'm ready for this?"

"Then we can keep playing," Tyce said. "But, honestly, it's mostly just a question of attitude. Remember that you're doing this because you love it. Sure, you're going to be up onstage with people staring at you, but that's exactly where you want to be. It's just a part of doing what you really want."

Sebastian looked around The Rose Chalet. "So playing weddings here is what you really want?"

No.

The answer came so swift and so clear to Tyce, he knew there was no hiding from the truth anymore.

What he really wanted was to be able to write a song again.

And he wanted Whitney, too.

CHAPTER TEN

THE HIGH SCHOOL auditorium was packed by the time Whitney arrived. Fortunately, Sebastian had reserved a seat for her. Even if he hadn't, she would have found a spot close to the stage, because she was the only member of the family in town and Sebastian needed to know his family supported his dreams. He might have spent the week pretending the talent show didn't matter, but Whitney knew he was nervous.

Not as nervous as she'd been for most of the week, however, as she'd told her relatives about Kenneth, one by one.

Her brother had been easy to tell, because Whitney knew he wasn't going to judge her. Annette had been easy, too. The hardest part was stopping her cousin from continuing to suggest other men to date to take her mind off the "pain" of losing Kenneth. It had taken a good quarter of an hour to persuade Annette that "we both decided to end it" was not code for Kenneth having run off with someone else.

Her parents had been the hardest ones to tell. She'd put it off all week, expecting her mother to cry and her father to say how disappointed he was in her for letting a good man like Kenneth go. The last thing that Whitney had wanted was to hurt them.

Despite her fears, her parents had actually been great. Once she'd finally managed to get the words out, her mother had hugged her. Her father had asked her if she was sure it was what she wanted, and when she'd said yes, he'd seemed almost relieved.

"All we want is for you to be happy, honey," he'd said. "I'm glad you realized this now, before you and Kenneth got married."

"We've always liked him," her mother had added, "but if the two of you don't have that spark, then you obviously aren't right for one another. I know one day you'll find someone who will make you truly happy."

It had been surprisingly easy to tell them the truth. So much easier than Whitney had thought it would be. So easy that sitting there in the darkening auditorium, she found herself wondering if she couldn't tell her parents the rest of it; that she wasn't sure she wanted to spend her life running their company.

Only, the truth was that resigning as head of operations of the Banning Wellness Corporation would affect everything. And Whitney couldn't possibly forget the conversation she'd overheard five years ago....

"I DON'T KNOW what we're going to do now that Whitney has decided to go to veterinary college," Graham Banning said to his wife.

"You aren't thinking of staying at the company, are you, Graham?" Jen replied. "You know what the doctor said about stress and your health."

"I don't know what else I can do, Jen. Whitney's the only one I trust to take over. Could you imagine one of her cousins doing it?"

"We could recruit someone else to take your place, someone who has been in the business for a while already. Your health isn't good enough to put in those long days anymore."

"I won't have a stranger running the family business."

"But if Whitney doesn't want to do it...?"

Graham Banning's voice was resolved. "Then I have to keep going."

HAD ANYTHING REALLY changed since then? Whitney wondered as the last few people came in to the auditorium.

No, it hadn't.

After thirty years behind a desk her father had been pale. Too thin. He'd traveled too much and hadn't eaten right. As soon as she'd taken over, his health had improved. Now when he traveled it was for pleasure. And he was full of laughter whenever they were together. She loved knowing she'd been there for him the way he'd been there for her her whole life.

Her parents still wouldn't want a stranger running the business they had worked so hard to build up. So who did that leave? Sebastian in a few years, after he graduated from college?

Whitney looked up at the stage and knew her brother's heart was in music, not running an international corporation.

The reserved seat next to her was the only empty one in the room. Just as the lights went all the way down, a man sat beside her. Whitney couldn't help staring; her pulse speeding up automatically, her breath coming fast.

"Tyce? What are you doing here?"

Even in the dark auditorium, she could see he looked particularly good tonight, wearing a dark shirt and slacks. Whitney thought that she could see the muscles moving under his shirt as he sat, then chided herself for noticing.

"I came down to support Sebastian," he said. "After all the work he's put in over the past week, I wanted to be here."

"All the work…" Whitney stared at Tyce for a moment or two, drinking him in. His nearness. His clean scent. The beautiful flash of his eyes as he stared back at her. She'd asked him for time and he'd given it to her, but now she wished he hadn't. "You've been helping him?"

"Shh!" a parent behind them hissed. "The show is starting."

It was so hard to keep her hand on her own lap, rather than slipping it into his. Tyce helping her brother was so sweet.

She had to forcefully remind herself that she'd only just told her parents about Kenneth. And that she hadn't even begun to work out what she really wanted when it came to her future.

All too aware of Tyce sitting next to her, she kept her eyes carefully glued to the stage as groups of high school students started to perform. Whitney did her best to focus on the acts that came on one after the other, but it wasn't easy. The kids were quite talented and she had to admit that the show was a lot more fun than she'd thought it might be. But when Tyce's hand brushed against hers on the armrest, Whitney simply couldn't concentrate on what was going on up on the stage.

She quickly refocused when Sebastian walked out onto the stage with his guitar, though. No, not walked. *He strode.*

Her brother strutted as though he owned the auditorium, and when he began to play, every eye in the room was on him. He looked around the crowd as he played, seeming to connect with all of them at once. It wasn't quite like watching Tyce perform, but it was close. Closer than Whitney would have believed it could be.

Tyce had obviously put in a *lot* of work with her brother.

Everyone in the audience seemed to think Sebastian was great, too, judging by the way they applauded. She could hardly bring herself to stay in her seat for the rest of the show, she was so eager to find her brother and congratulate him.

When the talent show ended, Tyce and Whitney both headed to the front of the stage.

She hugged her brother. "You were wonderful."

Beside her, Tyce nodded. "You did great. I knew you would."

"After all that time on the stage at The Rose Chalet, it wasn't so bad," Sebastian said. "It was fun being up there with everyone looking at me. Thanks for coming."

"I wouldn't have missed it for the world," Whitney assured him.

"Me, either," Tyce said, reaching out to shake Sebastian's hand. "Listen, I thought I could take you out to celebrate. After all the hard work you've put in, you deserve it."

But Sebastian's eyes had already wandered over to his friends. "A few of the guys from my class were talking about hanging out over at Connor's place, and I've kind of already said that I'll go. Plus, Michelle from my math class is going…"

"You don't need to say anything else," Tyce said with a smile that seemed to Whitney to be just a fraction too wide. It obviously had Sebastian convinced, though. "Go hang out with your friends. We'll jam together another time."

"See ya," Sebastian said, hurrying off to join a group of kids his age.

"You're very sweet," Whitney said, finally letting herself reach out to put her hand on Tyce's arm.

He was so warm. So *real*.

And so beautiful that she didn't know how much longer she was going to be able to stay away from him.

Or even why she should.

"Not just for offering to take Sebastian out to celebrate, but for helping him in the first place." She paused for a moment before adding, "If you've got a celebration plan in mind, it seems like a shame to waste it. Maybe you and I could—" The words got stuck in her throat, all the things she wanted mixing with all the things she didn't think she could have.

Tyce's eyes held hers. "What could we do, Whitney? Tell me."

She took a breath, or tried to, anyway. Being this close to Tyce made things like breathing hard.

"Maybe we could spend some time together tonight."

He grinned at her, obviously thrilled with her suggestion. "The place I had in mind is close enough to walk to."

WHITNEY LOVED WALKING beside him in the darkness. Just the way they once had.

"How are things going over at the Chalet? I hope Rose isn't too upset that I canceled."

"Honestly, she just wants people to be happy." His grin turned lopsided as he teased, "Even if it means losing the steady stream of Banning income."

"Maybe someday," Whitney said.

Tyce's smile fell away as he gave her another of those

burning looks that melted her insides. "Maybe someday," he echoed in a low voice.

They ended up at a small Italian restaurant, where he had a reservation. The place was nice without being too formal, plus it had great vegetarian food. Trust Tyce to know all the best vegetarian places in the city.

It wasn't a hugely romantic setting. In fact, Tyce waved away the candle the waiter tried to bring to the table, obviously not wanting to make things uncomfortable for her.

He really was sweet, Whitney thought as she found herself laughing when he started to give her the details of a few strange weddings he'd helped put on at The Rose Chalet over the years.

"They really wanted a *horse* up there on the stage with you?"

Tyce nodded. "Unfortunately it reared every time I played a loud chord. It ended up putting a hoof through one of my amps and I had to finish the set on an acoustic guitar."

Whitney laughed again, and told him a couple of stories about the chaos of trying to run a business with half her family underfoot.

Before Whitney knew it, they'd licked the plate of tiramisu clean, the check was paid and he was pulling back her chair as they got up to leave.

Walking back to their cars, it was so natural for Whitney to slip her hand into his. She stared up at the stars, admiring the beauty of the night sky, and when she looked back, Tyce was staring down at her.

She'd missed him so much this past week. Just as she'd missed him for five years.

"I'm glad you came to Sebastian's show tonight."

Tyce lifted their linked hands to her face and gently ran his knuckles across her cheek. "I am, too."

For a moment she thought he was going to kiss her. She would have let him this time, but right then a bird squawked loudly from a tree branch right above them.

Whitney jumped back in surprise. "My cat Clementine would be beside herself trying to get up the tree to that bird."

With that, she started to tell Tyce about her cat, about a fashion show her cousins had dragged her to, about anything that came to mind. He was so easy to talk to. So easy to be with. She could just be herself. Tyce was a great listener, and all night they had talked and laughed as if the past five years hadn't been lost. They'd talked so much, in fact, that they almost walked straight past the school parking lot where they'd left their cars.

"We could always just keep walking," Tyce suggested, and his expression turned serious. "Doesn't it feel like the night's only just started?"

Whitney could imagine spending the night walking hand in hand with Tyce all too easily. Of course, she didn't have to imagine, because she could *remember* what it was like last time. It would be fun, and magical, and it would end with a very sweet kiss before they went home again. It was the kind of thing great memories were made of.

But sweet memories weren't enough. Not anymore.

Not when Whitney wanted more.

"I don't want to keep walking."

"You don't?" Tyce looked a little confused. "But I thought—"

Whitney pressed herself tightly against him, feeling the strength of his muscles as she finally kissed him the way she'd been longing to kiss him all night long.

"I'd rather go back to your place. We can still talk, but…"

"But you don't just want to talk?" Tyce said it softly, almost cautiously, obviously giving her the chance to back out if she felt she needed to.

Right then, though, backing out was the last thing Whitney wanted.

"No," she agreed softly, "I don't just want to talk."

And then she kissed him again to show him just how much she meant it.

CHAPTER ELEVEN

When Tyce woke, Whitney was curled into him, her skin warm, her dark hair spilling out over the pillow. He loved being able to feel every tiny movement she made in her sleep, to hear every breath she took.

He'd thought for so long about what this would be like, but last night with Whitney in his arms had been so much better than anything he could have ever imagined. They had been two halves of the same whole, and even when the pleasure had taken them both over, their connection had been so much more than physical. Amazingly, lying with her as early morning light streamed in through the bedroom window was almost better than making love to her.

The truth was that whenever he'd pictured himself and Whitney together, it had always been this moment, holding her, with the morning sun streaming in through the window, and nowhere either one of them had to go.

At the sound of barking from the next room, Tyce winced. Well, *almost* nowhere to go.

He gently slid his arms from around Whitney, careful not to wake her. She looked so peaceful sleeping in his bed, and so tempting. It was all Tyce could do not to climb back into bed with her and wake her with a kiss.

There would be time for that later, though. To laugh. To kiss. To dream. To talk. To share.

And to love.

Tyce dressed as quietly as he could, then headed out into the living room where Milo was waiting for him to take him for his morning walk.

"You really know how to kill a great mood, don't you?"

Milo's ears twitched and Tyce scratched between them.

"I'm kidding. This morning is perfect. Let's take you for your walk so that I can get back to the woman I've waited for for five years."

Milo followed along happily as Tyce took him for a walk around the block.

Tyce thought about his plans to make Whitney breakfast in bed when they returned, then to wake her with a kiss. Maybe they'd stay beneath the sheets for the rest of the day together, or maybe they'd get up and just talk for hours, her hand in his, her beautiful face right there for him to memorize feature by feature.

The best part of it all was that it genuinely didn't matter to Tyce what they did. He'd been with women who had been exciting in the bedroom, but with whom he'd had nothing in common outside of it. With Whitney, he could happily spend the day simply being near to her. They could walk to her favorite coffee shop, then keep going after that, with no plans, just seeing where they ended up.

"Would you like that?" Tyce asked Milo. "Would you like to go for a long walk with Whitney?"

Milo wagged his tail. It was settled, then. Tyce would still wake Whitney up, but they'd go out after breakfast, and then... Well, there were so many possibilities. So many ways they could spend the day together.

So many ways they could spend the rest of their lives together.

When Tyce looked down again, Milo seemed to be shaking his furry head in warning.

"I know," Tyce said. "I need to take things easy and not plan too far ahead, but this is finally it, little guy. Me and Whitney, the way it should have been all along."

Milo barked.

"Okay, so we probably shouldn't push things too fast at first with her family, because Kenneth is fairly recent history. We can start off slow at first by dating, then deal with what comes next, one thing at a time. I mean, after last night…" Tyce shook his head. "Actually, you aren't old enough to hear about that, even if I factor in your dog years."

He started walking back toward his apartment with Milo following alongside. "She's the one. I'm sure of it. I've always been sure of it."

He'd known how he felt about Whitney from the moment he'd first met her.

Wanting to get back to her, he sped up until Milo had to trot along beside him. Knowing Whitney was probably still asleep, Tyce was extra quiet as he took out his keys and let himself in. Milo barked as Tyce started to open the door, and Tyce put a finger to his lips.

"Shh. You don't want to wake Whitney—"

Tyce didn't finish his sentence, because it turned out that they didn't have to worry about waking Whitney, after all. She was standing in his living room, fully dressed, with her bag over her shoulder.

"Whitney?" Tyce stepped inside, the door still open behind him. "You're leaving?"

Milo ran forward, and even as Whitney bent to pet him, Tyce could see the tension on her face. The beautiful features that had been so relaxed while she'd slept were tighter now.

"I have to, Tyce."

"Last night—"

"Last night was wonderful," Whitney said, cutting him off in a soft voice.

"But you're still leaving," Tyce said, unable to keep the bitterness from creeping in. "Again."

He'd been so certain that things were finally going right, yet here Whitney was, obviously ready to run away without looking back.

Whitney reached up to touch his face and, just for a moment, Tyce dared to look at her with hope. But then he saw the faint shimmer of a tear at the corner of her eye and knew…

He was losing her.

"In the past few weeks I've followed my heart on more things than in the whole of the rest of my life. Breaking up with Kenneth. Taking a chance on you."

"This isn't about Kenneth," Tyce said with absolute certainty.

"You're right," she said. "But it isn't entirely about you, either, even though last night was wonderful and perfect and you helped me see just how good things can be when I go after what I want."

He had to move a little bit closer. "So you do want me, at least."

Whitney wrapped her arms around his neck. "Of course I want you," she said before kissing him, too briefly.

As if she was kissing him goodbye.

"But you're still leaving, aren't you?"

Whitney unwound her arms from his neck. "Every time I've taken a chance recently, it has worked out so much better than I expected. I thought my family would be so upset with me when I broke up with Kenneth, but they were fine about it. I thought things couldn't possibly be as good as I remembered with you, but…"

She didn't finish that thought, but from the look in her eyes, she didn't need to.

"We could be good together, Whitney. We *are* good together." Tyce couldn't stand the thought of not being with her. "I thought you could see it, too."

Whitney nodded, and Tyce could see the pain in her eyes even as she agreed with him.

"I do see it," she whispered. "Please, Tyce, don't make this even harder for me." Whitney took a breath. "I'm going to give veterinary school a try."

Veterinary school?

For a moment Tyce had thought that there was a real problem. But school wasn't a problem. Not at all.

"UC Davis is one of the best vet schools in the country, isn't it? That's only an hour from here." He spoke quickly as the picture became clearer and clearer to him. "We can find a place in the middle that will work for both of us. Or I'll commute to the Chalet so you can be closer to school."

But she was shaking her head and he could feel his skin start to go cold in the warm room, even as the sun streamed in over them both.

"The school I've always dreamed of attending, and graduating from, is a combined ranch and veterinary college," she suddenly blurted. "It's the perfect place for what I want to do and when I called them, they told me they'll accept me again based on my records from when I applied before." She took a shaky breath before saying, "It's in Colorado, Tyce."

"Colorado."

Tyce repeated it flatly, the one word crushing his renewed hopes. He'd thought everything was finally going to work out, even if they each had to make a few sacrifices along the way. He'd thought that all *meant* something.

Yet here Whitney was, planning to move a thousand miles away.

She stepped back, clenching her hands together. "If I don't do this now, I'm afraid I never will."

In that moment Tyce knew how easy it would be for him to stop her.

A few words and Whitney would give up on the whole crazy dream.

A single kiss and she'd be his.

He could take her back to bed and make her forget that she'd ever thought about running off to another state to go back to school.

"You're right," he made himself say, each word tasting like dirt on his tongue. "You should go. I know how much you've wanted this. And how much you'll love being a vet."

"You aren't angry?"

What could he say to that? Of course he was angry.

Angry that the world could keep giving him brief tastes of the woman he was in love with, only to snatch her away again.

Angry at the part of him that still insisted he should stop her, even though he'd never forgive himself if he did.

"You're finally going to live your dream." Tyce pulled her back into his arms and kissed her gently. "I'm happy for you, Whitney. And so proud of you for going after everything you want."

Her eyes shimmered with unshed tears and instead of saying anything more, she kissed him one more time. It was a kiss full of deep emotion and boundless passion.

Her tears fell down her cheeks as she moved from his arms. Tyce made himself stay right where he was as she headed for the door and closed it softly behind her without looking back. But he could see the way her shoulders shook. And he could taste his own tears now.

BESIDE HIM, Milo whined and stared at the closed door.

"This is Whitney's dream," Tyce told him. "She's spent so long putting everyone else first. I'm not ruining this for her."

He picked up his bright, shiny Rose Chalet guitar, trying to find solace there. But before he knew what he was doing, he threw it down hard enough that the neck broke away from the body of the instrument.

"Damn it!"

Milo cowered in the corner, and Tyce realized it was the first time he'd ever frightened his dog. His chest clenched as he held out a hand and Milo came over cautiously, obviously worried about what his owner might do.

"It's all right, little guy," Tyce said, petting him. "I'm sorry about scaring you like that. I won't do it again, I promise."

Milo leaned into him, clearly using his warm, furry weight to try to be a comfort.

"If I did go after her, what then?" he said to the dog who had been there practically every second that he'd spent with Whitney. "We both keep working at things that aren't our dreams? We stay together for a while, then a year from now, or twenty years from now, we blame each other for getting in the way of those dreams? I don't ever want Whitney to feel that way about me." He paused. "And I don't want to feel that way about her."

He knew he'd done the right thing, but shouldn't the right thing feel better than this? Better than feeling as if his heart had been torn out of his chest, leaving a gaping hole that nothing could fill.

He picked up his old, beaten-up guitar. Sebastian was right when he'd said it matched Tyce more than his nicer one. He felt beaten and bruised, just like the guitar, but he'd once made beautiful music anyway.

Milo stared up at him, a pleading look in his brown eyes.

"Don't worry. I'm not going to break this one."

Tyce sat on his old armchair, cradling the instrument as gently as he'd held Whitney in his arms. Memories of being with her were fresh, and bright…and painful.

He'd told Sebastian genuine emotion was the most important thing when it came to music. Lord knew, he had more than enough feelings crashing around inside him.

Determined in a way he couldn't ever remember being determined before, Tyce put his fingers in place behind the frets and reached into himself. Deep. Farther than he'd reached before.

This time he wouldn't run from the pain that came with trying to do the right thing. Instead he would make himself feel every moment of the joy of being with Whitney…and then the loss.

Five years of waiting for her rolled over him, into him, through him, like the waves of an unstoppable tsunami.

Finally, when he wasn't sure that he could take any more, he began to play again.

And this time he kept playing.

CHAPTER TWELVE

WHITNEY LOOKED OUT over the ranch as a herd of horses ran around one of the paddocks. She could easily pick out the ones with small injuries after working with them for four months.

Had it really been that long already?

It seemed like only yesterday that she'd told her parents she was leaving the corporation—and San Francisco—to attend veterinary school. And then she'd told Tyce she wasn't staying in San Francisco, that she needed to take the biggest chance of her life. Leaving Tyce had been the hardest thing she'd ever done.

Looking back over the past few months she could critically say that everything had gone well so far. Her grades were great and she was currently top of her class. Her classmates were wonderful, too. They shared her passion for animals, which was so refreshing after working with the endlessly ambitious and business-focused people back in her old life.

Only, Tyce had been a part of that old life.

And she missed him terribly.

Every minute of every day, he was in her head. In her heart.

How she wished she could put her arms around him. Kiss him. See his smile somewhere other than in her dreams.

"Hey, Whitney." Rachel was a few years younger, with the tanned skin of a girl who had worked on a farm all her life. Joe, another student, was with her. "A few of us are going into town for a break. You want to come along?"

Whitney smiled at the invitation, but shook her head. "Thanks, but I've got a lot of work to take care of."

"I can't believe how hard you study," Rachel commented.

"It's obvious why your grades arc so much better than ours," Joe said in his good-natured way.

"All those books can't possibly be good for you," Rachel joked. "Are you sure you won't come?"

"Like the two of you need me in the way." Whitney watched as Rachel put an arm around Joe's waist. "You've been dating…what? Two weeks? I don't think I've seen you apart in all that time."

Her new friends smiled into each other's eyes. "When it's right, you know."

"Have a great time in town," Whitney said beforc heading back toward the cottage she was renting nearby in a town so small that some days it barely seemed like a town at all.

When she arrived home, she spotted a package sitting on her doormat and picked it up as she headed through the door. As soon as she walked inside Clementine pushed up against her, demanding attention. Her cat seemed to like Colorado, and they were close enough to the ranch that Whitney often found Clementine sitting on a fence post, staring at the horses.

She put the package down on the kitchen table while she made Clementine's dinner and set a pot of water on to boil for her pasta. The cat sniffed at the food in her dish before leaping up onto the kitchen table to circle the package.

"I doubt there's anything for you in there. Sebastian has already sent you a catnip mouse once."

The packages were a lifeline back to San Francisco. Her brother had a knack for finding things that were tiny reminders of home, whether it was a catnip toy in the shape of a cable car for Clementine, or the latest wellness product to roll off Banning Wellness Corporation's production line.

They came with old-fashioned, handwritten notes, too. Sebastian texted and emailed her, of course, but the notes always felt especially personal and thoughtful. He seemed to be determined to make sure that Whitney didn't miss out on any of the family gossip, and she was glad for it. She missed them almost as bad as she missed Tyce.

"I wonder what Annette is up to this time," she said to Clementine as she sat at the table to open the package.

As soon as Whitney had resigned, Kenneth had happily moved up to take over many of her responsibilities. But because he was still in China wrapping up the new deal, he couldn't take care of everything. Her entire family had been shocked when her cousin had offered to do more to help out.

Yet, amazingly, it had worked out.

Annette was surprisingly good at working out what people wanted. All those years of wheedling things out of Aunt Marge had made Annette an excellent negotiator. These skills were in sharp contrast to the odd story of how she had insisted on doing all the modeling for their current catalog herself, then had berated the photographer for taking "bad pictures." In the end, they'd had to redo the photo shoot with professional models.

But, on the whole, things were going really well for Banning. It was as if her cousin had been waiting for the opportunity to show what she could really do. It hadn't been easy for Whitney to be the responsible one all those years, but now she could see that it probably hadn't been much easier for Annette, with no one expecting anything of her except trouble.

"You know," Whitney said to Clementine, "I think my cousin might have hidden depths."

The cat stared back at her as if it was the most obvious thing in the world.

"Yes, I know *you* always liked her. And, yes, I know I'm putting off opening the package from home. It's called savoring the moment."

Whitney finally ripped open the paper on the small package. Inside there was a short note and a CD in a folded cardboard sleeve. When Whitney saw the name on the front, her hands started shaking: *Tyce*.

His name was typeset in large letters, with a picture of him in front and a band in the background.

Her cat brushed up against the picture of him on the CD. "I know you wanted to meet him, but I needed the space. I needed to figure out my own life first, before bringing someone else into it. I *couldn't* keep in contact, and he understands that. I know he does."

The cat settled against Whitney's chest as both of them stared at the CD sleeve. Finally she noticed a very familiar face in the cover photo.

"Sebastian?"

Clementine purred at the name, while Whitney opened the CD sleeve and stared at the list of musi-

cians in shock. It *was* Sebastian and, according to the
notes, he'd played all the lead and rhythm guitars Tyce
hadn't handled himself.

All those notes, all those emails and texts, and her
brother hadn't said a single thing about it.

Had he been worried about how she would react?

Whitney grabbed the note, looking for an explanation.

Hi, Sis,
I wanted this to be a surprise. Tyce let me play
on practically all of it, and he's set up the tour so
that I'm not going to miss school, so don't worry
about that. We're launching on the eighteenth, and
his boss is letting us use her place for the show.
Wish you could be there, but I know you've still
got a lot to do, so maybe you can play this at your
house and it will be like you're here with us. Gotta
practice our rock star moves now.
Sebastian

Sitting on the table, Clementine pawed at the CD and
Whitney turned to tell her cat, "I'm here in Colorado
because I want to be, remember? Things are perfect."

Perfect.

The perfect life…in the perfect little town…at the
perfect vet school. She was doing exactly what she'd
always wanted to do.

What more could she ask?

The water boiled over in the pot on the stove and
Whitney just barely managed to put down the note to
take it off the heat before the hot water really made a
mess. But she wasn't hungry anymore. She sat back at

the kitchen table knowing the hole inside her had nothing to do with needing something to eat.

Perfect didn't feel like this. So alone, as if half of her heart was missing.

Clementine mewed again. "What else could I have done?" she asked the cat. "A veterinary degree takes years. I couldn't expect him to wait."

The worst part was that he would have. Whitney knew that instinctively. If she'd asked him outright, Tyce would have agreed to wait for her however long it took. That, or he'd have given up everything he had in San Francisco, including his friends and his job, just to chase after her.

So she hadn't asked.

Oh, how she wished she had…

Whitney got up and grabbed her laptop, bringing it over to the table. She wasn't checking out flights because she actually *intended* to go to San Francisco. Really, she was just curious to see if she could make the trip to see Sebastian play at The Rose Chalet without missing too many classes at the ranch.

A little research revealed that she could go to her morning class, take a midafternoon flight that would get to the Chalet in plenty of time for the show and still make it back to Colorado the next day without missing too much.

Clementine pushed her furry head over the top of the laptop.

"You are incredibly nosy, even for a cat. You know that, right?"

Whitney tapped in a few details, then looked up to see Clementine staring at her. "No, of course I'm not actually *booking* it. I'm just, you know, seeing if I could. Hypothetically speaking. To see if I could get back to see Ty—Sebastian." Her cat blinked at her, a knowing look in her feline eyes. "What?" challenged Whitney. "I said *Sebastian*."

The online system had her log in so that she could see the finer details of booking the tickets, including whether there would be room for Clementine, since Whitney couldn't exactly just abandon her for a couple of days. Of course, she was going to get to the payment screen and cancel the whole thing. How could she justify a trip like this, right before finals at the end of the first semester? She had studying to do. Lots and lots of studying, just like the past few months.

At last, the payment screen popped up and she stared at it for several moments, not moving. She ought to close the page. The last thing she should ever do is hit the button to accept the—

Clementine stepped straight onto the computer, either deciding that she'd had enough of Whitney's dithering... or simply being annoyed that Whitney had been staring at the computer when she could be staring at her.

"Clementine!"

Whitney hurried to pick Clementine off the laptop. "What have you done?" she demanded, though the answer to that was obvious.

Her payment information had already been in the system...which meant the transaction had been accepted.

She was booked for a flight to San Francisco.

Whitney stared at her cat in what she hoped was a suitably stern way. "All right," she said at last as relief flooded over her at the knowledge that she'd see Tyce again. "It looks like we're going to San Francisco. But you're a very naughty cat."

Whitney headed off into the bedroom, trying to remember where she'd left Clementine's carrier while the cat yawned and started licking her paws in a spectacularly smug way.

CHAPTER THIRTEEN

TYCE SAT IN his living room at the center of a tangle of wires and amps and microphones, his laptop in front of him. The whole scene looked like the command center of a spaceship. He cradled his guitar, settling into the comfortable spot on the edge of his chair where he could play it without the armrests getting in the way. He hit the space bar to record and started to lay down a rhythm guitar part over a simple beat.

He had done this most mornings since Whitney had left, getting ideas down as quickly as they came, recording demo tracks to take to The Rose Chalet. There, he'd been regularly getting together after hours with old friends who formed his new band. They brought his songs to life.

After years of missing the joy of creating music, Tyce wanted more of it. But it was about more than that.

Music was helping to fill the hole in his heart that Whitney's absence had left.

His cell phone rang and, as with every time it had buzzed over the past four months, he hoped it was Whitney. Calling to tell him she missed him. Calling to tell him she wished he was with her. Maybe even calling to finally say, "I love you."

When he saw it was Rose, he worked to push away his disappointment, and instead focused his attention on how great his boss had been about his return to songwriting. Rather than being angry with him for not putting the Chalet at the center of his world, she was supporting him as a true friend. Not only by letting him use the Chalet as a rehearsal space, but by letting him throw his album release party there, as well.

"Hi, Tyce. I just wanted to go over the final arrangements for your show. Julie said that she's got the food taken care of. Phoebe will be running the invite list. RJ has reinforced the stage. And Anne said she's been working on your band members' looks. Is there anything else you need from me?"

Tyce grinned at the very sweet question from his brilliant and focused boss. He'd run the music at The Rose Chalet for so long that the whole place was set up exactly the way he wanted it. Still, he had to tease her with, "You do realize that most musicians would come up with totally outrageous demands at this point?"

"As you well know, I will not be supplying you with groupies, television sets to throw out of windows or bowls of M&M's with the brown ones taken out." Her amusement came through loud and clear.

"Seriously, Rose, everything's perfect. I really appreciate all you've done for me."

"You've always been a great friend, Tyce," she said simply. "To all of us."

No matter where music took him, he knew he'd be friends with Rose and the rest of the Chalet crew for life.

"Actually, Tyce, I have a favor to ask you."

"Don't worry," he teased, "I'm not going to set off fireworks from the stage."

"Definitely don't do that!" she agreed with a laugh before explaining, "I have another client hoping for a special song for his wedding. I tried suggesting an arrangement, because I know that's what you did with the last one, but—"

"Tell him yes."

"Yes? Just like that?" She was clearly surprised. "But I thought—"

"Things are different now. I don't think writing a song is going to be a problem for me anymore," he said with a smile.

When he slipped the phone back into his pocket, Milo ran over to him, ready for his morning walk.

Tyce took him out, walking over to the coffee shop the way he did every morning now. So regularly that the staff put out a water bowl just for Milo.

Things *were* different now. After losing Whitney again, he'd tapped into such a deep well of emotion— one he refused to run from ever again—and the songs had been coming fast and furious for the past four months. He'd written so many songs that he'd even passed a few he couldn't use for himself on to acquaintances in the recording industry. Amazingly, his songwriting credit was already on a couple of minor indie hits. Tonight, there would almost certainly be a few of the more important music journalists in the area attending his launch party.

The question was would the one woman who mattered most of all be there?

Milo tugged on his leash as they rounded the corner to the coffee shop and Tyce knew Sebastian must have arrived. Whitney's brother didn't meet them every morning, but when he did, he always played with the little dog.

The teenager had filled out over the past couple of months and had become more confident. The last time they'd spoken, he'd been talking about a girl at school he liked, but he was worried because they ran with different crowds. Tyce had advised him not to worry about their differences and to just ask her out to see if they clicked.

After all, he and Whitney had seemed so different on the surface. But they'd been perfect together anyway.

"Hey, Sebastian, are you looking forward to the show?"

Whitney's brother nodded, crouching to pet Milo. "It's going to be great."

"You aren't nervous?" Tyce asked with a smile.

"Of course not," Sebastian said right on cue. "You?"

Tyce dutifully shook his head. Then they both laughed. "We are *such* bad liars." Dying to know, he asked, "Who do you have coming to the party?"

"Well, there's my parents and Aunt Marge—"

"Tell her we're not playing anything from *Gone With the Wind,*" Tyce interrupted him.

"I already did. Oh, and Michelle said she would come, too."

"This is the girl you were going to ask out? The one from your math class?"

Sebastian nodded. "She didn't seem as impressed by the whole guitar thing as I thought she'd be, but she said yes anyway."

"That's good," Tyce said.

"I guess."

"It means she's actually into you, not just excited that you're in a band. And, trust me, sometimes having a little patience is the best way to go with things."

Or a lot of patience, in his case.

"Oh, and I also sent a copy of the CD to Whitney," Sebastian said with a careful look at Tyce, "but I doubt she'll be able to come all the way from Colorado."

TRYING TO TAKE a cat on an airplane at short notice was anything but straightforward.

"As I'm sure you know, ma'am," Steve, the manager at the check-in desk, said, "animals often get quite distressed in flight and—"

"Does Clementine look distressed to you?" Whitney said, cutting him off as she held up the carrier where her cat was currently fast asleep. She needed to get to San Francisco. She wasn't about to leave Clementine in the middle of an airport. And she would do whatever it took to get both of them on a plane in time.

"Actually," Steve said, "because we didn't receive notification that there would be an animal on board, the hold isn't pressurized, so—"

"So Clementine can't go down there unless you're expecting her to hold her breath for upward of a thousand miles," Whitney said in a voice that vibrated with her attempt at remaining patient. "I have copies of the paperwork when I notified the airline I'd be traveling with a pet right here."

She fished out printouts of the relevant screenshots from inside her jacket. If running the family business had taught her one thing, it was to always keep copies of everything. She put the papers down in front of the check-in desk manager, who looked at them dismissively.

"I'm sorry," he said, sounding anything but sorry, "but I will have to abide by what I see in our system. And there is definitely nothing here about a cat."

Ordinarily, Whitney wouldn't have done what she was about to do, but she couldn't afford to miss this flight. She just couldn't.

It wouldn't be fair to Sebastian.

Sure, a small voice in the back of her head said. *He's the only person you're thinking about.*

She took out her cell phone and scrolled through her contact list until she found the number for her secretary. Technically, Olivia was Annette's secretary now, and Whitney still got occasional emails from each of them complaining about the other, but she hoped that Olivia would still feel enough loyalty toward her to help her out. After all, aside from leaving her with her cousin, she thought she'd been a pretty good boss.

"Olivia, hi, it's me. Sorry to call you up out of the blue like this. Are you at the office? Annette has you doing *what?* Look, sorry to interrupt but could I ask a favor? We did business with a small airline a while back. I need the private number for Guy Jupp. You have it? That's great. Thanks."

Whitney punched in the number while watching Steve-the-Manager's face. He seemed to be caught between a mixture of disbelief, annoyance and continued arrogance, secure in his position behind his desk.

"Hi, Guy," Whitney said. "This is Whitney Banning. I don't know if you remember me?"

"Of course I remember you! That deal we did with you on transport was one of the best things to happen to my business. I had a great time when you and Kenneth came over for dinner. How is he?"

"He's fine," Whitney assured him. "I hate to do this, but I'm having a problem getting on one of your flights."

"If it's full it might be tricky—"

"It isn't full. I actually have a ticket. It's just that they won't let me take my cat, Clementine, on board, even though I have the paperwork confirming that it was okay." She hadn't forgotten that when she and Kenneth had gone for dinner at Guy's house, there had been three large Persian cats sprawled all over the furniture.

"Could you please hand me over to the representative you've been speaking with, Whitney?"

She smiled as she took the phone from her ear, mostly because Steve-the-Manager was still looking at her as if she was crazy. "It's for you."

"Mr. Jupp?" The man's face paled considerably. "That's right, sir." Steve looked down at the paper with Whitney's flight details. "Yes, I'm very sorry. I understand. Yes, of course, sir. Absolutely." He handed her phone back. "I'm sorry for the misunderstanding, Ms. Banning. If you'd like to go through to the first-class departure lounge, we'll call you when your flight is ready to board. In the meantime, Mr. Jupp has instructed me that if you want anything, you only have to say the word."

"Thank you, Steve." She picked up Clementine and carried her over to the waiting area just as another woman walked into the lounge, moving to sit next to her.

The woman's stark white hair was elegantly cut, and the handbag she placed next to her was designer. "Well done on handling the dictator at check-in," the newcomer said. She extended a hand. "I'm Yvette Markston."

Whitney knew that name, even if she'd never met the woman personally. "Whitney Banning."

"I know who you are. You look just like Marge did at your age."

"You know my aunt?"

"We meet occasionally. Charity events, usually. She speaks very highly of you. So, tell me, what is so important that it has you pulling out the stops to get onto the plane?"

"My brother is playing in a band and they're having the release party for their album. I haven't seen him for months and I want to surprise him."

"Have you been doing business in Colorado?"

"No," Whitney said, slightly defensively. "I'm not working for the Banning Wellness Corporation anymore. I've been training to be a veterinarian. Colorado has one of the best schools in the country for horses. And," she said, unable to stop the words from coming, "this way there are no distractions. And no one—" She cut herself off. "I mean, nothing to keep me from following my dream."

"Ah, distractions." Yvette's lips curved into a small smile. "I used to have my fair share of 'distractions' when I was a beautiful young girl like you." She raised an eyebrow and leaned closer. "What's his name?"

"I'm not with anyone," Whitney said quickly.

Too quickly.

"No?"

But it wasn't true. She and Tyce hadn't made any promises to each other, but he was still there with her, in her heart. The same way he always had been, right from their first night together five years ago.

"I left him to find out what it was I really wanted," she finally admitted.

"And do you have an answer?"

"Sometimes I think I do," Whitney said in a soft voice. "But then, I don't. All I know is that I miss him. Terribly."

The other woman patted her arm. "Just look at that aunt of yours. A brand-new husband she adores, a thriving business, and still she has time for her friends and for the causes that she believes in. Do you think she feels she has to choose?" Yvette didn't wait for her answer. "There is little worse in life than regrets. If you know what you want, reach out for it. Fight for it, whether it's your family, or your choice of career, or love."

"And if I don't know what I want?" Whitney asked.

"Then work it out." It was a no-nonsense answer, not meant to give offense. "Though I think you do know, or you wouldn't have put so much effort into getting on this plane, would you?"

CHAPTER FOURTEEN

SETTING UP FOR the CD launch at The Rose Chalet felt like a family affair. Julie and Andrew came early with several large trays full of food. Phoebe put a dozen rock-and-roll-inspired arrangements of flowers around the main room, then spent the rest of her time with Patrick, helping him decorate the main hall for the evening.

What Tyce wouldn't give to have Whitney there beside him.

THE FLIGHT WAS going well so far. No turbulence, and Clementine had behaved herself in her carrier. The cabin crew had gone out of their way to be courteous and friendly, so either they all liked cats or news of what had happened at the check-in desk had spread quickly.

Whitney didn't want to be the ex-executive who bullied people until she got what she wanted. Other people's feelings mattered.

Except…what she wanted mattered, too. And she'd forgotten that for so long.

For too long.

TYCE HEARD THE rumble of thunder as the storm clouds rolled in. It wasn't the best weather for a party, but they were all going to be indoors. Rose began to pull the shutters closed to keep the rain out, and RJ was there to help her, the way he always was.

Tyce started to lend a hand, but RJ shook his head. "We've got this under control. All you should be thinking about right now is putting on a great show."

Rose's phone rang and she put it to her ear. "Donovan? Really, you can't? Okay. I understand." She frowned as she slipped the phone back into her pocket. "It looks like Donovan won't be able to make it, Tyce. Between an emergency client and the weather… Well, you know how things can be for him."

Yes, Tyce knew exactly how things were with Rose's fiancé. In any case, Donovan wasn't the reason Tyce was keeping his eyes trained on the door.

WHITNEY LOOKED AT the sudden appearance of thick, gray clouds out her window and held on to her armrest while the plane shook with turbulence.

"Ladies and gentlemen, this is your captain speaking. We will be approaching San Francisco shortly, but I regret to inform you that due to the severe weather conditions, we will have to wait a little longer than usual to land."

"No!" Whitney didn't realize that she'd said it out loud, or quite how loud she'd said it, until one of the cabin crew rushed over to her.

"It's all right, Ms. Banning," the young flight attendant said. "It isn't anything serious. It might take a while longer than we were hoping, but we'll get there."

Whitney wanted to tell the woman that she couldn't wait, but she knew that wouldn't do any good. She was stuck in the sky until it was safe to land.

She checked her watch. How long would it be before Tyce's show started?

Would she still make it?

TYCE TAPPED HIS foot to the beat while the band warmed up. Sebastian broke off from the two-bar vamp they were working through to adjust his amplifier for controlled feedback. Guitarists were guitarists, no matter how young they were.

Anne moved up beside Tyce, the many-layered fabric of her party dress seeming to float around her.

"Isn't it wonderful that everyone is here for your big moment? Rose, RJ, Phoebe, Julie, Patrick, Andrew, me. It's just like one big happy Rose Chalet family." But when she caught him looking at the entrance one more time, she gently asked, "Is everyone you're waiting for here?"

Tyce made himself smile at his friend. "Thanks for coming tonight, Anne."

He headed for the stage to start the show, Milo beside him every step of the way, as if realizing his owner needed him close by.

WHITNEY HURRIED THROUGH the terminal with Clementine mewing from within her carrier.

"I know," Whitney said as she rushed out into the rain, "you hate getting wet, but it's for a good cause."

For Tyce...and for love.

Unfortunately there was a huge crowd of people waiting for taxis. For a few seconds Whitney waited along with them. But it didn't take her long to realize that if she remained the polite, good girl she'd always been she would definitely miss the show.

She pushed her way through, ignoring the occasional outraged shout as she ducked into any space that presented itself and took full advantage of those moments when people heard Clementine complaining from the carrier. Moments later, she clambered into a taxi, just ahead of a businessman.

"Hey!" he yelled as she closed the door on him.

The cab driver scowled at her. "What do you think you're doing, lady?"

"Sorry, but I'm in a hurry. Do you know where The Rose Chalet is?"

"The wedding place? Sure, I drive past it most days. But this isn't your cab and—"

Whitney took out her purse. "I have two hundred dollars to give to you if you can get me there *now*."

"Two hundred dollars?" The driver looked at her in disbelief. "Are you serious? That's a fifteen-dollar fare, max."

"Completely serious. And I'd like you to drive as fast as you can without getting pulled over."

The cab driver smiled widely. "Lady, I never get pulled over. You'd better buckle up. And hold on tight to that cat."

TYCE LOOKED OUT over the crowd. He'd taken as long as he could with the sound check, but now that The Rose Chalet was full, he couldn't wait any longer.

There were his friends, Sebastian's family, the girl Sebastian liked so much, the staff from the Rose Chalet, and strangers, too. Some were friends of friends, who had obviously been tõld about Tyce and his songs, and others were music journalists and bloggers who could make or break a new release.

He stepped up to the microphone and was glad to feel the familiar joy of being onstage. He'd missed this.

Tyce knew, deep within himself, that while Whitney might not be at his big comeback show, he wasn't plan-

ning to give up on his dreams again. Not on his dream
of being a songwriter.

And not on his dream of being with her.

"I'd like to thank you all for coming here tonight,"
Tyce said, then nodded to Al, the drummer, who
counted them into the first song.

WHITNEY'S CAB DRIVER was named Lyle. She knew that
because he liked to talk as he drove, the speed of the
words running neck-and-neck with the speed of the cab.

Currently he was talking very fast indeed.

"I had this one guy in the cab, he paid me just to go
see the bridge, drive over it and then turn around to go
back to the airport. Then there was this other guy—"
Lyle threw the car into a tight turn "—who paid me to
just drive around for a whole afternoon, making stops,
and I started to think he was a mafia hit man, but it
turned out that he was a computer technician and—"

"Watch out for that red light!" Whitney gasped.

But her driver kept going, making it through the
junction an instant before traffic started flowing
through it the other way.

"Relax," he said with a quick glance into the rear-
view mirror. "It was barely red for a second. Besides,
your cat doesn't seem to mind."

That was the strangest thing of all. Clementine was
calmly sitting in her carrier, looking straight forward
as though she were actually *enjoying* Lyle's kamikaze
driving style.

"So what's with the rush? If you're going to the wedding place, does that mean you're going there to get
married? Or maybe you're rushing to interrupt a wedding and win back the guy you love. It's something like
that, isn't it?"

"Yes," she said, her hands in a white-knuckled grip on Clementine's carrier as she realized the full truth of her feelings for Tyce…and just how deep they ran. "It's something like that."

THE MUSIC FLOWED. Tyce had seen this moment so many times in his mind's eye, but the reality was better. So much better. The band was tight. Sebastian was wailing on the guitar whenever he got a solo, and the applause for Tyce's new songs grew louder and louder.

Milo was sitting up on the stage, watching but thankfully not making any doggy attempts to sing along.

Tyce bent to scratch his ears. Then he straightened and nodded to the band.

"Guys, give me the stage for this one, would you?"

WHITNEY DUMPED HER wad of twenties into Lyle's hand, shoved open the taxi door, grabbed Clementine and ran through the puddles to the door of The Rose Chalet. Inside, the lights were low and for a moment her heart squeezed tight as she thought she'd missed the show.

But then a single spotlight came up, highlighting Tyce with his guitar.

"I'd like to play a new song for you. One even the rest of the band hasn't heard. Actually, it's not that new, since it's the last song I started working on before I hit a long dry spell with my songwriting. I didn't realize, until a little while ago, that was because I wasn't ready to say what I really needed to say." He paused. "I call this one *'Whitney.'*"

And then he started to play.

CHAPTER FIFTEEN

THE SONG WAS heartfelt and catchy and amazing.

It was about a man who had lost the woman he loved, and who kept on losing her, thinking that he would get close to finding her but never quite managing it. But he never gave up, either. Because, no matter what happened in their lives, or if they were apart, he loved her then, loved her now and would love her forever.

He loved her.

Whitney moved forward through the audience as Tyce sang, listening to every word and knowing with each one just how difficult it must have been for him to let her go to pursue her dreams.

She reached the front row and set down Clementine's carrier just as Tyce reached the end of the song. The lights were so bright, she knew he couldn't see her. Until, finally, the room lights came up a little bit and he looked at her, his eyes wide, as though he couldn't quite believe that she was there.

Even though he was in the middle of his show, Whitney couldn't wait any longer. She jumped up onto the stage, took Tyce's face in her hands and kissed him. She kissed him sweetly, lingeringly, wanting to savor the moment as much as she could and loving the taste of his mouth against hers.

"I love you, too," she whispered.

At least, it was meant to be a whisper. It was only

when the assembled audience cheered that she realized the microphone was live. They'd all heard her.

Once, that might have embarrassed Whitney, even shocked her. Right then, though, all she could think to do was to say it again. Stepping away from the microphone, she said, "I love you, and the song was beautiful, and I don't want to wait any longer. I want to be with you."

"But Colorado…"

"I want Colorado, but I want you, too. I'll do whatever I have to so I can be with you. Travel across the country, come to San Francisco on weekends."

"Or I could come to Colorado," Tyce suggested. "If you'll let me."

By way of an answer, Whitney kissed him again.

"We should talk about this," Tyce said. "I could end the show."

"Don't you dare!" Whitney insisted. "I'll be right here. Listening to my favorite singer. Now and always."

"And possibly trying to catch your cat," Sebastian said from behind her. "I think she just got loose."

Whitney got down off the stage before the crowd got too restless about the interruption of the show, and was about to go after Clementine. But then Tyce and his band started playing again, and a couple of nice-looking teenagers scooped up her cat and started spoiling her, which was a very good thing since Whitney couldn't have moved away from the front of the stage for the world.

The band played with so much energy, and while Whitney had thought Tyce was amazing before, now every word he sang came straight from his heart. She danced until the music finally faded on the last song.

When Tyce finally jumped off the stage, she met him

with another kiss. He kissed her back so thoroughly that it was all Whitney could do to keep from suggesting they should abandon the party to rush back to his place.

His family and friends came up to tell him how great the music had been and, at the back of the room, she saw Sebastian kiss a girl about his age on the cheek. Whitney grinned, thinking that her brother's friend from school had obviously appreciated the performance, too. And she was beyond thrilled when the journalists all assured Tyce that their write-ups were going to be spectacular.

One female journalist turned her attention to Whitney while the others crowded around Tyce. "It occurs to me that Banning Heiress in Relationship With Up-and-Coming Star makes a much bigger headline than Local Musician Releases Album," the woman said, "but I thought I'd check with you before I went with that one."

Not that long ago Whitney would have worried about what her family would say, or what it would do to the Banning corporate reputation. Now she just laughed. She *wanted* the world to know about her and Tyce. And she was so proud to be linked to him.

"If it means more people will hear Tyce's music, it sounds good to me."

Whitney felt two sets of warm, familiar arms come around her and belatedly realized that, of course, her parents had come to see Sebastian play.

"He's not the reason I broke up with Kenneth," Whitney said quickly. "Although the truth is that I never should have agreed to marry Kenneth in the first place."

Her mother smiled at her. "Tyce seems like a great guy, honey."

"All we've ever wanted was for you to be happy," her

father said. "And we're so sorry we didn't realize you were putting your dreams on hold for us."

She hugged them back. "All of my dreams are coming true now."

It was true, she thought as Tyce moved up beside her and she introduced him to her parents. She was finally learning how to put the pieces of a wonderful life together.

A family she adored.

Work she thrived on.

And a love she couldn't live without.

After her parents left, Whitney and Tyce walked back into the main hall holding hands. Most everyone had left apart from the band...and Clementine.

Whitney's cat was sitting in the middle of the floor washing herself sedately while Milo padded his way across the floor, obviously intent on sneaking up on her. The little dog kept low to the ground before barking in a way that made it clear he wanted Clementine to run away so that he could chase her.

Clementine just kept licking herself, barely even bothering to look at him.

Milo crept closer, and Whitney started forward to interfere before Clementine ended up as the little dog's chew toy. Only, just then, the cat whirled around and batted Milo with one paw, catching him squarely on the nose.

The little dog sat sharply, almost falling over with the sheer shock of it. He whined and then lay down, looking up at Clementine as though not sure what to do next.

For her part Clementine looked smug. She moved to sit beside Milo and pushed against him until he gave up the patch of floor he was on. Then she lay down with her head resting on the dog, using him as a pillow while she curled up and closed her eyes.

"I think we've worked out how that relationship is going to go," Tyce said, wrapping his arms around Whitney so that his head rested on the top of her head. "Poor Milo. He never stood a chance."

"I never did, either," she murmured, turning in his arms to brush her lips against his. She pulled back to look up at the man she loved. "So, now that the animals are settled, have we worked out how *our* relationship is going to go?"

"We will," Tyce promised. "I was thinking we could start with me moving to Colorado to be with you while you go to school."

"You'd do that? Just uproot and leave? I thought you loved it here."

"I love you more. And I can make music anywhere." He smiled. "At least, anywhere you are. We could look for a nice little house with plenty of space for animals out back and close enough to the veterinary practice you're going to set up."

"Have you been reading my mind?"

Tyce put his hands in hers. "I know you, sweetheart. And I want you to have your dreams. All of them."

She wrapped her arms around him. "I have one of them right here."

"We both do," Tyce assured her, pulling her close. But then, he was the one pulling back to stare down into her eyes. "Do you think The Rose Chalet might see another Banning wedding, after all?"

Whitney pressed tightly to him, loving the sensation of finally being so close when they'd been apart for so long. "I do," she said softly as a prediction of future vows. "After all," she said with a smile, "I never did get that dream wedding."

"You can have any dream you want, Whitney," Tyce said. "Just as long as it doesn't involve *Gone With the Wind.*"

Whitney laughed. "I think we can leave that one to Aunt Marge."

And then Whitney kissed Tyce, standing right in the spot where so many brides had kissed their grooms before.

EPILOGUE

As ANNE FARLEIGH headed off for home on foot after the concert, she couldn't help smiling at how sweet and romantic Tyce and Whitney were together. They were clearly perfect for one another, and Anne was so glad they'd finally worked everything out.

She hoped their relationship would be as good as her parents' had been. Her mother and father had become childhood sweethearts after her father had literally bumped into her mother in the high school corridor, helping her to pick up her books and asking her out on a date all at once. From there, they'd hardly ever been apart. They'd attended the same college, and married as soon as they'd graduated. He'd turned down a high-paying job opportunity so that he could be near her, and she'd later supported him while he wrote his novels.

Even after they died in a tragic accident, their love had shone through. The emergency personnel had found their car at the bottom of a ravine, her parents holding hands, as though they'd reached out for one last touch of each other's hands in their final moments.

One day Anne hoped to find a love that pure and perfect with a man who would love her every bit as much as her father had loved her mother.

Anne liked to think that she took after them, though obviously the wedding dresses she designed were in a different medium from her mother's sculptures and her father's novels.

It was why she did so much work with Rose and the brides at the Chalet. Rose was her friend, and it was a wonderful opportunity to make beautiful gowns for brides who really appreciated them. Ultimately, though, there was nothing better in the world than to watch the love on the bride's and groom's faces when they were both saying "I do."

Anne was only a couple of blocks from home when Tyce's van pulled up next to the curb.

"Why don't you hop in so that Whitney and I can give you a ride the rest of the way?"

"Thanks," she replied, "but it's a lovely night."

"Lovely?" Whitney said, both Milo and Clementine sitting on her lap looking out at Anne. "It's raining. And your dress is getting wet."

"Rain *is* lovely," Anne replied. True, her dress was getting fairly wet, but she'd only made it for this party and would likely alter it completely before she wore it again. She smiled at both of them. "You gave a great show tonight, Tyce. I'm so glad you were able to make it, Whitney." She waved them away. "Have a great night."

Her house had once belonged to her parents but was now hers alone. It was a large Craftsman style home not too far from The Rose Chalet. It had been built with a family in mind.

She was surprised to see a black SUV parked outside her house; a man standing in front of it in the rain. He was wearing dark jeans and a dark jacket. Even though he was staring at her without the barest hint of a smile, Anne couldn't help but think that he was very good-looking, with slightly long brown hair and piercing blue eyes that were hard to ignore even through the rain.

Assuming the shiver that went through her was simply a reaction to her cool, wet clothes pressing against her skin, Anne smiled over at him as she walked up her front steps to get out of the rain.

"Hello," she called out. "Are you looking for someone?"

"Are you Anne Farleigh?"

When she nodded, he moved toward her. When he was under cover on the porch, he reached into his black jacket and held out an envelope.

Surprised, Anne took it and immediately reached inside to see what it was. Her eyes widened slightly as she read the document.

"You've made a mistake," she said, holding out the envelope to the man in front of her. "You have the wrong person."

"Your parents were Edward and Chloe Farleigh?"

Anne nodded. "Yes."

The man shook his head confidently. "Then I'm afraid there hasn't been any mistake. I'm here to serve you with legal papers relating to your father's other daughter."

* * * *

Watch for Anne Farleigh's story,
THE WEDDING DRESS,
in the next ROSE CHALET *anthology,*
KISS THE BRIDE, available soon from Lucy Kevin
and Harlequin HQN.
In fine bookstores everywhere.

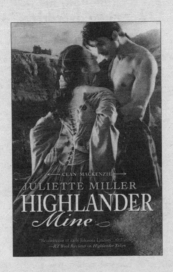

REQUEST YOUR FREE BOOKS!

2 FREE NOVELS
FROM THE ROMANCE COLLECTION
PLUS 2 FREE GIFTS!

New York Times and USA TODAY bestselling author

DIANA PALMER

**brings you back to Jacobsville, Texas, where
Hayes Carson is a man on a mission—for justice.**

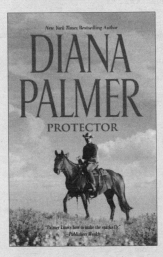

Hayes has always suspected
Minette Raynor had something to
do with Bobby Carson's death, that
the bright-eyed blonde gave his
brother the drugs that killed him.
As far as Hayes is concerned,
neither her looks nor anything else
will stand in the way of his righting
this grievous wrong.

Minette can't get handsome Hayes
off her mind, or off her back. His
investigation of her is annoying, but
as an undercover DEA agent, that's
the least of her worries. Until she
finds herself in great danger, and he's
the only one who can save her. Can
she count on Hayes to believe the
truth—and save her life?

Available wherever books are sold!

Be sure to connect with us at:

Harlequin.com/Newsletters

Facebook.com/HarlequinBooks

Twitter.com/HarlequinBooks